THE
BETRAYAL

Book **Four** in the
Munro Family Series

CHRIS TAYLOR

When much decorated Australian Federal Police officer **Declan Munro** is accused of illegally accessing confidential police files containing child pornography, his world is turned upside down. Fronting the investigation into his alleged criminal behaviour is Senior Internal Affairs Investigator **Chloe Sabattini**.

A veteran investigator, Chloe is taken aback to discover that not only is Declan likeable, but his protestations of innocence are believable. Furthermore, despite her best efforts, she finds herself drawn to him.

But the evidence can't be ignored and Chloe vows to investigate the matter with all of the resources available to her.

The more she delves, the more she's convinced of Declan's innocence. Someone is framing him. But who? And why? And what does a high ranking Government Minister have to do with it?

An innocent man's life hangs in the balance. Will she discover the truth before it's too late? And will she be able to handle the fallout when she does?

The Munro Family Series

THE PROFILER
(Book One—Clayton and Ellie)

THE INVESTIGATOR
(Book Two—Riley and Kate)

THE PREDATOR
(Book Three—Brandon and Alex)

THE BETRAYAL
(Book Four—Declan and Chloe)

THE DECEPTION
(Book Five—Will and Savannah)

THE NEGOTIATOR
(Book Six—Andy and Cally)

THE RANSOM
(Book Seven—Lane and Zara)

THE DEFENDANT
(Book Eight—Chase and Josie)

THE SHOOTING
(Book Nine—Tom and Lily)

THE MAKER
(Book Ten—Bryce and Chanel)

DEDICATION

This book is dedicated to my sister Nic, a remarkable woman who is both inspirational and funny. Without her, Chloe Sabattini would never have happened. And as always, to my amazing husband Linden, my very own honorable, hardworking hero.

Acknowledgements

As usual, no book comes into being without a lot of help and support by my friends and family. A world of thanks must go to my friend and fellow author Angela Bissell, critique partner extraordinaire, and a girl who loves the Munro family as much as I do.

To Pat Thomas, the best editor in the world, thank you for believing in my vision for Declan and Chloe. It wasn't always easy, but we got there in the end. To Alisha and Damon Za, thank you for yet another fantastic cover. To my sister, Nicole Guihot, thank you for your excellent editorial comments and suggestions. Nic, I hope you like the final result.

To Amy Atwell and her dedicated staff at Author EMS who are so much more than book formatters. Amy, once again, thank you for your magic.

To the fantastic writer organizations such as Romance Writers of Australia, Romance Writers of America and Romance Writers of New Zealand for all the help, support and encouragement they offer new and aspiring writers, including me.

To my readers, thank you for your support and love for the Munro family. Your encouragement and enjoyment make this journey all worthwhile.

And lastly, to my friends and family, especially my husband and children. Thank you for putting up with late dinners and even later conversations as I've emerged day after day from the sometimes scary but always enthralling world I've created on my computer.

PROLOGUE

The Master turned another page of the report with a lazy flick of his fleshy finger. A short distance away, Chip stood and watched in silence. With clenched fists, he willed the trembling in his body to cease. The pumping of his blood as it pulsed in his ears and the occasional rustle of paper were loud in the comforting dimness of the room.

The solitary source of light emanated from an antique lamp perched on the hand-carved desk near the Master's elbow. The meager illumination glinted dully off the silver in the Master's closely cropped hair, enhancing his air of urban refinement. This was further heightened by a costly suit and snowy-white shirt, tailor-made to fit the Master's considerable bulk. A five hundred dollar tie, a gift from Chip, had already been discarded and lay in a silken pile amongst the scattering of papers on the desk.

The Master continued to scrutinize the report in silence. The lines that marked his forehead deepened. With a nonchalant hand, he reached across the desk and picked up the black leather riding crop that rested there. He flicked it with apparent disinterest across his generous lap.

Nerves and excitement danced in Chip's gut. His throat tightened. He stared at the riding crop, as mesmerized by the rhythmic slaps as though it was a cobra, poised to strike.

A tiny moan escaped his parched lips and he instantly bit down on it. The Master's gaze flew upwards. Steely, black eyes pierced him. His breath halted. Three seconds passed. Then five.

The Master smiled.

The breath left Chip's body in a rush. He tried to stem the relief that poured into his gut. It wasn't over. Not yet.

The slap of the riding crop recommenced, but this time, the slaps were slow, measured, tantalizing. The Master looked up at him, his face now relaxed. A smile widened his lips to show a row of straight, coffee-stained teeth.

"You've done well, Chip."

The graveled voice rasped along the young man's nerve endings, leaving them warm and tingling.

"Th-thank you, Master," he stammered, basking in the satisfaction that now glinted in the other man's eyes.

The riding crop stilled and was returned to where it came from. The Master picked up the pages of the report and shuffled them together before setting them in a neat pile on the desk in front of him. The steely eyes found Chip's again.

"This is exactly what I asked of you. I like it when people follow my instructions. I like it very much."

Excitement and a little fear surged through him. The Master pushed back against his upholstered leather chair and re-adjusted his bulk. With his legs spread wide, he beckoned.

"Come over here, Chip. You deserve to be rewarded."

The Master's hand slid over his ample lap to the bulge now noticeable in his pants. He fondled his erection. Excitement exploded through Chip's veins. His body hardened. He took a hesitant step toward the desk. And then another.

A smile licked at the Master's lips. "Take off your shirt, Chip, but leave your tie on. Afterwards, we might talk about that little promotion I mentioned."

CHAPTER 1

Federal Agent Declan Munro tossed his canvas gym bag into the bottom of his government-issued locker and shrugged out of his charcoal-gray suit jacket. Hanging it up on the coat hanger that swung from the rod inside, he smoothed his hands over his thick wind-blown hair, straightened his bright yellow tie and then closed the locker door.

"Christ, did you collide with a shit-faced canary or something?"

Declan turned, a quick grin spreading across his face at the sight of his friend and colleague, Agent Charlie Stanford.

"No harm in standing out in a crowd, Stanford. It takes a real man to be brave enough to wear a color like this."

Charlie snorted, grinning back at him. "Whatever floats your boat, Munro."

Declan shrugged, his smile still in place. "It's a Christmas present from my mom. What am I supposed to do?"

"Hide it in the darkest, furthest place in your closet and plead ignorance every time she mentions it."

Declan gestured with his chin toward his friend's much more conservative navy-and-silver tie that hung meekly around his neck. "Is that what you do?"

Charlie's expression sobered and he looked away. "I can't remember the last time my mother gave me a present."

Declan shot him a look of surprise, but dropped the

subject. He'd known Charlie a little over a year, but they hadn't done much more than trade the basics about their families. He'd been grateful they'd hit it off the minute he'd stepped foot inside the Child Protection Unit, a division of the Australian Federal Police, and Declan had enjoyed Charlie's company ever since.

Having once been a senior detective with the New South Wales Police Service, Declan had expected to be greeted with a fair amount of badgering and distrust. Unfriendly rivalry abounded between the State and Federal law enforcement agencies and relations were often less than amicable.

But his welcome into the CPU as an AFP recruit couldn't have been warmer. Declan didn't know if the reasons had more to do with the fact two of his brothers were long-serving, well-respected agents or that budget cuts had seen fewer and fewer recruits come through their hallowed doors. Nevertheless, he accepted the welcoming attitude with more than a little relief.

Like him, Charlie was in his mid-thirties and hadn't yet succumbed to the anchor of marriage. Their budding friendship had been made even easier when they discovered neither of them had a girlfriend. They were among the few who didn't have significant others to be consulted about all things from what they might do after a long day at work to how they'd spend a free Saturday night.

With another weekend approaching, it was time to make plans. "What are you doing tomorrow?" Declan threw the question over his shoulder as he headed for the door that led into the squad room.

Charlie grimaced. "Working. The boss has me on a late shift on Saturday and an early on Sunday."

"I thought you were rostered off?"

"And now I'm not."

"Bummer."

"You can say that again. What do you have planned?"

"I thought I might go and watch the football game. The Raiders are playing on Saturday afternoon," Declan said, referring to Canberra's National Rugby League team.

"Who are they up against?"

"Manly." He winced. The Sydney team—an old rival of his local team—was currently at the top of the table.

"Should be a good game."

"Yeah." Declan reached his desk and pulled out his standard issue, faux-leather office chair. "Too bad you're gonna miss it."

Charlie nodded and turned away to take a seat at his desk, not far away. Declan pressed the power button on his computer. Tugging the keyboard toward him, he waited for it to boot up. Sensing a presence behind him, he swung around in his chair and greeted his boss.

"Morning, Gary. How are things?"

Detective Superintendent Gary Julian did not return his smile. "Declan, I need to see you in my office." With that, the boss turned on his heel and left.

Declan frowned and swung back around to meet Charlie's equally bemused gaze.

"What's that all about?" Charlie asked.

Declan shook his head. "Damned if I know. I guess I'd better get in there and find out."

Declan pushed back his chair and walked the short distance to Gary's office. With a brief knock on the half open door, he entered and came to a halt in front of his boss' desk.

"Close the door."

Mystified at Gary's brusque tone, Declan did as he asked and tried to ignore the tiny fluttering of nerves in his gut. The last time he'd been called into a closed-door meeting with his superior had been more than a decade ago when, as a cadet fresh out of the Academy, he'd fucked up a simple roadside breath test by failing to ensure the machine had been properly calibrated.

The offender had "walked" on a high range offence and his boss had impressed upon the young probationary constable that a mistake like that must never happen again. Declan could still feel the burn of humiliation at the memory.

Gary had remained standing. Even at six foot four, Declan had to look up at him. The man was a bear.

"Is something the matter, Gary?" Declan kept his tone even, refusing to pay heed to his nervousness.

Gary's gaze fell to a pile of papers on his desk. He shifted them around and then sighed. When he looked up, his expression was grim.

"There's no easy way to say this, Declan. I've been contacted by Internal Affairs. They've received a call from someone who claims he can prove you've been accessing sensitive computer files without proper authorization. Given that you work in the Child Protection Unit, I don't have to tell you how serious this is."

Shock and disbelief rendered Declan momentarily speechless. He frowned hard and tried to process what he'd just heard, but it was no use. He couldn't comprehend for even an instant how anyone could come up with something so preposterous.

"That's... That's utter bullshit," he eventually sputtered. "I assume you mean files containing child porn?"

At Gary's tight nod, Declan shook his head. "How the hell...? I mean, why...? *Fuck*..." He shook his head again. "You're joking, right?"

Gary's expression remained disconcertingly grim.

"I wish I was. To say that I'm shocked is an understatement. You've been a star agent from the moment you walked in here, a real asset to the team. I don't want to believe for even a second you're involved in something so fucked up."

Desperation clawed at Declan's insides. Fear nipped at the edges of his consciousness and his throat tightened. He took a step closer to Gary's desk, fists clenched.

"It's not true, boss. You have to believe me, it's not true."

Gary's shoulders heaved on another sigh. "I want to, Declan. Believe me, I want to, but you must appreciate how sensitive this is. You work in the CPU. Any allegation— no matter how insubstantial—that an agent under my command has illegally accessed files will be investigated to the full extent of the law. Do you understand?"

Declan stared at him, his mouth agape.

Gary was the first to look away. "IA has already opened an investigation. You have an interview with them at nine o'clock on Monday morning. I need you to step down, effective immediately. You'll be on full pay until it's sorted out, one way or another."

The fear Declan had tried to suppress erupted into full-blown panic.

"Fuck, Gary. No! No, boss. Listen to me. I don't know what you're talking about. I don't have a fucking clue." He shook his head violently. "There's been some mistake. That can happen right? A computer glitch, or something." He stopped his frantic pacing and snapped his fingers. "That's it! It must be! A computer glitch. A fucking computer glitch. We'll probably be laughing about this in a day or so."

Gary remained unmoved, although Declan thought he saw a glimmer of sympathy in his boss' world-weary eyes. The sight of it ignited his anger.

"Don't go feeling sorry for me, Gary. Don't you fucking *dare*. This is bullshit! It wasn't me. There's been a mistake. You'll see. It's all a mistake. A simple, fucking mistake."

Gary rested his hands on his desk and leaned over it, holding Declan's gaze.

"I hope for your sake that's true. But in the meantime, I have my orders. You're standing down until further notice."

Declan stumbled out of Gary's office and headed in the direction of his own desk, his thoughts a disjointed blur. A dull roar sounded in his ears. In a daze, he saw Charlie stand and move toward him, a concerned expression on his face.

"Are you all right, mate?"

Declan pushed past him and staggered toward the locker room. His limbs were heavy, like they were weighed down with concrete. The door to the locker room seemed light years away.

Reaching it at last, he put a shoulder to its hard surface. The door gave way and he collapsed against the bank of steel lockers and sucked oxygen into his depleted lungs. His heart hammered against his chest.

Christ, he was having a heart attack.

"Shit, mate, you look awful. What's going on?"

Charlie's hands grasped the material of Declan's shirt and steadied him. Declan was thankful for the support, not at all sure his legs would continue to keep him upright.

"I don't know; I don't know," he gasped, shaking his head. "Someone's setting me up. IA is involved. I have to go."

Pulling out of Charlie's grasp, he turned and stumbled to his locker. Leaning heavily on the wall of steel, he released the combination lock and tossed his things into his gym bag. Charlie watched him in silence, concern marring his handsome features.

"IA? Fuck. What are you talking about? What can I do, mate? Please, talk to me. Tell me what I can do."

Declan stopped what he was doing and spun on his heel, anger exploding through his fear and confusion.

"I'll tell you what you can do. You can keep your eyes wide open and your ears to the ground. And spread the word. I'll find out who did this and when I do, I'll make them regret they ever fucking knew me."

CHAPTER 2

The snooze button went off for the third time and Chloe Sabattini groaned. She lost another minute of sleep debating whether she could actually afford to spend any more time in bed... Then guilt won out and she reluctantly pushed off the blankets and climbed out—her weekend was officially over.

After her restless night, she thought briefly about skipping the shower, but one look at her thick, black hair standing on end changed her mind. Nothing but water, conditioner and a hairdryer would be strong enough to tame the long, riotous curls into the order and respectability expected of a senior Australian Federal Police Internal Affairs investigator.

Toweling dry after a few minutes under the steaming hot spray, she slid open the door to her closet and surveyed its contents. Like every other morning, an array of sensible black and navy suits and even more sensible tailored white or pastel blouses hung there.

Once, months ago, in a fit of daring she'd bought a fancy fitted-silk blouse in the hottest of pink, but she'd stowed it in the back of her cupboard as soon as she returned home. The price tag was still attached.

It wasn't that she didn't have a healthy self-esteem. She was more than happy to have inherited her parents' dark Italian coloring; that her flawless olive skin was envied by her school friends when she'd sailed through puberty with barely a zit and they'd been battling full scale acne; that her figure, although a little on the short side, was compact and curvy in all the right places—or so she'd been told by the handful of men she'd briefly dated since she'd been old enough to drive. She was even happy with her mostly straight, white teeth that had emerged without the aid of braces.

But despite these positive physical attributes, she'd never managed to completely overcome her shyness...and drawing attention to herself with bright, bold colors had never been something she was brave enough to entertain for more than a few wistful minutes.

The mantle of confidence, strength and unquestionable authority she exuded at work was a far cry from her private self. If she'd told any of her work colleagues about her affliction, they'd have rolled around the floor with laughter, not to mention disbelief. That was one of the reasons she'd chosen her occupation. Her job as a hard-nosed IA investigator forced her to become the woman she wished she could be and she lived in the vain hope that somehow, somewhere the professional confidence would rub off into her personal life.

No one had guessed that beneath the poised, self-assured exterior she wore to work, along with the classic, tailored suits, was a woman who wasn't even brave enough to flirt or ask a man out. She was sure it had something to do with the time way back in high school when, after weeks of agonizing, she'd finally found the courage to ask the boy of her dreams if he'd like to go to the library with her after school.

The humiliation of his emphatic 'No' and his subsequent retelling of the encounter to all of his friends had lived with her for many years and, if she were truly honest, even now, the memory of it still left her embarrassed.

Her glance fell on the snatch of hot pink silk that peeked out from underneath a shoebox on the top shelf of her closet, but then quickly skittered away. Today wasn't the day to trial bravado. She'd been up most of the night reading over the file of Federal Agent Declan Munro and was scheduled to interview him later that morning.

The allegations were serious—much too serious for a frilly, form-fitting, hot-pink blouse—even if it was teamed with a sensible, tailored navy skirt and matching jacket.

With a sigh, she reached for the nearest pastel blouse and pulled it off the hanger.

———————

Chloe glanced at her watch and wiped slightly damp palms down the sides of her skirt. The bare walls of the interview room suddenly seemed too close. She always got nervous right before a major interview, especially one involving such serious misconduct. Even when it was being conducted on her turf, the nerves still set in.

She'd obtained a photograph of Declan Munro from the AFP's personnel office and the image of the man with sparkling green-flecked brown eyes and a broad, cheeky smile looked better suited to a glossy magazine model than a sexual predator, but she'd learned the hard way not to be taken in by someone's more-than-pleasing looks and she was determined not to make the same mistake again.

A short rap on the closed door of the interview room interrupted her thoughts. Looking up, she caught the brief flash of light brown hair through the small square of clear viewing glass on the door. She drew in a deep breath and let it out slowly. Remaining seated, she called for him to enter.

Her first thought was that his photo hadn't done him justice. His hair was flecked with lighter pieces of gold. It was thick and wavy and looked ruffled in a sexy, straight-from-the-bedroom kind of way. A bold, lime-green tie, liberally embellished with navy and silver polka dots, eclipsed a well-cut navy suit and dazzling white business shirt. The fabric looked expensive, but the colors weren't for the faint hearted.

Then he smiled. Open, warm, honest. Her heart skipped a

beat and then hammered against her chest. In the flesh, Declan Munro was more than she imagined. He was beautiful. And incredibly tall.

He reminded Chloe of an athlete—all tanned, taut skin and long, athletic limbs. Even under his suit, his body looked hard.

She swallowed and then blinked, turning her attention to the hand that had been extended in her direction. Pushing away from the desk, she stood and returned his handshake. Her hand was engulfed in a warm, firm grip.

"I'm Federal Agent Declan Munro. I take it you're from IA?"

Retrieving her hand with undue haste, Chloe swiped at an errant strand of hair that had come loose from the sensible bun at the nape of her neck and tried to regain her composure.

"Senior Investigator Sabattini. And yes, I'm from IA. Th-thank you for coming in."

A gleam of surprised amusement lit up the green-brown of his eyes and sent her pulse skyrocketing. Heat flooded her face. Flustered, she turned away.

Get a grip, Chloe. So what if he's as good looking as... Her mind was in such a muddle, she couldn't even come up with an acceptable comparison.

Not that it was important. His looks were irrelevant, along with his expensive clothes. He was being investigated for accessing online child pornography. Nothing else mattered.

The thought sobered her. She regained her seat and opened the file on the desk in front of her and indicated for him to sit down opposite in the single remaining chair.

"I take it you know why you're here?"

His smile evaporated and his eyes narrowed. "Oh, I know all right. I know it's bullshit. Whatever you have in there," he pointed toward the file in her hands, "is total bullshit."

Chloe was used to anger. The offenders she interviewed usually cycled through an arsenal of emotions: shock, anger, disbelief, denial, guilt, remorse and sometimes back to anger again. It wasn't easy to get them to admit to their guilt, but she prided herself on having a knack for getting to the heart of a suspect.

Most of the time, deep down, they weren't bad people. After all, they'd gone into the AFP for noble reasons, wanting to serve and protect their community. It was just that somewhere along the way, things veered off course.

It helped her to think of it like this. Somehow, it made her job more bearable. She also wholeheartedly believed in the justice system that presumed a man innocent until he was proven guilty. It was this belief that helped her do what had to be done. After all, the ultimate decision about guilt or innocence lay with the courts.

Ignoring his outburst, she kept her expression neutral and tugged the blank legal pad and pen toward her.

"I need to ask you a few questions, Agent Munro, and I'd like you to answer them honestly. I'm sure you understand that when an allegation such as this is made, it must be thoroughly investigated. However, I'd like to remind you, this is an investigation, not an interrogation. Who knows? If you answer the questions to my satisfaction, this whole thing may not go any further."

He stared at her. Dragging her gaze away, she concentrated on the pad in front of her. "Do you agree to answer my questions, Agent Munro?"

The earlier glimmer of amusement was long gone. His lips tightened and his expression turned hard. "It's not like I have any choice."

"Of course you do. You have the right to seek legal representation and you are entitled to have your lawyer present during this interview." Chloe looked up from the notepad in front of her and caught his gaze. Green-flecked eyes stared back at her unflinchingly.

"Would you like to speak to a lawyer, Agent Munro?"

"No. I have nothing to hide. Ask your questions. Let's get this bullshit over with."

The anger in his voice was reflected in his eyes. Chloe held his gaze a few seconds longer, searching for signs of insincerity. So far, she'd been unable to detect even the slightest hesitation.

Still, the evidence was there in her file. She needed to get past the fact he was gorgeous and get on with her job— digging to get to the truth.

She nodded. "All right, let's get on with it. Try to keep in mind that if you provide me with honest answers, we'll get to the bottom of this very quickly. Tell me lies and it will take longer. Either way, I'll find out the truth eventually. It's your choice."

He eyeballed her again and she forced herself to remain unmoved. "I'm obliged to tell you this interview will be recorded." She reached for the remote control that lay on the desk and pointed it in the direction of the video recorder that was fixed to a shelf in the corner opposite to where they sat. High above it, hung a camera.

"For the sake of the video," she continued, "I will introduce both of us. My name is Senior Investigator Sabattini and I have with me Federal Agent Declan Munro." After confirming the time and the date, Chloe turned to him.

"Agent Munro, is your full name Declan Andrew Munro and do you live at 9-338 Jonas Road, Kingston Foreshore?"

The man seated opposite her gave a brisk nod.

"I'm sorry, Agent Munro, I must have a verbal response from you."

"Yes, that's my name and my address."

"That's a nice part of town, Agent Munro. Do you rent or own there?"

"Not that I see the relevance of your question to this interview, but I rent, Senior Investigator Sabattini."

She failed to rise to his bait. "How old are you, Agent Munro?"

"I turned thirty-four a few weeks ago."

Chloe hid her surprise. He held his age well. If she'd been asked to guess, she would have thought him younger, closer to her age. She filed the information away and continued.

"You've been requested to attend this interview for the purposes of answering questions regarding an alleged incident or incidents that occurred during the course of the week commencing August thirteenth this year.

Her eyes narrowed on his face. "Agent Munro, have you ever accessed confidential departmental computer files without proper authorization?"

His gaze remained steady on hers. "No."

"Can you tell me what your departmental username and password is?"

His lips twisted. "I'm sure you've already received that information or else I wouldn't be here. Surely, that's what you're hanging your hat on, isn't it? The fact that my username and password was used to illegally access files on my computer?"

Chloe's anger stirred, but she held it in check. "For the purposes of this interview, Agent Munro, can you please tell me your username and password?"

His face hardened. His words became clipped. "My username is declanmunro22@afp_cpu. My password is Cassie."

Chloe dropped her gaze, ostensibly to make some notes, but her thoughts snagged on his password.

Cassie. His wife, perhaps? She forced the thought from her mind, silently castigating herself. What the hell did she care if he was married? If the allegations proved to be founded, she'd have nothing but sympathy for his unsuspecting spouse.

"Agent Munro, have you ever told anyone else your username?"

"No."

"What about your password?"

"No."

She glanced back up at him. "Not even your wife?"

"I don't have a wife."

"Girlfriend?"

"No."

"No, you haven't told her or no, you don't have one?"

Irritation flared in his eyes and Chloe held her breath. The question wasn't work related. She prayed he wouldn't take issue with it.

She breathed a tiny sigh of relief when he shook his head and answered her, the anger easing out of his voice.

"No, Senior Investigator Sabattini, I do not have a girlfriend."

Chloe ignored the *zing* of satisfaction that arced through her and concentrated on the rest of his answer.

"And even if I did," he continued, "I wouldn't tell her my username or password. I've already told you: I've told *no one*."

Satisfied, she looked at the list of questions in front of her. "Have you ever written your username and/or your password down, either at work or at your home?"

He was already shaking his head before she finished. "No."

"You're sure?"

His eyes bored into hers. "I'm *sure*."

"Then, Agent Munro, how do you explain how your username and password were used to access files from four different investigations over the course of a week, none of which you were involved in, and all containing images of child pornography? These files were not only accessed by you, but they were saved onto the hard drive of your computer."

Chloe watched him closely. Tension returned to his body. His fists clenched and unclenched. Anger heightened the color in his cheeks—or was it guilt?

He looked at her, his eyes like flint. "Anyone could have done that. I'm only there for one shift a day. There is at least one other shift and sometimes two, every day, where someone else has access to my computer. You know that."

Chloe returned his stare. "Of course, I do. But that doesn't explain how they got hold of your username and password. You've already told me no one else knew it."

"So, they must have *stolen* it." His large frame moved restlessly in the chair. He ran a hand through his hair and tugged at the thick strands.

Chloe refused to be moved by his frustration, no matter how genuine it appeared.

"Usernames and passwords are issued out of the Home Affairs Office on the day you're entered into their system as an AFP employee. Are you seriously accusing a staff member in that office of stealing your details, sneaking into your squad room unnoticed, accessing files and saving them to a computer—I'm guessing one of about twenty or so in your squad room—that you just happen to use?" She shook her head. "Even I can't stretch my imagination that far."

Declan's shoulders slumped on a heavy sigh. He leaned forward and rested his elbows on the desk, his head in his hands.

Chloe's pulse quickened. He was going to confess. Feeling equal amounts of satisfaction and disappointment, she braced herself with her pen poised.

"You don't have to tell me how bad it looks, Senior Investigator Sabattini. All I know for sure is, it wasn't me." His words were muffled beneath his fingers.

"I'm sorry, Agent Munro, do you mind repeating that?"

He looked up and captured her gaze, his eyes imploring hers. "I said it wasn't *me*."

Compassion stirred inside her. She wanted to believe him. He looked so genuine, so honest, so...lost—like he didn't know what to do next. She cleared her throat and tried to regain her professional demeanor.

"Agent Munro, I've read your file. You had a long and impressive career with the New South Wales Police Service before you relocated to Canberra. I'm curious: Why did you transfer to the AFP, and more particularly, to the CPU?"

Long moments passed. She didn't think he was going to answer. When he did speak, his voice was pitched low.

"I transferred because of Cassie. My niece."

His niece.

Heat suffused Chloe's cheeks. She cursed under her breath. Damn her overactive imagination and damn her for caring that Carrie wasn't what she'd assumed.

She strove to keep her voice neutral. "What about your niece?"

Declan looked away, as if gathering his thoughts. Finally, he turned back to face her.

"It happened a little over a year ago. My niece was kidnapped and assaulted by a pedophile in Sydney. I was a State copper at the time. I assisted the AFP taskforce and helped capture him."

Chloe's eyebrows rose in surprise. It was the last thing she'd expected him to say and while his tone had remained flat and unemotional throughout his recital, she could well imagine how traumatic it had been for everyone involved.

As if he could read her thoughts, he spoke again. "I know what you're thinking. And the answer is, yes. It was one of the toughest cases I'd been involved in, probably more so because of my personal connection. I freely admit it did my head in for a good while afterwards. I was beyond furious at the sick fu—" He looked away. A flush stained his cheeks. "I mean, the sick men—and let's face it, it's usually men—who get off on little kids. I couldn't even get past the *thought* of it and then to have the evilness of it touch someone so close to me—it messed me up a bit. I took stress leave and attended counseling. I was halfway through my fifth session when I realized what I had to do. I had to go after them. Every last one of them."

Chloe stared at him, trying to gauge his sincerity. "There's no mention of any of this in your file."

Declan blew out his breath on a sigh. "I don't know what it says in there." He pointed to the file open on her desk. "But I told the powers that be when they interviewed me. I told them everything—about Cassie and what happened afterwards—but it didn't matter to them. My record as a senior State detective spoke for itself. As did the reputation of my brothers." He tossed her a wry grin. "I'm sure having two brothers with stellar careers in the AFP didn't harm my chances."

Chloe frowned in thought. She recalled reading about Clayton and Brandon Munro in Declan's personnel file. Clayton was a hotshot profiler and had been with the AFP for years. Brandon was similarly well thought of and had spent an impressive amount of time working as an undercover operative. On top of his brothers' achievements, Declan was the son of the first aboriginal District Court Judge to preside over a court in New South Wales. She could see how having relatives like them would improve his chances of gaining entry.

"So, that's why you applied for the CPU? Because of what had happened to your niece?"

He nodded, his expression sobering. "Yep. I found out firsthand what it felt like to be brushed by evil. Thank Christ we caught him before he raped her. She was spared that agony, but I vowed to do all that I could to make sure assholes like that could never harm children again."

His voice had roughened with emotion. When he looked back at her, his eyes were shadowed. A moment later, he shrugged and looked away.

"So, I transferred," he added.

"You could have worked in similar State-based units."

"Yep, I could have, but you guys go after the big fish, the huge pedophile rings that operate both here and overseas. I have big numbers in my sights. I want to bring down each and every one of them."

The passion and determination in his hard gaze shivered down her spine. She believed every word he said. It was so contrary to the preliminary file of evidence in front of her that she shook her head in confusion. Was it all a front? Or was he telling the truth?

"What happens now?"

She blinked. His quiet question brought her out of her kaleidoscoping thoughts and forced her attention back to him.

"I'll talk to the other witnesses and then a report will be prepared based upon my findings."

A frown marred the smooth tanned skin of his forehead. "What do you mean, other witnesses?"

"Your boss, your colleagues—including the one who came forward with the initial complaint."

Declan's eyes blazed. "A *colleague*? You're shitting me?

Who is it? Who's the asshole that started all this bullshit? They're who you should be looking at."

Chloe held his gaze, feeling genuinely contrite. "I'm afraid I can't tell you that, Agent Munro. If charges are laid and it goes before a court, naturally you and your lawyer will be given access to all of the evidence against you. Until then, the identity of the primary witness will remain confidential." She glanced at her watch and noted the time.

"It's ten-thirty in the morning. Unless you have any further questions, this interview will now be suspended. Please remain within close proximity of your usual address so that you can be contacted, if necessary. If you have to leave Canberra for any reason, you will need to let me know. Agent Munro, do you understand?"

He shot her a blistering look, his lips white with tension, but gave her a tight nod. She gathered the papers on her desk and put them back into the file.

"I suggest you call a lawyer or at the very least, talk to someone in our legal department," she added. "I don't need to remind you these allegations are serious."

"Are we done?"

She nodded brusquely. "For now. I'll be in touch."

CHAPTER 3

Declan stumbled toward the elevators that loomed a lifetime away down the hall, his head buzzing. *Unauthorized…witnesses…charges…lawyers…evidence.*

Fuck! How the hell had his life spiraled out of control so quickly? After his conversation with Gary, he'd spent the rest of Friday wandering aimlessly through Civic in a shocked daze. Over the weekend, he'd looked at possible scenarios from every angle he could think of and before the interview, he'd convinced himself that he'd blown the whole incident out of proportion and that it would be sorted out with an apology and a handshake within minutes of his meeting with the IA officer. He couldn't have been more wrong.

When he'd first spied the hot-looking investigator through the Perspex window, he'd even thought he'd be able to charm her into dropping the whole thing. The sensible navy jacket and skirt did nothing to conceal her shapely legs or the generous cleavage he'd glimpsed through the opening of her shirt.

The frown as she'd stared down at the notes in her file had only emphasized her high cheekbones and when she'd caught her full bottom lip between those even, white teeth, despite the seriousness of his predicament, his body had stirred.

But it had quickly become obvious she meant business. Even still, he'd been confident the truth would eventually win out. But now she was talking about laying charges…

Christ. Panic spiked at the edges of his consciousness and he brutally forced it back. Punching the 'down' button on the wall at the elevators, he drew in a deep breath. He had to remain calm, keep a clear head and think things through.

He had to call Clayton.

Pulling his phone out of his shirt pocket, he switched it off silent and dialed Clayton's number. He prayed his brother would answer and he sighed with relief when he did.

"Clayton, thank Christ I caught you." Tripping over his words, he gave Clayton a brief, jumbled explanation. Gratitude flooded through him when his brother replied without hesitation.

"I'll be right there."

———————

Declan answered the front door of his apartment and returned his brother's handshake.

"Thanks for getting here so quickly, Clay. I appreciate it."

Clayton's expression was somber. "Anytime, mate. I know you'd do the same for me. In fact, you have."

Declan's lips compressed, his thoughts full of the Clayton of six years ago, who'd mourned his wife's suicide. Declan was pleased to note there were no signs of that devastation now. The passage of time and Clayton's new wife, Ellie, had everything to do with that.

"How are Ellie and the kids?" he asked.

A soft smile tilted Clayton's mouth. "Great. They're great. Olivia's getting bigger and bossier by the day. Mitchell turned four last month and thinks he rules the house and Damon... What can I say? You were over at our place a few weeks ago. You saw him. He's twelve months old and into everything. This morning he pulled all the trash out of the bin and tossed it all over the kitchen. He's driving us all nuts." Clayton shook his head. "And Ellie keeps telling me she wants another."

Declan chuckled and stood aside to let his brother enter.

"You love every minute of it," he said, a little wistfully.

"Yeah, you're right. I do."

Declan pushed aside thoughts of the wife and children he didn't have, and started making coffee. His state-of-the-art machine had two steaming hot mugs of black brew ready in minutes. He handed a mug to Clayton.

"Thanks."

"It's the least I could do," Declan said and took a sip of his coffee.

After taking a couple of quick gulps, Clayton set his mug aside. Leaning back against the black granite countertop, he folded his arms across his chest and looked Declan squarely in the eye.

"All right, big brother, hit me with it. Your garbled explanation over the phone made my head spin. I'm still not sure I heard you right. I want you to start at the beginning and tell me what the hell you've gotten yourself into?"

Declan's shoulders slumped. All at once, the pressure of the past few days caught up with him. He needed someone to offload onto. Someone who wouldn't judge. Someone who would understand.

Declan might have been the older by three years, but Clayton had been an AFP agent for more than a decade. Declan both valued and respected his opinion.

"I'm in the shit, Clay. Christ knows how I got here. That's completely beyond me at the moment, but I need help and I need it fast."

Concern creased the folds around Clayton's eyes. "What the hell's going on, Dec?"

Declan turned and paced the length of the open-plan kitchen and living room. The stylishly appointed apartment boasted impressive views across Lake Burley Griffin, but he hardly registered the sparkling brilliance of the early spring sunshine as it bounced off the clear, wind-rippled water.

Starting at the beginning, he told Clayton about the accusation, then of the shock, the confusion, the disbelief and the anger when Gary Julian's words had sunk in.

He told him how he'd wracked his brains over the weekend following his meeting in his boss' office, trying to figure out who could be responsible, but had come up with nothing. And then he told Clayton about Senior Investigator Sabattini.

"Christ, Declan," Clayton muttered, running a hand through the disheveled length of his blond hair. "Who the hell would do something like this?"

Declan laughed humorlessly. "I've spent the last seventy-five hours or so asking the same thing and I still come up blank."

"Why didn't you call me earlier? I can't believe you've carried it around with you all this time."

Declan shook his head, his lips compressed. "I thought it would blow over. I know darn well I didn't do it. I assumed I'd meet with IA, set the record straight and be back at work in the morning. Never in my wildest dreams did I see it panning out this way."

Clayton pushed himself away from the kitchen countertop and went to stand near the floor-to-ceiling glass doors that led out onto the balcony. He gazed out at the view, but showed no signs of seeing the sparkling display from the lake below. Moments later, he spun on his heel to face Declan. "What about now? Have you called any of the others? Brandon? Tom? Riley?"

Declan shook his head.

"Tell me you've at least told Mom and Dad?"

"No, you're the first one to know. Like I said, up until now, I thought it would be resolved at the first meeting. When the IA investigator mentioned talking to other witnesses before she wrote her report, I started to panic. That's why I called you. You've been in the AFP longer than any of us. Besides, you live in the same town."

"You need a lawyer. I'll call the family. They'll want to know what's going on."

Declan opened his mouth to protest, but Clayton waved him off. "They're your family, your mom and dad. Wouldn't you want to know if it was one of your kids?"

"I don't have any kids."

Clayton ignored him. "We need a lawyer from Sydney. The best there is. Tom and Brandon will know who to call. Sydney's their turf. And that's before we talk to Dad about calling in a few favors."

Clayton tugged out his phone and scrolled through his contacts. Declan eased out his breath, already feeling better than he had since he'd been given the news. He moved back toward the kitchen and collected his mug from where he'd left it on the counter. His phone vibrated in his pocket.

Taking a slug of coffee, he checked the caller ID and then answered the call.

"Charlie, how are things?"

"Shit, mate, what's going on? I can't *believe* it. The things they're all saying at the office... That IA's all over you. I won't believe it. I told them all to shut the fuck up. I wanted you to know I'm here for you, mate. If there's anything I can do..."

Declan puffed out his breath on a heavy sigh and took another mouthful of coffee.

"Thanks, mate. I appreciate it. And thanks for the vote of confidence. I thought after working with those other blokes for more than a year, they'd know me better than that, but apparently not. I guess you never can tell."

"Well, as some poor bastard said, 'It's when you're down that you find out who your true friends are.'"

"Isn't that the truth," Declan replied with a grimace.

"I mean it, mate. If there's anything I can do..."

"Yeah, thanks. Do you fancy hitting a bar on the foreshore tonight? I know it's the beginning of the week, but right now, all I want to do is get good and drunk and forget I ever heard of IA."

Images of the good-looking investigator immediately came to the forefront of Declan's mind.

Too bad she worked for the enemy. He hadn't felt such interest in a girl since Alice and he broke up.

Not that he'd had much practise, lately. He'd given the whole dating scene a miss for the past year. Having the girl you thought you'd one day call your wife run off with a work colleague could do that.

It wasn't as if there hadn't been plenty of offers, but most of them had come from female officers he worked with and he'd always had a rule about mixing business with pleasure. It was fine when things were going well, but it all got too messy when the relationship went south.

But little Miss IA had sparked enough interest that under different circumstances he could almost see himself breaking his rule.

Declan shook his head and scoffed.

Who was he kidding? She was enemy number one—a woman to be avoided at all costs. He was grateful when Charlie accepted his invitation and his thoughts moved to the much safer ground of when and where they would meet and seek to eradicate the last few days.

Chip stood before him in the dimness of the Master's office and delivered his update in a voice shaky with nerves. The Master chuckled silently, his generous girth jiggling with the effort.

He loved their fear. The boy was past thirty, yet still he feared him. The sound and scent of it excited him, made him hard with wanting.

The sun had long ago vanished from the sky and the traffic outside the window had been reduced to a sporadic hum. The heavy, dark drapes had been drawn against the oncoming night, cocooning him in secrecy and warmth.

"And so it begins," he murmured under his breath.

The younger man's recital came to an end and the Master clapped his hands softly.

"Good job, boy. You've done well."

"Th-thank you, Master. I-I like to please you."

The Master chuckled again. "Oh, I like you to please me, too. I like it very much."

He pushed away from the enormous slab of cedar that formed his desk and eased his bulk from the chair. He made his way around the front of the desk and sauntered toward the tall, locked cabinet that stood on the opposite wall.

Chip's eyes widened with excitement and his cheeks grew flushed.

With great exaggeration, the Master jiggled around in the pocket of his suit pants and pulled out a key, which he fitted into the lock of the cupboard. From the corner of his eye, he saw the younger man shift his weight from foot to foot. The Master's cock stirred to life.

He retrieved the black leather riding crop from the cabinet and closed and relocked the door. Slapping the side of his leg with the stiff piece of leather, he turned and moved closer to Chip.

"Take off your shirt, boy and get down on your knees. It's time for your reward."

Chip hurried to comply and the Master positioned himself in front of the man's waiting mouth. He eased the zipper over his swollen cock and pulled his erection out of his underwear. He swiped the tip of it across Chip's lips.

Chip moaned and opened his mouth and the Master thrust all the way inside.

"Do what you do best, boy."

Chip complied. The Master tensed with pleasure. He raised the crop and ran it lovingly over the other man's back. The boy's naked skin glowed palely in the dim light. Chip shivered and renewed his efforts.

"Ah, that's it, boy, that's it. You know so well how to please me. Keep it up and you'll be in charge of your own Area Command before you know it."

CHAPTER 4

Chloe glanced at the bedside clock and sighed. It was a little after six, barely early enough for the sun to rise over the hills in the distance. She still had a couple of hours before she had to leave for work. It was a shame she'd woken so early. The only good thing about it was that she'd have time to call her mother.

Reaching across the double bed, she scrabbled for the telephone and dialed her mother's number. Giovanna Sabattini answered on the second ring.

"What are you calling so early for, bambina? I thought I was the only one who got up before the sun?"

Chloe smiled and settled herself back against the pillows. "Now, Mama, don't be like that. I woke early and thought I'd call you. Is there anything wrong with that?"

Her mother *tsk tsked* on the other end of the phone, but Chloe could tell she was pleased. Ever since Chloe had been promoted to senior investigator, calls to her mother had been squeezed into the tiny slivers of time she had between work matters. It had been weeks since they'd had a decent chat and even longer since she'd gone home for a family dinner.

Guilt shot through her at the thought. It wasn't as though her parents lived interstate. They were less than half an hour away, in Queanbeyan. She had no excuse. Other than the one that she kept repeating to her mother every time the conversation came up and which happened to be true: She was far too busy at work.

"How are you, bambina?" her mother asked and Chloe felt warm inside knowing her mother really wanted to know.

"I'm all right, Mama. Busy, you know."

"Work, work, work. That's all you ever do. You won't find a man that way, bambina."

Chloe sighed and braced herself for the usual, well-meaning tirade. Her mother didn't disappoint.

"When I was your age, I'd been married for nearly a decade. I had three children under eight and another one on the way."

Chloe had heard it all before and knew her protestations fell on deaf ears, but she made them anyway.

"Mama, I'm only thirty. That's hardly geriatric. And I have a career. A very successful career. Right now, I need to put my energies into that if I want it to continue to flourish."

"Oh, pooh to a career! How is a career going to keep you warm at night, bambina? Or give you babies? It's time you started putting your energies into *that*! And who's going to give me more grandbabies?"

Chloe rolled her eyes. "Mama, between Cathy, Carlo and Antonella, you already have ten grandbabies. How many more do you want?"

"I want *your* granbabies, bambina. I don't want you to get to be an old woman and look back and regret you don't have any. And that's what will happen, bambina. You mark my words! It's time you found yourself a husband. Even better if he's a nice strong Italian boy. A man who will do your family proud."

"Yes, Mama. You're right. I'll go right out now and find one. I can probably Google "Italian husband hunt" on the Internet. I don't know why I haven't done it already. Thank you, Mama. You're always right."

Chloe's answer was met with suspicious silence. She tried to hold back a giggle but failed.

"Chloe Maria Sabattini! You are a naughty, naughty girl! You shouldn't say such awful things to your mama. If I was over there now I would turn you over my knee. It's exactly what you deserve!"

Chloe laughed harder and swiped at the tears that formed in the corner of her eyes.

"Oh, Mama! *You're* exactly what I need. Thank you for brightening up my day!"

"Humph!"

"No, Mama, I mean it. I have a tough interview ahead of me and I'm grateful that you've managed to take my mind off it."

Her mother's voice sobered. "Are you okay, bambina? Are you eating right?"

Chloe thought of Agent Munro and the way he'd looked at her right before he'd stormed out. In a few short hours, she'd be interviewing the man who'd reported the incidents. A man who, according to the file, Agent Munro had previously called "friend."

———

The AFP headquarters was situated in the Edmund Barton building on the edge of the Parliamentary Triangle. A short drive away on the Hill sat Parliament House, an impressive example of modern architecture where life-changing decisions were often made on a daily basis.

The stark interview room on the fifth floor was exactly how Chloe had left it the day before. The same bland, blank walls surrounded her. The same gray-laminate desk and two hard plastic chairs took up most of the space in the small room. Not a single window broke up the sparse expanse of off-white walls. There was not a hint of the gorgeous spring morning she'd had a brief chance to encounter on her way inside.

Chloe placed her briefcase on the desk and pulled out the Munro file. After Agent Munro had left, she'd taken the time to make notes on the interview and in particular, record her overall judgement of his demeanor and level of sincerity. A copy of his ERISP, or electronic record of interview of a suspected person, was also in the file.

She had to admit, if she hadn't been presented with irrefutable evidence that he'd accessed the files, the light of honesty and integrity that had shone in his way-too distracting eyes would have swayed her. But, by his own admission, no one knew his login details, which meant that his guilt was almost assured. All that was left to do was to interview the man who'd first drawn the matter to the attention of his superior.

Promptly at nine o'clock, a knock sounded on the door. Chloe arranged her notepad and pen and then called for the person to enter.

A man she guessed to be somewhere around Agent Munro's age entered the room. A smile of greeting belied the wariness in his dark blue eyes. Surprise and a little nervousness barreled through Chloe's stomach. *What was it with the agents in the CPU?* Charlie Stanford was just as good-looking as his friend.

Tall and without an inch of flab in evidence under the expensive business shirt and tailored suit pants, she was sure the mop of fair, sun-bleached hair and baby blues would have the girls running from all directions.

Pushing the thought aside, she stuck out her hand. "Agent Stanford, I'm Senior Investigator Sabattini. Thank you for coming."

Her hand was engulfed in a firm handshake. "It's nice to meet you, Senior Investigator Sabattini and please, call me Charlie."

Chloe nodded. "All right, Charlie. Take a seat and let's get started."

After checking there was a fresh tape in the video recorder and going through the preliminaries, Chloe commenced the interview.

"How long have you known Agent Munro?"

Charlie leaned back in his chair, his body now relaxed. "A bit over a year. He transferred into the CPU just over twelve months ago. I was already working there."

"And how would you describe your relationship?"

"We're mates. Good mates. We spend a lot of our free time together. I thought I knew him pretty well."

"Did you know that before he joined the AFP, he was a detective with the New South Wales Police?"

"Yes, I was aware of that."

"I'm curious about his reasons for transferring. A State detective working in general crime is a long way from a Federal Agent chasing online pedophiles. Do you know why he transferred?"

Charlie shrugged. "No, I don't. It's not something we've ever talked about. In fact, I don't think I've asked any of the blokes I work with what brought them to the CPU."

"What brought *you* to the CPU?"

"The kids," Charlie stated simply. "I do it for the kids."

Chloe made a notation in her file and then looked up again. "Do you know anything about Agent Munro's family?"

"Only that he has a big one. Three or four brothers and a couple of sisters. I think a couple of his younger brothers work for the AFP."

"Have you met any of his family?"

"No."

Chloe penned a reminder to research them a little deeper. It would help her to get a sense of his family and his origins. With two of them being AFP employees, her search would be made a little easier.

"All right, Charlie. Let's talk about the incidents. I understand you reported them to Detective Superintendent Gary Julian?"

"Yes, that's right."

"I've read your statement, but I want you to tell me what happened."

Charlie's lips tightened and the wariness returned to his face. He drew in a deep breath and eased it out. With obvious reluctance, he answered.

"It wasn't one thing in particular that got me wondering. It was a series of things. About a month ago, I came into work early. I had some paperwork I needed to finish and I thought if I came in before my shift started, I'd have the time to complete it. I was surprised to find Declan already there."

"What time was this?"

"About five in the morning. My shift was due to start at six. I figured an hour would be all that I'd need."

Chloe noted down the time. "Did you say anything to Agent Munro about why he was there so early?"

"Yeah, I joked that he mustn't have scored with the hot blonde he'd been chatting up in a bar we'd been to the night before. Dec was getting it on with some chick in a tight red dress and I decided to leave him to it. I left a little after ten."

Chloe refused to acknowledge the twinge of jealousy that tightened her belly. She forged on.

"What was Agent Munro's response?"

"Something about him losing interest after the third drink. I don't know. I didn't pay that much attention. I was there to catch up on paperwork."

"What was Agent Munro doing?"

"See, that's where things got a bit weird. When I got closer to his desk, he closed the screen he had opened on the computer, kind of like he didn't want me to see it."

Chloe scribbled in her notepad. "Did you say anything to him?"

"No. I thought I might have been overreacting. I shrugged it off and got on with my day."

"What else happened? There must have been something else for you to go to Superintendent Julian? After all, this man is your friend."

Charlie's face turned grave. "Yes. There was something else. I wish to God I hadn't seen it, but I couldn't pretend any longer that I hadn't. I'd suspected something wasn't right for over a month. I'd tossed and turned and inspected the facts from all angles and there's only one explanation I came up with. Hence, my approach to the boss."

Chloe turned to a fresh page of her notepad, trying hard to ignore the anguish on Charlie's face. "Tell me what happened during that time."

A heavy sigh rumbled out of the man across from her. He leaned back further in his chair and folded his hands behind his head.

"After that first incident, there were a couple of other times during the same week that I caught Dec by surprise and both times he reacted the same way: Closing down the page he'd been viewing and acting kind of weird."

"And you still didn't say anything to him?"

"No."

"To anyone?"

"No."

"What made you change your mind?"

"A week ago, I stayed back after my shift finished. I was meeting a friend for a drink in town and I decided to shower and change at work rather than return home.

"I'd said good-bye to Dec earlier, when our shift had ended. I think he must have assumed I'd left. When I came out of the locker room, the squad room was quiet except for the handful of agents that had just clocked on for the night shift. They were gathered in the tea room making coffee and basically shooting the breeze.

"I'd left my wallet and keys on my desk. I sit right behind Dec. We're like...three or four feet away from each other. I'm not sure why he didn't notice me, but he didn't. I reached my desk and looked over in his direction and that's when I saw it."

"Saw what?"

"Kiddie porn all over Dec's computer screen. I recognized them as being images from one of my earlier investigations—an investigation that had finished months ago."

"Had Agent Munro been involved in that investigation?"

Charlie shook his head. "No. I'd been partnered with a few other agents."

"Was there any reason for him to be viewing those images?"

"None at all. As I said, that particular investigation had

finished four or five months earlier. We arrested eight men who are now on remand awaiting trial."

"Did you say anything to him?"

"No! Christ, it made me sick! He was my mate! I couldn't believe it! All I wanted to do was get out of there and pretend it had never happened!"

"Had Agent Munro ever shown inappropriate interest in children before?"

Charlie ran his hands through his hair and shook his head again. His cheeks were flushed and his breath came faster. "No! Christ, no!"

Chloe gave him a few minutes to compose himself. "What did you do?" she asked.

"That's the thing. I didn't do anything. I didn't know what to do, what to think. All the times I'd seen him closing pages on his computer whenever I approached, the furtiveness, the secrecy, the late nights, the early starts—all of a sudden, it all made a horrible kind of sense.

"Somewhere, deep down, I'd known what it all meant. But even then, I didn't want to believe it. Declan! A good mate! A guy I thought I knew quite well."

Drawing in a deep breath, Charlie eased it out, the tension in his body releasing. He looked up at her, his eyes full of distress.

"I couldn't eat, I couldn't sleep and worst of all, I had to keep working with him, pretending everything was normal, pretending I didn't *know*. In the end, I couldn't take it anymore. I told my boss."

Chloe frowned and continued to scrawl notes. What Charlie had told her sounded legitimate and the access records from Agent Munro's computer backed it up. But both men weren't telling the truth.

Chloe bit down on a sigh and closed her notebook. "Charlie, thank you for coming in. I appreciate it. I know how difficult this must be, given how much Agent Munro means to you and I want to assure you we will be giving this matter our utmost attention. We take every complaint of wrong-doing seriously, but I'm sure you can appreciate how very serious these allegations are."

Charlie nodded, his expression calmer. "So, what happens now?"

"Like I told Agent Munro, I'm going to interview Detective Superintendent Julian and thereafter I will review the evidence and make my recommendations."

"How long will it take?"

"I have yet to speak with your boss, but I hope to make a decision within the week."

Surprise lit up Charlie's face. "Wow, that soon?"

"Yes. I believe in moving quickly with something like this. It needs to be resolved one way or the other as swiftly as possible."

"Yes, I understand. When will—?" Color exploded across his lean cheeks. "That is, when will Dec know about...?"

"About your involvement?" Chloe asked gently.

"Yes. My...involvement."

Her heart constricted with sympathy. He was in an extremely difficult position.

"If I decide no further action is warranted, he won't ever find out, unless you tell him. In the more likely event that charges are laid, your statement, along with any others I deem relevant, will form part of the Brief of Evidence. It will be served upon Agent Munro and his lawyer within four weeks of my final determination."

Charlie's lips compressed and he nodded grimly. "Thank you, Senior Investigator Sabattini. I appreciate your time." He offered a grateful smile and Chloe couldn't help but return it.

"Thank you for having the courage to report your suspicions. It couldn't have been easy."

Charlie nodded and ducked his head and then stood and headed toward the door.

"Oh, one more thing," Chloe said.

He turned around and raised an eyebrow, his mouth tugging upward in a grin. Chloe tried to remain unmoved.

"Has Agent Munro ever told you his username or password?"

Charlie frowned and shook his head. "Never."

Chloe watched the door close behind him. She sighed and glanced at her watch. She still had an hour before her scheduled appointment with Gary Julian. Long enough to snatch some fresh air and a bellyful of strong caffeine. Grabbing her briefcase off the floor, she stowed her papers inside and left.

———

An hour later, feeling marginally refreshed from her large takeaway double-shot espresso latte´ and the bite of fresh spring air she'd squeezed into her lungs whilst waiting for her order, Chloe arranged her papers on the desk in front of her and prepared to interview Agent Munro's boss. When a brisk knock sounded on the door, she buttoned up her black pin-striped suit jacket and bade him enter.

Detective Superintendent Gary Julian was a mountain of a man. Chloe had thought Agent Munro tall, and he was. But he was no match for the man who towered in her doorway, ducking his head as he entered the close confines of the interview room.

Chloe stood and offered her hand. It was swallowed in a brief handshake and then set loose. Her gaze swept over the liberal sprinkling of silver in the man's closely cropped hair and she noted the fatigue in his world-weary eyes.

According to his personnel file, Gary Julian was a man of some reckoning. With more than thirty-six years as a Federal Agent under his belt, the last ten of which had been spent as head of the Child Protection Unit, Chloe could only imagine what he'd been subjected to and marveled at his resilience.

"Detective Superintendent, thank you for coming in. Please, take a seat."

The chair disappeared beneath his bulk and Chloe had a fleeting image of it collapsing underneath him. But, it seemed to adjust to the weight and she looked down and opened the file in front of her.

"I'm sure you're aware of the reason I've asked you to meet with me today?"

His lips remained tight. His only response was a sharp nod.

She cleared her throat, a little nervous at the thought of reminding such a seasoned law enforcement officer of basic procedures.

"I'm sorry, Detective Superintendent. Shortly, I'm going to be switching on the video recorder and this interview will be taped. It's important that you provide me with a verbal response to every question."

He seemed to take her request in the spirit she'd intended and nodded again. "Of course, I understand."

Chloe held his gaze. "Thank you. I'm sure you understand how difficult this is for everyone. I've already spoken to Agent Stanford and he's incredibly distressed at what's happened. I've assured him this matter will be resolved as quickly as possible. Agent Munro is also understandably upset."

"He didn't do it."

"I thank you for your opinion, Detective Superintendent Julian and I accept that you know Agent Munro far better than I do, but I'm sure you'll appreciate I have a job to do and the sooner we get on with it, the sooner this can be dealt with."

"Fine. But just so you know: He didn't do it."

Chloe plunged ahead. "I understand Agent Munro has been under your command for a little over a year. Is that correct?"

"Yes, he transferred in August last year. He came to us from the New South Wales Police Service."

"Do you know why he transferred? I imagine the Child Protection Unit isn't for everyone."

Gary hesitated and then replied, "His niece was kidnapped by a pedophile. From what I remember, she was rescued before she was raped, but I'm sure you can imagine how traumatic the whole thing was for her and her family. Declan submitted an application to the AFP a month or two afterwards. Once he'd finished his training, he applied for and was accepted into the CPU."

"Isn't that a little unusual? Going straight into a high tech operations group?"

"Yes, most agents don't commence their careers in a high tech operations group and especially not a group like the CPU, but Declan had a decade or more experience as a senior detective in the State system. He had the ability and, more importantly, the passion to see bottom-feeding scum like pedophiles hunted down and locked away. Besides, he also has a brother in the CPU. Brandon Munro's been with us about a year and a half. He's based in Sydney. Before that, he was undercover in Jakarta, rooting out terrorist cells. He has an enviable service record and we're more than happy to have him on our team."

Chloe added some notes under the heading "Family" and tried not to let her feelings show. To say that she was impressed was an understatement, but just because the man had a stellar family didn't mean that had rubbed off on him.

"Tell me about Declan Munro."

The superintendent drew in a deep breath. Chloe would have sworn the width of his chest almost doubled. He crossed his arms and eased the air out between his lips.

"Declan Munro is one of the best agents I've ever had the honor of commanding."

Chloe held Julian's gaze. It didn't falter. Sincerity was reflected in even the darkest corners of his eyes. She scribbled a note on the paper, feeling more and more confused.

"What do you think about the accusations made by Agent Stanford?"

Julian shook his head in disbelief. "To tell you the truth, I don't know what to think. Agent Stanford's been in the unit for years. He's a good investigator. Not necessarily as insightful or enthusiastic as Declan, but Stanford's been in the game longer, and had more time to wear out. We all wear out eventually."

"And what of the evidence? The computer access logs which clearly show unauthorized access from the computer Declan Munro has already agreed is the one he uses."

"There are other agents who use that computer," Gary protested.

"I know. That's why I asked you to bring your timesheets and clock cards for the last six weeks. Did you do that for me?"

"Yes. They're in here." The superintendent reached inside his briefcase and pulled out a folder. Flipping it open, he handed the records to Chloe.

"Thank you. I'll examine these later. I have the times and dates off the computer logs. If they match up with the times we know Agent Munro was on duty, it will be just one more burden he'll have to overcome."

She cleared her throat. "I understand agents are sometimes in the squad room outside their normal work hours. Is that correct?"

He shrugged. "Sure. Under normal circumstances, they usually pull an eight-hour shift. If we're under pressure to close something down, they'll work around the clock. But that doesn't mean they can't come in outside that time and finish paperwork, follow up leads, whatever. What they do in their own time is their choice."

"So, it's possible someone could have come in at a time when they weren't rostered on and accessed the Unit's computers?"

"Of course, it happens all the time."

"So, even if the computer logs don't match up with Agent Munro's time sheets, it's still possible that he was using the computer at the time the logs say he was?"

Gary nodded grimly. "Yes, it's possible, just as it is for any of the staff working there, but you're forgetting this is a man who goes above and beyond the call of duty. This is a man who has volunteered to do double shifts so he could make sure a ring of pedophiles operating out of Murrumbilla could be exposed and shut down forever. This is a man who's received the State's highest service awards. A man whose father is a former District Court judge. A man who has four brothers who are involved in law enforcement. This man cut his baby teeth doing the right thing. It is quite simply beyond my imagination to even begin to think he could be involved in this."

Julian's breath came fast. Chloe looked down at the notepad in front of her and gave him time to gather himself. She didn't have any hesitation in knowing that he believed every word he said, but that didn't necessarily mean his unshakable conviction wasn't misplaced.

That was her job: To sift through the evidence and separate the facts from the emotions. To discover the truth and then act upon it—and right now, despite the emotion involved, there was no getting away from the cold, hard facts.

She did her best to ignore the turmoil in her head and bit down on a sigh. She was a professional. She was good at her job. And that's all this was. Another job. So what if the offender in question sent butterflies hurtling around her belly? So what if she wanted to believe every word he said?

The facts were the facts. End of story. Her shoulders slumped. Some days even the healthy pay packet wasn't enough.

CHAPTER 5

Declan jogged along the walking track that skirted Lake Burley Griffin. The mid-afternoon heat of the sun on the back of his neck was comfortably warm. School children in wide-brimmed hats huddled at one end, listening with varying degrees of interest to the teacher in front of them.

It had been more than a week since Senior Investigator Sabattini had interviewed him. He hadn't heard a thing and the wait was slowly driving him mad.

Without the distraction of work to take his mind off things, he'd been forced into uncharacteristic idleness. He was a man who worked hard and played hard, but there had always been a balance. Now that one of those outlets had been taken away from him, he had no choice but to take the subsequent frustrations out on his body.

Sweat ran in rivulets down his face and soaked into his navy-blue Nike T-shirt. His chest was tight from exertion and the muscles in his calves screamed for rest. But he pushed himself on, knowing that only the sheer pain of excessive physical exercise could even come close to helping him forget, for a little while, the nightmare he was living.

In typical Munro fashion, his family had gathered around him in support. His father and Clayton and Brandon, after expressing their disappointment and anger about a system that could accuse him so unjustly, had made sure the best criminal lawyer in Sydney was standing by and they had done what they could to cheer up Declan. Brandon had even flown down to Canberra for the weekend and they'd hit the bars and clubs and had drunk enough alcohol to wake up more than a little seedy the next day. The distraction had worked, for a little while, and Declan had been grateful for their support.

But nothing changed the fact he was still on leave from the job he loved and no one could tell him when that situation would change. It was driving him crazy. Almost as crazy as not knowing how the investigation was going.

Christ. The investigation. The investigation he was at the center of. He still couldn't believe it.

Taking the path that led down the road to his apartment, he pushed himself hard through the final mile. His breath came in harsh pants and his shirt was soaked through. Still, the final burst of speed had given him something else to think about and he was grateful for even that momentary distraction.

Rounding the corner, he jogged across the footpath and through the gate of his apartment complex. From behind him came the sound of car doors closing, but he ignored it and continued into the foyer and strode over to the elevator.

Punching the button to his floor, he bent over and dragged more oxygen into his lungs, concentrating on slowing his breathing. A pair of expensive-looking, black leather heels came into view. His gaze traveled upwards, over shapely legs encased in black stockings.

A fitted, charcoal-gray skirt filled his vision. Moving slowly upward, his gaze rested on the merest hint of a generous cleavage cleverly concealed beneath a pale blue blouse. The top two buttons were undone, giving him a glimpse of creamy, gold skin.

His heart leaped and then thumped hard against his chest, but this time it had nothing to do with his recent exertion. Senior Investigator Sabattini stood in the foyer of his apartment building and she wasn't smiling.

Belatedly, Declan noticed the man beside her wearing a navy suit and an expression that matched hers.

"Agent Munro, we're placing you under arrest for accessing highly sensitive computer files without proper authorization. We will take you to your local station where you will be charged. You'll be given the chance to call someone—a lawyer, or a family member—from the station. We also have a search warrant for your apartment."

Shock slammed into him. His thoughts scattered like confetti in a windstorm. *He was innocent.* She couldn't be arresting him. There had to be some mistake.

"What—? How—?" He shook his head and tried to form a coherent sentence. "You're making a mistake. I didn't do it." He glared at her. "I've already told you. I didn't do it."

Ignoring his plea, the man beside her pulled out a set of handcuffs. Tugging Declan's arms none too gently behind him, her partner fixed the cuffs to Declan's wrists. Moments later, he was guided back out through the entryway and placed into the back seat of an unmarked police car. The stench of his fear-tinged sweat filled the air.

They hadn't even given him time to change.

———————

The next few hours passed in a blur that felt like a nightmare Declan struggled to wake up from. Within minutes of depositing him in the charge room of the local police station, Chloe and her partner had disappeared. He was placed in the dock, formally charged, fingerprinted, photographed and then left to sit in a daze of confusion and disbelief in the lockup that reeked of stale body odor, desperation and fear. The only thing he was grateful for was that it was empty.

As soon as they'd finished processing him, Declan had phoned Clayton. Praying his brother would get there soon, he rubbed at the marks left by the handcuffs.

Handcuffs, for Christ's sake! Who did they think he was? A common criminal? He now knew how it felt to be locked up for something he didn't do and he was helpless to do anything about it.

A sound in the corridor drew Declan's attention. He looked up from where he sat on the cold, steel bench and watched one of the arresting officers approach his cell.

"You've got a visitor," he said, his voice as cool and indifferent as his movements as he unlocked the padlock that secured the thick Perspex-and-steel door.

Declan peered over the man's shoulder and slumped with relief when Clayton's face materialized behind him. His brother strode through the cell doorway. Declan stumbled to his feet and almost collapsed against his brother as the door clanged shut behind him.

Clayton pulled him into a hard hug, anger and disbelief clouding his eyes.

"Christ, I can't believe they'd do this to you! What the fuck are they thinking? I've called Gary four times. I've left a pile of messages. He's not returning my calls. When I finally get my hands on him, I tell you what—"

"It's not his fault," Declan muttered, releasing his brother and stepping away.

Clayton ran a hand through his hair, further dislodging the disheveled mass.

"I've phoned the lawyer, like you asked me to. He's catching the first available flight. He should be here in a couple of hours. I'll meet him at the airport and bring him straight over. As soon as he gets here, they'll take you before the magistrate for a bail hearing. Once bail's set, we can get you out of here."

Declan threw himself back down on the bench and hung his head in his hands—beyond words, beyond...anything. Clayton lowered himself beside him and drew in a big breath.

"It's going to be okay, mate. We're going to find out who's behind this and make this whole nightmare disappear. I'm going to talk to that girl from IA and find out what the hell they're doing. She'd better have a mountain of watertight evidence against you or we'll sue everyone in her department. It's not right what they're doing to you. It's not fucking right!" Clayton made a sound of anguish in his throat. As if propelled by his anger, he turned and began to pace the tight confines of the holding cell.

Declan watched him move, as if in slow motion, listening with abstract concentration to the squeak of the soles of his brother's expensive leather shoes on the stained, cracked concrete. He wished he could offer words of comfort and reassurance, but they were simply beyond him. He couldn't even assure himself that things would be okay.

He'd been arrested, handcuffed, charged and locked up, for Christ's sake. Things he'd never imagined happening to him. And yet they had.

He was at the mercy of an investigator he knew nothing about, other than that she had amazing physical appeal. She held his life in her hands and he didn't even know her first name.

He punched his fist hard against his hand and growled his frustration. Clayton paused mid-stride and turned to look at him.

"Fuck, I'm sorry, mate. I shouldn't be going on like this. You're the one with the right to vent."

"It's all right, Clay. Vent all you like. I appreciate you coming."

"Of course I came! Christ, I'm just as shocked as you. I know you didn't do this and I swear to God, Dec, I'll find out who did."

Declan tried to smile, but his lips refused to move. "Thanks, Clay. That means a lot to me."

One of the other officers ambled into view and produced a set of keys, looking genuinely contrite. "Righto boys; time's up. I'm sorry, Clayton, but you're gonna have to go."

Clayton moved closer and squeezed Declan's shoulder. "We're going to get you out of here, bro. Keep your chin up. I'll be back before you know it."

Declan swallowed the lump in his throat and nodded. Clayton stood and made his way out through the opened doorway. Declan couldn't bring himself to watch. The clang of the metal as it slammed closed reverberated through his head.

The courtroom reflected the Government's well-meaning attempts to turn a room where the fate of the desperate and despairing were determined on a daily basis, into a pleasing, peaceful sanctuary. But not even the bright colors and modern décor could remove the air of fear and finality that permeated right through to the fabric of the furniture, and Declan felt the weight of his predicament like a barrel of concrete in his gut.

His last meal had been breakfast—a bowl of cereal and a slice of toast with vegemite. He hadn't bothered eating before his run, preferring to punish himself on an empty stomach.

He'd been offered a sandwich in the cells, but his stomach had churned at the thought and it had been all he could manage to hold everything together while he'd waited for his lawyer to arrive.

He'd had it on the good authority of his father and brothers that Roger White was the best barrister money could buy. With his impressive height, shock of long snowy hair, commanding voice and a don't-mess-with-me attitude, Declan could see some of why the man had earned his reputation. He was accompanied by a younger female attorney and together, they'd attended upon him at the police station.

"All stand." The Clerk of the Court announced the entrance of the magistrate and the thick fear that had been doing its best to erode Declan's composure since his arrest stirred in his gut. He stood in the dock, his wrists once again immobilized in handcuffs. 'Standard procedure,' he'd been told by a less-than-jovial corrections officer when he'd protested against what he considered an unnecessary show of force.

He looked around. Immediately to his right, he spotted Clayton sitting in the front row of the public gallery. His brother gave him a reassuring thumbs-up and Declan returned his silent greeting, thankful for the show of support.

His gaze narrowed on the lawyer representing the Commonwealth Director of Public Prosecutions office, or DPP, already seated at the bar table. The man's gray-speckled hair was in need of a haircut and there was a hard glint in his unfriendly eyes. There was no sign of Senior Investigator Sabattini.

Not that he'd expected to see her. This was only a bail hearing. A mere formality. A minor cog in the wheel of justice that had now overtaken his life.

The magistrate took his seat at the bench and brought his court to order. Declan sat and prayed for it to be over. A blur of brief arguments for and against his bail conditions were made by the men at the bar table. Declan tried hard to concentrate on what they were saying, but all he heard was the final slap of the gavel as the magistrate confirmed the terms and then rose and left the room, his black cloak swinging ominously behind him.

Roger White approached the dock, his face wreathed in a satisfied smile. "Unconditional bail, Declan. You're free to go."

"Thank you."

"Don't thank me yet, son. We have a long way to go. This is only the beginning. The court's given the DPP one month to serve the Brief of Evidence. Until then, you're to keep your head down and your nose clean. From what I've seen of the Statement of Facts tendered to the court just then, you're in a bit of trouble."

Declan glared up at him. "I didn't do it."

White held his gaze, his eyes assessing. After awhile, he nodded, seemingly satisfied with what he saw. "Your father speaks highly of you. So does your boss. But from what I've read, the evidence they have against you is strong." His eyes narrowed. "Who could be doing this and why?"

Declan shook his head in despair. "I have no idea. I've

wracked my brain for more than a week. I still come up blank."

"You have to tell me everything. Unless we can come up with a reasonable alternative to how your username and password came to be used, I can offer you little hope."

Desperation clawed at Declan's gut. "Please, you have to believe me. I didn't do it. I fucking didn't do it."

White eyeballed him again. "Then you'd fucking better come up with an explanation. And it's not *me* you have to convince."

Declan stared out of the tinted window of Clayton's secondhand BMW, lost in thought. His brother had offered to drive him home and he was inordinately grateful for the thoughtful gesture. Apart from the fact he was without a mode of transport, he wasn't in the frame of mind to cope with the noisy peak-hour traffic that crowded around them as everyday people left their everyday jobs and made their way home.

The events of the day continued to roll through his head like a terrible movie and his gut clenched tighter every time they replayed. He was almost numb with the shock and disbelief and he couldn't shake the thought that there was a very real chance he could be convicted. He didn't realize they'd arrived at their destination until Clayton turned to him and spoke.

"We're here."

Declan roused himself from his panicked thoughts and offered a grateful smile. It wobbled on his lips.

"Are you going to be all right, Dec? Do you want me to stay for a while?"

Declan shook his head. "No, but thanks, mate. You've done enough already. I appreciate it. Go home to Ellie and the kids. They need you, too."

Clayton's brow furrowed in concern. "Right now, it's you I'm worried about."

"I know and I'm grateful for it; but I'm fine. I'll go inside and have a beer or two and try and forget this day ever happened. Tomorrow, I'll start all over again and try yet again to work out who the hell is behind it all."

A knock on Declan's window startled them both. Declan turned and activated the button. The window slid down in silent sophistication, revealing Charlie. His expression was almost frantic.

Declan forced a smile. "Hey, Charlie. What are you doing here?"

"Christ, Dec! Where have you been? What the fuck is going on? Someone at work said you'd being arrested? I've been calling you for hours."

"I had my phone switched off," Declan said, turning away.

"Talk to me, mate. What's going on?"

Declan heaved a sigh and opened the car door. With a nod of thanks to his brother, he closed the door behind him and stepped up onto the sidewalk.

Leading Charlie into his apartment, Declan threw himself down on his leather couch and closed his eyes. "It's been a shit of a day, mate."

Charlie came closer, his eyes full of concern. "What happened? Is it true? Were you arrested?"

Declan drew in a deep breath and eased it out between tight lips. "Yep, it's true. Those assholes from IA ambushed me on my way in from the circuit. I was worn out and reeking with perspiration and they jumped me. Took me away in handcuffs." He spread his hands to indicate the crumpled and sweat-stained jogging clothes he still wore. "They wouldn't even let me change."

Charlie shook his head, his eyes wide with disbelief. "Christ, I don't believe it. I told that woman you hadn't done it. I told her I knew you as well as anyone. I told her you'd never even looked like being a kiddie fiddler."

Declan stared at him almost uncomprehendingly and then shook his head. "She talked to you, too? I guess I should thank you for the show of support," he said wearily.

"Was she there? The IA bitch with the big tits? Was she there when they arrested you?"

Declan pushed aside a twinge of irritation and nodded grimly. "Oh yeah, she was here. Her and some other IA meathead I'd never seen before. He was the one who slapped the cuffs on."

"Christ, you have to be kidding? They *cuffed* you?"

"Yep."

Charlie paced the length of the open-plan living room, shaking his head and muttering his disbelief. Declan hoisted himself off the couch and headed toward the bar in the far corner of the living room. It faced the view of the lake.

The myriad of twinkling city lights illuminating the wide expanse of water normally served to calm him after a stressful day, but right now, nothing seemed to be able to penetrate the dull fog that had descended upon him since his arrest.

He pulled open the door of the bar fridge and tugged out a cold Crown lager. Flipping open the bottle top, he slugged half of the contents in one gulp.

"Do you want one?" he asked, indicating the bottle in his hand.

Charlie stopped his pacing and nodded. He walked over to the bar where Declan stood and leaned his elbows on the countertop.

"I'm sorry, mate. I'm sorry you had to go through all that."

Declan tugged another beer out of the fridge and handed it to his friend. "It's not your fault, mate."

"Would it help if you talked about it?"

Declan's lips twisted in derision. "Probably not. Talking's not going to change anything."

"Did they tell you how they found out? Who it was who pointed the finger at you?"

Declan shook his head and took another slug from his beer. "Nope, but that's not going to stop me. It's obvious whoever the bastard was that went to them is the one who has set me up."

Charlie turned away and took a sip from his beer, peering

through the wall of glass on the opposite side of the apartment and into the night beyond.

"We'll get to the bottom of it, mate. I promise you."

Declan walked around the bar and returned to his seat on the couch. "I've been told to stand down until it gets sorted out. My access to the station has been restricted."

"But mine hasn't." Charlie turned around and looked at him, his face grim with determination. "I'll find out who did this to you, mate. I swear it."

CHAPTER 6

Charlie stared through the windscreen and into the darkness toward the Master's mansion on No. 32 Boland Drive. It sat well back from the road and was bordered by a high sandstone fence. Through the double black wrought iron gates, he could see that the place was ablaze with lights, warm and welcoming in the cool spring night.

They beckoned him inside, but he knew better than to fall for their light-filled treachery. The Master had made it clear: Charlie was welcome to spend time with him at his office; his house was strictly out of bounds.

It was one of the reasons why Charlie found himself drawn to the building. Time after time, during the restless hours when sleep eluded him, or like tonight, when his thoughts lay uneasy on his mind, he'd find himself outside No. 32 Boland Drive.

Thoughts of Declan weighed heavily. It had been more than a month since the arrest. A month where he'd had to keep up the pretense of friendship with a mate he'd betrayed. He thought of what he'd done and what he still had to do and experienced a twinge of concern.

Had he done the right thing? Declan had been nothing but friendly during the year they'd worked together. The two of them had enjoyed a lot of fun times, going to the football games, hanging out in bars, swapping shoptalk. But the problem was, Declan didn't know. Declan didn't know the truth. Only the Master knew and only the Master could truly make Charlie happy.

Familiar shame surged through him. He was in his thirties and he still hadn't found the courage to be himself, to stand up for what he believed in, to be proud of the man he was.

His mother's constant vitriolic criticism, which had started when he was a teenager, had set him back a lifetime. For years, he'd despaired of ever being brave enough to stand up to her and her narrow-minded prejudices. But then, he'd met the Master and his mother's approval no longer seemed important.

The meeting had been pre-destined. A memo had arrived on Detective Superintendent Julian's desk requesting the presence of Charles Stanford to assist in the implementation of a policy-related operation that was to be conducted from the Home Affairs Office. The memo was a little vague on details, but Charlie's interest had been piqued. Being handpicked by the office responsible for his employment was an honor he refused to take lightly.

When he met the Master and discovered the man's proclivities were peculiar to his own, he was buoyant with the possibilities. Here was the opportunity he'd been looking for: The chance to leave the dark shadow of his mother's disgust and revulsion behind him forever and to become the man he wanted to be. At last, he could live his life the way he wanted.

Of course, it hadn't quite worked out that way, but he hadn't given up hope that the day would come when he could throw off his mantle of deceit and live openly the way he dreamed of.

He was smart enough to realize the Master could help him achieve his goal. When he was with the Master, anything was possible. He felt as strong and as brave and as determined as he needed to be to throw off the constraints he'd lived under for so many years—and to be proud of the real Charlie Stanford.

It was a shame his friendship with Declan had to be sacrificed, but it was a small price to pay. Besides, the

Master needed Charlie. He needed him to help protect the Master against the very real danger Declan posed. The Master had told him all about it.

Being needed by the Master was the sweetest feeling in the world and Charlie cherished it like a child cherished a favorite toy. Nothing and no one would come between them.

He glanced at his watch. Its chrome-plated face was illuminated by a nearby street light. Registering the time, he sighed. It was late and he was rostered onto work in the morning.

Shooting a final, wistful glance at the Master's mansion, he started the ignition of his car and eased out onto the street. As the distance between him and the Master widened, he couldn't help but yearn for the day when he could be part of the Master's life—in every way possible.

Chloe frowned at the words on her computer screen and then deleted the paragraph she'd just written. She had two days left to serve the Brief of Evidence on Agent Munro's lawyer and there were parts of it that were still giving her a headache.

She'd requested the transcripts of the statements of the offender, the main witness and Gary Julian for inclusion in the brief, along with the CPU's computer log records and timesheets. What was giving her grief was her summary of the offences.

Declan Munro didn't fit the profile of a pedophile. It was as simple and as complex as that. Not that there was any magic formula, but this man was a pillar of society, well liked and respected by his family and his colleagues, including his boss. The statement he'd made to her and the demeanor with which he'd delivered it rang with truth and sincerity— and yet the evidence indicated otherwise.

Then there was the statement made by Agent Stanford. A

man who described himself as a friend of the offender. A close friend, if she was to believe Stanford's account. And why wouldn't she believe it?

He'd come across as an honest officer and appeared genuinely horrified at the thought that his friend might be a pedophile. Chloe had run a check on Stanford and although his family background left a little bit to be desired and his colleagues were not quite as gushing in their praise, he was nevertheless considered a good agent and sported an unblemished record.

With a sigh of frustration, she sat back in her chair and rubbed at the ache in her neck. Which one of them was lying?

"What's the matter, Chloe? You look like you can't find the word to match the last clue to a five thousand-word crossword."

Chloe summoned a tired smile and looked across at her work colleague. Jack Webber had been her partner and sounding block ever since she'd arrived in the somewhat stilted halls of the IA. Before he'd taken on the role of IA investigator, he'd had over twenty years of experience in the field. It was this kind of experience and his ability to read a situation with uncanny accuracy that Chloe had depended upon during her first few years in the job.

Being an investigator for IA was a difficult job and one that not a lot of agents were willing to do. But while Chloe found it incredibly stressful at times, especially when her gut instincts were in full argument with her head like they were now, she also found it enormously rewarding.

The majority of Federal agents were hard-working, honest people who took pride in keeping their country safe. Every now and then a rogue officer slipped through the ranks and put the whole organization in jeopardy. The media could rarely be found when the AFP got something right, but invariably turned up in force if things turned sour—particularly if the source of the problem came from within. Journalists salivated about breaking the story of a cop who'd turned bad.

"It's this case I'm working on. The one involving Declan Munro. It's...complicated."

Webber pushed away from his desk and closed the short distance between them. "How so?"

Chloe's shoulders slumped. "He's an exemplary officer. Everyone I talk to sings his praises, even his superiors. He's been in the game for more than a decade and there's not even a hint that something might be amiss. He's sinfully good looking and has the charm of the boy next door. I spoke to some of his female colleagues. Nobody had a bad word to say about him. The only thing I will say is I couldn't find a woman in his office that he'd dated. Not that it means he's a pedophile," she hastened to add. "There could be any number of reasons why he doesn't date his coworkers."

"I know a certain young woman who's never gone out with a man from her office," Webber teased, the crows' feet at the corners of his eyes crinkling with humor.

Her lips turned up in a tiny smile. "Exactly. Refusing to date coworkers isn't a crime in anyone's book." She sighed again and shook her head. "I've looked at the witness statements, I've made my own enquires, I've studied the hard facts, but no matter how I consider it, when looked at as a whole, it doesn't fit."

Webber propped a hip against her desk and shrugged. "Evil comes in all guises, Chloe. It's often the ones who least look the part that are the most dangerous. Believe me, even I've been caught out."

Chloe grimaced, recalling another man who'd duped her with his easy charm. It had been a decade and a half ago, but she could still remember like it was yesterday—*and* she couldn't forget her solemn vow never to be taken in by a Colgate smile again.

Determination surged through her. There had to be something on Declan Munro that she hadn't found, something that explained his penchant for child pornography.

With a nod of thanks in Webber's direction, Chloe straightened in her chair and reached for her keyboard.

Within moments, she'd accessed the New South Wales Police database. A few keystrokes later and she'd found what she was looking for: Declan Munro's State Police file.

Scanning the first few pages, she digested the enviable array of recommendations and honorable mentions he'd been awarded over the course of his career as a New South Wales police officer. They were impressive; but then, she knew they would be. She'd already read his AFP file.

His initial application to the AFP had included references from his State colleagues and commanding officers, as well as mandatory background checks. Everything had come back clear, which was no more than she expected—he'd been accepted into their ranks, after all.

Tabbing through the various entries on the screen in front of her, a small heading caught her eye. Clicking open the file, she discovered a report from five years ago that involved a complaint against one Declan Andrew Munro.

She scanned the contents. Uneasiness morphed into shock. Discovering the proof she'd been seeking should have filled her with elation, but instead she felt nothing but coldness and an overwhelming sense of disappointment.

The phone at her elbow rang. With her eyes still focused on the screen in front of her, she answered it.

The IT expert on the other end didn't mince words. The laptop confiscated from Declan Munro's apartment during the execution of the search warrant had been forensically examined. More than a hundred deleted images of child pornography had been found on the hard drive.

Chloe's shock of only moments ago congealed into icy anger. She couldn't believe that even for an instant, he had taken her in. It just went to show, as far as her instincts went, that lately she couldn't be more off kilter.

Reaching for the phone again, she punched in the number for Munro's lawyer.

Declan pulled into a parking lot within walking distance of the AFP headquarters. It was just after lunch in the middle of the working week and the car park was nearly full. Despite the fact he was on a motorbike, he rode through several levels before he eventually found a vacant spot.

As he made his way into the building which housed Senior Investigator Sabattini, he wiped his damp palms on his suit pants and tried desperately to hide his nerves.

He hated feeling this way. He hated that his life had spiraled so far out of control that he no longer recognized it as his own. He hated the fear and uncertainty that stared back at him in the bathroom mirror. But mostly, he hated the feeling of hopelessness that enveloped him every time he thought of the charges that had been brought against him and the nameless, faceless witness who had instigated all this.

The telephone call from his barrister had taken him by surprise. Apart from his family, calls to his cell phone had been few and far between. He hadn't even heard from Charlie for over a week. Busy at work, Declan assumed, wishing he could make the same complaint.

In accordance with the timetable set down by the court, the prosecution had two more days before the brief had to be served, so it was unlikely Roger was calling about the contents of that.

After the briefest of greetings and an exchange of even briefer preliminaries, Roger had gotten straight to the point: Senior Investigator Sabattini wanted to speak with him and she'd requested the presence of his lawyer.

Declan refused to get his hopes up that the nightmare of the last few weeks could soon be over. Surely, that was the reason for the summons? Why else would she contact his lawyer and order both of them to her office without delay?

Declan entered the elevator, grateful to find it empty. Punching in the number of the floor that housed the IA offices, he moved toward the back and waited for the doors to close. In less than a minute, he was transported to the fifth floor.

The sleek, silver doors slid open and he stepped into the hall, his footsteps muffled by the light gray-and-navy colored carpet that lined its length.

The nerves he'd managed to suppress returned in full force and he swallowed with a throat that was suddenly sandpit dry. The sight of his lawyer waiting for him outside the interview room helped only slightly to ease his tension.

"Roger, thanks for coming at such short notice."

The barrister held out his hand and Declan shook it. "That's what you're paying me for, son."

"Yes, well, even so, I appreciate it." Declan angled his head in the direction of the closed door. "Do you have any idea what this is all about?"

Roger shook his head, his expression grim. "I couldn't get anything out of her, which makes me nervous."

"So, you don't think she's called us here to tell us she's dropping the case?"

Roger's lips compressed. "There's nothing that would please me more, Declan, but unfortunately, experience tells me something different."

The lawyer noticed Declan's disappointment and stepped forward to give him a comforting pat on the shoulder.

"I'm sorry, son, but I'm not going to bullshit you. If this was good news, I'm sure it would have been relayed over the telephone. Chloe Sabattini knows I've had to drop everything and hop a plane from Sydney to be here. I wish I could give you more hope, but you're not paying me for fairy tales."

Roger looked uncomfortable, but Declan barely noticed. His thoughts had snagged on one word: *Chloe.*

So, that was her name.

Chloe. Somehow, it suited her.

His thoughts were interrupted when the door to the interview room swung open and he was treated to another close-up of Senior Investigator Chloe Sabattini.

She greeted both of them with a firm handshake, her expression unreadable.

"Mr White, Agent Munro. Thanks for coming." She turned and moved across the room to check the video recorder on the shelf in the corner. Declan's gaze shifted around the stark interview room.

The only difference he could ascertain since his last visit was a second plastic chair had been added, he guessed in deference to his barrister. Seemingly satisfied with the status of the video machine, Chloe indicated the seats with a wave of her hand and then made her way around the standard-issue laminate desk.

Declan busied himself with taking a seat and did his best not to notice how well her knee-length, tailored, navy skirt cupped the curve of her rounded butt or how her pale yellow blouse set off the golden tones of her skin. When she took the only remaining chair, he averted his gaze, but not before he caught an enticing glimpse of shadowed cleavage.

Christ, what was wrong with him? This woman held his life in her hands. Surely, he could lift his thoughts above his navel and concentrate his efforts on convincing her of his innocence?

Opening up the file in front of her, she appeared not to notice his preoccupation. Declan drew in a deep breath and eased it out, willing himself to relax.

"Senior Inspector Sabattini, both Agent Munro and I are keen to find out what this is all about. We have yet to receive the Brief of Evidence from you. As far as we know, your number one witness could be little more than a figment of your imagination. Agent Munro's life is on hold. We would appreciate it if you would be direct."

The woman held White's gaze for a moment and then her gaze flicked to Declan. He caught his breath at the anger that sparkled in their dark depths.

"I can do direct," she said, her gaze still drilling his. She addressed him, despite the fact his barrister had opened the conversation.

"For a start," she continued, her eyes sparking fire, "the brief's not due for another two days, as I'm sure you very well know." Her gaze narrowed and her eyes turned hard. "Secondly, why didn't you tell me about Meg Harvey?"

Shock ricocheted through each and every one of Declan's nerve endings. Roger turned in his seat to face him, a question in his eyes. Declan felt the weight of his barrister's stare.

Declan's gut churned with dread. "What the hell does Meg have to do with all of this?"

The expression on the investigator's face didn't change. "You've been charged with unauthorized access to secure police files, files that contained pornographic pictures of children. You can't possibly expect me to believe you didn't think the fact that a woman who complained about you improperly touching her four-year-old daughter would be relevant?"

Her voice had risen, along with her anger. Color crept up her neck and spilled over into her face. Declan glanced at his lawyer, who had paled beneath his tan. With admirable brevity, White regained his wits.

"Don't answer that, Declan. In fact, I suggest you say nothing further until after we've discussed the matter at length." He turned and shot an intimidating look toward the woman who sat across from them. "In private."

Chloe's lips thinned, but she gathered her file and pushed away from the table.

"Wait," Declan said. "I want to answer."

Roger reached out to him as if to stop him. "Declan, we need to talk. Don't say anything until we've had a chance to—"

"No," Declan interrupted, shaking off his lawyer's cautionary hand. "I have nothing to hide. I didn't touch Meg Harvey's daughter and I didn't access files containing kiddie porn."

He turned away, sickened by the thought.

Chloe slowly regained her seat. She eyeballed him, her gaze steady.

"Are you sure you want to continue?"

"Yes."

Roger opened his mouth to protest again, but Declan shook his head.

"Roger, it's fine. Like I said, I have nothing to hide." He turned back to Chloe. "Ask your questions."

The barrister crossed his arms and made a sound of disgruntlement. "For the record, I'd like it to be clear you are doing this against my advice. I will not be held accountable for what this may or may not cost you."

The barrister's words and his somber demeanor gave Declan pause. The man was the best criminal defense lawyer in the country. He knew what he was talking about. But to leave the allegations hanging without a word of explanation was something Declan was simply not prepared to do. He was innocent. He had to make her see.

He offered White a brief nod of acknowledgement. "Thank you for your advice, Roger. I appreciate you being here, but I would like to answer Senior Investigator Sabattini's questions. I've already told you, I have nothing to hide."

White studied him closely and seemed comforted by what he saw in Declan's eyes.

"As you wish," he murmured.

Declan drew in a deep breath and steeled himself for Chloe's questions. He met her gaze without flinching.

She stared back at him. "Tell me about Meg Harvey."

CHAPTER 7

Chloe stifled a surge of surprise when Declan agreed to be interviewed. She'd been sure he'd lawyer up and refuse to answer any of her questions, especially given the sensitive nature of this development.

But he hadn't. In fact, he'd even gone against the advice of his barrister to answer her. She couldn't help but feel a twinge of admiration and she wouldn't deny his cooperation had pushed the balance ever so slightly back in his favor.

She hadn't been required to allow him the opportunity to explain himself, but despite the damning evidence she'd discovered in his State Police file, something about the inconsistencies in the case that were still keeping her sleepless had prodded her into offering him the chance.

She eyed him closely, eager to note every miniscule expression. His voice was low and without inflection when he spoke.

"Meg Harvey and I dated for nearly a year. She was the daughter of a wealthy South African businessman. I was introduced to her through mutual friends at a charity function in Sydney. She was about my age, single, blond and beautiful. We hit it off straight away."

Chloe swallowed the twinge of jealousy that went through her at his words. It was the second time she'd heard him mentioned in reference to a blonde. *Did he have a type? Did he prefer blondes over brunettes?* She hated that she'd even thought that and hated it even more that she cared even a little bit about the answer. She cleared her throat in annoyance.

"When did you meet her daughter?"

Declan ran a hand through his hair. Chloe watched the movement of his fingers, knowing that he was completely unaware of the effect his looks had on others. Even messy hair couldn't detract from them.

"We'd been dating constantly for a couple of months before she introduced me to Ella. I didn't even know she had a daughter until the week before she introduced us. We'd met for dinner and parties many times during weeknights and weekends and not once had she mentioned anything about a daughter or the need for babysitters."

He drew in another deep breath and let it out on a sigh. "I'm not sure why it took her so long to say anything. Perhaps she thought it would scare me off."

"Did it?" Chloe asked, not daring to breathe.

"Of course not," he retorted. "I love kids, but not in the way you're implying. My brothers have enough between them to just about fill a theme park. The only reason I don't have any of my own is that I haven't found anyone I want to have kids with."

He flashed a disarming smile, a roguish glint in his eyes. "It takes two, you know."

Chloe felt the heat of it, all the way down deep in her belly and even lower. His humor was all the more surprising given the gravity of their conversation. She squirmed on the chair.

His gaze turned knowing and it was all she could do to prevent the heat from spreading up her neck and across her face. He spared her from replying by continuing his story.

"My parents have always told me the best thing I can do for my kids is to love their mother." He shrugged. "I guess I haven't found her yet."

"You've never been in love?" she asked and then immediately regretted it.

Declan's barrister sat forward. "Are these questions necessary, Investigator?"

This time she did flush and there was nothing she could do to stop it. With unsteady hands, she shuffled the papers in front of her and prayed her question would be ignored.

Sneaking a peek in Declan's direction, she stifled a groan. He watched her closely, his eyes sparkling with mischief.

"Of course I've been in love. It started from the time I was three. Jennifer Doyle was her name. She was the prettiest girl in preschool. I gave her my lunch every single day for at least a week."

Chloe forced herself to meet his teasing gaze. "A whole seven days? That *is* dedication."

"Five, actually, but who's counting?"

His grin widened and Chloe clamped her lips together lest they move upwards of their own accord.

What was she doing? Was she *flirting* with him? He was the suspect in her investigation. *What was she thinking?*

Tearing her gaze from his, she cleared her throat and tried desperately to restore a professional demeanor.

"So, Meg told you about Ella...?"

Declan rearranged his position in the chair, his body relaxed. "I'm not sure how it came up, but one night, Meg told me she had a daughter. I was surprised she hadn't told me earlier, but it didn't make any difference to me or to our relationship."

"Did you ask about the child's father?"

He shook his head. "It wasn't important. Meg said something about going through a messy divorce and that a lot of her money was still tied up in the courts, but I wasn't that interested. It was early days in our relationship and I was still a little uncertain about how serious things would get."

"You'd been dating regularly for two months. You didn't think you were past the early days?" Chloe asked, a little disbelievingly.

He shrugged with unconcern. "Call me old fashioned, but I like to take things slowly. Build up the anticipation. I like to get to know the woman I'm dating before it becomes complicated."

Chloe was desperate to ask whether that meant refraining from sleeping with Meg, but the question would be totally out of bounds and one that he and his barrister would justifiably have reason to object to.

"When did you meet Ella?"

"I think it was the weekend after Meg told me about her. I hadn't freaked out at the news she was a mother and I guess she felt comfortable enough to introduce us. We went to a movie, chosen by Ella, and afterwards went out for ice cream."

"And Meg was with you?"

Declan pulled a face. "Of course she was with us. Do you think she'd introduce her four-year-old to someone and then just leave? Is that something you would do, Senior Investigator Sabattini?"

Heat seared Chloe's cheeks and she looked away.

"Do you have kids, Investigator?" Declan asked.

She resolutely kept her gaze fixed on the paperwork in front of her and shook her head.

"I see. That explains your question, although I can't for the life of me think of anyone who'd be willing to leave their young daughter with a complete stranger."

Anger tightened her throat. "That's not what I said, Agent Munro and you damn well know it. This woman accused you of fondling her child. She claims to have caught you on two separate occasions in her daughter's bedroom. I'm trying to establish the truth of what happened and what weight, if any, should be given to her claims given that you have come before me charged with illegally accessing child pornography."

Chloe's eyes blazed into his, her breath coming in short pants. She felt a brief surge of satisfaction at the remorse that filled his eyes.

"I'm sorry. I shouldn't have said that. Can we try again?"

Chloe swallowed and drew in a deep breath, focusing on her notes.

"You said you and Meg dated for nearly a year. That's a reasonable amount of time to put into a relationship. Why did it come to an end?"

For the first time, he looked uncomfortable. His gaze fell away and he moved restlessly in his chair. Chloe sat forward, her body tense.

"It didn't work out. Simple as that."

"I don't believe you."

Anger flashed in the depth of his eyes. "I don't know what else you want me to say?"

She narrowed her eyes on his face. "I want you to tell me the truth."

He held her gaze for an interminable few seconds and then looked down at his lap.

"All right, you want the truth? The truth is, I wasn't ready to take her on, to take *them* on. She was looking for a husband and a father for her child. While I'm not against either of those roles, I couldn't see myself in that role with *her*. For a little while, perhaps, but not forever."

His gaze caught and held hers. "As I said, I'm a little old fashioned; that's what it would be for me. Forever."

Chloe tried to look away and couldn't. The sincerity in his eyes beckoned to her, pleaded with her to believe him. She dragged her gaze away and cleared her throat.

"Tell me what happened."

Declan's shoulders slumped on a heavy sigh. "She went psycho. Completely off-her-brain out of control. The night I broke it off, she pelted me with anything and everything out of her kitchen cupboards. Thank Christ she didn't have any sharp knives at hand or else I might not have lived to see it through."

"Did you report her assault to the police?"

He shook his head and grimaced. "Of course not. Have you taken a look at me? I'm six-foot-four and weigh over two hundred pounds. Meg barely came halfway up to my shoulder and weighed less than half that. I'd have been the laughing stock of the office.

"Besides," he added, squirming a little. "I guess some part of me thought she was allowed to vent a little anger. After all, I'd just told her we were over. She'd invested the best part of a year into us and I'd gone and called it off. I kind of felt she had a right to beat up on me."

Chloe made a few notes on the paper in front of her, digesting his explanation. She had to admit, it made sense and she couldn't imagine him complaining to a random general duties officer about how his featherweight ex-girlfriend had assaulted him.

"What about Ella? How did she take the news?"

A fond smile flickered at the corners of his mouth. "Ella was a trooper. I found her curled up on her bed. I thought she was asleep, but she wasn't and I went in and sat down beside her. I told her I wouldn't be seeing her for a while. She asked me why, so I told her the truth. She was a smart kid. She gave me a hug and thanked me for telling her. I left soon after."

"Did you hear from Meg again?"

Declan made a noise of disgust. "She rang me constantly and when I gave up answering the phone, she started texting me. I can't remember exactly what she said but the flavor of it was always the same: I was the biggest asshole in the world; I'd led her on; I'd wasted twelve months of her life; I'd never loved her." He shook his head. "It went on and on."

"Did she ever say anything about Ella?"

"No. Meg wanted me back. She *begged* me to come back. She told me we'd work things out, that she'd do anything to have me back. She wanted us to be one big happy family."

"Why do you think she came forward with the accusations?"

He eyed Chloe balefully. "You're a smart woman, Investigator Sabattini. It doesn't take much working out."

"So it was nothing more than a woman scorned? Is that what you're saying?"

"Not just me, Investigator. This was thoroughly looked into by the New South Wales Police Internal Affairs Department. They arrived at the same conclusion: The allegations were groundless."

Chloe continued to stare at him, saving the best for last.

She couldn't wait to hear his explanation for the next bombshell.

"Do you own a laptop, Agent Munro?"

His hard gaze remained on hers, but his expression stayed neutral. "Yes. I have a Toshiba I have for personal use."

"A Toshiba laptop was seized during the search of your apartment. Would that be the laptop you're referring to?"

He shrugged. "Without seeing it, I can't say for sure, but if you say it came from my apartment, then I'd guess it was mine."

"Is your laptop protected with a password?"

"No, as I said, I only use it for personal stuff. I don't keep anything of importance on it and I live alone. There's no need to prevent anyone from logging in."

Chloe made a note of his response. "Do you ever take the laptop with you when you travel away or for any other reason?"

"No. If I'm traveling for work, I sign out a work laptop. If I'm traveling for leisure, I leave as many technological devices as I can at home. That's the whole point of getting away, isn't it?"

His lips tugged upwards in a tiny smile. She tried hard to ignore its effect on her.

"Have you ever loaned your laptop to anyone? A friend? A colleague?"

"No."

"Are you certain?"

"I'm certain."

Declan's barrister made a sound of impatience. "Is there a point to any of this line of questioning, Investigator? I thought we'd agreed you'd be direct."

Chloe compressed her lips together and nodded. The moment had come.

"As you wish, Mr White." She turned her stare on Declan. "As I mentioned, the laptop taken from your apartment has been examined. A substantial number of pornographic images of children were found on the hard drive. Would you care to explain how they got there?"

Declan's face leached of color. Shock and disbelief widened his eyes.

"What the fuck are you talking about?" he choked.

Roger White was on his feet. "Declan, don't say another word." He turned blazing eyes toward Chloe.

"Investigator Sabattini, how dare you! How dare you ambush my client like this! You could have had the decency to give me a little prior notice of your discovery."

Chloe shrugged, unmoved. She'd done nothing wrong. Her narrowed gaze remained fixed on the man seated across from her.

"Are you prepared to answer the question, Agent Munro?"

"No—"

"Yes," Declan declared.

They spoke simultaneously and then squared off in silence.

"I have nothing to hide," Declan stated, his voice cold. "Not now, not ever."

"We need to talk about this before you say anything that might be used against you," White pleaded. "Don't give them anymore ammunition."

"I have nothing to hide," Declan repeated, his hard gaze now fixed on Chloe's.

She drew in a deep breath and waited the men out. Long seconds passed before White's shoulders slumped in defeat.

"So be it, but I reiterate my earlier warning," he growled and regained his seat. He looked far from happy.

Tension emanated from every part of Declan's body. Chloe picked up her pen and tugged the notepad closer, waiting for him to speak.

"I have no idea how those images came to be there. That laptop never leaves my apartment. Most of the time, it's not even charged. There's nothing else I can say, other than to tell you again: I am not a pedophile and I did not download pictures of child pornography: not then, not now, not *ever*."

Chloe eyeballed him, but remained silent, digesting his clipped words.

Declan's expression turned grim with emotion. His eyes narrowed. "Investigator Sabattini, have you ever been accused of doing something you haven't done?"

She held his gaze and tried not to flinch. "No," she lied.

"You're lucky. It's not a nice place to be. I don't know what else you want me to say. I'm being set up. Someone is trying to bring me down. Why? I have no fucking idea, but I will find out who's behind it. While you're hell-bent on putting me behind bars, I'm going to be looking for the asshole who started this because there's one thing I'm certain of: It sure as hell wasn't me."

He pushed back his chair and prepared to leave. "You know," he added. "It's so easy for someone to ruin a man's life over shit like this. Pedophilia is an ugly topic and one we're all rightly sensitive about. It's the reason I joined the CPU—to put as many of them behind bars as possible.

"But, it's so easy for a mother, or anyone for that matter, to play the child molester card to destroy someone they want to punish. When it comes to something like this, it's their word over mine. In Meg Harvey's case, all I had is the knowledge of my own innocence, plus the fact that I was pulling a twelve-hour nightshift with more than five police witnesses to verify my whereabouts on at least one of the occasions I was supposed to be fondling her four-year-old. With respect to the images found on my hard drives, I'm not so lucky. All I have is my word that I didn't do it and right now, that seems to be worth shit."

Chloe closed the file and folded her hands on top of it. His explanation about Meg Harvey's complaint supported the fact that her State counterparts had taken the matter no further. He'd answered her questions with forthrightness and what appeared to be honesty and she couldn't help but feel he told the truth. But the fact was, pornographic images of children had been found on his hard drive, on *both* of his hard drives. It was evidence that simply couldn't be ignored. He'd admitted he'd never given anyone his login information. He'd admitted the laptop never left his apartment. At this point, she had no choice but to accept it was him who'd downloaded the images, for whatever reason.

Swallowing a sigh, Chloe forced herself to meet his gaze. "Thank you for coming in today, Agent Munro. I appreciate your candidness. Unfortunately, this matter will continue to proceed through the courts."

A tiny frown marred the smooth skin of Declan's forehead and then deepened to a groove as her words sank in.

Tearing her gaze away from the anger and desolation on his face, she turned to the barrister. "You'll have the Brief of Evidence on your desk by tomorrow morning."

Chapter 8

The mid-afternoon sun shone brightly off the aluminium garden furniture that graced the balcony of Declan's apartment. The air was filled with the scent of perfume that drifted from the flower-laden Murraya hedge that grew directly below. Despite the beauty of the day, Declan remained indoors, pacing from one side of his living room to the other as he waited for a phone call.

As if on cue, the phone in his hand vibrated. When he recognized the number on the screen, his belly somersaulted with nerves. With fingers that weren't quite steady, he answered the call.

"Roger?"

"Declan, I told you I'd call as soon as I'd had a chance to look at the brief and I'm as good as my word."

Declan's stomach clenched tight. "Hit me with it."

"Well, it looks like our star witness finally has a name. Federal Agent Charles Stanford. I take it you know him?"

Declan bent over, gasping. *Charlie? It couldn't be.* He felt like he'd been hit in the gut with a baseball that had been headed out of the park.

"Declan, are you all right?"

He could hear the concern in his lawyer's voice, but it was all he could do to force air into his constricted lungs.

"Declan, can you hear me? Say something."

"They've made a mistake. It can't be Charlie," he wheezed.

"I'm afraid so. I've read through his statement. He says he works with you. Is that right?"

Declan let out a humorless laugh, shock making him dizzy. He collapsed onto the couch and attempted to slow his frantic thoughts.

"Yeah, he works with me. He's also a good mate."

Roger swore loudly on the other end of the phone. "I'm sorry, Declan. I truly am. I can't imagine what a shock this must be for you."

Declan shook his head, still unable to accept it. "I have to see it. I have to see that statement. Can you fax it to me? I have to see it right away."

"Of course. I'll get someone to do it now. After you've had a chance to read it, we need to talk. Call me, okay?"

Declan ended the call, his mind in a spin. The thought of Charlie being the one behind the allegations was incomprehensible, and yet, according to Declan's barrister, it was true. Was Charlie the man who'd set him up? And if so, *why?*

The sound of the fax machine whirring to life in the next room pulled him out of his seat. Striding into the spare bedroom where he'd set up a desk and computer and other basic office equipment, he snatched at the papers that were streaming onto the tray.

His gaze was drawn to the bottom of the page. Charlie's signature, with all its extravagant loops and curls, was scrawled across each one with the date printed neatly next to it.

Nausea billowed in his gut. He dashed into the toilet and leaned over the bowl just as hot, acidic vomit burned a path through his esophagus and into his throat.

Declan didn't know how long he sat slumped on the hard tiles of his bathroom floor with his arms wrapped around the cold porcelain, but the sun had made a beeline for the horizon when he eventually found the strength to stand and make his way into the living room. He bent and picked up his phone from where it had fallen onto the carpet and noticed the list of missed calls. Most of them were from Roger.

With limbs weighed down with shock and disbelief, he dialed Charlie's number.

Charlie Stanford looked at the number on his screen and his hand trembled. Anxiety knotted his belly and he wondered again whether he'd done the right thing.

Ignoring the call, he let it go through to voice mail and then dialed the number he knew off by heart. The Master answered it on the second ring with his customary brusque greeting.

Charlie drew in a deep breath and then let it out in a rush. "It's…it's me. I-I think it might be time for that transfer."

Chapter 9

Chloe woke to the sounds of early morning traffic passing outside the window of her one-bedroom condominium. Nestled in a quiet corner of Belconnen, a northern suburb of Canberra, she escaped most of the noise from the highway nearby and was once again grateful for the sacrifices she'd made to afford it. The monthly mortgage payments still made her cringe, but it was the place she loved to call home, even if it did make her mother scowl.

Chloe had been born in Canberra Hospital and had lived in and around the city her entire life. Apart from the occasional jaunt north to Sydney to spend the weekend with friends or the even more infrequent trip to the coast at Batemans Bay, she spent the majority of her time either behind her desk on the fifth floor of the AFP Headquarters or pottering in the postage stamp-sized backyard she loved to call her garden.

As the scent of star jasmine and petunias wafted through her open window on the light breeze, she already longed to put the day behind her and escape into the haven of her garden.

If only it was that easy.

Knowing that the dread that had already settled in the pit of her stomach at the thought of what the day would bring wouldn't subside until she faced it, with a heartfelt groan she pushed back the covers and climbed out of bed.

Stepping into the shower, she turned the water on full force and enjoyed the feeling of the warm spray on her body. Reaching for the shampoo, she squeezed a generous dollop into her hand and lathered it through her hair. She wasn't prepared to face this day without clean, controllable hair.

Declan's committal hearing was due to commence that morning. She hadn't seen or heard from him since their last meeting, more than three weeks ago. Sometimes it could take months to obtain a date for a committal hearing, but due to the sensitive nature of the case, the matter had been expedited. It was thought best for all concerned.

Nerves jangled in her belly at the thought of seeing Declan again. Not only seeing him again, but confronting him inside the close confines of the courtroom.

He probably hated her.

She grimaced and wished things could be different, but they weren't. She was only doing her job. Surely, he understood that? From the little she knew of him, he seemed to be a man who took his work responsibilities seriously. She hoped he'd understand she felt the same way. It was nothing personal. It was just the way it was.

She squeezed the water out of her hair and turned off the faucets. Stepping out of the shower, she wrapped a towel around her and padded into her bedroom. She stared at the row of navy and black and charcoal-gray suits in her closet and felt like *Groundhog Day*. Though tempted to tug out the hot-pink silk T-shirt that skulked in the back of her closet, she shrugged off the momentary insanity and dressed in her usual sensible garb.

Her thoughts strayed to the family dinner she'd finally made time to attend over the weekend. All but one of her three siblings had been there and she'd been smothered in sticky hugs and wet kisses from their myriad offspring.

Not that she minded. She loved having her family around her and most of the time, a stint with her nieces and nephews was enough to satisfy the occasional urge she had to have a child of her own.

Not that she'd ever admit to such fantasies aloud. Her mother and sisters would have a field day. Even at the weekend barbeque, her mother had managed to pull her aside and give her the "your clock is ticking, bambina" lecture in between serving the tiramisu and the coffee.

Chloe suppressed a sigh. She knew her mother meant well—and to some extent, she had a point. Chloe was already thirty. Her body wouldn't wait around forever.

Thoughts of Declan in his impeccably pressed suit and bright lime-green tie surfaced. He'd said he loved kids. He'd said he wanted to be a husband and a father. Images of him running around with a football tucked under his arm and a swag of curly, brown-haired children running behind him crystallized in her mind and her face flamed.

She frowned. *What the hell was she doing?* He was the defendant in a criminal matter she'd instigated. While she still very much believed in the presumption of innocence, the fact was, she'd found there was enough evidence to prosecute.

But there was something about Declan Munro that resonated with her and she could only put it down to the fact that they had something in common. Despite what she'd told him, she knew what it was like to be accused of doing something she hadn't.

Before she could stop them, the memories washed over her. She remembered it as if it was yesterday and yet a decade and a half had passed since that awful day.

She was fifteen and a plump, gawky teenager. She may have been spared the humiliation of braces and requiring acne cream, but her body had been reshaping itself and forming into the curvaceous woman she'd become.

At thirty, she was proud of her rounded hips and D-cup bras, but at fifteen, it had been a nightmare. Although her best friend, Mandy, had stood by her, Chloe's life was never the same after Juliette Garbutt, the most popular girl in school, accused her of stealing Juliette's underwear.

Chloe had been a day pupil at an all-girls boarding school and even though there hadn't been any boys around to witness her degradation, she was humiliated just the same.

Nobody seemed to care that Juliette Garbutt's bras were two sizes too small for Chloe. The fact was, they'd been found in her locker. The locker was secured with a combination lock and only Chloe knew the code. Despite her protestations of innocence, the evidence was there for all to see.

Even now, years later, she didn't know how Juliette had managed to discover the code, but obviously she had. There was no way Chloe had stolen the bra. It took years for the scandal to die down. Even then, there were still people who didn't believe her. She'd left high school, to be forever known by some as the "bra snatcher."

Okay, her plea of innocence wasn't up there on the scale of what Declan Munro claimed, but she knew how agonizing it was to know you were innocent and be unable to prove it. She was also sure it was the reason Declan Munro kept intruding upon her thoughts and why she continued to rest uneasy, even though the evidence pointed overwhelmingly toward his guilt.

Then there were the rare glimpses of his charm and sense of humor. They'd thrown her off balance, being so at odds with the black-and-white facts she'd accumulated on the pages in his file.

The fact was, she *wanted* to believe him. She'd been in the system long enough to know if there had been any real substance to the complaint made by Meg Harvey, he would not only have been charged in New South Wales, he would have been thrown out of their police service and he would not have made it through the rigorous screening carried out by the AFP.

As to the images found on the computer hard drives, Declan had told her his laptop wasn't password protected. In theory, it could have been open to anyone to download the pictures. Even his work computer wasn't used solely by him.

Her thoughts shifted to Charlie Stanford. *What kind of*

person jumped to such horrific conclusions about a friend without first talking to them about it? Surely, it wasn't beyond reality to expect that if you had cause for concern about a friend's behavior, you'd approach them for an explanation instead of reporting it to IA where you knew they were obligated to investigate?

The doubts and misgivings she'd endured for weeks stirred in her belly, but she had no further time to dwell on them. In less than two hours, she was due to meet the lawyer representing the Crown to go over her statement—and here she was still wrapped in a towel.

With an impatient groan, Chloe strode back into the bathroom. Reaching for a comb, she went to work on the thick strands of her hair. Declan Munro would be tried before the courts. It was the right course of action. Let the evidence she'd collected be tested in a court of law and let the judicial system she believed in do its job. There was nothing more she could do and it was probably for the best, despite the fact she sensed there was so much more to him and this case than what was written on paper.

———————

Declan paced inside the cramped confines of the interview room that had been allocated to the defense team inside the courthouse and did his best to keep his nerves in check. He still couldn't believe matters had gone so far. It was like he was weighted down under water, screaming for help, with nobody able to hear.

He looked over at his family huddled together in the corner of the room. His parents and his brother Riley had flown down from the country—the dark scowl on his father's face testament to the way all of them felt. Two other brothers, Brandon and Tom, and their wives, had driven down from Sydney. Clayton stood near the door.

Declan appreciated their show of support and took comfort from their presence, but it also brought home the stark reality: He was in a serious position. Family did not gather *en masse* like this unless the situation was more than grave.

"How are you holding up?" Clayton murmured.

Declan tried to smile, but failed.

"It's going to be all right, bro. We're all here for you. We're not going to let this happen to you."

Declan pressed his lips together and blinked back the sting of tears. The love he felt in the closed room strengthened him, even though his family was powerless to call a halt to the proceedings. Duncan Munro was a recently retired District Court Judge and yet everyone in the room knew justice would take its own course here. Declan could only pray for a magistrate that saw reason.

The door to the interview room opened and Roger strode inside, his shock of white hair streaming behind him. His confident demeanor lifted Declan's spirits and he shook his barrister's hand with relief and gratitude.

After warmly shaking his father's hand and greeting the rest of the Munro family, Roger turned to him.

"I'm not going to bullshit you, Declan. We're in a bit of a tight spot here. We've elected to have a committal hearing rather than a paper committal. It means we'll at least get to hear the evidence they have against you and test the balls of your friend. He must know that *you* know he's lying. Let's see how he holds up under pressure."

Declan's mother stepped forward, wringing her hands. Marguerite Munro looked a decade older. Declan was overcome with guilt, knowing he was the cause of her concern.

"Is it possible the magistrate might throw the matter out today?" she asked.

Roger turned to face her. "It's always possible, Mrs Munro. That's what I'm here for. The committal hearing gives us a chance to test the Crown's evidence. They have the burden of proof in these matters and it's set high—beyond reasonable doubt. It's one of the tenets of our criminal justice system."

He took her hands and gave them a reassuring squeeze. "If their evidence doesn't stack up, we're entitled to make an application for dismissal. I'll be doing that anyway, regardless. We have nothing to lose."

"And if they satisfy the burden of proof?" The quiet words from former Judge Munro fell into the tense silence.

Roger nodded gravely. "You know as well as I do what will happen after that."

No one spoke. No one dared. Most of the people in the room had grown up around law enforcement. They knew what would happen if the Crown proved its case beyond reasonable doubt: Declan would be committed to stand trial.

It would be a savage blow. Although that was still some way from being found guilty, it still meant that a magistrate—a representative of the court—believed the prosecution had enough evidence to solicit a guilty verdict.

"Please, let's not dwell on this," said Roger. "Right now, we have to think positive. We all know Charlie Stanford's lying. Declan's told me it's possible he even accessed the laptop. Let's see if we can shake the truth out of him. I say, bring it on."

CHAPTER 10

Declan should have realized the first person to give evidence against him would be Senior Investigator Chloe Sabattini. She was, after all, the officer in charge of the investigation. But it still felt like he'd taken a hard right hook to his gut when she took the stand, averted her gaze from him and swore to tell the truth.

She looked as cool and professional as she always did, dressed in a subdued but nicely fitting charcoal-gray suit and a pale pink blouse. He zeroed in on her shapely legs, visible beneath her knee-length skirt, and did his best not to be impressed. This woman was the reason he was there. She had no right to look so good.

He brought the uncharitable thoughts to a halt. Chloe Sabattini wasn't the reason he was there. She was only doing her job and he could tell from the way her hand kept moving to push back a wayward strand of hair that had escaped the tight bun at her neck, she wasn't as calm and collected as she appeared.

Maybe she had doubts about his guilt? Perhaps she'd garnered something in his explanation about Meg that had made her think he was telling the truth after all?

Declan bit down hard on the surge of hope. She was here, wasn't she, giving evidence for the prosecution? If that wasn't enough proof she thought him guilty as sin, she hadn't once looked his way. That told him all he needed to know.

He turned slightly from where he sat in the dock and caught sight of his family seated behind him. They filled the first three rows of the public gallery and another surge of gratefulness for their presence flooded through him.

Clayton gave him a somber thumbs-up and Declan acknowledged it with a slight movement of his head before turning back to face the witness box.

With quiet efficiency, Chloe went through her evidence. She recounted how Detective Superintendent Gary Julian had contacted IA. How she had combed through computer records, which clearly showed the defendant, Declan Munro, or someone using his username, password and computer, had accessed child pornography unrelated to any investigation with which he was involved.

Neil Abbey, the young, newly appointed DPP lawyer with a reputation for being a hard-nosed player, questioned her about her interview with the defendant.

Chloe's gaze collided with Declan's. Her eyes widened. He could tell she was as surprised as he was that she'd glanced in his direction. His heart thumped. The courtroom receded. For a few seconds it seemed there was nothing but the two of them, staring at each other.

And then she looked away.

Declan felt the absence of her gaze like the sun receding on a frosty morning. He took stock of what happened then cursed under his breath, knowing that being interested in the officer investigating his case was one of the stupidest things he could think of.

But he couldn't help it. There was something about the cool sophistication of the IA officer and her staunch belief in the justice system that he too believed in... Her dedication to her job was another thing he grudgingly respected. They may have been on opposing sides, but that didn't mean he didn't admire the way she went after the things she believed in.

The thoughts lingered in his mind, her effect upon him powerful enough to push away, even for a miniscule segment of time, the threat she presented when she entered his life.

"During the course of the defendant's record of interview, did you ask him about his username and password?" Neil Abbey asked, his tone deceptively conversational.

"Yes," Chloe replied, her gaze now firmly trained back on the prosecutor.

"And did the defendant answer you in relation to those questions?"

"Yes, he told me he'd never supplied his username or password to another person."

"Not another living soul?"

"That's what he told me."

The prosecutor picked up a sheaf of papers that lay on the bar table. "Is this the defendant's record of interview?" He indicated the papers in his hand, passing them to the clerk of the court who handed them to Chloe. After taking a few moments to check them over, she nodded.

"Yes. This is both the first and second record of interview."

Abbey addressed the magistrate. "Your Honor, I'd like to tender a copy of this record of interview. I have already supplied my learned friend with a copy."

"Is that correct, Mr White?" the magistrate asked, peering over the top of his reading glasses.

Roger stood. "Yes, Your Honor. We have no objection to the tendering of the record of interview."

"Very well. I will mark it Exhibit A." The judge looked toward the prosecutor. "Will there be anything else?"

"Nothing further, Your Honor."

Then it was Declan's turn, or more accurately, his barrister's. Roger went in confidently, but both of them knew there was little he could do with Chloe's testimony. The computer records spoke for themselves. Everything hinged on whether anyone else could have obtained access to Declan's login details. Chloe was not in a position to know that information. But what she could do was vouch for his character.

"Tell me, Senior Investigator Sabattini, you interviewed my client on two separate occasions. Is that correct?"

"Yes, that's correct," she replied, her gaze on the defense lawyer.

"And during that time, did you come to any conclusions about his integrity?"

Chloe frowned. "I...um, I'm not sure what you mean."

"What I mean is, did you form any opinion as to whether my client, Agent Munro, was telling the truth?"

Declan sat forward, his heart pounding. It seemed that at least half of the occupants of the courtroom were holding their breath along with him.

Color crept up Chloe's cheeks.

"Answer the question, Investigator," the magistrate prompted quietly.

"Yes. I-I did."

"Yes, you formed an opinion about my client's sincerity? Is that what you're saying?"

Chloe cleared her throat and sat up straighter in her seat. "Yes, Mr White. I formed an opinion."

"And what was that opinion, Investigator?"

The blood pounded so loudly in Declan's ears, he was afraid he wouldn't hear her answer. He strained against the noise.

And then she looked at him again. Another fleeting moment and her gaze was gone.

"In my opinion, Agent Munro was telling the truth."

A murmur ran through the courtroom. The prosecutor sent Chloe a glare that looked like he wished it had the power to turn her to stone. Declan held his breath.

"And yet, Investigator," Roger continued, "here we are."

Chloe bowed her head. A moment later, she looked back at Declan's lawyer. "There was a lot of circumstantial evidence that Agent Munro was unable to explain away. I thought under the circumstances, the proper place to decide his guilt or innocence was in a court of law." She looked around the room, avoiding Declan. "And here we are."

Knowing he wasn't going to make any further ground, Roger returned to his seat. The magistrate made a few notes on the paper before him and looked over toward the lawyer representing the Crown.

"Is there any re-examination?"

"Yes, Your Honor." Abbey jumped to his feet.

"Senior Investigator Sabattini, is there any doubt in your mind that this matter should be heard right here, before His Honor in a court of law?"

Declan stared at her, willing her to answer in the affirmative. It seemed to take a lifetime, but eventually she replied, her voice low, but firm.

"No."

The breath rushed out through his mouth and his shoulders slumped. Yet he hadn't expected anything else.

"Nothing further, Your Honor," the prosecutor said, tossing Roger a look of victory.

The magistrate cleared his throat. "Very well, Senior Investigator Sabattini you may step down." He looked over toward the prosecution. "Please, call your next witness."

The courtroom door opened and Detective Superintendent Gary Julian strode down the aisle and stepped up to the witness box. After being sworn in by the clerk, he took the seat Chloe had recently vacated and rested his hands on the ledge in front of him, his fingers folded. His gaze found Declan's and he offered a reassuring nod.

Gratitude warmed Declan's gut and he returned the imperceptible greeting. At least someone was on his side. Within moments, the preliminaries were established and Abbey got down to the real reason Declan's boss had been called to testify.

"Detective Superintendent, I have here a copy of the staff roster prepared by you over the month of August. Would you take a look at it and confirm that it is correct?"

A copy was passed across the bar table to the defense team. Roger glanced at it briefly and then nodded his assent. Declan didn't need to see it. He'd checked the roster the minute he'd been able to after his first interview with Chloe. He knew he'd discover he'd been rostered on during the relevant times the illegal access had occurred. Stanford wasn't stupid.

As expected, Gary confirmed that the roster was in order. The prosecutor then asked him to confirm that the defendant was rostered on duty on the dates in question. Again, Gary confirmed that this was so.

Abbey then picked up another piece of paper. "I have here a print out of the usage of a particular computer in your squad room. I'd like you to take a look at it."

The same procedure was followed, with a copy being supplied to the defense before being handed to the witness.

"Is it true that every single desktop computer and government-issued laptop have individual identification names and numbers?"

"Yes, that's true. It's standard procedure."

"Do you recognize the identity of that computer?"

"Yes."

"Can you tell the court whose computer that is?"

"Well, it belongs to the AFP, but it is a desktop computer located on the desk of Federal Agents Munro, Black, Angus, Timms and Cannister."

"So all of those agents have access to that computer?"

"Yes, we generally run two or three shifts over a twenty-four hour block, depending on what's going on. All of those agents use that desk while they're at work and hence, they use that computer."

"Does each officer have their own username and password?"

"Yes."

"Do they ever login as someone else?"

"No, that's something none of them would do. Every keystroke made by a user is tracked and recorded. Everyone in the office knows it. Sharing usernames or disclosing passwords simply wouldn't happen."

"So, if I told you the records show that someone using Federal Agent Munro's username and password illegally accessed child pornographic material, you would be satisfied that the person who carried out that activity was Federal Agent Munro?"

"Objection!" Roger was on his feet. "It's not for this witness to say whether or not he's satisfied as to Federal Agent's guilt."

"Sustained," the magistrate agreed. "Please continue, Mr Abbey."

"Detective Superintendent Julian, of all the officers you mentioned who use the very same computer Agent Munro uses, how many of them were on duty during the times which are the subject of this hearing?"

Julian drew in a deep breath. His shoulders slumped. "A couple of them were on duty at one time or the other, but Agent Munro was the only one on at all of those times."

"I seek to tender the staff roster and the computer records, Your Honor."

The magistrate looked over at Roger. "Do you have any objection, Mr White?"

"No, Your Honor."

"Very well, I'll mark them as Exhibits B and C respectively."

"I have no further questions," the prosecutor said.

Roger got to his feet. "Detective Superintendent, were you surprised when you were told Agent Munro had been charged with these offences?"

Gary straightened in his seat. "Yes, I was very surprised. Agent Munro is an excellent agent. He's part of a first-class team. I can't imagine that he would be involved in such a thing."

"Agent Munro has been under your command for approximately twelve months. In that time, what have you observed of his character?"

"As I said, Agent Munro has been an exemplary employee. He's always the first to volunteer for extra duties and he's pulled more than his fair share of doubles when it's been required. He has excellent investigative initiative and an agent I've been proud to have on my team."

"Detective Superintendent, you've been a Federal Agent for many years and a team leader for more than a decade. Is that correct?"

Gary nodded. "That's correct. I joined the AFP at the age of twenty-two. I'm now fifty-eight. Apart from holidays, I've spent all of that time fighting crime in an effort to keep our country safe."

"So it's fair to say you've had considerable experience working with other officers and getting to know them."

"If you call thirty-six years considerable time, I'd have to agree with you."

There was a murmur of laughter through the courtroom. Roger acknowledged it with a smile and continued.

"Detective Superintendent, who else has access to your employees' login information?"

Gary's expression sobered. "No one, as far as I know. They're generated out of the Home Affairs Office when an agent is first employed and given directly to the agent."

"Are there any hard copies of such information left in an employee's file?"

Gary frowned in thought. "I'm not sure. When I first started at the AFP, there were no such thing as logins and passwords. From my recollection, when computers became part of our daily life, my login details were generated by the computer system. I have no knowledge how it works these days."

"Thank you, Detective Superintendent. I have no further questions."

Abbey jumped to his feet. "I'd like to re-examine, Your Honor?"

The magistrate nodded. "As you wish."

"Detective Superintendent, you mentioned that Agent Munro was part of a first-class team and that you couldn't imagine that he would be involved."

"Yes," Gary agreed warily.

"So thinking about the rest of your first-class team, which one of them do you think could have done this?"

A knot of dread tightened in Declan's gut. He watched the color disappear from his boss' cheeks.

Gary shook his head. "I-I can't believe any of them would be capable of it."

Abbey's voice lowered. "And yet, one of them is."

Gary's head bowed.

Declan's shoulders slumped.

Chloe saw the defeat in Declan's eyes and wished she could go to him and offer words of comfort. She'd always prided herself on being a good judge of character and despite the fact she stood by the testimony she'd given, everything she'd seen this morning had reinforced her growing conviction that, notwithstanding the evidence before them, Declan Munro was exactly what he said he was: an innocent man.

The next witness was the IT technician employed by the AFP who had carried out the forensic testing on Declan's laptop. Within a few moments, Terry Higgins had given testimony to the effect that more than a hundred images of child pornography had been found on a laptop located in Agent Munro's apartment and believed to be one owned by Agent Munro.

White got to his feet. "Mr Higgins, the laptop you examined from Declan Munro's apartment wasn't protected by a password, was it?"

"No, it wasn't," the witness replied. Declan frowned and whispered to his lawyer.

Roger asked the technician, "Were the images downloaded at one time, or over a period of time?"

The technician looked confused by the question. "They were all downloaded and saved to a file on the hard drive on the same day. From memory, it was September eighth."

"And that date was after the defendant was laid off work, isn't that right?"

"I wouldn't know the answer to that, sir."

"For the record, you're saying the pictures were put on the home computer in a single download operation. This means whoever did it wasn't in the habit of downloading this kind of material to his home computer. With no password, anyone could have logged into the laptop, correct?"

"Yes, that's correct. That's the reason most of us use passwords."

"In fact, someone else could have put those pictures there for forensics to find, isn't that true?"

"Yes. That's possible."

White returned to his seat. Chloe sighed, knowing there was nothing more he could do to dispute the forensic evidence. Declan's only hope was proving that someone else had accessed his laptop.

The clerk called out the name of the next witness and her attention was drawn to the door of the courtroom as it opened again. Charlie Stanford strode through the doorway, staring straight ahead. He wore a dark navy suit, white business shirt and a conservative blue tie. He looked like any other federal agent she might encounter over the course of her day.

Her gaze slid to Declan. He'd straightened in his seat. Even from across the aisle, she could see the tension in his body.

After taking the oath, Charlie took a seat in the witness box and proceeded to answer the prosecutor's questions. Abbey established that Charlie was an officer with an enviable service history and an unblemished record. The court also heard how Charlie was Agent Munro's friend.

"Can you tell us, Agent Stanford, about the events that occurred on or about the week commencing August thirteen?"

Chloe listened as Charlie relayed the story he'd given her. He seemed a little more nervous than before, but then, who wouldn't be? It wasn't every day you had to give testimony against your friend in a court of law.

She glanced across at Declan. His lips were compressed into a thin line, his hands clenched into fists. Chloe could almost feel the anger that radiated off him. Her gaze returned to Charlie.

"Agent Stanford, it couldn't have been easy to do what you did and the law applauds your bravery. You've been friends with the defendant ever since he arrived in your unit." Abbey took a piece of paper that was handed to him by his associate and glanced at it.

"Tell me, Agent Stanford," he continued, "has the defendant ever expressed unhealthy interest in children in the past?"

Chloe knew the answer to that one. It was a question she'd already put to him.

Charlie stared straight ahead, toward the prosecutor.

"Yes," he said.

CHAPTER 11

Chloe's mouth gaped open in shock. A ripple of unsettled murmurs went through the courtroom. She didn't dare look at Declan.

"I'm sorry?" Abbey said, frowning slightly.

"Yes. I said, yes."

"Yes, the defendant has shown unhealthy interest in children in the past?"

"Yes." Stanford looked away, appearing suddenly fascinated with the wall on the far side of the courtroom. "At the time, I didn't know what to make of it."

Roger White got to his feet, his expression livid. "Your Honor, this is the first time we've heard about this. Agent Stanford gave a record of interview about the events before you today and not once did he mention anything about this. In fact, his answers were quite to the contrary. I seek an immediate adjournment so that I can consult with my client about these fresh allegations."

With a dubious expression on his face, the magistrate turned to look at the prosecutor.

"Is that correct, Mr Abbey? Is this the first notice the defense have had of this evidence?"

"Yes, Your Honor. I believe so."

The magistrate frowned. "We have rules about this kind of thing, Mr Abbey. Those rules are there for a good reason."

"Yes, Your Honor. I understand and I apologize for the lack of notice given to my learned friend. In my defense, I-

I was unaware until now this evidence was available."

The magistrate's lips compressed. He stared down at the papers in front of him. Eventually, he raised his head and looked at Roger.

"I find myself in an unusual position, Mr White. How do you wish to proceed?"

Roger turned to Declan. An angry flush had spread across Declan's cheeks. Chloe could understand how he felt. She was more than a little angry herself. She'd asked Stanford the very same question and he'd denied it. Either he was lying then, or he was lying now. Either option was unacceptable and said something about his character.

A frantic, whispered conversation ensued between Declan and his barrister. A few moments later, the barrister turned back toward the bench.

"Your Honor, I would like to reiterate my request for a short adjournment in order to seek further instructions from my client. Agent Stanford's most recent evidence has taken both of us completely by surprise."

The magistrate nodded. "Very well. We'll resume in fifteen minutes. This court is adjourned."

With a bang of the gavel, the court was dismissed.

Fifteen minutes later, the spectators and lawyers filed back inside. Chloe risked a glance in Declan's direction. His face was as dark as a thundercloud. Roger White didn't look any happier.

When the magistrate took his position at the bench, Charlie Stanford returned to the witness box. Neil Abbey jumped to his feet.

"Agent Stanford, before the break we were talking about how the defendant had previously given you cause for concern about his behaviour. Tell us what you remember."

Charlie kept his gaze directed toward the prosecutor. "It happened about six months ago. We were heading toward Fyshwick to interview a witness. I can't remember what the matter was about. Anyway, Agent Munro was driving and he pulled up near a park not far from our destination."

"Did you ask him why he'd stopped?"

"Yeah, I said something like, 'What are we doing here?'"

"And what did he say?"

"He didn't say anything. He just sat there, looking at some little kids who were playing on the swings."

Chloe saw Roger White scribbling furiously on his legal pad. She couldn't even imagine how he was feeling. She felt like she'd been blindsided.

"When you say, "looking," what do you mean?" Abbey asked.

"I don't know. Just looking. Staring. I don't know... It felt weird, that's all."

"Thank you Agent Stanford. No further questions." Abbey took his seat.

Roger shot to his feet seconds later. "Agent Stanford, you were interviewed about this matter at length by Internal Affairs, were you not?"

Charlie nodded cautiously. "Yes."

"And yet, you didn't think to tell the investigator then anything about what you've just revealed, even when asked directly, isn't that correct?"

Another cautious nod. "Yes."

"It's rather convenient, wouldn't you say, that now, more than a month after your initial interview and smack bang before a crowded courtroom that you decide this little morsel of information best be shared."

Stanford colored. "It's not like that. I-I must have forgotten. With all the stress and pressure of coming forward to report something like this—something so...so *horrible*—I didn't remember every detail."

"Time had brought this forward in your memory, though you denied this in your original interview? Is that what you want us to believe? A rather convenient lapse of memory, Agent Stanford."

Chloe stared at the witness, her heart thumping. If she hadn't put the very question to him that was now the subject of the fresh evidence, she would have believed Charlie's explanation. Everyone would believe coming forward to report a colleague for such heinous behavior would be stressful and could cause a lapse in memory, but she'd asked Charlie about whether Declan had exhibited any unhealthy interest in children before and he'd replied with an emphatic *no*.

Something was off. Rather, another piece didn't fit. Charlie remained tight lipped on the witness stand. Roger White eyeballed him.

"I put it to you, Agent Stanford, that no such event happened. I put it to you that at no time did my client stop at a park and spy on children. I also put it to you that you are lying when you say you saw Declan Munro view child pornography on his computer from a previously finalized investigation of which he had no part."

Stanford had begun to shake his head even before White had finished. "No, no, no. You're wrong. He did it. I saw him. I *swear*."

Chloe watched as fury ignited behind Declan's eyes. He stared at Charlie without flinching. It was Charlie who averted his gaze.

White shuffled some papers and then chose another tack. "Agent Stanford, you're a friend of Declan Munro's, aren't you? In fact, the two of you are good mates."

"Yes," Stanford answered cautiously.

"And that's what makes this so hard for you, isn't it?" White continued in an understanding tone.

"Yes. That's what I tried to tell you earlier. This has been just *awful* for me."

Chloe frowned, wondering where Declan's barrister was going with this.

"You and Declan spend a lot of time together, don't you? You work together; you socialize together; you hang out at each other's apartments?"

"Yes."

And then she knew.

"In fact, it wouldn't be unusual for you to spend at least one of your days off every week in the company of Declan Munro, kicking back, chugging down a few beers in front of the television at Declan's apartment, would it?"

Once again, Stanford nodded. "That's right. We were mates. Good mates. We spent many a weekend together watching football from Dec's TV. He has a big screen."

"Of course," White agreed amiably. "That's what mates do. Tell me, did you ever spend the night at Agent Munro's apartment?"

Stanford looked a little more cautious. "Sometimes. If I'd had a few too many to drive, Dec would let me stay in the spare room."

White eyeballed the witness, his eyes hard. "He's been a good mate to you, hasn't he?"

Color exploded across Stanford's cheeks. He lowered his gaze. "Yes," he muttered.

"I put it to you, Agent Stanford, that while you were in Declan Munro's apartment, you accessed his laptop and downloaded the evidence they found there, over a hundred pornographic images of children."

Stanford went pale. "No, no, I had nothing to do with it. You've got it all wrong."

White glared at the witness. "I don't think so, Agent Stanford. I have nothing further, Your Honor." With that, the barrister returned to his seat.

The magistrate looked across at Abbey. "Any re-examination from the Crown?"

"Yes, Your Honor." Abbey got to his feet.

"Agent Stanford, it's fair to say you've visited Agent Munro's apartment, correct?"

"Yes, of course. He's a mate."

"Have you ever used Agent Munro's laptop?"

"No, never."

"Nothing further, Your Honor."

"Very well. We'll adjourn until ten o'clock tomorrow morning. Bail to be continued." The gavel banged sharply in the silence.

The magistrate departed amidst a flurry of black robes. Chloe let out her breath and glanced at Declan. The fury was still there, but he also looked shell shocked. He stood, fists clenched, lips taut, face pale. Flanked by two of his brothers, he stepped down from the dock and made his way into the aisle.

She sat less than ten feet away. His gaze clashed with hers. Pain and anger and a hint of vulnerability burned in his eyes. He shook his head, once, twice and then strode past her without a word.

Charlie hastened down the steps of the courtroom and strode toward his car. His gut still churned with nerves and fear, despite the worst of it now being over. He spared a glance over his shoulder and was relieved to see Declan, surrounded by people he presumed to be his family, headed in the opposite direction. There was no sign of the little IA investigator.

At the thought of her, his gut clenched again. She had to know he was lying. She'd put the very same question to him during his interview and he'd denied it. He'd told the Master as much when he insisted Charlie ramp up his evidence to include that extra tidbit.

Despite the breach of protocol when it came to giving evidence, the Master was certain once the evidence had been heard, the magistrate would be hard pressed to ignore it and it wasn't as if the committal hearing was the real deal. It had been little more than a formality. Everyone knew the decisions that really mattered would be made in the Supreme Court. Right now, the Master insisted it was Charlie's responsibility to ensure the matter made it that far.

Charlie thought of the Master and the assurances the man had given that Charlie's cooperation in this matter was vital to the Master's position—hell, to his very life. It made Charlie feel warm all over knowing how much the Master trusted and depended upon him. Only good things could come of having such a charismatic, powerful man in his debt.

That thought made Charlie smile. Reaching his car, he

unlocked the door and slid behind the wheel. He tugged out his cell phone and switched it off silent. There were three missed calls, all from the Master.

A surge of love and loyalty rushed through him. He dialed the familiar number. It was picked up immediately.

"Tell me."

"It's done," he murmured. "Just like you asked."

CHAPTER 12

Chloe took a sip out of her wine glass and sighed. It had been hours since she'd listened to Stanford change his evidence, and her thoughts were still in chaos. The memory of Declan's parting look had contributed to her unrest. Despite hurrying from the courtroom immediately after the magistrate had adjourned the matter for the day, and waiting outside, she'd seen no sign of Declan or Charlie.

Disappointed and disgruntled, she'd returned to her office and had immediately pored over Stanford's statement, wondering again about the possible reasons why he'd changed his story. An hour later and still clueless, she'd tried to catch a moment with her colleague to get his take on it, but Webber had been in meetings all afternoon and she'd finally left for home, no more the wiser.

After watering her plants and feeding the neighbor's cat, she'd filled a glass from the half full bottle of Shiraz she found on the kitchen counter.

What she needed was an unbiased opinion, from someone who would listen and then tell her what they honestly thought of the situation. Someone who was smart and perceptive. Someone like Savannah O'Neill. Reaching for her phone, Chloe dialed her best friend's number and sighed in relief when she answered.

"Chloe, how goes it?"

Chloe smiled at the habitual laughter in Savannah's

voice. No matter the subject, speaking with her friend always made her feel better. She was exactly what Chloe needed now.

"Hey, Sav. I've had a shit of a day and I needed someone to offload onto."

Savannah laughed. "Whinge away. I've had writer's block all day. The way I'm going, I'll never meet my deadline. Maybe lending you a sympathetic ear is just the thing I need. Besides, that's what friends are for."

"Thanks. It's not so much of a whinge as a need for a sounding board. I'm in the middle of an investigation that's twisting me up in knots."

"They always twist you up in knots, Chloe. I keep telling you not to care so much."

"What can I say? It's an occupational hazard."

"Yeah, yeah, yeah... That's what you always say."

"Perhaps I should have a career change? Take up journalism, like you?"

Savannah's throaty laughter brought a tired smile to Chloe's lips.

"Oh yeah, baby. Do it! I tell you, you'll never have the problem of caring too much again!"

"Come on; you love it, Savannah. All that political intrigue on top of the Hill. It's the reason you left the city lights of Sydney to venture down south. Isn't that what you told me?"

"What I told you was that you'd end up doing your back in trying to twist your body into those impossible yoga poses, but you refused to listen."

Chloe didn't fall for the innocent tone. She laughed wholeheartedly at the memory and felt a sympathetic twinge in her spine.

It was how they'd met, not quite six years ago during a yoga class at a gym in Civic. Chloe had been attending for only a month when she'd noticed the new girl at the back of the room.

It was impossible not to. With her mass of auburn hair and a body that would put Pamela Anderson to shame, there hadn't been a person in the room who failed to observe the arrival of Savannah O'Neill in her hot-pink leotard and matching yoga mat.

Dressed in a conservative black-and-silver leotard and black leggings, Chloe had secretly envied the girl's confidence as she'd laid her mat on the floor and started straight in with the exercises.

Being a little short on coordination and a lot short on height, Chloe had felt squat and gawky alongside the leggy beauty in the back row. But afterwards, while Chloe had been mopping her sweaty brow with her old, worn towel, Savannah had approached and stuck out her hand in greeting.

"Savannah O'Neill, investigative journalist extraordinaire. I saw some of your moves back there. I have to tell you, I'm impressed." The girl's brilliant green eyes had sparkled with humor.

Chloe couldn't help it. She'd grinned back at her and then laughter had spilled over. It was common knowledge amongst the group that even the instructor had given up on Chloe and her coordination.

She'd offered her hand in greeting. "Chloe Sabattini, professional yoga person."

Savannah had shaken her hand and had raised a single, dark auburn eyebrow. "Pleased to meet you Chloe Sabattini, professional yoga person."

From that moment, their friendship had been sealed and even though Savannah was three years her junior, Chloe had come to rely on her friend's uncanny ability to see through to the heart of a matter. It was one of the things that made her such a reputable journalist.

"So, what is it that has you all churned up this time?" Savannah asked.

She said it without recrimination and Chloe picked up her glass of Shiraz and headed into the living room, prepared to unload on her best friend.

When Chloe was finished recapping the events that had led up to the hearing, Savannah was silent for a few moments.

"I heard something about this earlier. One of the journos at work was heading down to the courthouse to get a quote."

"This conversation's off the record, Sav," Chloe warned.

"Of course it is, silly. Everything you tell me is off the record."

"I don't know what to do," Chloe admitted. "On paper, everything points to his guilt, but there's something about him, something indefinable, that just screams innocence."

"And of course, you've already told me how good looking he is."

"Savannah O'Neill! That's unfair! You know I'd never consider a person's guilt or innocence based only upon their looks! I demand that you take that back!"

"Okay, okay! I take it back," Savannah laughed. "*Mm*, you seem a little sensitive about it. Now, why would that be?"

"No reason at all and definitely not one I'm going to share with you," Chloe replied tartly.

"*Ooh*, I knew it! You *like* him! You like your number one suspect! Oh, Ms Sabattini, whatever are we going to do with you?"

Chloe's cheeks burned, even in her solitude. She wisely refrained from arguing. Savannah was a pit bull when she smelled a story. It was another thing that made her so good at her job. It wasn't nearly as endearing when that tenacity was turned on Chloe.

"I called you to get your advice, Savannah. You're supposed to be my best friend. You're supposed to be here for me in my hour of need."

"Oh, we both know what you need, baby and it isn't me."

Chloe couldn't help it. She giggled, even as heat spread through her body.

"You have to call him, Chloe. Do it. Your star witness is lying. You're beginning to doubt your defendant's guilt. You owe the man a chance to explain, away from the pressure of the interrogation. And he's cute. You owe it to yourself to find out once and for all if he's in the running."

Butterflies multiplied in Chloe's stomach. Could she call Declan out of hours and ask him to meet her? Did she dare?

———

Declan lay sprawled across the couch, a half empty glass of scotch in his hand. Tilting his head, he poured what remained of it down his throat, relishing the slow burn. Reaching down, his fingers closed around the neck of the bottle. He brought it up to eye level and discovered it was empty. Cursing savagely, he struggled to a sitting position.

Oblivious to the beauty of the cool, spring night wafting in the air moving across his balcony or the occasional murmur of late-night traffic on the road below, he moved across the living room and hunted behind the bar for another bottle. Coming up empty, he cursed again.

He wasn't much of a drinker, especially when it came to hard liquor. A few beers on a Friday night or at a social function on the weekend were about the sum of it, but he liked to keep his bar well stocked for times when friends came over. Too bad he'd forgotten the scotch had run low.

His gaze scanned the labels of the assortment of other bottles lined up on the shelf. There was an unopened bottle of rum, but he'd never been a rum drinker. The one and only time he'd tried it was after a police union football game and he'd been so ill he'd vowed never to touch the stuff again.

A headache began to make itself known behind his eyes and with a sigh tinged heavily with regret and disappointment, he set his empty glass down on the countertop and headed back to the couch.

The image of Chloe sitting across from him in the courtroom, watching the proceedings—proceedings she'd instigated—wouldn't leave him.

He'd noticed her right away, of course. There was something about her that drew him. As the hearing had drawn on, he'd felt her gaze upon him. He'd fought the urge to look at her until he'd lost the battle.

The surge of heat that had traveled through his gut and down to his groin when their eyes connected had taken him by surprise. Of course, from the moment of their first meeting he'd found her compelling, but so far, the reasons for bringing them together had managed to quell any real thought that things could go any further.

Under normal circumstances, he would have flirted with her, maybe even asked her out, but these weren't normal circumstances. She was investigating him for a crime and the heinous nature of that prohibited any attempt at normality between them.

And yet, he'd sensed a change in her attitude sometime after Charlie had taken the stand. She'd sat up straighter in the hard plastic seat and her gaze had narrowed on the witness. A frown had marred the flawless skin of her forehead and she'd bitten down on her lip.

He'd noticed all of this and had wished he'd been able to keep his attention on what had been unfolding in front of him. Even the shock of hearing the lies fall from Charlie's mouth couldn't completely divert him from the investigator's distracting presence and curious response to Charlie's statement under oath.

But nothing changed the fact they were on opposite sides of a serious criminal investigation—an investigation that pointed the finger squarely at him.

It was an unsettling thought. Apart from the odd speeding ticket when he'd thrown caution to the wind and had opened the throttle on his 1199 Panigale Ducati on the freeway north to Sydney, he'd never imagined he'd find himself on the wrong side of the law and not in a million years had he thought he'd be the defendant in a criminal trial.

But that's how it was, and any future with the delectable Chloe Sabattini would be doomed before it started. The system advocated innocence until proven guilty, but everyone knew the prosecution was convinced of the defendant's guilt before they stepped foot inside the courtroom. They wouldn't bring a case before a magistrate or a judge unless they were confident they could win.

Chloe Sabattini was the senior investigator. She was the one who'd put together the brief, the one who'd interviewed the witnesses, prepared the statements, met with the prosecutor. It didn't take much to work out how she felt about his status. Under these circumstances most men would give up on thinking there could ever be something between them.

But he wasn't most men.

His parents had taught him to strive for the unreachable, to ignore hardships and setbacks and never lose sight of his goal. Being of mixed race, life hadn't always been easy and his parents had known he'd face additional obstacles because of it. He'd learned to set aside prejudices and narrow-minded opinions and forge on, regardless. He'd never let anything stand in his way of creating a successful life and career he was proud of.

A surge of determination brought him upright. He straightened on the sofa and dropped his feet onto the floor. He'd never taken the easy way out and he'd never given up on something that was important to him. There was no way he was going to go down without a fight. He was innocent. One way to clear his name was to convince the woman who was responsible for him being there.

With renewed energy, he strode with purpose to the kitchen and picked up his phone from where he'd left it on the counter. Scrolling through his contacts, he found her number and listened as it dialed out.

Chloe stood right inside the doorway and glanced around the dimly lit bar, trying to quell the nerves in her stomach. Although it wasn't the usual place she chose to hang out, with its dated interior and pervasive smell of stale alcohol, it wasn't hard to guess why Declan had suggested it.

The clientele were few. A couple of men with grizzled cheeks and graying hair were deep in conversation at the far end of the bar. The only other occupant was an older woman with heavy makeup and deep wrinkles around her mouth that told the story of a chronic smoker. She sat alone at one of the scarred wooden tables scattered around the room, a half empty glass by her elbow.

Although Chloe had never been there before, the bar wasn't far from her condominium and the short drive hadn't given her nearly enough time to fully think through her actions.

Why had she agreed to meet him? It was nearly ten-thirty at night. She should be home in bed going over her notes for the witnesses due to appear at the committal hearing in the morning, not meeting with the defendant...

Had she totally lost her mind?

She cursed Savannah under her breath. Meeting with Declan was wrong on so many levels. She shouldn't have accepted his invitation, despite Savannah's encouragement and Chloe's misgivings about Stanford's evidence. Halting mid-stride, she turned on her heel to leave.

Pushing open the door she'd just entered through, she glimpsed the back of a cab, its taillights receding in the distance. She tugged out her car keys and swung around, intending to head back to her Honda. She gasped when she ran into a hard, hot wall of male.

"Going somewhere?"

Chloe jumped back as if she'd been scalded. His hands reached for her arms and steadied her.

"Whoa! I didn't mean to startle you." He offered her a quick grin.

Heat seared her cheeks. Flustered, she looked anywhere but at his face. If it were possible, he looked even more delectable in his casual white T-shirt and jeans than he had in his formal suit and tie. The stretchy fabric of his shirt hugged the impressive expanse of his chest and she was sure she could still feel the warmth of his fingers where they'd touched her.

"I'm sorry, I-I was just leaving. This isn't a good idea. I shouldn't have agreed to come."

"And yet you're here."

When she turned to face him, his gaze captured hers and wouldn't let it go. Her heart thumped crazily. She swallowed, and tried to speak.

"Declan, look... I'm sorry. I can't do this. It's not right."

"Stanford's lying. *That's* what isn't right."

CHAPTER 13

Chloe stared at Declan and bit her lip—torn. Stanford was lying, at least about part of what he'd said. It stood to reason if he'd lied about one thing, he might have lied about others. He might even have lied about it all. He'd agreed he had regular access to Declan's apartment. It was possible he'd also accessed the laptop. She didn't know and the confusion and uncertainty of all this was driving her crazy.

On top of all that, she wanted to believe the man who stood in front of her, looking more scrumptious than any man had a right to look. When he called, she'd been shocked. It was like he had ESP. From the time she'd ended her call to Savannah, she'd vacillated about calling him and there he was, on the other end of the phone. It was more than a little surreal.

She'd barely given herself time to brush her hair and throw on some makeup—so much was her haste to meet with him. Despite the lateness of the hour, she still hadn't changed from the suit she'd worn to court.

He continued to hold her gaze, his eyes encouraging her to stay. Knowing if she left now she might never get to the bottom of it, Chloe nodded and followed him inside. Declan headed toward the bar.

"What are you drinking?" he asked.

Chloe eyed the barman whose overgrown hair and ragged black T-shirt had seen better days and knew instinctively that ordering a margarita was probably something best not done here. She looked back at Declan.

"I'll have a beer, thanks," she said.

One dark eyebrow lifted in surprise. "You don't look like the kind of girl that drinks beer."

She shrugged. "What does a girl that drinks beer look like?"

His gaze held hers for a significant moment before sliding down her very sensible pale-pink blouse and even more sensible tailored suit, which now looked more than a little rumpled. Despite everything, heat followed in the wake of his gaze, tingling her nerve endings.

"Not as prim and proper as you, that's for sure."

She didn't know whether to feel flattered or insulted, but the teasing gleam in his eyes cooled her indignation.

"Looks can be deceiving," she murmured, shocking herself. Was she actually *flirting* with him?

His eyes flared with some indefinable emotion and Chloe's stomach somersaulted. God, she was so out of her league. *He* was out of her league. Girls like her didn't get to go out with guys who looked like they'd stepped out of the pages of GQ. Boys who looked like that were the exclusive property of the cheerleaders, the popular girls, the girls with bodies to die for and hair to match. Not short, shy Italian girls with hair that could only be controlled by a decent drenching—and even then it was a struggle.

In an effort to restore the conversation to a level she could handle, Chloe forced her pulse to slow and cleared her throat.

"I'm actually more of a margarita girl, but I thought I might offend the barman's sensibilities if I asked for one."

Declan looked around at their surroundings and grimaced. "Yeah, I'm sorry about the venue. I'm trying to fly under the radar. I passed a handful of reporters and a couple of photographers outside my apartment this afternoon. They were yelling out at me about the hearing." He shook his head. "It's already started."

Chloe felt a pang of sympathy, mixed with a fair dose of

guilt. "I understand." She shrugged. "This place is fine."

Their drinks arrived in frosted glasses. Declan slid some money over the bar and Chloe murmured her thanks. Collecting their beers, Declan turned and headed in the direction of one of the abandoned tables in the dimmest part of the room.

"We can talk over here," he said and pulled out a chair for her.

Warmth seeped through her at his chivalry. For all her hard-fought independence, there was something inside her that still appreciated that kind of attention from a man. She reached for one of the glasses and took a sip from it. It was yeasty and cold. The froth stuck to her lip and she licked it off.

Declan's gaze followed the movement. Even in the dimness, when she glanced up she saw the flare of awareness in his eyes. Desire kindled low in her belly. She gritted her teeth against it; now wasn't the time to let her hormones dictate her actions. A man's life and career was at stake.

And that man sat across from her.

Declan seemed to come to the same conclusion. He shook his head and his forehead creased in a frown.

"You must know Stanford's lying. I read his statement. There was nothing in it about a visit to the park." He shook his head in disgust, as if still unable to believe it. "I don't get it. Why haven't you called off the dogs?"

"How do you know I haven't?" she challenged.

"Because I wouldn't have had half a dozen media personnel ready to ambush me outside my apartment the minute I stepped outside, if you had."

Chloe's shoulders slumped and she gave it up, unsure why she'd felt the need to challenge him in the first place. The truth was, apart from her efforts to talk her concerns over with Webber and her telephone call to Savannah, she'd done nothing more than toss arguments back and forth in her head ever since she'd heard Stanford's evidence at the hearing.

"What do *you* make of Stanford's evidence?" The words were out of her mouth before she realized she'd spoken aloud. And no wonder; the question had been at the forefront of her thoughts all afternoon.

Declan's lips compressed. "I don't know how to explain it and for the life of me, I can't come up with a reason why Charlie would lie—about everything. That's the problem." He stared at her, his eyes pleading with her to understand. "All I know is that I didn't do it."

"What does he have to gain?"

"Nothing." Declan shook his head helplessly. "It's what makes this whole thing so unbelievable."

Chloe leaned forward and took another sip of beer. "He's the same rank as you, isn't he?"

"Yes. He's been an agent a few years longer, but we're the same rank."

"Has that caused friction?"

"No!" He's been a good mate from the day I started. I'd have trusted him with my life. It just goes to show how wrong I was."

"Perhaps he thinks you did it? Perhaps someone else is loading the gun and using him to fire the bullets?"

"But why would he lie about me being at the park? There's no way in the world it happened and yet he says he was with me." Declan ran his hands through his hair, his frustration evident. "It doesn't make sense."

Chloe nodded thoughtfully. She knew exactly how he felt. Well, probably not *exactly*. After all, it wasn't her reputation and freedom on the line. But there'd been times in her life when she'd known the same sense of bewilderment that now emanated from him in almost-palpable waves.

"Let's think about it. As far as I see it, everything revolves around your login details. Somehow, he's gotten hold of them."

"But how?" Declan exploded. "The username was issued to me when I commenced my employment with the AFP. I chose the password. I gave them out to no one."

"So the only possible explanation is that someone stole

them. Let's back up a minute. What department issued the username?"

Declan shrugged and sat back against his chair. "Human Resources, as far as I know. That's what I was told at my induction."

"And what about your password?"

"I was asked to provide one at the induction. Someone from HR spoke with the newcomers. We all filled in a mountain of paperwork, had photos taken for our ID's, provided tax file numbers, bank accounts, superannuation details and a bunch of other stuff...and then we were asked to come up with a password to use for computer access."

Nervous excitement tightened Chloe's stomach. "How did you provide your password?"

Declan looked momentarily confused.

"Did you give it verbally or were you asked to write it down?"

"We were asked to write it down," he said slowly, comprehension dawning.

"See!" Chloe grinned. "Someone else knew the procedure. I bet it's still stored in your personnel file, along with all the other forms you filled in. It's not too great a stretch to imagine someone accessed that file and discovered your login details."

"But who? And more importantly, why? As far as I know, I've done a darned good job since I started. I've had my fair share of successes and was well on the way to a promotion. In fact, Gary Julian encouraged me to apply for the team leader's position that's about to be advertised."

Chloe sat forward. "Did Charlie Stanford know you wanted to be a team leader?"

"Of course. He was one of the first people I told."

"And how did he react?"

Declan shrugged. "Like you'd expect. He offered me congratulations and agreed that I'd make a great team leader."

"And that was it? You didn't sense any undertones?"

"No. It's like I told you before, I can't, for the life of me, fathom why he'd say those things about me when he knew they were just plain false. It doesn't make sense."

"Maybe he was hoping the additional evidence would put you away that much quicker," she responded dryly.

Declan took a healthy swallow of his beer and then set the glass down. Chloe tried not to notice how strong and masculine his hand was or remember how his fingers felt, firm and warm around her arms when she'd stumbled into him outside. She took another gulp from her beer.

"You *are* a beer girl," he teased, a grin tilting the side of his mouth upwards.

Heat rushed through her and her cheeks flamed with embarrassment. She was inordinately grateful for the room's lack of lighting.

Declan's smile faded and his expression turned serious. "All of these questions you're asking—does this mean you believe me when I tell you I didn't access those files?"

His gaze searched hers. She saw the uncertainty that warred with hope in their green-flecked depths. She nodded, her eyes not leaving his.

"Yes, I believe you. I think I always have, but the evidence dictated otherwise. In the end, I took the only way out I knew. I chose to have the system do its work and let the courts decide."

"What a perfect world you live in," he mused.

Chloe shrugged. "Perfect or not, it's my world. I'm an IA investigator. I have to believe, above all else, that justice will be served and that the truth will prevail."

Declan's lips twisted in a grimace. "I wish I could be so idealistic."

Irritation surged through her and she sat up straighter in her chair. "Don't patronize me, Agent Munro. I don't know what happened to make you so cynical, but don't foist your preconceived notions on me. You know nothing about me."

"I was referring to my own experience. But you're right, I don't know much about you. We could change that," he murmured, his gaze lingering on her lips.

Chloe gasped at the heat in his eyes and tried not to let it affect her. She might as well have tried stopping a tsunami.

Desire ignited a path of need deep inside her and she was reminded of how long it had been since she'd been intimate with a man. She could barely remember the details, but the wanting was still the same. It hadn't changed.

Declan must have seen something in her eyes, or maybe he heard the tiny whimper of need that escaped her parched lips? Either way, her hand was suddenly engulfed inside the warmth of his.

He drew her fingers up to his mouth and pressed his lips against the soft skin of her wrist. She watched his progress in fascination before reality crashed into her. She pulled back as if she'd been branded.

"Please. Don't."

His gaze held hers. "I like you, Chloe. And I think you like me. Now that we've established we're no longer on opposing sides, what's wrong with that? We're both adults. What's wrong with getting to know each other a little better?"

Chloe's mind struggled to keep up with how quickly things had changed. Yes, she found him attractive, but they were in the middle of a committal hearing. She'd given evidence for the prosecution. He was the defendant. There was a real chance his case would go to trial.

What was she thinking?

She was shaking her head even before the words formed on her lips. "I'm sorry, Declan. I-I... No. This is not a good idea."

Bewilderment clouded his eyes. "I thought you said you believed me?"

Chloe pursed her lips. "I did. I do. At least, I think so, but that doesn't change anything. I can't just waltz into the courtroom and tell everyone Charlie Stanford's lying and by the way, can you please let the defendant go? Be serious. The allegations are still on the table. The evidence is still there. Good evidence. Solid evidence. With, or without Stanford. The computer records don't lie. It's the reason I recommended the laying of charges in the first place."

Declan groaned in frustration and thumped the table with his fist. "Then what the hell can we do? I'm not going to sit back and let some overambitious prosecutor convince the court to commit me for trial for something I didn't do. Who's to say that a jury won't look past the obvious and convict me? Would you sit by and let them send me to *prison*?"

Chloe hunted for her purse, now eager to bring their meeting to a close.

"Of course not. But it's not that simple. You, of all people, know that. We need to find out who's behind this. It's becoming obvious this is bigger than Charlie Stanford. You've admitted you can't think of a single reason why he'd do this. There must be more to it and we need to be discreet. If whoever is responsible for this gets wind that we're onto them, we might lose them and whatever tracks they've left behind."

"So, we just sit back and take whatever comes?" he said angrily.

"Yes. At least, for now."

"Easy for you to say. It's not you being led to the dock in handcuffs. It's not your face being splashed all over the national papers."

Chloe drew in a breath. He looked so desolate. Against her better judgement, she reached across the table and took his hand and squeezed. His gaze bored into hers.

"Do you trust me?" she asked.

It took him eons to answer and when he did, his response was grudging. "I guess I don't have a choice."

She withdrew her hand and sighed. That would have to do.

CHAPTER 14

Chloe glanced at her watch and hurried inside the elevator. It was a smidgen past eight-thirty in the morning. She'd deliberately chosen the time to reduce the chances of running into other staff members who worked in the AFP's Human Resources Department. It also meant she'd be able to conduct the interview and still make it to court before the second day of Declan's committal hearing commenced at ten.

She'd arranged an appointment with the manager of HR on her way into the AFP building and was grateful Marcia Slater was an early starter. The woman had expressed polite curiosity at her request, but Chloe had been quick to keep the conversation to a minimum. At this point, she didn't know who was involved in framing Declan and until she did, she had no choice but to treat everyone as a suspect—or at the very least, an accomplice.

The elevator reached the seventh floor and slid open with barely a sound. She stepped into the carpeted corridor. Frosted glass doors lined either side of the hall. About halfway down the corridor, she stopped at the floor-to-ceiling window with the words "Human Resources" stenciled in neat script. She pushed open the door with her shoulder.

The large open-plan office was filled with partitioned desks and looked much as it did when she'd last been there more than six years ago, on the eve of taking up her career with the AFP.

A couple of people sat in front of computers and two more employees stood in the doorway to what Chloe recalled led to the tea room, steaming cups of coffee in their hands. They chatted together in low tones.

An elegantly attired older woman with perfectly coiffed silver hair approached Chloe with a smile of welcome.

"Senior Investigator Sabattini?"

Chloe nodded and briefly shook the woman's proffered hand.

"Yes. You must be Mrs Slater."

"Please, call me Marcia. Follow me; we can talk in my office."

The woman turned and with quiet efficiency made her way across the room and into an enclosed office. Chloe trailed behind her.

The glass windows surrounding the office looked out onto the plethora of partitions and afforded the HR manager with an excellent view of most of the occupants in the room. Marcia Slater was someone who liked to know what was happening in her domain. Chloe felt reassured that the woman would be able to help her.

Taking a seat behind a scrupulously tidy desk, Marcia indicated one of the empty chairs across from her.

"Sit down, Senior Investigator Sabattini and tell me what I can do for you."

"Call me Chloe, please." Chloe sat and tugged a legal pad and pen out of her briefcase. Leaning forward, she eyed the woman solemnly.

"I'm in the process of conducting a very sensitive investigation into the actions of one of our agents. I can't impress upon you enough, how important it is that our conversation remains absolutely confidential. Do you understand?"

"Of course. I would assume any IA Investigation requires complete confidentiality. What is it that you want to know?"

"One of the agents involved in the investigation is Declan Munro. He's been with the AFP for a little over a year. I'd like to see his personnel file."

"Declan Munro? Well, he's certainly popular all of a sudden," the woman replied with a smile.

Chloe's heart skipped a beat. She fought to keep her voice casual. "Why do you say that?"

"It seems like it was only the other day someone else requested access to his file."

"What a coincidence. Do you know who asked for it?"

Marcia frowned in thought. "I'm sure it was someone from the Minister's Office. I remember thinking it was a little strange. It's not often someone from the Hill pays us a visit down here. I assume this has something to do with the court case. I saw it on the news last night."

Chloe drew in a breath and forced her pulse to slow, unwilling to allow the woman any hint of the importance of what she'd just shared.

"Would you mind retrieving the file for me, please?" Chloe asked.

"Of course. It won't take me a minute. All of our personnel files are stored on site. I'll be back shortly."

"Thank you," Chloe managed, exhaling in a rush as the woman left the room.

Unable to sit still, Chloe stood and paced, her thoughts barely keeping up as she sifted through the possibilities. To discover her instincts were on the mark was little consolation. If someone from the Home Affairs Office was involved, this was way bigger than even she had imagined. The office was headed by an elected Minister who had the Prime Minister's ear—or so it was rumored.

A niggle of disquiet filled her with unease. *Surely this couldn't be coming from the top?* What could the Home Affairs Minister possibly have to do with a new agent like Declan Munro? From all accounts, he was an exemplary officer and he hadn't been in the system long enough to have trodden on anyone's toes.

Had he?

The Home Affairs Minister had jurisdiction over the thousands of people employed by the Australian Federal Police across the country and those stationed overseas. It was an enormous responsibility and she could only imagine it would be quite often a stressful task. He was constantly under scrutiny from the media for the success or otherwise of his troops and his job security was only assured until the next election.

Chloe didn't envy his position, but she knew that if anyone could carry off the role with efficiency and the minimum of fuss, it was current Minister for Home Affairs, Ronald Sabattini.

Her uncle.

Marcia's return startled Chloe from her thoughts. The woman held a slim manila file. Chloe swallowed her disappointment. It was obvious it contained very little.

Marcia took her seat behind the desk and handed the file to Chloe, a slight frown marring her features.

"There's not much inside. I must admit, I thought when I retrieved it for Eric there was a little more in it than that." She shrugged. "I must have been thinking of someone else."

"Who's Eric?"

"Eric Stoltenberg. He works in the Minister's Office."

Chloe took the seat opposite Marcia and flipped through the file. The usual employee documents were inside. Tax file number declarations, superannuation details, bank details, next of kin contact details and computer login details. Her heart thumped.

Computer login details.

There they were, just as Declan had said, written in what she presumed was his handwriting. She forced thoughts of the discovery aside and focused on what Marcia had said.

"So, it was Eric who recently requested this file?"

"Yes, I checked the record book when I retrieved the file for you."

Chloe raised an eyebrow and looked at her expectantly. Marcia hastened to explain.

"I keep a record of all of the files that are taken out of our filing storage and who has requested them. Whilst I don't allow the files to be taken off site, personnel with the proper authorization are allowed access to employee files and can view them at their leisure in one of the empty offices on this floor."

"Are people allowed to copy things from a file?"

"Yes, but they need to come to me to do it. The photocopiers are all controlled with codes. It's easier for them to bring the item to me and have me do the copying. This system also enables me to keep a little control over who is copying what, and when."

"I see. I assume it's possible that things could be copied by hand without your knowledge and without removing anything, is that true?"

The woman frowned. "Yes, I guess so, but why would they waste time doing that?"

"How does someone get proper authorization?"

"Well, of course, in reality it's only a handful of people who have it. I'm sure you understand not everyone has access to our personnel files. Generally, it is someone from the Pays Department and occasionally we get a request from the Legal Department, mostly in relation to a family law matter, or from someone like you, who is involved in an IA investigation."

"How often do you get a request for access to a personnel file from the Minister's Office?" Chloe held her breath and waited for the answer.

Marcia shook her head, looking perplexed. "Not very often at all, actually. I guess that's why I remembered it. Eric said the Minister was putting together a new funding initiative and needed to look at some of our recent recruits. Declan Munro's file wasn't the only one he looked at."

Chloe made a note of the names of the other agents Eric had accessed. "Did he ask you to copy anything out of any of those files?"

"No."

"Are you sure?"

"Yes. I remember because after requesting so many files, I was sure he'd want something copied. I made myself available, expecting him to ask, but he didn't. In fact, he was only here a few minutes and then he returned the files to me and left." She shrugged. "I wondered at it because he couldn't have possibly have gone through all of them in that time, but I assumed he must have been called away for something more important."

"How long ago was he here?"

"It didn't seem that long ago, but I checked the date when I looked at the record book. It was three months ago."

"And has he been back to finish what he started?"

"No, he hasn't."

Chloe made a few more notes on her writing pad and then packed it away in her briefcase.

"Would you like to have anything copied from the file?" Marcia asked, indicating the folder still in Chloe's hand.

Chloe shook her head and handed it over. "No, but thank you for meeting with me this morning. You've been very helpful."

Chloe stood and held out her hand. Marcia took it and returned the brief pressure.

"If there's anything else I can do for you…?"

"Thank you. I appreciate the offer, but that will be all for now." Bending, Chloe retrieved her briefcase and headed toward the door. Through the glass windows, she could see more employees at their desks, holding take-away cups of coffee and other beverages in their hands. Turning back, she offered Marcia a smile.

"I'll see myself out. Thank you again for your time."

"My pleasure. I hope you found what you were looking for."

Chloe refrained from answering. With a polite nod good-bye, she left the office. Looking neither left nor right, she made her way past the partitions and into the corridor. If she hurried, she'd still make it to the courthouse before the committal hearing ended.

———

Declan glanced around the courtroom and tried not to let his disappointment show.

She wasn't there.

He'd thought after all they'd shared last night... He'd even kissed her, for Christ sake. Okay, it had only been a kiss on the wrist, but he thought they'd had a connection— enough at least that she'd be here this morning to show her support.

Maybe the kiss had been a mistake? She'd certainly appeared shocked when it had happened and had left shortly afterwards. If the kiss was the reason for her no-show, he was regretful, but he wasn't going to wish it hadn't happened.

She was all he'd been able to think about. Her keen intelligence, her sense of justice, her passion when she argued for something she believed in. Then there was the way she looked, the way she'd tasted. It had kept him sleepless until the early hours of the morning. He'd woken to the sound of his alarm, in the throes of a fantasy that involved far more than hand kissing. His cock had been rock-hard and he'd had to settle for a quick pull in the shower to relieve the tension that had settled heavily in his balls.

It was crass, but he couldn't help it. He wanted her, pure and simple. Niceties, be damned, he wanted to bend her cute little ass over the back of his leather couch and fuck her hard and fast. He wanted her writhing and moaning beneath him, begging him for more. At least, that's how it had gone in his dream.

With a sigh, he turned back to face the bench and waited for the lawyers to assemble.

———

Chloe eased open the door to the courtroom and slid into the nearest vacant chair. Declan's family was seated where they'd been the day before. A cluster of journalists filled the back row, more than there had been the day before. It stood to reason: The committal hearing was due to conclude today. Gazing across at them, she was surprised and pleased to see Savannah, notepad and pen in hand, waving surreptitiously back at her.

Chloe acknowledged the greeting and then focused on the broad back of Declan Munro.

He wore another dark suit that emphasized the width of his shoulders. A snowy-white shirt collar was visible just below his hairline. Although his face was turned away, she could see the tension in his shoulders and wished she could ease it.

She'd purposefully steered away from all thoughts of his kiss and had been determined to brush the memory of it away, at least until after the hearing was over. While she'd done nothing illegal by meeting with him, it may have been a little unethical and it was certainly not something she wished to advertise, especially not while his position under the law was so tenuous.

Her meeting with Marcia Slater had made it clear that someone else was likely involved. Declan's file had been accessed a month before the alleged incident had been brought to her attention. While nothing appeared to be missing and Marcia had assured her nothing had been copied, it was still more than possible the login details had been stolen.

Most people carried a cell phone and every cell phone she knew of housed a camera. It wasn't too much of a stretch to imagine someone photographing the contents of Declan's file, including his login details. Particularly if they were accessing them for nefarious reasons.

The prosecution's case depended upon the Crown proving Declan was the only person with access to his username and password. After her interview with Marcia, it was clear that wasn't the case.

It might have been unusual for someone to request access to an employee's file, but the fact was, from time to time it happened and she now had proof that it had happened to Declan. What she didn't know was why?

She bit her lip in consternation. The magistrate entered and she stood automatically, bowing in his direction, as was the custom before he took his place on the bench.

She now knew she needed to see her uncle. For some reason, it appeared his office was involved. She didn't believe for an instant her much-loved uncle—an intelligent, affable family man who'd made good in politics—was responsible, but someone close to him was and she needed to identify them.

As the spectators and lawyers took their seats, Chloe gazed across at Declan. He had half-turned in her direction and was now looking at her over his shoulder. Their gazes met and he smiled at her as if she was the best thing he'd seen all morning. Her breath caught at the intensity of emotion in his eyes.

Her lips moved of their own volition and she found herself smiling back. He'd been put through hell, mostly by decisions that had been made by her and yet, he still managed to smile at her. His thoughtfulness and consideration in the middle of his committal hearing warmed her through.

With a final lingering glance, he turned away to face the barrage of lawyers and court personnel in front of him.

Chloe drew in a deep breath and tried to concentrate on the proceedings. Neil Abbey was making his closing arguments. His voice rose with heat and passion as he asked that the magistrate find sufficient grounds to commit the defendant to stand trial.

The gravity of Declan's position suddenly hit her hard. A flood of nerves knotted her stomach and made it difficult to breathe. If the magistrate sided with the prosecutor, the next time Declan appeared in court could be in front of a jury. Being committed for trial was a long way from being found guilty, but she hated knowing she was responsible for putting him there in the first place, especially now she knew someone else was involved.

With a sigh, Chloe forced herself to let it go. Besides, she still had no idea who was behind it. The best thing she could do for Declan now was to help him prove the charges false by discovering the real person or persons responsible for plotting his downfall.

Regardless of what Declan had to say about his friend, she still hadn't written off Charlie Stanford. He seemed completely convinced Declan was a pedophile. He showed none of the loyalty Declan had showed to him. What kind of a friend wrote another friend off so quickly, believing the worst of a mate with barely a second thought?

Not the kind of friend she wanted—that was for certain. Recalling Savannah's presence in the courtroom, Chloe looked across at the huddle of media and caught her friend's eye. She indicated with her head for Savannah to meet her outside. Savannah nodded and a few moments later, stood and left the courtroom.

Chloe looked back toward the bench where Abbey was still engaged in his ardent oratory. With a quick motion, she shouldered her handbag and slipped quietly outside.

Savannah waited for her right outside the door.

"Hey, you!" she said and smiled. "I can see why you're so tied up in knots about this guy. He's absolutely *gorgeous*! If I wasn't so madly in love with Jonathan, I'd snatch him up myself!"

Chloe grimaced and looked around to make sure there was no one nearby. "*Shh! Someone might hear you!*"

"So what?" Savannah replied nonchalantly, lifting an elegant shoulder. "It's not a crime to find a man attractive and I'm only engaged, not blind."

"You're talking about the defendant in a matter I investigated. I need to keep up some semblance of propriety."

Savannah grinned knowingly. "Ah, I see you're not denying he's the hottest thing you've seen in quite some time."

Heat scorched Chloe's cheeks. "Savannah, stop it! It's not as if we're dating. Hell, we're on opposite sides of the law. It's not something we can simply forget about."

"But I thought you said you were having second thoughts

about his guilt? Isn't that why you went to meet him last night? To clear up the confusion?" A sly smile widened her full mouth. "Or did you spend the time getting to know each other better?"

Chloe slapped at her friend without malice. "Stop it! You're incorrigible. Can't you raise your thoughts above your navel for just a nanosecond?"

Savannah pretended to look hurt. "Now, now, Chloe. There's no need for you to be like that. It's not my fault Jonathan spends every waking moment sexting me. He's insatiable and it's starting to rub off. I just can't help thinking lascivious thoughts when I see a guy who could double as Hugh Jackman."

Chloe stifled a groan. The analogy was spot on, despite the differences in hair color. Thinking about the comparison made trying to concentrate on her friend's conversation even more difficult.

"So, did you kiss him?"

Chloe suddenly zeroed in on Savannah's question. "*What?* You have to be *kidding*. He's the *defendant*." She hoped she sounded suitably outraged and that Savannah wouldn't notice Chloe's cheeks were about to combust.

Savannah laughed. "Just joking, but I have to tell you, I don't know if I'd have that much self-control. He's one fine specimen."

"You need to go and find Jonathan and cool your libido, Savannah. Go and surprise him in his office. Despite your boastful references to the contrary, it's obvious you're not getting anywhere near enough satisfaction."

"Look who's talking?" she replied with a cheeky grin.

Chloe returned her smile. "Yeah, well maybe I can cope with it better than you."

Savannah grinned and Chloe grinned back at her. "Enough of this, I need to get back in there and find out what's happening."

"So, did you find out anything during your meeting with the hottie?"

"Off the record?"

Savannah perked up, suddenly all ears. "Of course."

"I mean it, Savannah. Strictly off the record."

Savannah's shoulders slumped. "Dammit, Sabattini, you're no fun at all."

Chloe sobered. "I'm not sure what's going on, Sav, but I need to talk to my uncle. I think his office is involved."

Savannah's eyes widened. "You mean the Home Affairs Office?"

"Yes. A clerk from my uncle's office accessed Declan's file a few months ago. The file contained details of his username and password."

"Wow, that *is* interesting. Have you told anyone? Declan? His lawyer?"

"No, I haven't had a chance and I want to speak to my boss first. I'm sure he won't want to make anything public until we know for sure what's going on, so don't say anything to anyone, agreed?"

Savannah nodded. Chloe blew out a breath on a sigh.

"The closing arguments are almost finished. It's too late to bring fresh evidence forward at this stage. If there is anything worth bringing to someone's attention, it will have to wait."

"I guess you're right. It won't make any difference to the outcome now and I'm sure you'll bring whatever it is to the attention of the defense prior to the trial."

"Of course. As soon as I have anything concrete, I'll pass it on. I've always believed in playing fair."

"Does that include the media? Please tell me that if anything comes of this, I'll be the first person you call?"

Chloe smiled. "Savannah O'Neill, you'll be the first person I call."

Savannah stepped forward and gave her a brief hug. "Thanks, Chloe. You're the best friend *ever*."

Chloe tried to hide her pleasure. "Yeah, yeah, yeah. That's what you always say."

Savannah collected her handbag off the floor and started down the corridor. "I'll talk to you later," she called over her shoulder.

Chloe opened the door to the courtroom and quietly

regained her seat. Declan's barrister now had the floor.

After summarizing the evidence against his client, Roger White concluded his measured address to the magistrate by asking that the matter be dismissed. Whilst lacking some of the prosecutor's passion, his charismatic baritone rumbled through the courtroom with sincerity and conviction.

Chloe watched Declan take a deep breath and exhale it on a heavy sigh. He rolled his shoulders and neck. She could see the tension in his tautly held body.

The committal hearing was over. It was now up to the man who sat high above them on the bench, to decide Declan's fate. A fifteen-minute recess was called and the occupants of the courtroom stood as one and waited for the magistrate to depart. A murmur arose from the small crowd the minute the magistrate's black robes disappeared from view.

Chloe watched as Declan acknowledged his family with a nod of gratitude. Moments later, his gaze moved on and found hers.

The distance between them became almost nonexistent. Chloe held her breath and tried hard to pretend her heart rate hadn't accelerated the minute his gaze locked on hers. The more she delved into it, the more it appeared Declan Munro was exactly what he said he was: an innocent man who cared about the safety of his family and of his community; a man who had pledged his life to the service of others; a man who was fighting for his very survival.

He paused to speak briefly with his barrister and then stepped down from the dock and began to head in her direction. Her belly clenched in panic.

Surely, he couldn't intend to speak with her here, in front of everybody? She looked left and right in an effort to formulate an escape.

"Good morning, I'm glad you're here."

Too late.

His deep voice rumbled over her. She bit her lip and forced herself to look up at him.

His gaze tangled with hers. Her heart tripped over, but she resolutely refused to pay it heed.

"How do you think it went?" she said, determined to keep things on a professional level.

He grimaced and offered a halfhearted shrug. "I guess we'll know shortly when the magistrate returns with his decision."

Her lips compressed. Despite her earlier decision, she wondered if she should just come right out now and tell him of her discovery. But what could she say? She didn't know if what she'd found meant anything yet, and she needed to speak with her uncle before she said more. He was family, after all. He deserved her loyalty.

"I guess all we can do is hope for the best."

Declan's shoulders slumped, as if he'd been hoping for something more. Guilt surged through her, but she determinedly pushed it aside.

"I'm going to reinterview Charlie Stanford," she offered in an effort to lift his spirits.

"What for? He's hardly going to admit he lied."

"He's lied to me or he's lied to the court. Either way, I'm going to ask him why. He knows more about this than he's letting on. I'm sure of it. There's no other reason for him to have been dishonest."

The door to the courtroom opened and people began to file back in. Chloe glanced at her watch. Declan's fifteen minutes were up.

"I need to return to the dock," he said. "The magistrate will be back soon with his decision."

She bit her lip. She hated to see him treated like this, like a common criminal. She reached out a hand and then just as quickly withdrew it. "Good luck," she murmured, feeling inadequate.

He acknowledged her with a tight nod and turned away. He gazed quickly across at his family. Chloe followed his line of sight. A blond-haired woman she presumed was his mother, looked drawn and pale. A tall man with dark hair liberally splashed with gray who conducted himself with an obvious air of authority pulled the woman close, his expression grim. A younger man with messy fair hair gave Declan a halfhearted thumbs-up. With equal looks of dread and resignation, they all took their seats.

Declan turned away. Chloe watched as, with another heavy sigh, he headed back to the dock.

CHAPTER 15

Chloe, from her position in her Honda Civic, took in the sight of Parliament House perched high up on the Hill. While she looked upon the building every day during her commute to her office, it never failed to inspire her.

The sun bathed the building in warm light and glinted off the enormous steel structure that crowned the roof. The rich green grass that surrounded the building covered the steep slope it sat on and looked like it was growing up to meet the sky. It was smooth enough to double as a carpet.

She slowed for the security guards who were perched inside a booth at the entrance to Parliament House and the underground car park. Pressing the button on her armrest, she lowered the window, her security pass at the ready.

Within moments, her credentials were checked. Blinking against the dimness, she pulled her Honda into the first available parking space. The darkness of the underground car park was a little disorientating after the bright noon sunshine.

When the magistrate announced there was sufficient evidence for Declan's matter to proceed to trial, she'd waited only long enough to offer him brief commiserations and had then made a beeline for her car. Although she was conscious of the necessity of touching base with her superiors and bringing them up to speed, the need to speak with the Minister was more urgent. It was possible he could enlighten her about Eric Stoltenberg and the reason why he'd accessed Declan's personnel file.

Phoning ahead, she arranged to meet her uncle for lunch in the building's cafeteria. It had been awhile since she'd seen him and if the situation hadn't been so grave, she would have been looking forward to the catch-up.

He was already there when she arrived and greeted her with a smile and a warm hug.

"Princess! How wonderful to see you. It's been too long."

She returned his embrace and then moved to take a seat opposite him at the small wooden table.

"It's lovely to see you again, too, Uncle Ronnie."

"What have you been up to?"

She drew in a breath. "Until now, I've been involved in a committal hearing. I've come straight from the Magistrate's Court in Civic."

"Busy as usual, I see," he replied with a fond smile.

Chloe shrugged. "You know how it is."

"Yes, unfortunately I do. Sometimes I wonder what in hell I was thinking when I put my hand up for this job. I go from morning to midnight—and often well after—six, sometimes seven days a week. There always seems to be something that needs to be done."

The twinkle in his eyes belied the brusqueness in his tone. Genuine affection surged through her. Her uncle looked so much like her father, they could be twins. With only thirteen months between them, people had often mistaken them as such, but unlike her father, her uncle carried an extra fifty pounds.

"You love every minute of your job, uncle. You wouldn't have it any other way," she teased.

He sighed dramatically. "Yes, you're right, princess. I wish your aunt was more understanding. She never stops haranguing me about getting home so late."

"Perhaps you should surprise her one day. Get home before dinner time. Better still, take her *out* to dinner."

The Minister smiled and let the comment slide. "What are you having for lunch?"

Chloe scanned the extensive menu in front of her and quickly decided on her usual. "I'll have chicken, avocado and mayonnaise on a toasted Turkish bread roll, no butter. And a skim latte´ in a mug."

Her uncle shook his head. "What's this skim nonsense? You're fading away to a shadow. I'm the one who should be ordering skim."

Chloe laughed, but refrained from commenting. Her uncle had always been self-conscious about his weight. Not that it was enough to make him do something about it. Her earliest memories had him larger than life.

He stood and went over to the counter to place their orders. Chloe glanced around her while she waited for him to return. The usual scattering of public servants dressed in dark, conservative suits surrounded her. From all the chatter, they appeared to be making the most of their lunch hour to catch up on office gossip. Her uncle returned, tucking away his wallet inside his suit jacket.

"Thanks for treating me lunch, Uncle Ronnie."

"It's my pleasure, princess. We don't do this half as often as we should." He seated himself at the table and his expression turned somber.

"Now, what's going on? I assume you need to speak with me about something more serious than the family's latest exploits?"

Chloe smiled ruefully. "What gave me away?"

"Well, your office isn't exactly next door to mine. You're busy. It's the middle of the working week. Yet, you're here. Out with it, princess."

"You know me too well. You're right. There is something I wanted to talk with you about."

"Fire away."

Chloe took a deep breath. Her pulse picked up its rhythm and all of a sudden, she didn't know what to say. Then she thought about Declan and the look on his face when the magistrate handed down his decision. The memory of that spurred her on.

"I've been investigating a case involving an agent by the

name of Declan Munro. There was a brief mention of it on the news last night. Do you know him?"

Her uncle's expression didn't change. "I don't think so. Sandra Callan, my personal assistant, mentioned it this morning at our daily debriefing. She said something about a committal hearing. I didn't realize you were involved in it. Given that Munro's under my jurisdiction, I guess the media will be looking for a sound bite from me at some stage." He eyed her curiously. "What are the charges?"

"Unauthorized access to confidential police files. The agent works in the Child Protection Unit, so you can understand the serious nature of the charges."

Her uncle nodded and Chloe continued. "Despite Agent Munro's protestations of innocence, there's enough evidence pointing to the contrary. His best friend and fellow agent, Charlie Stanford, is the one who brought it to our attention."

Her uncle glanced surreptitiously at his watch. Chloe plowed on, speaking quickly.

"Stanford's the prosecution's main witness. He was also mentioned on the news."

Her uncle shrugged. "I'm not familiar with the name, but Sandra may have spoken about him this morning."

Chloe continued. "The committal hearing finished about an hour ago. Agent Munro's been committed to stand trial. The media will be all over this soon."

The Minister spread his arms wide, his expression curious. "Naturally, I'm concerned that an officer under my control will be tried for something so heinous and of course, I'll give a statement to the press, but I have full confidence in our legal system and I'm sure justice will be done. My attitude surely doesn't come as a surprise to you, princess, so what are you here for?"

Chloe took another breath. "You're right, uncle. There's more. Today, I discovered a member of your staff accessed Agent Munro's personnel file, along with some other files. Coincidentally, it happened about a month before the allegations were made." She paused and then said in a rush. "I think someone from your office is setting him up."

His eyes widened in astonishment. "You can't be serious?"

"I'm afraid so."

He shook his head. "No, it's not possible. I handpicked each member of my staff. I would vouch for every one of them."

Chloe's gaze remained steady on his. "I understand, but the truth is, someone by the name of Eric Stoltenberg requested access to Agent Munro's file a month before the allegations were made. It's been noted in the record book kept by the HR Manager, Marcia Slater. I understand from Ms Slater that Eric Stoltenberg came from your office."

Her uncle looked mystified. "She's right. Eric works in my office, but why in the world would he do something like that?"

"According to the HR Manager, Eric said you were putting together a new funding initiative and needed to see the files for some of the more recent recruits. Agent Munro has only been an agent for twelve months."

"Funding initiative? I have no idea what you're talking about."

Chloe was at a loss. She'd been sure her uncle would be able to clear things up.

"You don't? B-but…? I don't understand. What does Eric Stoltenberg do, anyway? Who does he report to?"

"He's a junior in the office. He works with Sandra. Runs errands, fields phone calls, that kind of thing—a general dogsbody. I guess he ultimately reports to me. They all do."

"What need would he have to access personnel files?"

The Minister shook his head. "None that I know of and I'm completely mystified that he'd tell anyone he was acting on my behalf." He cleared his throat. "Leave it with me, princess. I'll talk to Sandra. Maybe she knows something about it."

Their meals arrived and they picked up their utensils. Silence fell between them while they enjoyed their lunch. After a few moments, Chloe broke it by asking about her cousin.

Her uncle smiled. "Maria's great. So independent these days. She's already halfway through her degree at the Australian National University. It seems like we only see her when she needs a change of clothes."

A chuckle escaped Chloe's lips, remembering the days when she was similarly consumed. "Is she still keen on horses?"

"Yes. More than ever. I thought when she started Uni, she'd lose interest, but she's even worse than you were at that age."

Chloe smiled at the memory. Horses had been her life a decade ago. "Does she still have my old riding crop?"

"You bet. I saw it the other night when I went to tell her goodnight. It has pride of place on her nightstand, always within easy reach." He winked.

Chloe laughed and finished her lunch. It was good to spend time with her uncle. She always walked away from a meeting with him thinking nothing was too hard to deal with, after all. She loved that about him—that he could lighten her load without even trying.

When he glanced at his watch again, she swallowed the last of her coffee and bent down to collect her briefcase off the floor.

"Thanks for lunch. I appreciate you making the time to meet with me."

He smiled. "I'll always make time for you, princess."

"Let me know about Eric, won't you?"

"I promise. I'll speak to Sandra as soon as I get back upstairs. At the moment, I'm as perplexed as you are, although I'm sure there's a reasonable explanation."

"Thank you," Chloe replied, knowing he was probably right, but hoping for Declan's sake he wasn't. If there was nothing suspicious about Stoltenberg's actions, the conspiracy theory lost most of its momentum and they were back to square one.

Even so, that she now believed Declan's protestations of innocence didn't surprise her. She wasn't sure when her attitude toward him had changed, but it was probably somewhere between his arrival in a bright lime-green tie on the morning of their first meeting and the warm kiss he'd bestowed on the inside of her wrist last night.

Either way, she needed to find out who was behind all this. Someone inside the CPU had created the access trail on Declan's computer. Someone else had downloaded images on his laptop—and deleted them. If Declan hadn't done it, who had?

She smiled grimly. It was time she had another little chat with Charlie Stanford.

———————

Declan paced the generous confines of his apartment and did his best to control his frustration. Knowing there was nothing more they could do, Brandon and Tom, along with their wives, had left to return to Sydney. Riley had flown back to Grafton. As the Local Area Commander of a large rural command, he didn't have the luxury of too much time away from the job. On top of that, his wife, Kate, had her hands full with three-month-old twins. From what Declan could recall of them, Daisy and Rosie were more than a little challenging and he understood Riley's need to return home. Declan appreciated the time Riley had given to him. Riley's support, along with the rest of their family, had kept him sane.

Clayton and his parents occupied the couch. Varying degrees of concern and strain had etched itself onto their tired faces.

"What did Roger say?" Clayton asked.

Declan turned to face him. "He's going to review the evidence. See if he can find another angle to pursue at the trial. He told me I had to find out who stole my login details. Without that, I'm fucked."

"Declan," his father admonished him quietly, "not in front of your mother."

Declan looked at the woman in question, his chest

tightening with emotion at the shock and disbelief that still lingered on her face. She'd aged overnight.

"Sorry, Mom."

"It's okay, Declan. I can understand you might misplace your manners under the circumstances."

"At least with the magistrate committing the matter for trial, we have a few more months to come up with a strategy," Clayton said. "Did Roger say anything about when he expected to receive a trial date?"

Frustration surged through Declan anew and he clenched his fists. "No, he didn't. I have to speak to Charlie. He's not returning my calls. I rang the squad room. He's been transferred. No one will tell me where he's gone." He paused for effect. "I'm going to ambush the bastard at the gym. He goes there every other day, like clockwork. He should be there first thing tomorrow."

Clayton frowned at him in concern. "Is that a good idea?"

Anger ignited inside Declan. He turned on his brother. "No, Clayton," he bit off. "It's probably not a good idea, but if you can come up with some other way I can force the asshole to explain to me why the hell he perjured himself yesterday, I'll be happy to hear it." Declan's breath came hard. Rage tinged with panic burned from every pore of his skin. He turned away, ashamed of his outburst. The people on his couch cared for him, were hurting for him. That's why they were here. And he was treating them like shit.

He drew in a deep breath. "I'm sorry, Clay. I didn't mean—"

"It's all right, Dec. I know you didn't." Clayton ran his hand through his hair. "Christ, I can't imagine what you must be going through. You've devoted your entire adult life to upholding the law and keeping society safe and this is how they repay you."

"I agree. It's not right, son," Duncan Munro stated, weighing in at last. "But we have to fight fairly. Let's not stoop to their level, whoever "they" are. Didn't you say this Sabattini woman was following up some leads?"

Declan nodded, refusing to acknowledge the tiny spark of hope that ignited low in his gut at the mention of Chloe's name.

"Chloe Sabattini. She's the senior investigator working for IA," he said. "She's the one who did the initial investigation and recommended the charges."

"And now she's on *your* side?" His father shook his head, his scepticism plain to see. "How does that work?"

Declan offered a grim smile. "It's a long story, Dad. Hopefully, when I tell you about it one day, we'll look back and laugh."

"Yeah, well right now, laughing's the last thing on my mind," his father said.

"You and me, both, Dad," Declan replied grimly. "You and me, both."

———

The Master flicked the leather switch in his hand, enjoying the raspy sound of it against the fine cloth of his suit pants. Earlier, he'd enjoyed a thoroughly pleasurable hour with his office junior. It had been much too long since he'd availed himself of the boy's talents. The boy was more than eager to please a boss who could do so much for his career.

A word in the right ear could make the difference between permanent employment and all the benefits that came with it, or having to go from one temporary contract to another. Applying for a bank loan to purchase a house, or even a car, could be extremely difficult without a permanent pay packet.

The intercom on his desk buzzed and he strode over to answer it. His secretary announced he had a visitor: Federal Agent Stanford was waiting for him.

A smile tugged at the Master's lips. The day was about to get even better.

"Send him in and hold all my calls."

Charlie glanced around the dim interior of the Master's office and surreptitiously wiped the perspiration off his hands. He always felt nervous when he came there. It had more to do with excitement than fear, but he couldn't deny a visit to the Master caused a little apprehension. He never quite knew what mood he'd find the man in.

"Chip, come in. It's good to see you." The Master came toward him and flung an arm around his shoulders. Charlie relaxed slightly and savored the other man's nearness. He closed his eyes briefly and breathed in the Master's scent.

The man's arm dropped and he took a seat behind his desk. Leaning back, he looked up at Charlie expectantly.

"What can I do for you? I hope the transfer's working out?"

Charlie nodded. "Thanks, it's working out fine. The Fraud Squad is happy to have me. The commute to the office is even shorter. But that... That's not what I wanted to see you about."

The Master raised a single, bushy eyebrow. "Oh?"

Heat exploded across Charlie's cheeks. "I-I wanted to see you. I wanted to see *you*."

A knowing smile spread slowly across the Master's face. "Why, Chip, I'm flattered, but I did meet with you a couple of days ago, right before the hearing. You know we're not due to get together again until Friday afternoon."

Charlie's desperation ratcheted up another notch. He was prepared to do anything for the Master, even betray a man he'd considered a friend, but he needed to know his sacrifices were truly appreciated. Lately, it had begun to feel like the Master's attention had waned.

Stepping closer, Charlie grabbed hold of the other man's sleeve in an effort to convey to him the depth of his feeling. The Master stared at Charlie's hand and then slowly reached up to remove it.

"I don't have time for you today, Chip. I have several

engagements that need my attention. You'll just have to wait—I'll see you on Friday."

"I can't wait that long," Charlie shouted. "I need to be with you, to touch you. Ever since this thing with Munro started, I've been a mess. I can't eat; I can't sleep... I've done everything you asked. I need to know it was worthwhile. I need to know you appreciate it. All of it."

The Master stared at him thoughtfully—at last seeming to realize the depths of Charlie's despair. Sliding his chair backward, he beckoned him closer.

"Come here, Chip."

Charlie trembled with excitement and relief. He stepped forward and fell to his knees, his head bent low. The Master reached out and caressed his cheek. Charlie gasped at the gentleness in the other man's hand. He leaned into the Master's touch, silently begging for more.

"Of course I appreciate it, Chip," the Master murmured tenderly. "There's nothing about you I don't appreciate. You're my right-hand man, Chip. You know that. Your evidence at the committal hearing was nothing short of brilliant."

"Y-you were there?" Charlie whispered hopefully.

"No, Chip. Unfortunately, I wasn't able to make it, but I have my sources. I heard all about it, including the fact Agent Munro was committed to stand trial, just like I wanted."

The Master's fingers had continued to caress Chip's face while he spoke. Then his fingers wandered higher and tangled in Chip's thick, fair hair.

Charlie groaned at the pure deliciousness of it and his body burned with need. "Please, Master," he gasped. "*Please.*"

With a sigh, the Master stood and reached for the riding crop. Charlie's cock pulsed with desire.

"All right, Chip, but we're going to have to be quick. As I said, I have pressing matters to attend to."

Charlie bobbed his head in agreement, grateful for whatever attention the Master chose to bestow.

"Of course, Master, of course. All I want to do is please you."

"Then pull off your pants and show me."

Charlie struggled to his feet. With trembling fingers, he undid his belt. He loosened the button on his pants and undid the zip. His gaze remained fixed on the thin hard piece of black leather in the Master's hand.

"Turn around."

The order was issued in a voice that was as soft as steel. Charlie hastened to do as he was asked.

"Bend over."

The kiss of the whip sent fire across his ass. The agony of it was excruciating. He bit his lip against the pain, even as his cock stood to attention.

"Stroke yourself, Chip. I want to see you stroke yourself."

Another stripe across his buttocks and Charlie flinched and reached for his cock. His hand tightened around the thick shaft. He stroked slowly, rhythmically, in time with the riding crop until his desire had reached a fever pitch.

"Show me, Chip. Turn around and show me how much you love what I do to you. I want to watch you come."

The Master's words sent him catapulting over the edge. He spun on his heel. An arc of white fluid spurted out of his cock and filled his hand. He shouted in relief. Gasping, he fought to regain his breath.

"Well done, Chip. I hope you now realize how much I appreciate you. I'll always appreciate you. Don't forget it."

Charlie kept his head bowed, his eyes fixed to the floor. "Yes, Master. Thank you, Master. I promise, I won't forget."

The Master loosened his pants and dropped them to the floor. His underwear quickly followed. His cock sprang thick and hard from his groin. "Good. Now, clean yourself up and get over here. I have something else you need to attend to."

Eric stared through the crack in the opened door, his eyes wide with shock. His boss stood half naked behind Agent Stanford, his cock thrusting rhythmically in and out of the younger man's pale ass.

He'd known the Minister was gay, of course, or at the very least, bi-sexual. The Minister had never pretended he wasn't married, but Eric had been under the impression his boss had chosen him and him alone for his pleasures, not this buffed up try-hard that looked like he had a decade or more on Eric.

Hurt and disbelief flooded through him. How could the Minister prefer Stanford to *him*? And how could his boss go from loving Eric deep and slow on the couch less than two hours ago and whispering sweet platitudes in his ear, to fucking this wannabe Arnold Schwarzenegger like an animal?

It wasn't right and if he hadn't seen it for himself, he'd never have believed it. For nearly a year, he'd been at the Minister's beck and call, fulfilling his every need and he'd loved every minute of it. The Minister continually assured him of his appreciation of all that Eric did for him and Eric was more than happy to deliver.

But that was when he'd thought he was the only man in the Minister's life. Now it was clear that wasn't the case.

He thought back to when he'd first come across Agent Stanford in the Minister's Office and realized it was more than three months ago—about the same time his boss had approached him with the task of attending HR and obtaining access to a list of personnel files. He'd been given strict instructions to pay particular attention to the file of one Agent Declan Munro, including photographing every page of the file.

At the time, Eric hadn't questioned the order. He did what he was told and he gladly waited for his reward. The Minister hadn't failed to deliver. The memory of their encounter after Eric had downloaded the photos onto the Minister's computer still had the power to make him hard.

But that was then, before he knew. Before he knew it was

all a lie. He wasn't the Minister's special boy. He wasn't the favored one. He wasn't the only one the Minister loved…

He wanted to charge into the room and tear the men apart. He wanted to scream out his pain and disillusionment until he was hoarse from the effort…

But where would that get him? It was obvious the Minister had been playing him. For nearly twelve months, Eric had done everything his boss had asked of him—and more—without complaint and now he knew it had all been for nothing. God knows how many others had been in the game, taking the kind of pleasure from the Minister that Eric had believed was his alone. All this time, he'd been blissfully unaware.

Heartbreak and disillusionment nearly made him weep. Rage like he'd never known burned behind his eyes. He'd been played the fool, pure and simple. Well, not anymore. He'd find a way to make the Minister pay…

The Minister watched with a narrowed eyed gaze as Chip departed the way he'd arrived. The boy had come in handy, but his usefulness was at an end. Now that Declan Munro had been committed to stand trial, the need for Chip had dissipated. Even if Munro was found not guilty, the damage to his credibility would be irreparable. The man could continue to spout his innocence to all and sundry, but who would listen? He'd been charged with accessing child pornography. His career and reputation would never recover.

Besides, the meeting with his niece a little over an hour ago had unsettled him and the increasing desperation in Chip's eyes was more than cause for concern. Desperate men were unpredictable and the Minister hated when things went beyond his control. No, it was time to put an end to the man's dependence upon him, before he became more trouble than he was worth.

He'd do it as gently as he could, of course. It wasn't as if he hadn't had plenty of practice. He'd ended more relationships than he could remember. More often than not, they'd ended amiably with a promotion and reward. History assured him the odds were in his favor.

He'd begun to tire of Chip, anyway. He'd only sought the man out as a way to get access to Munro. Now he'd achieved his aim, it was time to let him go. Besides, cutting Chip loose would give him more time to devote to his young clerk. During the year they'd been working together, he and Eric had grown close, but with most of his efforts concentrated on Chip over the past few months, the Minister had been more than a little neglectful of the boy.

It was time he paid the clerk a little more attention.

Chapter 16

Chloe bent over the sink in the staff restroom and splashed cool water onto her face. She patted it dry with some paper towel and then stared at her reflection in the mirror. Her cheeks were flushed; her eyes were overbright. Tendrils of hair that had escaped the tight confines of her bun, now curled riotously around her face. Overall, she looked like she'd run a marathon around Lake Burley Griffin. Twice.

The lunch with her uncle had left her feeling dissatisfied. She'd hoped he would answer her questions with facts; that one way or the other, she'd know the truth about why Declan's personnel file had been accessed. But her uncle had been anything but enlightening and when she left, she'd felt even more unsettled.

With a sigh, she pulled out hairpins and loosened the elastic band that contained her bun. She released the heavy mass on another sigh. Grabbing a brush from her handbag, she ran it through her wayward locks before twisting it back into its customary bun. With a last look at her reflection, she left the bathroom and headed back toward her desk.

Straight after her meeting with her uncle, she'd returned to her office and had placed a call to Charlie Stanford's cell phone. The call had gone through to his voice mail. It was now nearly two hours since she'd left a message for him to contact her and she had yet to hear from him.

Impatience churned in her belly and she reached for the internal police phone directory and found the number for Detective Superintendent Gary Julian. Snatching up the phone again, she punched in the numbers for Stanford's boss and waited for someone to pick up.

"CPU."

"Detective Superintendent Julian, please."

The call was redirected and a few moments later, the familiar, deep voice of Gary Julian answered the call. Chloe cut to the chase and told him she was waiting for Stanford's call.

"I'm sorry, Senior Inspector Sabattini. I wish I could help, but Charlie transferred out of my unit a fortnight ago. I didn't even know it was happening. The transfer papers turned up on my desk out of the blue. Stanford never said anything, although given what he's had to say of late, I can understand why he wouldn't want to hang around here. The rest of the unit isn't exactly overflowing with understanding for him."

"What do *you* think about his evidence?" she asked.

There was a long sigh on the other end of the phone. "If it was anyone else but Stanford, I'd have said it was a load of bullshit. But Stanford's a good agent. He's been here for years. Then again, I'm still not willing to believe Declan's guilty of the charges."

Julian sounded tired and bewildered. "I've been a copper for most of my life and yet *I* don't even know what to make of it."

Chloe bit her lip. She could totally empathize with his confusion. She'd felt exactly the same way and she hadn't known the men involved even a skerrick of time compared with their boss.

"I think there's someone else behind it," she stated, wondering if she was doing the right thing. Until she knew exactly what was going on, she didn't know who was involved, but something told her she could trust the superintendent.

"What do you mean?" he asked sharply.

"I'm not sure yet, and I'd rather not say anything officially until I know more, but I'm with you. I don't believe Declan did this and I don't think Charlie Stanford is acting alone, but he knows more than he's saying. I need to talk to him again."

"He's been transferred to the Fraud Squad. Their office is in Woden. That's about all I can tell you."

"Thanks, I'll give them a call. I've already tried his cell. It keeps going to voice mail."

"As far as Stanford knows, you're still on his side. You brought the charges against Declan, based on Stanford's evidence. I'm sure he'll contact you as soon as he's able."

"I hope so. I can't imagine what Declan and his family must be going through. It's my fault things went this far and it's now my responsibility to set things right."

"Don't be too hard on yourself. You had to do your job and work with the evidence available."

Chloe appreciated the superintendent's sentiments, but right at that moment, they didn't mean squat.

The cell phone, sitting on the desk in front of her, illuminated an incoming call. She glanced at it and froze. Charlie Stanford was on the other end of the line.

"I'm sorry, superintendent. I have to go. It looks like you were right. Agent Stanford's calling me on my cell phone. I'll talk to you soon."

Hanging up, she answered the incoming call. Not wanting to spook him, she remained professionally polite and requested that he meet her at her office in half an hour.

The doors to the elevator closed behind Charlie and it made its speedy ascent to the fifth floor. His heart hammered against his chest and he fought hard against the panic that threatened to overwhelm him.

In a few minutes, he'd face Senior Investigator Sabattini and provide her with an explanation for the reason he'd lied to her. The nerves in his gut swirled. Nausea threatened.

He'd listened to her message as he was about to leave the Master's office. Together, they'd come up with a reasonable explanation and he returned the call straight away. Charlie only hoped she fell for it.

His thoughts turned to the other handful of missed calls listed on his phone, all of them from Declan. He'd purposefully ignored them. He didn't have anything to say. He'd done as the Master bid and that was the end of it.

Warmth spread through him and his cock twitched at the thought of the Master. Their encounter a little over an hour ago had been their most memorable yet. It had taken him back to his youth, when he'd been nothing more than a lonely teenager who'd caught the eye of the boarding school dorm master.

He could remember those days like they'd happened yesterday. His introduction into the joys of sex had started innocently enough. A touch here, a lingering look there. Charlie had enjoyed the attention. Having never known his father, the interest of a man had felt at once strange and exciting. It wasn't long before he was summoned to the dorm master's private rooms and had been asked to suck the man's cock.

At fourteen, Charlie had barely had an inkling about what to do, but the dorm master had been patient in his efforts to educate the young boy in the delights of the male flesh.

Charlie had blossomed under the man's tutelage. Until that first time, he hadn't realized he was gay. Girls had held little interest for him, but he'd assumed that would change in time. The dorm master made Charlie see himself as he truly was for the very first time and he'd been inordinately grateful.

Within weeks, they'd graduated to intercourse. Charlie had basked in the pleasure and satisfaction on the dorm master's face as he'd eagerly applied all the skills he'd been taught. He'd reveled in the tenderness he felt in the other man's arms when the dorm master had gathered him close. For the very first time in his life, he'd felt loved.

His mother had noticed the change in him, of course. The confrontation had happened soon after he'd arrived home for the spring break. She'd narrowed her eyes at him, staring at him through eyes reddened from cheap whiskey, and had demanded he tell her what was going on.

He'd resisted for as long as he could, not wishing to sully the beauty of his relationship by sharing his experiences with the filth and detritus that was his mother. She'd been a good-for-nothing alcoholic for as long as he could remember. He'd only been able to afford to attend the posh boarding school through the generosity of his grandparents, both of whom had long since wiped their hands of their daughter.

But she'd eventually worn him down. She'd pestered him for days and days and finally he'd told her: He was in love with his dorm master.

His mother's eyes had filled with anger and disgust. She'd ranted and raved about the filth of it until it was all he could do but hold back the tears. Then she'd threatened to throw him out on the street.

The house they lived in had never been much, but it was the only home he'd known. His grandparents' philanthropy had never extended toward him visiting them and he had nowhere else to go.

At fourteen, he'd been tall and sturdy for his age, but he knew there was no way he'd make it on his own. He also knew better than to think his dorm master could help him. The man had a wife and children. Charlie did the only thing he could: He never spoke of it again.

Chloe waited with barely concealed impatience for the knock on her door. When it came, she swallowed against the sudden onset of nerves. This could be it. Charlie Stanford could provide her with the explanation she needed—the link she was certain was missing.

Taking a few seconds to pat down her hair and straighten her skirt and jacket, Chloe stood and opened the door.

"Agent Stanford, thanks for coming in. Please, take a seat."

Stanford nodded a brisk greeting and took the chair indicated. Chloe seated herself at her desk and opened the file in front of her. Tugging out a copy of Charlie's statement, she placed it in front of him.

"Do you remember making that statement, Agent Stanford?"

He stared at her without flinching. "Yes."

"Is it the same statement the prosecution tendered to the court yesterday?"

"Yes."

His gaze remained steady, almost disconcertingly so. Chloe cleared her throat. "I want to draw your attention to paragraph sixty-three." She waited while he flipped over the pages.

"Do you remember me asking you if Agent Munro had ever given you cause to suspect him in the past of behavior consistent with a pedophile?"

Stanford's expression remained closed, but he nodded.

"At paragraph sixty-three, I asked you that very question. Please read your response, Agent Stanford."

A frown marred Stanford's forehead, but he read the response as she'd requested.

"So, eight weeks ago, when you made this statement, you told me your friend, Agent Munro, had never given you cause to suspect him in the past and yet, yesterday you told the court, under oath, that he had. When were you lying, Agent Stanford? Then, or now?"

Stanford's cheeks reddened. Chloe felt a surge of satisfaction that at last, she'd managed to elicit a reaction from him.

"Perjury is a criminal offence punishable by imprisonment, Agent Stanford. I'm sure I don't have to remind you of that."

She waited a few moments to give him the chance to let the gravity of his situation sink in.

Leaning forward, she rested her chin on her hands and contemplated him in silence. Purposefully, she gentled her tone. "How about you tell me what's going on, Charlie?"

His struggle showed plainly on his face. Chloe held her breath and prayed she'd done enough. Moments later, his expression hardened and all signs of his inward battle disappeared. Her spirits sank, knowing she'd lost him.

"I was lying when I told you I hadn't had any cause to suspect Declan in the past. I thought if I told you the truth, like I did in court, it would make things worse. I didn't know when you first interviewed me that you would charge him. I knew what he'd done was wrong, but a part of me hoped he'd be stood down and given help—some counseling, or...or something. I never wanted him to end up like this. He's my mate."

Confusion and doubt once again made their presence known among the whirling thoughts in Chloe's head. Stanford looked so genuine. If she hadn't come to know Declan better, she'd have believed Charlie's account and believed it unquestioningly.

She was reminded of how convincing he'd been at his first interview—an interview where he now admitted he'd been dishonest. Was he that good at deception? She shook her head, trying to clear it.

"Do you know Eric Stoltenberg?" The question left her lips without any forethought. She didn't know where it had come from, but all of a sudden, it felt right.

Stanford frowned, but then nodded. "Yeah, I've seen him around."

Chloe sat up straighter in her chair. "Around? Can you be more specific?"

He shrugged and looked away. "Around. What do you want me to say?"

"What about Ronald Sabattini?"

"The Minister for Home Affairs?"

Chloe nodded.

"Yeah, I know him."

She sought clarification. "When you say you know him, do you mean you know *of* him or that you know him personally?"

Stanford's expression turned guarded. Chloe stilled.

"I've...met him a few times."

Her heart rate accelerated and her chest felt tight. All of a sudden the room felt hot and constricting.

"How many times?"

"I already told you. A few. Three or four, maybe five."

"At work functions?"

"Yeah, something like that."

"Did he speak to you? Make conversation?"

A smile tugged at Stanford's lips and then was quickly squashed. "I guess you could call it that."

The confusion in her head compounded. Her uncle had said he'd never heard of Charlie Stanford and yet Stanford was telling her different.

Why would her uncle lie? Or was Stanford playing her again?

The perplexity of it was giving her a headache. She shoved her chair back abruptly and stood, her hand outstretched toward the agent.

"Thank you for coming in, Agent Stanford. I appreciate it."

"No problem. Happy to help where I can."

"I'll be in touch," she managed and dropped her gaze to the desk, busying herself with the papers that were spread across it.

The door closed with a soft click. Chloe collapsed into her chair and wondered when her life had gotten so complicated. Her uncle had denied knowing Charlie. He'd also denied sending Eric Stoltenberg to access Declan's file.

Charlie Stanford knew Eric Stoltenberg. Charlie had also met and spoken to her uncle on more than one occasion— or so he said. Someone was telling lies—but who?

Charlie Stanford had form. He'd already owned up to being dishonest, but was he lying then—or now? And who was he lying about? Declan? Her uncle? Or both?

Whichever way she looked at it, something wasn't right. It was time to speak with her boss.

Detective Superintendent Tony Hammond always stayed well after his shift ended. Being the last person to leave the office every day was his thing. Chloe thought it had more to do with the enormous workload he carried and his exceptional dedication to his job rather than any quirk of character, but nevertheless, she was reassured that, even though the sun had nearly called it a day, Tony would be in the office.

Pushing away from her desk, she stood and made her way through the maze of partitioned offices until she came to the one at the end, enclosed by glass. Her boss glanced up from the pile of paperwork on his desk and moved his head slightly in greeting.

"Heading off?"

Chloe nodded. "Shortly, but I wanted to speak to you about something before I left. It's about the Munro matter."

Hammond pushed his glasses further up his nose and nodded. "I heard he was committed for trial. Good work on that one, Chloe."

Chloe grimaced. "Yeah, well I'm not sure it was. I've discovered evidence that indicates someone else was involved. In fact, I'm almost certain Agent Munro had nothing to do with the unauthorized access."

Hammond's expression registered surprise. "Really? What are you saying? That your witness got it wrong?"

Chloe held his dubious gaze. "That's exactly what I'm saying. I now believe there wasn't any unauthorized access at all. I think Agent Munro was set up."

Hammond leaned back against his chair and shook his head. "Wow, that's a long way from the summary of your Brief of Evidence you submitted to me a month ago. You were all but convinced of Munro's guilt."

"You're right, I was. At least, enough to allow the matter to proceed through the courts."

"So what happened?"

Chloe sighed and wondered yet again if she was ready

for this. Once she'd shared her suspicions, there would be no going back.

"Agent Munro has always insisted upon his innocence. I started thinking about different scenarios for how a computer trail could exist that clearly demonstrated his guilt. I realized everything revolved around the computer login."

"But Agent Munro was adamant he'd never given those details to anyone," Hammond said.

"Exactly. It's the reason I couldn't see past his guilt. Even now, the thought of it annoys me. From the time I knew what the presumption of innocence meant, I've believed in it. It's the backbone of our criminal justice system, but to tell you the truth, once I had those computer printouts that confirmed Agent Munro's computer login had been used to illegally access those files at a time when he was at work and then when the images were found on his laptop, I couldn't see beyond them."

"Chloe, I think you're being a little hard on—"

"No, I'm not. I'm just being honest. As Agent Munro was concerned, apart from a lapse of certainty every now and then, I was convinced of his guilt before we ever stepped foot inside the courtroom."

"I still think you're being too hard on yourself, but anyway, let's move on. What's happened to make you change your mind? In fact, not only to change your mind, but to take the investigation in a completely different direction?"

Chloe held his gaze. "I discovered this morning that Agent Munro's personnel file was accessed by a staff member from the Home Affairs Office a month before Agent Stanford came forward with the allegations. Agent Munro's file contained his computer login details."

Hammond pursed his lips and slowly nodded his head. "Wow, that's...interesting. The Home Affairs Office? Who was it?"

"A clerk by the name of Eric Stoltenberg. I've yet to speak with him, but I did speak to the Minister."

"Your uncle?"

"Yes." Chloe took a deep breath. "He denied knowing anything about it."

"Who sent Eric to HR?"

"I don't know yet. As I said, I haven't had a chance yet to talk to Eric. My uncle assured me he'd find out what was going on. I'm still waiting for him to call me."

"Is that all you've got?"

"Yes, at least for now, but it proves that someone else, even if it was only Eric Stoltenberg, had access to Agent Munro's login details. It provides reasonable doubt. Even I would argue for a not guilty verdict."

"But where's this Eric fellow's motive? And how would he gain access to the computer used by Agent Munro in the CPU? How would a clerk from the Home Affairs Office even *know* which computer Agent Munro used?"

"You're right. There is still a lot we don't know, but it's enough to cast serious doubt on Agent Munro's guilt."

"What about Agent Stanford? Didn't he give evidence yesterday that Agent Munro had exhibited an unhealthy interest in young children in the past?"

"Yes, he did, but I'm beginning to wonder about that, also. In fact, I'm now almost certain it was Stanford who downloaded the illegal images onto Agent Munro's laptop. He was a friend of Agent Munro's and he admitted under oath he had regular access to Agent Munro's apartment, where the laptop was kept. It's not beyond the realms of possibility that he downloaded the images."

Hammond blew out his breath on a heavy sigh. "It's a lot to take in, Chloe. Where are you going from here?"

"Fortunately for me, the magistrate has now committed Agent Munro to stand trial. It means that I have a little time to dig deeper and find out exactly what's going on and who's responsible."

"Does Agent Munro know this Stoltenberg fellow? Is there any reason why Stoltenberg would try to frame him?"

"I'm not sure. I haven't put either of those questions to Agent Munro. I only found out about Stoltenberg today.

Interestingly, Agent Stanford admitted to knowing him. As I said, I have yet to speak with Eric."

Hammond's eyebrows disappeared into his hairline. "There's a link between Stanford and the clerk? That *is* interesting. After all, it was Stanford who you say, started all of this in the first place."

"Yes, I agree Stanford is in the thick of it. Whether or not he was the one to make the request of Eric, we'll have to wait and see."

"I think Stanford's a real possibility. It makes sense, especially given his connection to Munro and the laptop. If Stanford and the clerk are friends, it's not too much of a leap to imagine Stanford obtaining Agent Munro's login details and creating the computer trail. Stanford's evidence against Munro then makes perfect sense. All we need to find is a motive."

From out of nowhere, Chloe's thoughts landed on her uncle and the inconsistency in his story. It appeared more than likely that he was also connected to Stanford, but yet again, there was the problem of motive. Her uncle didn't even know Declan.

Hammond eyed her quizzically, but her lips remained compressed. She wasn't ready to sully her uncle's name just yet. Until she had irrefutable proof of his involvement, she'd leave the Minister out of it.

"You're right," she said, "and as soon as I interview Eric, I hope to be a little closer to finding that out. Unless the clerk's in this right up to his neck, I would have thought he'd be more than willing to tell me who requested he access Agent Munro's file and whether or not it was Stanford."

Hammond eyed her solemnly. "Let's hope it is. I'd rather it be Stanford than someone high up in the Home Affairs Office. Things could get nasty for all of us."

Determination flooded through her. She thought of Declan and of the honorable way he'd conducted himself throughout both of his interviews and throughout the hearing. If what she suspected was true, he'd been treated abominably. He had every reason to hate her and everyone associated with her.

She stared at Hammond and straightened her spine. "Our job is to seek out the truth and see justice done. I say, bring it on."

"You're going to have to inform Agent Munro's lawyer as soon as possible about these developments, at least the part about the personnel file being accessed."

"Yes, you're right. I guess it's only fair."

Hammond pursed his lips and nodded. "Yes, it is. I'll see you tomorrow."

CHAPTER 17

After leaving Hammond's office, Chloe returned to her desk to log off her computer and collect her things. Unable to help herself, her thoughts once again centered on Declan. She was now more convinced than ever of his innocence. Whether it was Stanford or Stoltenberg or a combination of both, it was obvious there was far more at play than a simple case of an agent gone bad.

Her boss was right. The information she'd discovered from HR and from Stanford were game changers. She could no longer justify keeping her findings from Declan, or at the very least, from his barrister.

She flicked through Declan's file until she found the number for Roger White. A cheerful sounding receptionist answered the phone after the third ring.

"I'm sorry, Mr White has left for the day," the woman informed her when Chloe asked if she could speak with the barrister.

Chloe politely declined to leave a message and ended the call. She glanced down at the file on her desk and her gaze landed on Declan's number. Her heart skipped a beat. Did she dare call him? What was she afraid of? Just because he had the power to send her insides to jelly didn't mean she'd lost the ability to speak.

She hadn't seen him since the end of the committal hearing earlier that day, when the magistrate had announced he was committing Declan to stand trial. That was when Declan had turned and looked at her, his eyes shadowed with devastation and disbelief. It felt like a lifetime ago.

Then there was the problem of what she would tell him. Her news was not something she wanted to give to him over the phone. But what if he refused to see her?

For goodness sake, Chloe, just call him and get it over with! Her mind taunted her. She smiled a little ruefully. Before she could change her mind, she picked up the phone again and dialed Declan's number.

Declan peered at the caller ID illuminated on his phone and his heart leaped. With an effort, he slowed the pounding inside his chest with a few quick breaths and answered the call.

"Chloe."

"Declan. Hi. Um... How are you?"

"I've had better days, but I'm sure you know that."

"Yes, sorry. That was stupid of me. I was... Well I was wondering if we could meet? I need to talk to you."

"Now?"

"Yes, if it's not too late for you."

"Of course it's not too late. It's not even six o'clock. Is this about Charlie? What did you find out? I've been trying to get hold of him all day."

"I'd rather not say over the phone. Is there somewhere we can meet? What about that bar in Civic?"

Declan spied the five empty beer bottles that stood accusingly on the kitchen counter and pursed his lips. "Um, look, I'm at home and I've had a few too many to drive. What can I say? It's been a shit of a day. How about you come over here?"

Silence greeted him on the other end of the phone. He could almost see her debating the pros and cons of his invitation.

"Forget about it," he said. "I'll get a cab. We can meet at the pub."

"No, no, it's fine. I'll meet you at your home."

"Are you sure?"

"Um...yeah. I'm sure."

"I assume you remember the way?" he said, a little dryly. It felt like a lifetime ago when she'd turned up to arrest him.

"I'll see you in an hour."

His pulse jumped again. "No worries."

Chloe braked at the traffic lights and for the thousandth time debated the wisdom of her decision. She should have insisted she meet Declan on neutral territory, a place where she wouldn't be tempted to remember how good it felt to have his lips touch her skin, but it was too late now. In minutes, she'd be at his apartment.

Besides, she'd never been a coward, at least not in that way. She might not be confident enough to wear colors that would make her stand out in a crowd, but she was sure she could keep her distance and handle an early evening meeting with a man she was trying to help, even if he was the hottest-looking man she'd come across in a long, long time.

Cruising along his street, Chloe slowed when she got to his apartment block. Pulling into the curb, she shut off the ignition and sat there for a few moments, gathering her courage. With an impatient shake of her head, she reached over and collected her briefcase off the floor and opened the door.

Get on with it, Chloe. She silently admonished herself. *And stop being so damned ridiculous.*

With that, she strode up the short walkway and pressed the button for the elevator.

Declan heard the buzzer outside his door and his heart skipped a beat. Ever since Chloe's phone call, his pulse had been doing double time. In a sudden panic, he ran his fingers through his hair in an effort to bring it under some sort of control. Glancing down, he realized he still wore the clothes he'd been in all day. Hours of angst and pacing later, they looked a little worse for wear. Unfortunately, he'd left it too late to change.

With a resigned sigh, he took a deep breath and opened the door. Chloe stood in the corridor, looking uncertain. Declan suddenly realized that for all of her outward confidence, she harbored a degree of insecurity outside working hours. It had been obvious at the bar the night before, but he'd put it down to her being in an establishment that clearly made her uncomfortable. Now he wondered if there was more to it. Or perhaps it was just him who made her nervous? The thought intrigued him.

"Come in. Please," he said, remembering his manners at last.

He stood back and allowed her to enter and then closed the door behind her. Noting she was also dressed in the clothes she'd worn to court, his nerves eased and he headed toward the bar to fix her a drink.

"Can I get you a beer? Or perhaps you'd prefer a margarita?" Her eyes widened in surprise and he could tell she was pleased he'd remembered.

"Um, yes. A margarita would be lovely."

After fixing her drink, he opened a bottle of mineral water and took a healthy slug.

"You're not drinking?" she asked.

He shook his head. "I think I've had my quota for today. Besides, something tells me I want to have a clear head—well, as clear as possible, for what you're about to tell me."

She moved further into the room and set her briefcase and cocktail glass on the coffee table. He followed her. Perching on the edge of the sofa, she took a deep breath, drew up her shoulders and looked him straight in the eye.

"I've discovered someone out of the Minister's Office accessed your personnel file about a month before Stanford came forward with his accusations."

Shock immobilized him. His jaw fell open. "Are you talking about the Minister for Home Affairs?"

Chloe bit her lip and nodded. Declan shook his head in disbelief.

"Look, let's not get ahead of ourselves," she said hurriedly. "All I know is that a clerk by the name of Eric Stoltenberg who works in the Home Affair's Office accessed your file. I went to HR today and checked the file myself. While there didn't appear to be anything missing and the HR manager assured me nothing had been photocopied, I can't be certain nothing was photographed."

Declan seized upon her announcement. He threw his arms up into the air. "Christ. Don't you *see*? It's like I told you before. Someone stole my login details. It's obvious I'm being framed. I wish to hell you'd had this information earlier. It could have made a difference to the magistrate's decision."

Guilt suffused her features. Declan's heart stopped. Comprehension slowly dawned and anger consumed him.

"You *did* know earlier...?"

Chloe swallowed and averted her gaze. Declan's temper rose. He advanced toward her.

"Yes or no, Senior Investigator Sabattini? Did you have this information prior to the time the magistrate handed down his decision?"

He held his breath and waited for her reply. When the tiny nod of acquiescence came, he clenched his fists and exhaled on a vicious oath.

"Why the hell didn't you *say* anything?" he yelled. "You were there, in the courtroom. All you had to do was step forward and inform the court that you'd come into new information that you believed could make a difference to the outcome. And yet, you didn't say a word. Even to *me*."

He scraped a hand through his ragged hair and stumbled

away from her, unable to face her for another second. He couldn't believe what she'd done. Rather, what she hadn't done. Charlie's betrayal was still a raw wound and now *this*. His fury spread through him until it threatened to consume him. He spun on his heel and lasered her with his eyes.

"Do you have any *idea* what it feels like to be treated like a *criminal*? To be arrested, handcuffed and put in a cell. To be sneered at, led into the dock, with my family watching on. Do you know what that *feels* like? Do you even *care*?"

Chloe's face paled. She looked like she was going to be sick. Declan forced himself to ignore the distress in her eyes. He opened his mouth to berate her again, but she beat him to it.

"I'm sorry I didn't say anything. At the time, I didn't think it was enough. Yours wasn't the only file Eric Stoltenberg accessed. I didn't know what it meant, at least, not enough to petition the court to reopen the hearing."

She drew in a breath and continued quickly, as if to prevent him from interrupting again.

"I've since found out there's a connection between Stoltenberg and Stanford. What I don't know is whether the clerk was acting under orders or acting alone." She sighed. "The other thing I keep coming back to is motive. Even you agreed you couldn't think of a reason why Stanford would do this to you. Do you know Eric Stoltenberg? Is there any reason why *he* would be framing you?"

The fury went out of him, replaced with a coldness that seeped into Declan's veins. He'd never heard of Stoltenberg. There was only one person he knew who worked in the Home Affairs Office.

Memories of his meeting with the Minister filled him with foreboding. He could barely bring himself to voice the question, but he had to know.

"Ronald Sabattini, the Minister? He's not... He's not your father, is he?"

"No."

Declan's breath *whooshed* out and his shoulders sagged.

"He's my uncle."

He gasped. Christ, of all the people to fall for—not that he was falling for her, he hastily amended.

Did she know about her uncle? Surely, she did? No family could keep something like that a secret.

But what if she didn't? He damned well wasn't going to be the one to enlighten her. Any chance they might have of making a go of it would be destroyed before it had started.

"Do you know him?" she asked, curiosity plain on her face.

For more than five seconds, Declan was sure his heart had ceased pumping. He stared at her, his mouth opening and closing as he waited for her to tell him she knew: She knew about him and the Minister.

But her expression remained open, filled with nothing more than keen interest. He searched frantically for the right words.

"Um, yes, I do. We... We met at a police function about six months ago. It was kind of a meet-and-greet night for the latest recruits."

Chloe frowned. "That's strange. My uncle said he didn't know you." A moment later, she shrugged. "I guess he attends numerous functions every week. My Aunt Nellie's forever bemoaning the fact he's never at home. I can understand why she chooses to stay in most of the time. It must be tiring going out night after night."

Declan nodded wordlessly, his mind turning furiously.

She didn't know.

She couldn't know. If she knew she wouldn't be babbling on about the social life, or lack thereof, of her family—as if that mattered.

Declan clenched his fists, at a loss about what to do next. He turned away. His thoughts continued to churn.

"Are you all right?"

Her concern nearly undid him. He couldn't tell her. He couldn't. "I'm fine," he managed, his voice strangled.

She eyed him curiously. "You didn't answer my question," she said at last.

He cleared his throat and prayed for strength. "What question?"

"About Eric Stoltenberg. Is there any way he could be behind this?"

Declan blew out his breath on a sigh, relieved the conversation had moved away from her uncle.

"I've never met the man. I've never even heard of him, until tonight. I can't imagine what reason he'd have to do this."

"You said the same thing about Charlie and yet it's more and more obvious he's involved. Why else would he give sworn evidence and risk a charge of perjury if he had nothing to gain? Either for himself, or someone who matters to him."

Declan shook his head in disbelief, even knowing what she said made sense. Charlie may not have done it for himself, but what if someone close to him had something to gain from Declan's fall from grace? Someone Declan wasn't even aware of?

Chloe paced the length of his living room with her arms crossed defensively over her chest. He could almost feel her agitation. A moment later, she halted and drew in a deep breath. She turned to him, her expression grave. "There's something else."

Her words reverberated against his brain. He stared at her, his heart pounding. *Christ, how much more could he take?*

"I think my uncle's involved."

He felt her words like an elephant kick straight to his gut. He stepped back and instinctively raised his hands, as if to ward off a blow.

"Whoa, what are you telling me...?"

She stared at him, her expression grave.

"*Fuck.*" He shook his head, not wanting to accept the reality of the awful thought he'd skirted around ever since she'd mentioned the connection to the Home Affairs Office.

As if unable to stand still, Chloe recommenced her pacing. Wringing her hands, she paused intermittently to gaze blindly out at the night through the balcony window.

Declan understood her agitation. His thoughts were in turmoil. But he needed answers. He needed to hear how she'd arrived at such an appalling conclusion.

He walked back to the couch and took a seat at one end and set the water he'd all but forgotten on the coffee table in front of him. Reaching across to the small end table that housed an antique lamp, he switched it on to better illuminate the room. He turned back to the woman whose steps had slowed with the onset of the soft glow of light.

"Talk to me, Chloe," he implored quietly. "Tell me what you know."

She turned to him with stricken features, looking lost and vulnerable. "I tried to call your lawyer. It's-it's time he knew about this. I-I wanted you to know, but this—this is so hard." He stifled the urge to close the distance between them and take her into his arms. He needed answers and she was the only person who could provide them. He patted the leather beside him, but she shook her head.

"No, I need to do this from over here. Please."

He nodded. She drew in a deep shuddering breath and he braced himself against what was to come.

"When I found out about Eric, I went to see my uncle."

"Right."

She grimaced. "It wasn't only because Eric works in my uncle's office that I went to see him."

Dread stole through Declan's veins, but he kept his tone as light as he could manage. "Okay."

"The HR manager told me that Eric had said he was there at the Minister's request. When I told my uncle what Eric had said, he flatly denied knowing anything about it."

"And you believed him?"

Chloe stopped moving and sighed. Turning to face him, she picked up her margarita and took a gulp.

"Until now, yes. He's my uncle. I've known him all my life. I had no reason to think he'd lie to me."

"So, what happened to change your mind?"

Lifting her glass again, she emptied its contents in two

swallows. As if coming to a decision, she closed the distance between them and took a seat beside him on the couch.

Declan's gaze locked with hers. He steeled his heart against the surge of emotion her nearness evoked. Her eyes were wide—whirlpools of confusion and disbelief.

Again, he resisted the urge to offer her comfort. He tightened his fists and forced his arms to remain by his side. His jaw clenched with the effort.

Chloe drew in a ragged breath. "A little while ago, I asked you if you knew my uncle and you told me you did, but when I asked my uncle about you, he couldn't recall you."

Unease held Declan in a death grip. He ignored it and forced a grin. "Like you said, he probably goes to hundreds of functions a year. I only met him once."

"That's true, but I also asked him about Charlie. He told me he didn't know him, either."

"Okay," Declan managed, relieved that the topic had shifted away from him. "Is there any reason why you think he'd know Charlie?"

Chloe scrubbed her fingers through her hair and scrunched her eyes closed. A few moments later, her hands lowered and her shoulders slumped. She looked at him.

Tears welled in her eyes, sparkling like diamonds in the golden glow of the lamp. Her mouth opened. Declan heard her soft intake of breath. The pain on her face almost killed him.

"I don't know why I asked him about Charlie," she whispered. "There was no reason for my uncle to know him. It just came out. When my uncle told me Charlie's name wasn't familiar, I didn't think any more about it." She looked away and then continued.

"Uncle Ronnie's a busy man. He deals with thousands of officers under his command every day. There's no way anyone would expect him to remember every single one of them."

Despite himself, he reached for her hand. "What happened, Chloe? What happened to change your mind?"

She shuddered and returned the pressure of his fingers. "I re-interviewed Charlie," she whispered.

Declan sat upright, shock and excitement arcing through him. "You spoke to the son of a bitch? I've lost count of the number of messages I've left for him. He's refusing to answer my calls. How did you get hold of him?"

"He's transferred to a different department. Fraud Squad. Once I found out, I left a message for him and he eventually called me back. He came into my office late this afternoon and we talked."

"Did you ask him about that bullshit performance he put on at court?"

"Yes, of course. His claim that you'd exhibited interest in children six months ago was totally contrary to what he'd told me in his first interview. I had to find out why he'd lied. And when."

She lowered her gaze and the significance of her comment slowly sank in. His anger stirred.

So, his guilt or innocence was still under consideration. He tensed and pulled his hand out of hers.

"You still think he might have been telling the truth in his court testimony? Are you *kidding* me?"

Chloe ignored him and continued speaking. "I asked him if he knew Eric Stoltenberg. He said he did. That's how I know there's a connection between the two of them. Then I asked him if he knew my uncle." She drew in a raspy breath. "He said he did."

"So what? There wouldn't be a single agent who doesn't know the Minister and if Charlie's ever had cause to go to the Minister's Office, he'd probably see his clerk."

"Charlie told me he'd met my uncle on several occasions. That they'd shared conversations."

"Big deal. That hardly—" Declan jumped up, his fists clenched. "Wait a minute, didn't you say your uncle denied knowing him?"

Chloe nodded, her face grim. "Now do you see where I'm going with this?"

Excitement and adrenaline rushed through him, leaving

him tingling. He moved closer to the couch, his arms spread wide.

"Don't you *see*? It *has* to be him. He lied about knowing Stanford and he lied about knowing me. Why would he do that unless he had something to hide? Even better, his clerk told the HR manager he was there on the Minister's orders. It all makes sense."

Chloe sat forward on the couch. "I think you're right. The only thing I don't understand is *why*."

Time stood still. Declan's heart thumped hard against his chest. Blood pulsed in his ears. She lifted her head and stared at him and whispered the words he'd been dreading.

"Tell me again how you know my uncle."

CHAPTER 18

A cold pit of dread formed a hard lump in Chloe's belly. She stared at Declan, almost willing the words back. Did she really want to know why her uncle would deny any memory of meeting him? If there was nothing to hide, why would he pretend it had never happened? After all, according to Declan, they'd only met six months ago, nowhere near long enough to forget about it.

A raft of emotions darkened Declan's features until they hardened into a mask of cold anger. Chloe shivered and almost wished again that she'd kept her mouth shut.

"Once I tell you about this, things will never be the same for you and your family. I'm assuming since your uncle denied any knowledge of me, he's also denied who he is—or more to the point, *what* he is—to everyone who knows him."

At his words, fear and foreboding congealed in her heart. Her pulse pounded in her ears. Chloe gripped the soft leather of the couch, digging her fingernails in until it hurt.

As if sensing her unease, Declan moved closer, his eyes searching hers. "Are you still sure you want to know?"

No, she wanted to scream. She didn't want to know. She could tell by the look on his face that what he was going to say would tear her apart, would destroy her world as she knew it...would devastate her family.

And it could never be taken back.

But she was an officer of the law. A seeker of the truth. Hadn't she spouted that very phrase to her boss not more than ninety minutes ago? How could she turn her back on an innocent man in the name of protecting a member of her family who may not even be worthy of her protection? Her respect? Her *love*?

Determination surged through her. She held his gaze with a steely resolve.

"Tell me."

He stared at her, probing her with eyes that pierced through her uncertainty and laid it bare.

"Are you sure?"

"*Tell* me."

After another long moment, Declan broke eye contact and stood and moved away, almost as if putting physical distance between them could soften the blow. He drew in a deep breath. Chloe braced herself.

"I met your uncle at a work function. I'd been with the CPU about six months. Although it was touted as a meet-and-greet thing for the latest intake of AFP recruits, they were also raising money to be donated to a charity that arranged for counseling for children whose lives had been touched by crime.

"We were all urged to attend. It was held at the Hyatt in Yarralumla. A really swanky affair. Tuxedoes, ball gowns and five hundred dollar tickets.

"I went with my oldest brother, Tom. He's been a police officer for most of his adult life. It was his daughter who'd had a narrow escape from a pedophile a little over a year ago."

"Cassie," she murmured, remembering.

Declan nodded, his mouth grim. "Yes, Cassie."

"Go on," she urged quietly.

"Neither Tom nor I had a date. Tom's wife, Lily, was sick at home with the flu. They live in Sydney and she didn't want to make the trip down. Tom was reluctant to go without her, but she'd urged him to go along and show their support. I was single, footloose and fancy free."

He threw her a wry look. "Long after Meg Harvey, I'd been seeing a lawyer. We'd been together a few years, but it didn't work out. The breakup was pretty rough on me and finding a replacement girlfriend had been way down on my list of priorities."

Chloe remained silent, even though a part of her was dying to know more. She bit her lip and waited for him to continue.

Declan scrubbed at his face with his hands, seemingly lost in his memories. His voice was deeper, hoarser when he began again.

"I was alone at the bar when your uncle approached me. I knew before he introduced himself who he was—hardly a week goes by that his face isn't pictured in the news for one reason or another—but I'd never met him. I was drinking beer and he asked the bartender to refresh my drink. Then he introduced himself."

Chloe shivered with unease and rubbed her palms up and down her arms. Declan grimaced.

"It's not too late, Chloe. Say the word and I'll stop. You'll never hear another sound."

A part of her jumped at the offer, wanting nothing more than to run screaming from the room with her hands jammed tightly against her ears. She drew in another breath and shook her head. "Go on."

A spark of admiration lit up the depths of Declan's eyes. He seemed to come to some decision and nodded.

"Your uncle asked me about myself, how old I was, how long I'd been with the AFP, whether I was married. I didn't find his interest rude; in fact, I was kind of flattered. Although I'd been an officer for more than a decade under the New South Wales system, I'd never come to the notice of anyone at the top. And here I was, barely six months into my new career and the Minister for Home Affairs, the boss of bosses, was interested in me."

Declan paced the length of the living room, his movements becoming more agitated. He drew in a deep breath and continued.

"We ordered another round of drinks and the banter remained friendly. I had my leg propped up on the rail that ran along the bar. Without warning, he moved closer and put his hand on my thigh and squeezed."

Chloe gasped. Shock ricocheted through her, turning her rigid. Blood pumped hard in her veins. She strained to hear him over the roar in her ears.

"I jumped back like I'd been scalded. I had no idea he was gay. In some confused part of my brain, I could even remember thinking I'd heard about a wife and a child somewhere. I told him rather abruptly that I wasn't gay and his advances weren't welcome. He didn't take it well. I could tell by the look on his face that I'd made a dangerous enemy."

Chloe's mind reeled with Declan's revelations. With every fiber of her being, she wanted to scream at him that he was wrong. This was her *uncle*! Her father's brother. A man who had always been there for her. A man who treated her like his very own daughter.

An angry denial instinctively forced its way into her mouth. She shook her head back and forth. Leaping up, she confronted Declan, her hands on her hips. "You must have misunderstood him."

Declan stared at her, his eyes unfathomable. "No."

Her heart pumped furiously. "He's been married for forty years. He has a daughter. It can't be right. You might have thought he was coming on to you, but did he actually *say* anything in that vein?"

"No, he didn't *say* anything. He didn't have to. It was obvious what he meant."

She spun on her heel, still unwilling to accept the possibility her beloved uncle was living a double life. "Okay, okay, maybe he touched you—"

"*Maybe?*" His eyes narrowed dangerously. "What the hell are you implying? That I don't know whether the man touched me or not? Are you for *real?*" A flush crept up his neck. Anger glittered in his eyes. Chloe took a deep breath and backed up a step.

"Okay, he touched you. I get it. But, there must be some mistake about his intention. Maybe it was accidental? Maybe he leaned over to pick up his drink and he accidentally brushed your leg?"

This time, there was no mistaking Declan's ire. He strode toward her, coming to a halt inches from where she stood. The tension in his body emanated fury with every step.

"He *squeezed* my thigh, Chloe! With his fingers. He leaned toward me and *squeezed my thigh*. How you could even think that might be accidental is beyond me."

Her thoughts whirled around inside her head. Panic dimmed her vision.

It couldn't be true. It couldn't. There had to be some mistake. There *had* to. The alternative was inconceivable.

She had to get out of there.

The thought had barely registered when she whirled around. Finding her briefcase, she rifled inside for her keys and then strode toward the door.

"Chloe, we need to talk about this. We need to—"

The sound of blood pounding in her ears blocked out the rest of Declan's plea. She made it to the door and flung it open. Stumbling into the corridor, she headed for the elevator.

She didn't look back.

CHAPTER 19

Chloe cracked open her eyes and shielded them against the morning light that seeped through her open curtains. In her haste to get home and hide beneath her covers, wanting nothing more than a chance to block out the world and the recent shocking blows it had dealt her, she'd forgotten to draw them.

She glanced at the clock on her nightstand and groaned. If she didn't get moving, she'd be late for work. The thought of fronting up to her office and to her boss filled her with dread. She'd tossed and turned and paced up and down her bedroom for most of the night. Declan's words echoed in her head. Images of her uncle, her aunt, Stanford and Stoltenberg had chased each other in a kaleidoscope of frenzied color and motion. She'd done her best to block out the roaring in her ears.

But it hadn't worked. She realized it was just as Declan had said. Now that it was out there, her life could never be the same again. The words couldn't be taken back—and neither could their effect.

It wasn't Declan's fault. She'd begged him to tell her. She'd practically forced the words out of his mouth and now she had to live with the consequences. No matter how much she'd wanted to deny it, during the long, lonely hours before dawn, she'd come to accept that what Declan had told her about her uncle made an awful kind of sense.

She'd struggled with a motive for both Stanford and

Stoltenberg, but Declan had presented her with one for her uncle that was as old as time.

That he'd set out to ruin a man's life over a mere rejection seemed extraordinary, but then everything Chloe had learned over the past twenty-four hours had been extraordinary. Her uncle knew Eric, Charlie and Declan *and* he had a motive. The Minister was the common denominator. What Declan said was true and the reason was blindingly simple.

Declan had no reason to lie.

Until last night, he hadn't even known that she suspected her uncle was involved. She and she alone had arrived at that conclusion and it had only been after she insisted on knowing about the details of his meeting with her uncle that he'd reluctantly told her about his introduction to the Minister.

If Declan had been using the encounter as a reason to cast suspicion onto her uncle, he would have made her aware of the possibility at the earliest opportunity, long before charges were laid. He wouldn't have waited until he'd been arrested, charged and dragged before the courts, his life in chaos, before saying something. It was ludicrous to suggest otherwise. In all of the sordid, soiled mess, it was Declan who'd remained the only one untouched by dishonesty and deceit. He, alone, had maintained his integrity and self-respect.

A sudden thought occurred to her and she dashed out of bed and ran down the hall, searching for her briefcase. She found it on the couch. Tugging it open, she riffled through the papers until she found what she was looking for.

She pulled out Declan's file and opened it. She flipped through the contents with fingers that shook. And then she found them: the images taken from the hard drives of Declan's work computer and his laptop. They were labelled with the names of each taskforce investigation the images had originated from, none of which Declan had been involved in.

Five different investigations.

Acting on a hunch, she went into the kitchen and took her cell phone off the charger. Scrolling through her contacts, she dialed Gary Julian's number. Despite the early hour, he picked up.

"Chloe, what can I do for you so early in the morning?"

"I'm sorry, Detective Superintendent, but I really need to talk to you."

His voice sharpened. "What is it?"

"The images that were downloaded to Declan Munro's work computer and his personal laptop were from five different investigations. I was wondering if you could tell me who was involved in each of the taskforces?"

"Sure. Tell me the name of the taskforces you're interested in and I'll look into it."

Chloe provided him with the information he required. "I'd appreciate your earliest reply, Detective."

"Of course. I'll get straight back to you."

Chloe ended the call, her heart thumping. If her suspicions were right, this could be the proof she needed. She sat back against her chair and sighed. Now all she had to do was wait...

In less time than she thought possible, Julian was back on the phone. "I've checked the staff records against each of those taskforces. There were several agents working them. A couple of those investigations happened quite awhile ago."

"Were there any agents who worked on all of them?"

There was a moment of silence. Chloe held her breath even as her pulse picked up speed.

"Only one. Federal Agent Stanford."

Chloe knocked on the door to Hammond's office and waited for him to bid her to enter. Her legs were leaden; she was weighted to her very soul. She'd passed Webber on her way to Hammond's office, but had brushed by her partner with barely a nod of acknowledgement. In ordinary circumstances, she'd have been grateful for his ear, but telling Hammond about her uncle, about everything, was going to be hard enough—she couldn't bear the thought of having the same conversation twice. Webber would find out soon enough.

"Chloe, come in. What can I do for you?"

She drew in a deep breath and held it until it burned. She stepped inside Hammond's office and took the seat opposite his desk.

Hammond frowned. "Is everything all right?"

She closed her eyes and bit her lip to hold back the tears that burned behind her eyelids. All through the dark, anxious hours before dawn, she'd managed to hold it together. She'd clung to her shock and to her anger and had forced any weaker emotion away. She hadn't shed a tear, not a single one.

But here, in the harsh light of day and with the bulk of her anger depleted, she had to not only face the truth, but to put it into words. The thought of doing so now, both exhausted and terrified her.

At her continued silence, Hammond's frown deepened. "Chloe...?"

"I think my uncle—no, I *know* my uncle, the Minister for Home Affairs, is responsible for framing Agent Munro."

Her words tripped over themselves. Hammond stared at her in shock. "S-sorry, can you run that by me again?"

Chloe shook her head, her burst of courage nearly depleted. "You heard me."

"I may have heard you, but I don't understand. How...? Why?" He looked as bewildered and shell shocked as she'd felt last night. She drew in another deep breath and blew it out between her lips.

"I told you yesterday afternoon about Stoltenberg and Stanford. At the time, I was aware my uncle knew both of them. Stoltenberg works in the Minister's Office and Stanford had told me he'd met my uncle on several occasions. My uncle had denied knowing Stanford, so whilst I was curious that Stanford's story was in conflict with what my uncle had told me, I wasn't immediately alarmed." She paused and gathered the remnants of her courage for what was to come.

"What I didn't know until last night was that my uncle also knew Agent Munro—another connection my uncle had denied."

"How did you discover the link between the Minister and Munro?"

"I met with Agent Munro last night, at his apartment." Chloe couldn't help the blush that stole into her cheeks, even though she had done nothing wrong. She sneaked a look at her boss. His frown had deepened. She hastened to explain.

"I tried to call Agent Munro's barrister yesterday afternoon, like we talked about, but he'd already left for the day. I decided Agent Munro deserved to know as soon as possible about the developments with his case.

"I phoned him and suggested we meet somewhere, but he advised me he'd had a little too much to drink and wasn't able to drive. He suggested I meet him at his apartment." She shrugged and held his gaze.

Hammond nodded, appearing to be satisfied. "What's Agent Munro's take on all of this? Does he believe your uncle's behind it?"

Chloe briefly closed her eyes again and then opened them. "Yes. Once I told him about the Minister's connection to both Stoltenberg and Stanford, he revealed he'd also encountered my uncle. He gave me reasons to believe that my uncle is the person responsible for framing him."

Hammond's gaze sharpened. "Such as?"

Chloe sighed, knowing there was nothing for it but to come completely clean. It had to happen sooner or later, anyway. She dreaded the thought of what would happen when the media got hold of it.

With another deep breath on board, over the course of several long minutes, she recounted the facts as she knew them, including filling him in on her recent discovery about Stanford's links to all five of the CPU investigations. After she'd finished, she felt drained. The shock on Hammond's face reflected the way she'd felt when she'd first been told. Hammond shook his head.

"You have to talk to Stoltenberg and confirm it was the Minister who asked him to access Munro's file. It appears Stoltenberg was an innocent pawn in your uncle's game, but let's make sure. Bring Stanford in again. It's obvious he was the one who downloaded the images. We need to put more pressure on him to find out why he did it. The Minister must have fed him the login details and Stanford must have been the one who created the computer trail. He left additional evidence on Munro's laptop. It's the only thing that makes sense."

Hammond's expression hardened. "The only other possibility is that Stanford and Stoltenberg are in cahoots and it has nothing to do with your uncle. Despite the evidence that appears to indicate your uncle has a strong motive, it's possible Stoltenberg accessed the login details off his own bat and provided them to Stanford who then created the computer trail and everything else."

Chloe looked at him dubiously. "It's possible of course, but the only problem with that scenario is that neither of those men have a motive. At least, not one that we know about."

Hammond sighed. "Bring them in and let's see what we can shake out of them. After that, we'll regroup."

It was late in the afternoon when Chloe eventually made contact with both Charlie and Eric. She'd located Eric easily enough at the Home Affairs Office. Charlie had been harder to find. His superior at the Fraud Squad had told her Charlie was on a rostered day off. Calls to his cell had gone unanswered.

When she'd finally made contact, she'd purposefully arranged the interviews so that both men would pass in the corridor. She wanted Charlie to know she'd spoken to Eric.

She started with Stoltenberg, whose youth surprised her. She expected someone with a little more experience to be working in a prestigious environment such as the Home Affairs Office.

After going through the preliminaries and obtaining his permission to record the interview, she got straight to the point.

"Mr Stoltenberg, do you know an agent by the name of Declan Munro?"

The man nodded. "Yes."

Chloe's jaw dropped in shock. Her heart felt like it would thump itself right out of her chest. She did her best to regain her equilibrium and continued.

"When you say you know him, what do you mean?"

Stoltenberg shrugged. "Well, I don't exactly know him. What I meant to say was that I know *of* him. I saw him on the television a couple of nights ago. Something about a committal hearing."

Chloe sucked in a breath, her tension easing. She cleared her throat and tried again. "I see. Approximately three months ago, you attended upon the Human Resources Department of the AFP and requested a number of personnel files. Do you remember doing that?"

Eric fingered his cheap, bright orange tie. It was liberally embellished with purple polka dots that matched his lilac shirt. His thin, manicured hand fluttered nervously, but he eventually replied in a voice that was almost steady.

"Yes, of course. It wasn't that long ago."

"Good. Do you remember who you spoke to at HR?"

A frown crinkled the smooth, pale skin of his forehead. "An older lady...Mary Slater, was it? I can't quite remember. I do recall she was very pleasant and most accommodating."

Chloe nodded in agreement. "Could it have been perhaps Marcia Slater?"

"Yes, you're right. It was Marcia, not Mary."

"Do you remember who asked you to access the files?"

Eric's gaze fell away. His fingers picked at lint on his dark gabardine suit pants. Chloe held her breath and waited.

"It was the Minister, of course." The lightness of his tone belied the anger in his eyes. He followed his response with a laugh that somehow seemed forced.

Chloe stared down at her notes and once again tried hard to slow her breathing. Despite what she knew, hearing confirmation directly from Stoltenberg that her uncle had requested the files caused pain deep in her heart.

She refused to pay it heed. She'd devoted her life to discovering the truth and she would see this through to the end, even if everything inside her demanded she turn and run the other way.

"Do you know why the Minister wanted those files?"

"He told me he was applying for extra funding for a program directed at AFP agents who had recently joined the ranks. He gave me a list of agents who had been with us for less than a year. He wanted me to check their employment dates to ensure they corresponded with the ones he'd obtained. What I found curious was that the only details he asked me to make a record of was the page containing the computer login details of Agent Declan Munro."

Stoltenberg eyeballed her, his eyes alight with challenge. It was almost as if he was daring her to ask the next question. Despite the hammering of her heart, she didn't disappoint.

"And did you?"

"Of course. I aim to please. I photographed the page with my phone and bluetoothed it to the Minister's computer, just like he asked." Eric smiled, but even that didn't ease the tension around his mouth. Chloe shivered. There was more to this than he was saying.

"How long have you worked for the Minister?"

"Nearly a year."

"And do you enjoy what you do for him?"

Stoltenberg tugged once again on his tie. A smile turned up his lips. "Of course. The Minister's an easy man to work for. Whilst he can be...demanding, he's also incredibly generous. Until recently, it was a pleasure to arrive at work."

Chloe sat forward. "What happened recently?"

Eric pursed his lips in thought. A moment later, he shook his head. "Let's just say, working there is not quite so exciting anymore." He shrugged. "I think I'm bored. It's time I moved on. I've put in for a transfer."

Chloe's eyebrows raised in surprise. "Really? What does the Minister have to say about that?"

Eric shrugged again and averted his gaze. "He doesn't know."

Chloe digested the information and then tried another tack. "Do you know an agent by the name of Charlie Stanford?"

Stoltenberg tensed. His cheeks paled. Anger once again sparked in his eyes. "That useless lump of muscle? Why would you want to ask me about him?"

"So you do know him?"

"Of course I know him. It seems like every time I turn around these days, he's there. With the Minister. It's been going on for months."

Chloe couldn't breathe. Her chest had tightened to suffocating levels. She gasped and dragged in a breath. Stoltenberg frowned at her.

"Are you all right? Should I call someone?"

Chloe shook her head. "No, no. I'm fine. It's...nothing. Don't worry about it. You were saying how you know Agent Stanford; that he's always underfoot. I'm curious, what does he do for the Minister?"

Eric's lips curled up in disgust and the anger in his gaze flared brighter. "Nothing, as far as I can tell, but it doesn't stop him from dropping by every other day, disturbing the Minister."

Chloe stared hard at him. It was obvious there was no love lost between Stanford and the clerk. She glanced at her watch. If Charlie was on time, he should be waiting for her right outside the door. She gathered the papers together on the desk.

"Thank you for coming in, Mr Stoltenberg. I really

appreciate your time. If there's anything else you'd like to add or anything you remember later, please feel free to give me a call." Chloe handed him her card that listed her direct line.

Eric pocketed it without glancing at it and pushed back his chair. Chloe stood with him and opened the door. Stoltenberg brushed past her, then froze.

Charlie lounged against the wall outside the interview room. Dressed in a pair of designer jeans and a Nautica polo shirt, he eyed Eric's colorful ensemble with barely disguised disdain.

Eric flushed under the other man's scrutiny. Fury glittered in the clerk's eyes. Chloe eyed the silent exchange with interest. Moments later, all hell broke loose.

"You fucking prick!" Stoltenberg shouted. "You bastard! How dare you! How *dare* you!" The clerk launched himself at Charlie who outweighed the younger man by more than a hundred pounds. Eric bounced off the hard wall of muscle and hit the adjacent wall. Tears streamed down his face, but he paid them no heed.

"You couldn't help yourself, could you? You had to do it!"

Charlie took a step toward Eric who cowered against the wall. "What the fuck are you talking about?" Charlie poked the other man in the chest and Eric whimpered.

"For Christ sake, you worthless piece of shit. What are you, a girl?" Charlie turned away, his expression full of disgust.

Regaining her composure, Chloe stepped between them, forcing them apart. "Whoa, gentlemen. Take it easy. What was that all about?"

Eric sniffed and swiped a hand across his eyes. "Ask *him*. I've had enough. I'm through," he choked and ran toward the elevators.

Chloe's mind spun.

What the hell had just happened? Any thought that Charlie and Eric were in this together had just been blown out of the water. Not that she'd given the theory any real credence, but it was satisfying to have that question put to bed. Not that the alternative gave her any comfort...

Indicating the open doorway with her hand, she swallowed a sigh and followed Charlie into the interview room. He took a seat and she sat down opposite him.

"Thanks for coming in again, Charlie. I hope I didn't drag you away from anything important?"

Charlie shook his head. "I'm on a day off. That's why I missed your call. I was at the gym and didn't hear my phone."

Chloe nodded. He looked like someone who spent a lot of time at the gym.

"What's with you and Eric?"

Charlie's expression turned belligerent. "I already answered your questions."

She turned her glare on him, suddenly completely out of patience. It was clear Stanford was in it up to his teeth. There was no other way the trail of evidence could have been left on Declan's computer. She eyeballed him again. "I have more. Tell me once more about Minister Sabattini."

Charlie stared at the investigator and his unease intensified. He forced it aside. There was no way the Minister had ratted on him. It wasn't possible. He shrugged and carefully schooled his expression into one of polite blankness. "There's nothing else to tell."

"Agent Stanford, I asked you a question. Tell me again how you know Minister Sabattini."

Charlie crossed his arms over his chest and leaned back against his chair, buying time while his mind spun in frantic indecision.

How much did she know?

If she knew the truth and he lied to her, it wouldn't go well for him. Then again, if she was clueless and he confessed like a wimpy schoolboy, it would be even worse. He chose to bluff it out.

"Like I told you before, we've met a few times. So what? I

bet he's met thousands of officers over his time. He's the Home Affairs Minister. That's what he does. He meets and greets."

"Except that he's done more than meet you, hasn't he?" she said.

Fury and disbelief arced through him. *Fucking Stoltenberg*. It had to be. The little asshole knew about him and the Master and he was jealous. It was the only thing that made sense. No doubt the prick had been overjoyed to spill his guts to the investigator.

Charlie drew in a deep breath in an effort to calm himself. Tension held him in a vice-like grip. He wondered again how much she knew.

"Talk to me, Charlie."

It was the kindness in her voice that got to him. All of a sudden, he was weighed down by depression and disappointment. Yet again, he'd been forced to live a lie, to hide who he really was in order to satisfy someone else's needs. First his mother's and then the Master's.

He'd thought the Master would be different. He'd thought the Master would be happy to parade him by his side—after all, Charlie was young, fit and good looking enough to draw attention.

But it hadn't worked out like that. The Master had been happy to keep their relationship a secret. In fact, he'd insisted upon it. It wasn't until about a month after they'd started sleeping together that Charlie discovered the Master was married. He happened to see a photo of a woman and girl on the Master's desk. It was then that the Master had told him.

Charlie had worked hard at concealing his shock. He'd admitted to the Master that he hadn't breathed a word of his own homosexuality to anyone since the fateful conversation with his mother all those years ago. The Master had been more than pleased at Charlie's revelation.

The Master's attitude had disappointed him at the time, but not enough to dim the burgeoning feelings he had for his lover who so often reminded him of his dorm master.

Now, he stared at the investigator and wished he could read her mind. Regardless of what she knew, he wasn't ready to blow his cover. He had to assume she was still in the dark. Opening his mouth to reply, he did his best to sound outraged.

"Where do you get off accusing me of things like that? The Minister's a happily married man. He's—"

"Also gay," Chloe interrupted. "Maybe bisexual, if that makes you feel any better."

Shock ricocheted through him. How the fuck did she know? *Nobody* knew. At least, that's what the Minister had told him. Not even that prick Stoltenberg would know something like that. She was bluffing. She had to be. He shook his head slowly back and forth, an instinctive denial rising to his lips. "No, you're wrong."

"When did you start sleeping with him?" she asked quietly.

He reeled backwards as if she'd struck him and his hands came up reflexively to protect his face. He gasped for air, his chest tight. Leaning forward with his elbows on the desk, his held his head in his hands and tried with increasing desperation to get control of himself.

"Talk to me, Charlie. You've been carrying this burden around for way too long. Longer than anyone—even the Minister—could expect. It hasn't been fair the way he's made you shoulder the responsibility for all of this, expecting you to betray your best friend, to lie to me, to lie to the court. It must have been so hard for you, Charlie."

He lifted his head and stared at her, throwing off her sympathetic words and drawing on rage to stiffen his spine. He wouldn't allow her to break him. The Master was his life, his everything. He wouldn't let anyone destroy what they had.

"No, no, you're mistaken! You have it all wrong!"

"I don't think so, Charlie. I know a lot more than you think. You see, the Minister is my uncle." Her calm voice hammered through the fog in his head, her words all the more powerful for their quiet, but firm delivery. He fought against a wave of dizziness, refusing to show weakness in front of her. He wouldn't betray his lover.

"What happened, Charlie?" she persisted.

Her gentle words, laced with kindness and concern, seeped into his veins. He cringed and put his hands over his ears, hoping to block the words out. He didn't want her compassion. He didn't want her understanding. He'd lived all of his life guarding his secret, knowing that anything worthwhile, anything beautiful, anything beloved had to be protected and nurtured behind an impenetrable wall of lies and concealment.

For more than twenty years, he'd concealed his secret. He'd learned the hard way that the only ones who truly understood were the men who invited him into their lives: the father figures who took him in, showed him tenderness, showed him love.

He wouldn't betray them, *any* of them. He stared at the investigator, his unrelenting gaze fierce with determination, but despite his best efforts, a voice echoed with increasing stridency in his head.

She was his niece. His niece! She probably knew everything... His resolve began to fade.

"The Minister asked you to frame Declan, didn't he? Just like he asked Eric to steal Declan's login details. For all I know, the Minister's sleeping with his clerk, too."

Charlie's chaotic thoughts snagged on her last words. He frowned in confusion and then anger stirred inside him.

"What the hell do you mean, he's sleeping with Stoltenberg? Of course he isn't sleeping with that little asshole. Stoltenberg is nothing to him, a nobody. He's in love with m—"

"You're right, he is in love with you. And you're in love with him. It's why you agreed to help him. It's why you agreed to betray a man you'd once called your friend."

Her words spun by him in a blur. His mind caught on the image of the Master as he'd been the last time Charlie had seen him, offering Eric an encouraging smile and a lingering pat on the arm when the clerk had entered the Master's office with a pile of papers.

Charlie hadn't wanted the gesture to mean anything—had even convinced himself he'd imagined it, but the investigator's words tore him apart. He was flooded with uncertainty.

Had he been wrong about the Master's feelings? Was it possible the man he adored didn't feel quite the same way? Had he been used in the worst possible way? Had his destruction of a friendship with the only mate he'd ever known been for *nothing?*

He dragged his head up and stared at the woman who sat across from him, his devastating thoughts shredding him from the inside out.

As if sensing his fragility, she reached out across the desk and squeezed his arm in reassurance. "Tell me what happened, Charlie."

He held her gaze. She squeezed his arm again and gave him a nod of encouragement.

All of a sudden, his anger dissipated. His life had spiraled out of control and yet he felt completely detached from it—as if it was someone else's train wreck he watched from afar with nothing more than mild interest.

He drew in a deep breath and eased it out. "I-I'd been...seeing the Mas—the Minister for about a month when he...asked me about Declan. He asked me if I knew him. He wanted to know what he was like to work with and things like that."

"When did this happen?"

He shrugged and drew in another breath. "I'm not sure. Maybe some time back in July?

"I thought nothing of his interest in Declan. I knew he was interested in *me* and I thought he was merely being polite, expressing interest in my place of work... After awhile, it became obvious his interest in Declan had nothing to do with me and everything to do with him. Every conversation we had seemed to include a reference to Declan in some shape or form."

Charlie lifted his head and challenged her with his gaze, a spark of his anger returning. "About three months ago, I found out why."

"You mean to say he *told* you he propositioned Agent Munro?"

Shock ricocheted through him. He shook his head in confusion. *That wasn't right.* The Master wasn't the one who'd made the first move.

"No, no, no… That's not how it happened. Declan was the one who approached *him*. It was Declan who wanted a relationship. I think about all the times Declan flirted with this woman or that, playing hard to get—it was all a front.

"The Minister sent him packing, but the prick threatened to go to the media. The Minister's life and the life of his family would have been ruined. He had no choice. He *had* to get rid of him."

The investigator shook her head in disbelief. "Think about it for a minute, Charlie. You've worked with Declan for more than a year. If what you say is true and Declan was the one who made the first move, do you honestly believe he'd stoop to something as low as *blackmail* when the Minister turned him down? The entire scenario is ludicrous."

Charlie's thoughts spun out of control. "But that's what the Minister said. That's why I had to help him fix the problem. I had to help him get rid of Declan. If everything came out, the Minister would be forced to end our relationship. We'd be over. Just the thought of that sent me into a panic. I couldn't eat. I couldn't sleep. I couldn't think straight. My life would be *nothing* without him. I was willing to do whatever it took."

The woman stared at him, aghast. Charlie frowned, his confusion increasing. For a moment, neither of them spoke.

With a heavy sigh, she finally broke the silence. "Tell me how you did it, Charlie."

He thrust out his bottom lip. "What does it matter? You already have my confession."

"It matters," she replied.

He shrugged, almost beyond caring. "The Minister told me he had to arrange for Declan's removal from the AFP. He couldn't take the risk that Declan would make good on his promise to expose him. The Minister assured me it would be nothing permanent, just enough to buy him some breathing space." He looked up at her and implored her. "He said nothing about sending Declan to jail, I swear."

The investigator stared back at him, her face a mask of stone. Charlie averted his gaze and kept talking, suddenly feeling the need to justify his actions.

"He... He asked me to *help* him. He said it would please him very much if I did what he wanted. I was in love with him." He shook his head helplessly. "I'm *still* in love with him."

The investigator remained unmoved. "You left the trail on Declan's computer, didn't you, Charlie?"

"The Minister gave me Declan's login details. I already knew which computer he used. We were often on the same shift together. It was easy to login under his name while he was out on a job or even just in the bathroom. All it took were a few clicks of the mouse every now and then and the Minister had everything he needed."

"What about the laptop?"

"That was the Minister's idea. He assumed Declan had a personal computer at home. He thought it would look more authentic if child porn was also found on it. I copied some images from old investigations to a USB stick. When Declan went to the bathroom one Saturday afternoon when I visited him at his apartment, I saved them onto his laptop. It was the Minister's idea to delete them. He said it looked like Declan had been trying to get rid of them."

"What about Eric?"

Charlie frowned. "Eric? Why do you keep going on about Eric? He's a nobody. All he did was access the HR file."

"So he didn't know anything about the Minister's plans, is that what you're saying?"

"That's exactly what I'm saying. He's just the errand boy," he scoffed. "The Minister would never trust him with something as important as this." A smile he couldn't quite maintain wobbled on his lips. He hoped beyond hope he was right.

"I take it he rewarded you well?"

Charlie smiled widened in memory. "Oh yes, he rewarded me very, very well. We even used the crop."

The investigator's mouth gaped open. Her face leached of color and she wore a look of horror.

"W-what do you mean, the crop? As in a *riding* crop?" Her voice sounded strangled.

"Of course." He smiled. "Is there any other kind?"

Chapter 20

Chloe's body felt weighed down by concrete. The day was drawing to a close and she could barely keep her eyes open and yet, her job was still not done. She had yet to report back to her boss with her findings after her interviews with Eric and Charlie. Knowing she was only delaying the pain by putting it off, she dragged herself out of her chair and headed toward Hammond's office.

As quickly, and with as little emotion as she could manage, she brought him up to speed. His expression turned grim, but his voice was gentle when he spoke.

"I'm so sorry, Chloe. I really am."

His apology almost undid her. She bit back tears, determined to see it through. Quietly and efficiently, Hammond outlined a plan of attack, starting with putting together a taskforce who would carry out the arrest of Minister Sabattini. Given the fact that the suspect was a government minister, it was vitally important that every protocol was closely followed.

Chloe nodded in agreement. "I agree. We need to dot all the I's and cross all the T's. The last thing we need is to bungle this. The media is going to have a field day as it is."

"I'm going to have to bring the Attorney General in on it, too. I wouldn't be surprised if he wants to liaise with the Prime Minister."

Chloe compressed her lips, even more fatigued at the thought of what lay ahead. To top it all off, was the heavy sadness that plagued her knowing her family still had to be told. Her shoulders slumped on a sigh. Misunderstanding its cause, Hammond looked at her.

"Go home, Chloe. Get some rest, if you can." His expression turned grimmer. "You're going to need it."

Chloe stared up at Declan's apartment building and wished she had the courage to go inside. After the way they'd parted, she didn't know if he'd ever speak to her again. She owed him an apology. It was the reason she found herself there, parked on his street, when she should have been home in bed.

It was after eight and she was emotionally drained, but she'd never be able to sleep until she'd cleared the air with him—or at the very least, offered him a heartfelt apology.

The lights that shone from his apartment assured her he was home. All she had to do was find the courage to climb out of her car and ring his doorbell. Surely, after all she'd been through, apologizing to him was the easiest part of all?

With that thought in mind, she opened the door and stepped out onto the pavement. Turning to lock the car with her remote, she walked the short distance to his apartment block and headed for the elevator before she changed her mind. All too soon, she stood outside his front door. With a deep breath, she pressed the buzzer.

The door opened almost immediately. Declan stood on the other side, a wary expression on his face.

"Chloe."

"Declan. Um...hi, I was just in the neighborhood and I thought... That is, I wondered..."

His lips compressed and his arms came across his chest. Chloe lowered her gaze to the floor. She got it. He didn't want to speak with her. Disappointment flooded through her. She turned to leave.

"Chloe, wait. Please, come in."

She turned back to face him. He'd stepped away from the doorway and was indicating with his hand that she should precede him inside. After a slight hesitation, she nodded her thanks and walked slowly into the apartment.

Once inside, her carefully rehearsed apology flew out of her mind. She'd left him in the middle of shouted denials about her uncle—denials she now knew were misplaced. The burden of that knowledge anchored her to the spot. She couldn't imagine how she was going to find the strength to tell her parents.

The thought sent a surge of determination flooding through her. At the very least, she could get this apology over with. She turned to face him.

"I interviewed Eric Stoltenberg and re-interviewed Charlie Stanford today. You were right. About everything. My uncle's responsible for framing you."

Declan's eyes widened in shock. It was a moment or two before he spoke. "I take it your witnesses gave you what you needed."

His tone wasn't accusatory, but she flushed with guilt. The evidence she'd gained from Stoltenberg and Stanford only cemented what Declan had told her, what he'd begun to suspect.

"Yes, they did. Stanford admitted to downloading the images to both computers. He told me about the Minister. My...my uncle will be arrested tomorrow and brought in for questioning. It's my guess your name will be cleared within twenty-four hours."

Declan nodded, accepting her pronouncement with little show of emotion. "That's great news."

"Yes. I-I'm sorry. I'm sorry I didn't believe you. I was in shock and I didn't *want* to believe you, but that still doesn't make it right. This mess wasn't about me; it was about you. It wasn't my life that had been turned upside down and inside out for something I hadn't done. My actions were inexcusable."

She stared at the floor in silence.

"Are you finished?"

Her head snapped up. A slight grin tugged at the corner of his mouth.

"How can you smile about this? For more than two months, your life has been torn apart through no fault of your own and you're *smiling* about it!" She shook her head in confusion. "I don't get it."

He stepped forward, closing the distance between them. Reaching out, he tilted her chin up until she was forced to look at him.

"It wasn't your fault, Chloe," he said. "Don't get me wrong, I've been mad as hell since it started, but not at you. Never at you. How could I? You were only doing your job."

She stared back at him, wanting to believe him. Without thought, she stepped into his arms. He dragged her close against him and groaned into her hair. She slumped against him.

"I'm sorry, Declan; I'm so sorry." Her voice was muffled against his shirt. His hand came up and stroked her hair. He whispered words of solace.

"It had nothing to do with you, Chloe. Like I said, you were just doing your job. A job you're good at. You had no reason to suspect there was anything more to it."

"But I was the one who recommended the charges." Emotion tightened like a steel band around her chest and she gasped in an effort to contain it. Her eyes burned. She bit her lip to hold the sobs inside, but one escaped and then another and another. With them came a deluge of pain.

Declan's arms tightened around her. "*Shh*, sweetheart. Please don't cry. Never once during this nightmare have I blamed you—and my life's far from ruined. Please believe me, Chloe. You have to believe me."

His words penetrated the fog of her misery and she raised her face to his. Tears blurred his features. She reached up and touched his cheek, delighting in the contrasting textures of the soft warmth of his skin against the roughness of his stubble. Her gaze dropped to his mouth and she heard his intake of breath.

His heart thumped hard beneath her hand. Nerves

tingled and warmed her to her core and she suddenly felt heady at the thought of kissing him. She met his searching gaze and basked in the desire that burned like fire in his eyes.

She yearned to feel his lips on hers.

A tiny warning voice in the back of her head reminded her she was the senior investigator in a case that had ended in criminal charges laid against him—a case that was still before the courts, at least for now. But her libido was having none of that.

When his lips lowered, her mouth parted in anticipation. His kiss was so light she thought she'd imagined it until heat ignited in her belly and quickly moved lower. Her arms came up around his neck and she pressed herself against him, desperate to get closer.

He increased the pressure of his mouth, seeking, taking, discovering. She groaned when his tongue sought the inside of her mouth.

Time ceased. There was nothing and no one but Declan. His chest was taut with muscle beneath her fingers. She squirmed against him, desperate to feel his skin against hers.

His erection pressed through her silk blouse and suit jacket into the softness of her stomach, turning her to liquid. He lifted his head, panting for breath and smiled down at her.

Her breathing was just as unsteady and she fought to regain control. She leaned heavily against him.

"Easy, sweetheart. We have all night."

Her belly clenched with excitement and nervousness. The last time she'd slept with a man, she'd been in college. The encounter had been less than satisfactory, more a grope and a grunt in the darkness rather than any kind of meaningful encounter.

To say that it hadn't exactly inspired her to continue an exploration of her sexuality, was putting it mildly. In fact, she'd often wondered what the authors of steamy romance books were going on about when they described in bold, black, descriptive prose the excitement and passion of sexual intercourse.

But as Declan's body ground against hers and his mouth continued its onslaught, she gained an inkling of what might have inspired those heated scenes. His lips trailed fire everywhere they went. He nuzzled her ear and then her collarbone. His hand came up and cupped her breast. Through the silk of her blouse, his fingers sought the tautness of her nipple and she gasped from the unfamiliar contact.

Desire ricocheted through her from her head to her core. Her clit pulsed and tingled. She tightened her arms about him and dragged his head up for another kiss. She drank in the feel of him, the scent of him. Every inch of him was delicious…

She couldn't get enough.

With impatient fingers, he made quick work of the buttons on her blouse and then brushed both her jacket and blouse off her shoulders. They fell to the floor in a silent pool of silk and gabardine. A whisper of cool night air sighed over her skin. She shivered.

"Are you cold?" he murmured.

Sudden shyness kept her head down. She crossed her arms over her breasts. "No."

With tender fingers, he brushed a coil of hair off her face and then tilted her chin upward until her gaze met his. He stared at her with eyes that were dark with desire. Their tumultuous depths seared right through to her soul. Her heart stilled.

"Don't be shy," he whispered. His gaze dropped to her chest and his hands came up and gently moved her arms until they hung by her sides. "You're so beautiful. Please, let me look at you."

Even still clothed in her bra, Chloe fought the instinct to cover herself. Heat scorched her cheeks. "I-I'm sorry, Declan. I'm not used to…to getting naked with someone." She shrugged self-consciously. "I…"

His eyes widened. "Are you a virgin?"

Despite his gentle tone, she tensed. "No, of course not. I'm thirty years old. It's just that…I-I've only been with a couple of men and the last one was…quite some time ago."

He smiled, his expression soft and tender. "It's been awhile for me, too. But you know what? It's like riding a bike. You don't forget how."

"I know, but I'm not exactly an expert. No one becomes a proficient rider after only two lessons."

"Who said anything about wanting an expert? I'm more than happy to show you everything I know."

His arms went around her and he drew her close. He pressed a kiss against her hair—his heartbeat, a reassuring thud under her ear. She relaxed into the warmth of his arms.

"Thank you for trusting me enough to tell me," he murmured and then shook his head. "You're such a delightful contradiction."

She tensed. He pulled back to look at her, a slight frown marring his forehead.

"Please don't take that the wrong way, sweetheart. I'm thrilled beyond words to know how particular you are with your bed partners."

Embarrassment crept up her neck and into her cheeks. She tried to turn away, but he would have none of it. Gripping her chin lightly, he encouraged her to look at him.

"Why now? Why me, Chloe?"

There was no suspicion in his eyes, only a tender curiosity and Chloe's defenses melted away. So what if she wasn't as experienced as most single women her age? It wasn't a crime not to sleep with every half presentable male that came by. She'd been busy building a career and she was choosy—that's all it was.

She was here with the most beautiful man in the world, and he was kissing her, worshipping her body with his eyes and his mouth and telling her he couldn't care less about her inexperience. She sighed and drew his face closer, pressing a soft kiss on his lips.

"Why not you? You're gorgeous, smart, sexy, kind, caring. What's not to like?"

Even in the pale glow of the lamplight, she could tell he was blushing and she loved him for it. His humility, though totally misplaced, was endearing. "You can't honestly believe you're not appealing to every woman with a heartbeat?"

His blush deepened and it was his turn to look away. "I might not look half-aboriginal, but to tell you the truth, growing up in a small country town and being of mixed race wasn't the easiest thing to do. I'm lucky Mom and Dad instilled in me such a healthy self-esteem or I might never have had the confidence to aim so high. I think in some ways the prejudices I suffered as a child only urged me to greater heights. I was determined to achieve success far beyond that of my schoolmates. I was lucky my father provided so much inspiration."

Chloe nodded. "The first aboriginal appointed to the New South Wales District Court. I can see how that would have inspired you."

Declan shrugged a little self-consciously. "I have a job I love and a family I couldn't be more proud of. I have nothing to complain about."

"Until now. Until you met me."

He was shaking his head before she'd even finished. "No, Chloe. I won't have you blaming yourself. The Minister for Home Affairs is the reason my life went to hell. It had nothing to do with you."

"Thank you, it's nice of you to say it, but nothing you say can change the fact that if I'd believed you during that very first interview, nothing would have come of it. Your life would have continued along on its merry journey, free from angst and blemish. It's as simple as that." Saying the words out loud felt like a confession and she stepped back.

Moving away from him, Chloe looked around for her clothes. Retrieving her blouse from the floor, she tugged it over her shoulders and hastily did up the buttons.

Declan reached out to her. "Chloe, listen—"

"I'm s-sorry," she stuttered. "I-I should go."

His hands closed gently around her upper arms. "Don't be sorry, Chloe and please don't go. Okay, so you recommended the charges and that decision set in motion a series of events I hope never to repeat, but if you hadn't, we'd have never arrived at this—with you in my arms. This feels so right it scares me."

His words warmed her heart, but it wasn't enough. She tried for a smile, but didn't quite manage to pull it off.

"Thank you, Declan. I appreciate what you're saying, but I need to go. It's getting kind of late and I have to work in the—"

"Then, come for a ride with me."

She gaped at him in surprise. "Excuse me?"

"Come for a ride with me. Now. On my motorbike."

Chloe's eyebrows rose and she shook her head. "Oh no, I don't do motorbikes."

A smile tugged at his lips. "What do you mean, you don't do motorbikes?"

She searched around in her mind for a suitable explanation and became a little panicked. She couldn't imagine anything more terrifying than being perched on the back of a motorcycle at the mercy of a man she barely knew—and every other crazy motorist out there.

"I dare you."

Oh, God, now what was she to do? It wasn't so much a matter of bravery; it was more that she was terrified. She'd never trusted anyone with that much control over her life.

And yet she'd trusted him enough to sleep with him. Well, almost. If they hadn't gotten off track, she'd more than likely be lying relaxed and replete in his bed after an amazing session of lovemaking. How she knew it would be amazing, she wasn't quite sure, but instinctively, she was certain he would deliver.

"I've never been on a motorbike."

His smile widened into a grin. "Then tonight, lady, you're in for a treat. The 1199 Panigale Ducati isn't just a motorbike. It's a freaking legend."

She grinned back at him. She couldn't help it. And suddenly, the fear melted away. She looked down at her clothes. "I'm not exactly dressed for riding."

He strode toward a hall she guessed led to the bedrooms. "No problem. My younger sister, Josie, leaves a few clothes here for when she visits." His gaze ran over her. "She's about your size."

"What about a helmet?" she protested weakly.

"I have a spare one. Josie's a speed fiend. She loves to ride pillion. Besides, it's the only mode of transport I have. If she wants to go to the shops, she has to climb on the bike."

He disappeared down the corridor and Chloe took a moment to catch her breath and regain control over the surge of excitement and anticipation that now threatened to overwhelm her. She could hardly believe it. She, sensible Chloe Sabattini was about to double on the back of a motorcycle and ride through the darkened streets of Canberra. All of a sudden, it seemed a perfect way to get away from all the disturbing revelations and the guilt. *Why not give it a go?*

Within minutes, Declan returned brandishing a pair of jeans and a T-shirt in one hand and a pair of boots in the other.

"I'm not sure what size shoe you take, but these should go pretty close. They're probably a bit safer than those stilettos of yours."

Chloe took the clothing with a murmur of thanks and slipped past him into the hall. A well-appointed bathroom with mismatched towels stood off to her right. A little further down, light spilled out of what she assumed was the second bedroom. She walked inside the room and closed the door.

Two single beds lay bare of bedding, a pillow and neatly folded bedspread lay on the end of each one. A large desk and chair took up half of the wall opposite. A laptop, telephone and fax machine were lined up on the desk in almost military precision. The spare room obviously doubled as Declan's office.

Apart from a couple of generic prints on the wall and a framed photograph on the nightstand, the room was devoid of any other decoration.

Unable to help herself, Chloe picked up the photograph and stared at the people who smiled back at her. She recognized Declan's parents and his brothers straight away. The two younger women who completed the picture were unfamiliar, but resembled the others closely enough that she presumed they were their sisters.

One of the girls stood beside Declan. He looked a little younger than he did now and his hair was worn slightly longer. His arm had been thrown around her shoulders in a casual pose. Chloe guessed her to be somewhere in her late twenties.

The other woman looked younger. Standing beside Declan's father, her blond good looks were in stark contrast to her father's black hair and swarthy skin. Her long, slim legs sported a pair of tiny denim shorts. They'd been teamed with a purple and green tank top. Her cheeky grin gave a hint of her personality and Chloe surmised she was a lovable handful.

Replacing the picture where she found it, Chloe removed her blouse and laid it carefully on one of the beds. Slipping the T-shirt over her head, she blushed at its snug fit. Her breasts pushed against the soft fabric, and would leave an observer no doubt as to her generous cup size.

Knowing there was nothing she could do about it and liking the feeling of being a little bit naughty, she slid out of her skirt and deposited it on the bed before stepping into the jeans. They were also a little tight. She'd barely be able to hoist her leg over the bike the way she was going.

A rap on the door drew her attention. "Is everything all right in there?"

Chloe tugged at the jeans in an effort to stretch them. "Um, yes. Everything's fine. I'll be out in a minute."

"Okay. Don't be too long."

She took a seat on the bed and pulled on the borrowed boots. The smell of leather filled her nose. They slid easily over her stockinged feet.

When she emerged into the living room, Declan eyed her with appreciation. His gaze paused at her chest. Excitement fluttered deep in her belly.

Her gaze swept over him, taking into account his fresh

attire. He now wore a pair of black jeans and a T-shirt that hugged him like a second skin, emphasizing the broad expanse of his toned chest. In each hand, he held a helmet.

He grinned and she felt it all the way down to her core.

"Ready?"

Chapter 21

The night sky, sprinkled with starlight, surrounded him when Declan wheeled the bike out of his garage and flicked down the stand. The glow from the streetlights nearby illuminated the paved driveway and glanced off the tall hedge of Murraya that bordered the edge of his apartment block. It was laden with sweet-smelling flowers. He breathed in deeply of the orange-scented air.

Chloe sidled closer, a mixture of anticipation and panic warring in her eyes. He swept another appreciative glance over her tight T-shirt and even tighter jeans.

Blood pulsed into his groin and his body hardened. Images of her bent naked over his bike flooded his mind and he squeezed his eyes shut against the tempting fantasy. He'd promised her a ride on his motorbike and a ride she would get.

Thrusting the erotic thoughts aside, he climbed onto the Ducati and adjusted his weight on the seat.

"Swing your leg over and hold onto me around the waist."

She looked at the bike dubiously and hitched up her jeans. He swallowed a smile.

"You'll need to come a bit closer. Those jeans don't have a lot of give in them."

Even in the dimness, he saw her blush, but she looked at the bike with determination and holding onto his arm, she hoisted herself onto the bike.

"That'a girl! I knew you could do it. Now, put your arms around my waist and enjoy the ride."

Pressing the electric start button, he opened the throttle and enjoyed the familiar rumble of power that roared out of the engine. Kicking it down into first gear, he eased the machine out of the driveway and onto the road. The evening traffic was light and Declan made good time, zipping through the darkened streets of his neighborhood.

Within minutes, he was on the main road that became the freeway north to Sydney. He leaned forward and opened up the throttle, enjoying the familiar rush of exhilaration.

Chloe was silent behind him, but he took that as a good sign. Her death grip around his waist during the first few miles had eased to a comfortable embrace. Conversation over the noise of the bike was impossible and he hoped she was enjoying the intoxicating freedom of being almost one with the elements as much as he was.

They rode in comfortable seclusion, cocooned by the night. Declan tried to concentrate on keeping the bike riding smoothly along the highway, but the feel of her body pressed up against his kept distracting him. He cursed aloud when he hit another pothole.

Sighting a truck stop up ahead, he slowed the bike down and indicated to take the turn. A few minutes later, they cruised to a stop. Careful to keep the bike balanced, he held the machine upright while his passenger alighted.

Chloe fiddled with her chinstrap and tugged her helmet off. Declan removed his too and grinned at her.

"What do you think? Are you cut out to be a bikie moll?"

The lights from the truck stop illuminated the blush that stole into her cheeks. She gave him a wide grin.

"That was *fantastic!* I don't think I've ever been so scared and so exhilarated in all of my life. How come nobody ever told me how thrilling one of these can be?" she said, nodding toward the Ducati.

Declan's grin widened, his insides warming from her

enthusiasm. "I don't know. All I can say is, you've lived a sheltered life, Senior Investigator Sabattini."

Chloe nodded soberly, her eyes twinkling. "I think you might be right, Federal Agent Munro."

Although it wasn't that late, they were the only motorists outside the truck stop. Declan glanced through the brightly lit glass windows of the building and spied a bored attendant slouched behind the counter, his gaze fixed on something in his hand. Declan indicated the shop with his chin. "Do you want to grab a Coke or make a bathroom stop?"

"A Coke sounds good, thanks."

Dismounting from the bike, he wheeled it off to one side, out of the way of any other traffic and kicked the stand down.

"I'll be back in a minute," he said and walked toward the store. Moments later, he handed a cold can to Chloe. She cracked it open and took a long gulp.

"Ah, that tastes lovely."

"Doesn't it just?" he said. "And what about the night? Could it be any more mild? Perfect motorcycling weather." He winked at her. "Glad you came?"

Chloe tilted her head and peered up at the blanket of sparkling stars that surrounded them.

"It's so beautiful out here." She looked back at him, her expression turning serious. "I'm so glad I came. Thank you for asking me."

He grinned back at her. "Thank you for coming." His gaze locked with hers. Heat flooded to his groin and his heart rate picked up its pace in response. Chloe was the first to look away.

"The stars seem so close out here. Almost as if I could reach out and pluck one out of the sky."

Declan forced his lascivious thoughts aside and concentrated on her words. "Yeah, it's hard to believe it's the same sky we gaze at in the city. With all the buildings and lights and all the other man-made paraphernalia crowding Canberra, it's easy to forget all of this is up there."

"It is," Chloe agreed. "A chandelier of stars. It's nice to take time out every now and then and appreciate it." She took another mouthful of Coke. "How often do you take your bike out?"

"Not as often as I'd like. And not once since the charges were laid. My head's been too crowded with everything else going on. A bike like this requires concentration. I didn't want to risk an injury."

"Well, I'm honored to have been taken along."

Declan stepped closer and brushed a loose strand of hair off her face. "Just so you know, apart from my sister, you're the first girl I've ever doubled on it."

His hand cradled her cheek and his thumb stroked her smooth skin. Her eyes widened and her breath caught on a soft gasp. His chest tightened with emotion and his body hardened with anticipation. This time, he refused to be denied. Drawing her up against him, he kissed her.

His lips moved slowly at first, tasting the sweetness of the Coke on her lips. His tongue skimmed inside her mouth and delved deeper. She moaned against his lips and he tightened his hold on her, cursing the half empty can in his hand that restricted his ability to draw her closer.

She moved against him, and he felt her inhibitions dissolving. Her arms went around his neck and he luxuriated in the feeling of her breasts pressed against his chest. He deepened the kiss, knowing that this was madness, but unable to stop himself. He could hardly bend her over the back of his bike in the shadows of the truck stop, no matter how much he wanted to.

Ice-cold liquid ran down his neck and inside the collar of his T-shirt. He tensed and pulled slightly away. Another gush of liquid dampened his skin.

Chloe's arms fell away from around his neck. "Oh, my goodness, I'm so sorry. I've spilled my drink all over you."

Declan tugged at the wet fabric behind his head, the smile on his face belying his scowl.

Chloe covered her mouth with her hand in an attempt to stem her amusement, but Declan wasn't fooled. In a single stride, he closed the distance between them again and grabbed her around the waist, spinning her around until she had her back against his chest.

With his other hand, he upended the rest of his Coke down the front of her shirt. She squealed and tried to pull out of his hold, but he only grinned and tightened his grip.

Her T-shirt was soaked. Her nipples hardened from the contact. Blood rushed to his groin. He groaned under his breath and wondered what kind of hell he'd made for himself.

Loosening his hold, he tossed the empty can into a nearby trash can and then returned his attention to her. She was brushing ineffectually at the large brown stain that graced the front of her shirt.

She looked up at him and smiled. "I hope your sister doesn't ask you how her shirt got stained."

Desire pulsed heavily between his legs. His cock lay rock-hard against his jeans. They were miles from home and his comfortable bed, but try as he might, he couldn't get the image of her spread naked across his bike out of his head.

He stared at her, unable to hide the emotion that held him transfixed. "You're nipples are hard."

She sauntered toward him, desire flickering in her eyes. Reaching out, her fingers pressed against his jeans and tightened about his erection. Shock and desire ignited in his veins. He stood rooted to the spot.

"They're not the only thing that's hard," she murmured, giving him another squeeze.

Declan grabbed her hand and held it against his cock. He couldn't believe how brazen she was and from the look on her face, neither could she. Not that he was complaining. He couldn't get enough.

"I've been fantasizing about you bent over the Ducati naked, with my cock buried deep inside you."

She gasped and blushed, but she held his gaze and Declan's desire for her skyrocketed.

"I want to feel you inside me," she murmured, her gaze fixed on his chest. "I've never felt this way before. All hot and funny and...tingly. I want to touch myself, relieve the pressure down there and then I think about you and I want *you* to touch me there."

Declan was going to explode. No woman had ever made him feel so wanted. Sex had been something he'd enjoyed without much thought or effort. He'd never stopped to analyze how he felt about it or the women he'd been with. Even with his long-time ex-girlfriend, Alice, sex had been a mutually satisfying pastime that he'd never spent much time contemplating.

But with Chloe, it was different. He wanted to talk about everything that was happening to him, everything she made him feel and he wanted to know what was happening to her and what she was feeling. Listening to her halting admissions aroused him more than he could ever remember and he wanted more of it. Much more.

But not here. Not in the middle of a truck stop where anyone could pull in without a moment's notice. And not over the back of his bike, no matter how tempting. At least, not for their first time.

He wanted comfort and privacy and time to get to know every inch of her delectable body and even more delectable mind.

Yes, at thirty-four years of age, he'd had a sudden revelation. Sex was just as much about the mind as it was about the body, perhaps even more so. And it had taken Chloe for him to discover that.

A frown marred the smooth skin of her forehead and her eyes clouded with uncertainty. Realizing he hadn't responded to her admission, he cursed silently under his breath and drew her hard against him.

"You won't believe how much your words turn me on, sweetheart. I'm so hard for you, I feel like I'm going to come in my jeans. In fact, I'm not sure how the hell I'm going to climb back on that bike and ride all the way home. I'm going to break every speed limit and hope like hell the highway patrol are on their break because I'll be flouting the speed limits to get us home. When I get you back, I'm going to spend the rest of the night loving you like you deserve—on a mattress, with clean sheets, flowers, champagne."

She looked up and offered him a soft smile. "Flowers and champagne? Really?"

He smiled back down at her. "Okay, probably not flowers and champagne. I'm a little unprepared on that scale, but I can definitely offer you a cold beer and a super-firm bed."

Her smile widened. "Okay."

"Okay?"

"Yes."

"Because if you don't want to, that's all right. I mean, just because I said what I said, doesn't mean we have to—"

She placed a finger across his lips and they stilled. His gut clenched at the softness of her skin and he breathed in the heady scent of her.

"I want to. I think I've wanted to from the moment I saw you."

Hot need ricocheted through his veins. His cock throbbed painfully. He drew her hard against him and ground his hips against hers.

"Do you feel how much I want you?" he murmured.

She pressed even tighter against him and reached up to draw his head down to hers. Their lips met in a fiery kiss that he felt all the way to his balls.

Gasping for breath, he broke off the kiss and tried to regain some control.

"Whoa, sweetheart. Any more like that and we mightn't make it back to my apartment. Let's get going before I change my mind about doing it in this truck stop car park."

Chloe's arms fell away and he suddenly felt bereft. Stepping backwards, he waited for her to catch her breath then helped her with her helmet. Tugging his own in place, he secured it under his chin.

After making sure she was all set, he kicked up the stand and climbed astride the Ducati. Chloe hitched up her jeans and swung her leg over and within moments they were on the freeway headed for home.

The powerful motorbike ate up the miles and it seemed hardly any time at all before Declan pulled into his driveway and cut the engine. Chloe's belly somersaulted with nerves and excitement at the thought of what lay ahead.

Declan helped her off the bike and undid the chin strap on her helmet before lifting it off her head. Removing his, he hung both of them off one of the handlebars and wheeled the Ducati into the communal garage under the building.

Chloe followed him more slowly. Never before had she gone home with a man for the sole purpose of having sex. Both experiences she'd had in college had occurred in her room after she'd invited her dates in for a drink. She'd known then what was going to happen, of course, but she'd been barely out of her teens and the men hadn't been any older.

Now she was thirty. A grown woman, but not nearly as worldly as the average thirty-year-old. Most women her age would know exactly how to take the lead. Chloe didn't have a clue. She suddenly felt panicky and way out of her depth.

Declan must have seen something of her uncertainty. After putting his bike away, he came over to her and tilted her chin up to face him. His gaze roamed over her face, concern and tenderness in his expression.

"You're over-thinking it, Chloe. I can see it in your eyes. You want me; I want you. That's all there is to it."

He moved closer, so close she could see the green flecks in his brown eyes. "There's nothing wrong with what we're doing. Okay, so we met in less-than-ideal circumstances. That matter will very shortly be resolved. It doesn't matter. It doesn't change us. We're two consenting adults who find each other attractive." He closed the distance between them and pressed a lingering kiss on her lips. "Very, very attractive," he whispered, his voice husky and low.

She bit her lip in indecision. He smiled at her with a look on his face that was so damned sexy that she melted inside.

He cocked a single, brown eyebrow. "Yes?"

Heat warmed her all the way through and left her tingling. A need so strong almost took her breath away. "Yes," she whispered.

His eyes darkened with emotion. His lips claimed hers in another fiery kiss that she felt all the way down to her toes. Her heart pounded. She pulled away with a gasp.

"Declan, I-I... Please, slow down. It's...like I told you before... I'm not very experienced at this kind of thing."

"Going home with a man or having sex?" he teased.

"B-both," she stammered, silently cursing the heat that exploded in her cheeks.

His face sobered and he cupped her cheeks in his hands and held her face still. Chloe had no choice but to look at him.

"Like I told *you* before, I want you. I don't care that you're not experienced. Only a fool of a man would. I love that you haven't chosen your bed partners indiscriminately. There's not a lot of that out there anymore, on either side. It's refreshing." He pulled her hard against him and pressed his erection into the softness of her belly. "It's a turn-on. Feel how much it turns me on."

Chloe's limbs liquefied with desire. Heat stirred deep down in her core and she moved against him. He groaned and another thrill went through her. That she could bring a man like him to that point of need made her feel invincible.

She reached up and pulled his mouth down to hers. His lips moved across hers with increasing need. She opened her mouth and gasped when his tongue swept inside and tangled with her own. Her hands buried themselves into the thickness of his hair. She returned his kiss with a passion that stunned her.

In one swift movement, he bent and lifted her into his arms and headed for the elevator. Sliding her down the length of his body, he held her close against him, their fingers entwined, while they waited.

Within minutes, he'd shouldered open the door to his apartment and was tugging her inside. She'd barely cleared the doorway when he drew her close once again and kissed her.

Chloe's heart pounded in her ears. She slid her hands across the soft fabric of his T-shirt, loving the feel of the hard wall of muscle beneath her fingers. She found the taut peak of his nipples and teased them with her fingernails.

Declan sucked in his breath and she smiled, loving the sense of power that surged through her.

His hands reached down to cup her backside and he molded her against him. She threaded her hands through his hair and held on, wanting the moment to last forever.

"I want you naked," he murmured against her mouth.

She tensed in sudden nervousness, but he was having none of it. Tugging her still-damp T-shirt out of her jeans, he lifted it over her head and dropped it to the floor. Her bra quickly followed. His hands stilled. He stared at her.

"You're beautiful," he whispered. "Just as I knew you would be." He reached out and cupped her breasts and rubbed the pad of his thumb across her nipple.

She gasped. Desire surged through her and pooled into moist heat deep inside her. His thumbs rasped over her tender flesh again and she clutched at his arms in an effort to steady herself.

Declan growled low in his throat. Taking her by the hand, he led her down the darkened hall and into the bedroom at the far end.

He let go of her hand and moved to switch on a lamp that stood on the nightstand. A king-sized bed made of some dark kind of wood took up most of the room. It was neatly made and the room was tidy, with not even a shirt or stray sock visible.

Declan tugged off his T-shirt and tossed it into a laundry hamper that stood inside the door of the ensuite. Taking a seat on the end of the bed, he pulled off his boots and dropped them on the floor and then made short work of his jeans. They, too, made it into the hamper.

He strode toward her, dressed only in a pair of boxer

shorts. Chloe glimpsed his erection straining against the cloth and averted her gaze.

"Look at me, Chloe. I want you to look at me."

The request was softly issued. She drew in a deep breath and grabbed hold of her courage. Her gaze met his. The nervousness and tension left her body when she recognized the need in his eyes.

Her gaze dropped lower, skimming over the impressive breadth of his well-muscled chest before pausing at the waistband of his underwear. Her mouth went dry at the thought of touching him again.

As if he could read her mind, he moved forward and took her hand and pressed it against his hardness. Her heart thumped at the magnificent feel of him beneath the silk of his boxers. She ran her hand up and down the length of him and was rewarded by another low growl.

"Feel how much I need you, Chloe. God, I can't wait to be inside you."

His words sent a surge of heat to the heart of her core and her clit tingled. She squeezed her legs together against the rush of feeling and tightened her hold on his cock.

"Oh, God, sweetheart, you don't know how good that feels. Touch me like that again."

Emboldened, Chloe did as he asked, desire building within her. Declan reached out and undid the button of her borrowed jeans and slid the zipper down. She let him tug her toward the bed.

A gentle push on her shoulder and she sat down. Kneeling at her feet, he pulled off her boots and threw them toward his. Still on his knees, he moved between her legs and inched her jeans down her hips. When his gaze fastened on her white lace panties, nerves once again warred with desire in her belly.

"I want to touch you," he murmured, sliding his fingers inside the satin of her underwear. His questing fingers skimmed over her clit and she jumped.

"It's okay, sweetheart," he murmured. "Let me love you."

His fingers moved lower and swept across her dampened

flesh. She moaned against the torment and moved restlessly against his hand.

"Easy, sweetheart. Easy."

He slid her underwear down her hips and it too went the way of her jeans. He feasted his eyes upon her and Chloe was glad for the dim lighting. With his hands on her thighs, he drew her closer toward him. When his tongue touched her tender flesh, Chloe almost came off the bed.

"Declan!" she gasped. "That feels…"

"Incredible?" he murmured, parting her lips with his tongue.

Chloe's hands clenched into fists against the indescribable pleasure. "No one's ever done that before," she whispered.

He looked at her in surprise and smiled. "Then you're in for a treat. Hold on tight."

With that, he buried his face between her legs and laved her with his tongue. Chloe clutched at his hair and marveled at the feelings deep inside her. The pleasure of his loving was almost painful as need built within her—need that only he could assuage.

Her legs moved restlessly under his ministrations and she thought she would die from the pleasure of it. He murmured sweet words of encouragement and Chloe found herself setting aside her shyness and embracing the feel of his magical tongue.

The desire inside her reached a fever pitch. She moaned and moved against him and searched for release.

"That's it, sweetheart. Let go. Come for me, Chloe. Come for me."

His gentle encouragement was the final straw. With a gasp, she climaxed. The tremors of it lasted long after he rose from the floor and joined her on the bed.

"That was…unbelievable," she said, reaching up to stroke his stubble-roughened face.

He stared down at her, his eyes forest dark with emotion. "*You* were unbelievable."

Chloe's shyness returned. She flushed and looked away.

"You're adorable, do you know that? You've just allowed yourself to have the most amazing orgasm and now you feel embarrassed about it? You have a beautiful body, Chloe. A body built for loving. Don't be ashamed of your feelings. Don't be ashamed of letting your body feel loved."

Chloe took a deep breath and looked back at him. "Okay." She ran her hand over his shadowed jaw. "You make me feel beautiful." Reaching up, she brought his head down to hers and kissed him.

He pulled her close, pressing himself against her. His erection prodded her stomach and she reached down between them and encircled his hardness with her fingers.

"It's your turn, now," she whispered.

"*Mm*, I was hoping you'd say that." Flipping her over, he stretched out above her, holding his weight on his elbows. Chloe reached for his boxers and within seconds he lay naked beside her.

Gathering her close, he kissed her mouth and then slid his lips over her neck, nuzzling the tender spot beneath her ear. She wrapped her arms around his shoulders and held him close against her, loving the feeling of the hardness of his body pressing into hers.

He found her lips again and deepened the kiss while his knee pushed aside her legs until she lay open beneath him.

"I need to be inside you. God, I want you so much."

Desire rekindled in Chloe's belly and she moved restlessly beneath him.

"I want you, too."

Needing no further encouragement, Declan reached across to the nightstand and pulled out a condom. Swiftly sheathing his cock, he reared up above her. The strain on his face, visible in the dim light, showed her how much he wanted her.

Chloe opened her legs wide and encouraged him to enter her. His cock prodded at her entrance, slick from her earlier orgasm. He moved slowly, inching into her until, with one smooth stroke, he surged inside, filling and stretching her like no other had. She gasped and held on tightly as he began to stroke.

Feeling awkward, she tried to match his rhythm. With gentle hands, he gripped her around the hips and guided her until they moved as one.

"Oh, Christ, Chloe. You feel so good. You're so tight, so wet, so hot."

His pace increased. She clung to his shoulders. The tension in her body tightened, became excruciating until she toppled over the edge in another mind-blowing orgasm.

Seconds later, Declan groaned and drove himself hard inside her. His body stilled for a second or two before he collapsed on top of her, spent. Breathing hard, he lifted his weight and grinned down at her.

"Not bad for the first time. The best thing is, we have all night to perfect it."

Heat flooded Chloe's cheeks, but she couldn't help but return his grin. "I don't know about that. I think that effort's going to be pretty hard to top."

"Yes, you're right. I'm certainly not complaining. But think of the fun we're going to have trying."

Chloe stifled a yawn and then flushed with embarrassment. Declan shot her a playful look.

"Great. Just great. I mention an all-night sex-a-thon and my girlfriend starts to snore. Talk about a blow to the ego."

Chloe grinned, but refused to apologize. She'd had a long day and it was getting late. Besides, she'd never felt so relaxed and sated in her life. And had he really called her his *girlfriend*?

Turning on his side, Declan drew her up against him and pressed a kiss against her hair. Chloe snuggled in close and laid her head on his chest.

"*Mm*, this feels so nice," she whispered.

His arm tightened around her. "You bet it does."

CHAPTER 22

The sun glinted through the undrawn blinds and bounced off the pillow, registering on Chloe's drowsy senses. She opened her eyes and squinted against the light, her gaze drifting around the unfamiliar room. Declan was asleep beside her and as she studied him, memories of their night together returned in force.

She didn't know what time it had been when they'd eventually fallen asleep curled around each other, exhausted and replete, but her eyes felt gritty and she groaned inwardly at the thought of facing the day.

She looked across at Declan. He'd kicked off the sheet and lay naked and exposed before her wandering gaze. Even relaxed in sleep, he was incredibly good-looking. Unable to resist, she inched closer and ran her palm across the smooth expanse of his chest, her nails grazing his nipple.

A single, greenish-brown eye opened. An instant later, he grabbed her hand and flipped her onto her back, straddling her hips.

"Is that your way of asking me to perform my manly duties?"

She met his gaze and nodded, a smile tilting the edges of her mouth. "Maybe, but first, I really need to use the bathroom." Ducking her head, she dragged the sheet around her and padded into the small room adjacent to the bedroom.

As she lay down on the bed a few minutes later he leaned over and pressed his lips against hers.

"You'd have thought after our marathon session last night, I'd be satisfied, but one look at you all naked and sexy in my bed and I'm desperate to have you again."

His husky admission sent a shaft of desire straight to her core. She reached up and kissed him again. He adjusted his legs until he lay flat against her, his burgeoning cock pressing against the juncture of her thighs. His head dipped and he tongued her nipples, sucking them into taut peaks.

Chloe moaned under the delicious torture, but she was having none of it. She moved out from under him. He stared at her, one eyebrow cocked, silently questioning her intentions.

"My turn," she murmured. Pushing him back down onto the bed, she straddled his hips and began her mission to drive him crazy.

Leaning over him, as he'd done to her only moments before, she found his small flat nipples amongst the light scattering of brown hair and tweaked them with her fingers.

He sucked in his breath. "*Mm*, that feels good."

"What about this?" She alternated her fingers with her mouth and nipped and tugged at the hard nubs.

Declan moaned louder, wordlessly encouraging her to continue. Moving lower, Chloe kissed her way to his navel, pausing to flick her tongue inside the slight indentation before continuing lower.

His cock stood thick and hard amongst the cluster of dark tight curls between his thighs. She encircled his length with her hand and squeezed him with her fingers.

"Ah, Christ, sweetheart. That feels so good."

Emboldened by his enjoyment, she swiped her tongue around the head of his cock before taking him into her mouth. Inch by inch, she took him in as far as she could, sucking and squeezing him with her fingers and her lips.

"*Mm*, yes. That's it, sweetheart. Don't stop."

Despite her lack of experience, Chloe went with her instincts, encouraged by Declan's moans and mumbled assurances that what she was doing felt good.

Lifting her mouth from his cock, she moved even lower. Cradling the heavy weight of his balls in the palm of her hand, she teased them with the tip of her tongue, swirling through the soft hair that covered them.

Declan groaned louder and lifted his hips off the sheet. "Christ, I can't take any more. I need to fuck you."

Chloe loved the urgency in his voice. It made her feel powerful, confident in her ability to arouse him. Sliding up over his body, she once again straddled his hips.

He twisted beneath her and reached for a condom and then handed it to her. She blushed and took it from his fingers. Frowning in concentration, she worked it over his erection, feeling triumphant at her success.

Positioning herself over his straining cock, she pressed her wetness over his tip, teasing him with slow, sensual movements of her hips.

"Christ, Chloe. Fuck me," he groaned hoarsely.

Without warning, she sat down hard on his thighs. They gasped in unison and Chloe couldn't help but think how good it felt to have him deep inside her again.

Moving slowly, she set the pace of their lovemaking. Leaning over him, she laced her fingers through his and stared into his eyes. They were wild with desire.

The pressure low in her belly grew. She picked up the pace and slid up and down on his cock with increasing frenzy. Moments later, she reached her peak. The waves of her release washed over her. Her inner muscles contracted. She leaned forward and squeezed Declan's hands, crying out in relief.

An instant later, he wrenched his hands free and grasped her hips, holding her still while he plunged into her again and again. With a hoarse cry, he tensed and emptied himself inside her.

It was long moments later before either of them was able to speak. Declan broke the silence.

"You're unbelievable."

Chloe turned in his arms and smiled. "I'm glad you think so."

He put his arms around her and squeezed her hard. "Oh, I don't think so, I *know* so. If I'd been any more turned on, my balls would have exploded."

Chloe ducked her head but couldn't help the grin. "You didn't do too badly yourself. You might not believe this, but last night was the first time I'd had an orgasm."

Declan's eyebrow rose in surprise. "Wow. I can't believe I'm the first to make you come. What the hell was wrong with those other blokes? You're a natural."

Chloe did her best to retain eye contact, but it was difficult with her face burning hotter than a summer bushfire.

"There were only two, remember? Not exactly a football team and we were teenagers."

Declan pulled her closer and growled in her ear. "And I'm jealous of even those two. I want to be the only one who gets to watch you orgasm. Agreed?"

Chloe stared at him, her smile evaporating. "What are you saying?"

Declan's eyes darkened and his expression sobered. "I really like you, Chloe. I know we met in...unusual circumstances, but I don't care about any of that. I want us to get to know each other, go out and date like normal people. What do you think?"

All of a sudden he sounded very uncertain. His gaze lowered, but not before she caught the vulnerability that shadowed his eyes. Her heart tripped over. She reached out and cupped his cheek in her hand, forcing him to look at her.

"I'd love to."

A torrent of emotion filled his eyes. "Really?"

She nodded and smiled. "Yes, really."

Declan pulled her close and kissed her softly on the mouth. Chloe reveled in his tender display. A shaft of sunlight landed on his head, burnishing the brown streaks in gold.

"What time is it?" she asked.

"Nearly seven."

"I'm going to have to go. They're putting together a

team to arrest my uncle this morning. I-I wanted to go and see him beforehand."

Declan frowned. "Why?"

Chloe struggled to make him understand. "It's not what you think. I'm not going to warn him, although I assume Stanford's already called him. I just want to...you know, ask him *why?*" Her voice cracked on the last word and she turned away so that he didn't see her tears.

"Tell me about him."

She closed her eyes against another surge of emotion and compressed her lips. Taking a deep breath, she began to speak.

"Forty-eight hours ago, I would have told you that, apart from my father, he was the man I most admired. He's strong, intelligent, funny, loyal. He's all the things I look for in a man. He's my number one support and has always been there for me."

"Christ," Declan muttered. "This must be devastating for you."

Her breath hitched. "He's been married for more than forty years. Okay, it took a long time for my cousin to come along—twenty years, in fact, but none of us thought anything of that. We all sympathized with their plight and prayed that somehow, some way they would experience the joy of having a child. It was all that my aunt wanted."

"Your aunt's obviously younger than your uncle?"

"Yes, she was twenty when they were married. He was twenty-seven. When she turned forty, they'd just about given up hope of having the much-longed-for child. We were all shocked when they announced she was pregnant." Chloe shook her head in disbelief. "All along, the family assumed it was my aunt who had the fertility problem. Now I can't help but wonder if it had more to do with my uncle."

"Who knows? At the end of the day, it probably doesn't matter. I wonder if your aunt is aware of his double life?"

Dread settled like concrete in the pit of Chloe's belly.

Her aunt... Did she know?

She tightened the sheet around her. She could hardly ask

her parents. She couldn't believe either of them knew the truth, yet something that big couldn't have been concealed from her family for so many years. *Could it?*

One of the often annoying things about a good Italian family was the lack of privacy. There was no such thing as minding your own business. If you had a problem, everyone from Great Aunt Marietta to the second cousin's three-year-old knew about it and that's just how it was. She had to believe her much-loved and well-respected uncle had hidden this shocking secret very well, or everyone would have known about it.

She was certain that no one in her family knew Ronald Sabattini was gay—or bisexual. She shook her head. She didn't even want to think about that.

Another thought struck her and she flinched in horror. Could *she* have also been a pawn in her uncle's quest to destroy Declan? As a close relative, Ronald Sabattini knew her better than most.

He would have known her senior position within IA would increase the chances of the investigation coming across her desk. He would have known if she believed a crime had been committed, she would prosecute to the full extent of the law. He would also have been comfortable that, in the event suspicion fell upon him, she would be the last person to give credence to the idea.

Had she also been part of his evil plan? The thought made her ill.

"Talk to me, sweetheart."

Declan's gentle request roused her from her dark thoughts. Keeping the sheet around her, she wriggled to the top of the bed and joined him with her back against the headboard.

"I have to confront my uncle and get some answers."

Declan pulled away from her, his expression reflecting his concern. "I'm not sure that's a good idea, Chloe. Surely you should let someone else in your office deal with this? No one knows how your uncle will react. It could be dangerous."

Chloe shook her head, refusing to believe her uncle

would hurt her. "He's not going to do anything like that. I'm not sure how he's going to react... Maybe shocked that his secret's been discovered and anxious that his role in why you were arrested has come to light—both of those things, I expect—but he's my uncle and he loves me. He'd never do anything to hurt me."

Declan looked unconvinced. "Be that as it may, you shouldn't be the one to speak with him. Or at the very least, you shouldn't be going alone. We have to assume Charlie's spoken to him since yesterday. Your uncle will know the net's closing in on him." His expression turned grim. "I'm coming with you."

Chloe opened her mouth to protest, but he cut her off. "This isn't up for negotiation, Chloe. Relative or not, the man's proven he's totally without scruples and he has to be feeling desperate. I'm not going to have you risk your safety when you don't know what he's going to do. We have no idea what he's truly capable of."

She stared at him. All the reasons why there was no need for him to accompany her ran through her head. Instead, she found herself nodding.

"All right."

Relief flooded his face. "Thank you."

"But we'll travel separately and you'll wait outside. You won't have clearance to get into Parliament House. It will be easier this way."

Declan nodded his consent. "Okay, but if he threatens you, if he even raises his voice to you, you get the hell out of there and call me. We'll set up your phone to dial me with the push of a button. I'll be right outside the building. Got it?"

"Got it."

"Good." Declan glanced at the clock. "What time does he normally get to his office?"

"Around eight. He likes to get in early."

Declan climbed out of bed, oblivious to his nakedness. "We'd better get moving then."

Chloe averted her gaze, unused to having a naked man

parade around in front of her. When he walked into the ensuite, she sighed quietly in relief. Moments later, she heard the sound of running water.

Scooting across the bed, she picked up the sheet and wrapped it around her. Slipping out of the room, she collected the clothes she'd arrived in from the spare bedroom and headed back to Declan's room. The sound of running water stopped. Declan filled the bathroom doorway, a towel wrapped around his waist and another one in his hand. He scrubbed at his hair.

Eyeing her and the sheet she held tightly around her, he grinned, a knowing glint in his eye. "Shower's free."

She refrained from commenting. Nodding her thanks, she slipped past him.

———————————

Declan barely had a chance to pull on his jeans when there was a loud knock at the front door.

"Declan, if you're in there, you'd better open up this instant. You're worrying the shit out of all of us. We've been calling you since last night. Mom's beside herself with worry. Christ, if you've gone and done something stupid, I'll never forgive you." Another loud thump sounded against the door.

Declan pulled on a clean T-shirt just as Chloe appeared in the doorway of the ensuite, wrapped only in a towel.

"What's all that noise?"

"It's Clayton. He's outside."

Chloe blushed. "What's he going to say when he finds me here?"

Declan grinned, delighted at her bashfulness. "If you hurry up and throw some clothes on, he doesn't actually have to find you *here*." He looked meaningfully at the rumpled bed. "I mean, we can kind of ease him into the idea of us being together. Clayton might be three years younger than me, but he's way more conservative. We don't have to hit him over the head with it."

She grabbed a pillow and threw it at him. "*I'll* hit you over the head in a minute." With that, she turned on her heel and headed back into the bathroom.

Declan chuckled and hurried down the hall, knowing Clayton wouldn't give up until he'd broken the door down. When another bang sounded, he called out to his brother.

"Clayton, it's okay. I'm here. Hang on a minute and I'll let you in." Smoothing down his hair with his fingers, he reached for the doorknob.

Clayton's worried frown warmed him all the way through. "Hey, there little brother," Declan said, grinning. "What are you up to?"

Clayton pushed passed him, his scowl deepening. "Don't play all innocent with me. Why haven't you answered your phone? I tried half the night to get through to you. I even came by here twice and I called you again this morning. Where the hell have you been? We've been worried as shit. Mom was about to start calling hospitals."

Declan sobered and considered what conclusions his family must have drawn when he couldn't be reached. When they'd left his place yesterday afternoon, he'd been down on everything. He'd asked them to leave so that he could have some time alone. He could only imagine what they'd thought when they couldn't contact him today.

"I'm sorry, Clay. I didn't think. Chloe came over last night and we spent some time talking about the case. There's been a breakthrough—"

Clayton's gaze moved beyond Declan's shoulder, his eyes widening in surprise. Declan turned and spied Chloe behind him, now dressed in the clothes she'd worn to his apartment the night before. He reached out and drew her close. Clayton started coughing.

Declan stepped forward and thumped him on the back. "Are you all right, mate?"

Clayton shook his head and fought to catch his breath. "Yeah, sure," he wheezed. "I'm just a little...surprised."

"I told you Chloe was helping me."

"Yes, you did. I didn't realize you meant..." Clayton flushed and averted his gaze.

Declan laughed at his brother's discomfort, but then took pity on him, after catching sight of the color that also bloomed in Chloe's cheeks.

"I'm sorry, Clay. I should have explained. Last night, Chloe and I realized how much we've come to care for each other. It sounds corny, but it's true. Right, sweetheart?"

He turned to her and squeezed her hip. Chloe's face turned crimson. She glared at him. He could almost read her thoughts: *I thought you said you were going to ease him into it?*

Anger suffused Clayton's cheeks. "I'm sorry, Chloe. Excuse me for a minute." He rounded on Declan. "What the fuck are you doing? Are you out of your mind? She's the senior investigator, instrumental to your case. Have you forgotten that? Do you know how much this could jeopardize your trial?"

Declan narrowed his eyes and did his best to control his temper. "Don't talk like she's not here, Clay. She's on my side, now."

Clayton shook his head in disbelief. "What the hell are you talking about? How can she be on your side? She's the reason you're in this mess!"

Declan forced himself to remain calm. He could understand his brother's confusion, even his anger.

"You're not listening, Clay. We've had a breakthrough. We know who set me up."

Clayton's jaw dropped. "You've found out who's behind it? Tell me! I want to know the name of the bastard."

Declan nodded grimly. "I'll fill you in on everything, just as soon as I've had some caffeine. He headed toward the kitchen. "Anyone for coffee?" He switched on the state-of-the-art coffee machine that sat on the kitchen counter.

"*Coffee?*" Clayton strode around the countertop and pulled up only a few feet from Declan. "How the hell can you think about coffee after dropping that bombshell? When the family left here yesterday, you were still talking about confronting Stanford. Is that the breakthrough you're talking about, or did something else happen?"

Declan stopped what he was doing and turned to face his brother. He glanced at Chloe. She met his gaze and then nodded.

"It's a long story, Clay and one I can't do without at least one cup of caffeine in my veins. I promise we'll tell you everything, but first, I need coffee." He looked back to Chloe and lifted an eyebrow. "Coffee?"

She sent him a look of gratitude and nodded. After setting out two mugs, he was about to add sugar, but pulled up short. He didn't have a clue how she drank her coffee. He'd touched every inch of her body, but still didn't know if she liked it black or white, cream, sugar or none of those.

His hand froze. "Black, no sugar," she murmured, sidling up to him. He breathed a sigh of relief and flashed a smile.

"Same as me."

She lifted an eyebrow in pleased surprise. "That makes it easy."

Handing her one of the mugs, he picked up the other one and turned to face Clayton. "You sure I can't get you one?"

"No, thanks. I just want to hear what's happened that's made you so different from the beaten man we left yesterday."

Taking a sip out of his cup, Declan guided Chloe out of the kitchen and into the living room. Seating himself beside her on the sofa, he waited while Clayton took a seat in the armchair opposite.

"It's hard to know where to start," he began. "The short version is Charlie used my login details to create the computer trail which led to the illegal access of the files. He got access through a clerk in the Minister's Office. He also left the images on my laptop."

"Christ, that's fantastic! What about the long version?" Clayton asked, undeterred.

Declan turned to Chloe. Her eyes darkened with sad shadows, but she drew in a deep breath and nodded.

"I think Chloe should tell you that one. Is that all right with you, sweetheart?"

"Yes," she replied, her voice husky with emotion. She cleared her throat. "I'll do it."

Declan took her hand in his and squeezed it. In halting sentences that gradually grew more confident, Chloe recounted the events leading up to the discovery of her uncle's involvement.

Clayton moved through various levels of shock and disbelief to outrage and finally, to a grim kind of acceptance.

"What happens now?" he said, directing the question to Chloe. "I assume you've spoken to your boss?"

"Yes, of course. He's putting together a taskforce as we speak. They…they expect to arrest my uncle this morning."

Declan squeezed her hand again, offering silent reassurance. Chloe turned to look at him. Tears glistened in her eyes. Declan pulled her into his arms and kissed her.

When he let her go, her face was aflame, but her embarrassment only endeared her to him even more.

His brother cleared his throat. Declan looked across at him and shrugged, grinning cheekily. Clayton stood and wiped his hands on his pants.

"I still don't understand why you didn't answer when I knocked last night? There were lights on in your apartment. You must have been home."

Declan ducked his head. "Yeah, we…ah… We went for a ride."

Clayton looked from Declan to Chloe and back again. "I see. And this morning?"

"I…ah… I switched my phone off last night. I forgot to switch it back on again this morning."

Clayton nodded and pursed his lips. "The only reason I ask is because Mom was on the verge of hysteria when I couldn't get a hold of you."

Declan had the grace to feel embarrassed. "Yeah, I'm sorry about that. Please give my apologies to Mom and Dad. I didn't even consider that they might be worried about me."

"Yeah, well they'll be thrilled to hear this nightmare's almost over."

Declan nodded as relief surged through him. Finally, the burden that had hung over him for more than eight weeks would be lifted. Charlie and the Minister would be arrested. The charges against Declan would be dropped. He could put it all behind him and resurrect his life.

That couldn't come soon enough.

CHAPTER 23

Ronald Sabattini took a sip of coffee and sighed in contentment. He always loved this time of day, before the noise and hubbub of the office found its stride. As far as he knew, he was the only one there and that suited him just fine. It was barely seven-thirty. He had plenty of time to enjoy his solitude before the administration staff arrived.

He drew the pile of papers that awaited his attention toward him and signed them with a flourish of his gold embossed pen. The pen had been a gift from a former staffer, a young man he'd always remember with fondness. It was too bad the boy's weakness for party drugs had brought their promising relationship to a premature end.

Drugs had given the boy a loose tongue and the Minister couldn't afford a scandal. It was one of the things he'd promised his wife. Without her support, his life could never have continued the way it had for more than forty years. Even the thought of it coming to an end was unbearable.

For almost his entire marriage, he'd lived a glorious double life. He had the best of both worlds. With a young and beautiful wife by his side, the opportunities to see and be seen were endless. Invitations to one social event after another crowded their letterbox. He'd rubbed shoulders with the mega rich and powerful members of Sydney society and his desire to be a formidable presence in politics had been fulfilled beyond his wildest imaginings.

The very same beautiful wife, with only a little persuasion, had also been willing to give him the freedom to fulfil every fantasy he'd ever had in the bedroom with an almost endless stream of fit, young men who were easy pickings within his domain. She willingly, if not always happily, turned a blind eye to his proclivities.

He'd known from the time he was a teenager that he was gay, but coming out in the sixties to his devout Catholic family wasn't an option. Instead, he'd been forced to enjoy illicit liaisons with teachers and fellow students and later, with some of his university professors under the cover of darkness with some flimsy pretext or other placing him within their very close proximity.

Even now, the memory of those secret liaisons made him hard. One professor, in particular, had made a lasting impression. Professor Greene, a man well into his fifties at the time, had introduced him to bondage and sadomasochism. The kiss of the whip across his bare ass still sent him into ecstasy.

It was too bad the man had died prematurely from a heart attack whilst at home one evening with his wife. It had left Ronald bereft and reliant only upon his imagination to finish the education the professor had so adeptly started.

Over the ensuing years, he'd found plenty of willing participants who allowed him to experiment and refine his craft. The pleasure had been willingly and graciously shared and had heightened the experiences for both him and his partner. Being appointed Minister for Home Affairs had been like a sign from above. All of a sudden, he had thousands of men—many not long out of high school—at his beck and call.

It wasn't long into his first term that he instigated a biannual tradition of hosting an elaborate welcome party for the new intake of AFP recruits. It was held under the guise of a charity event and was a perfect opportunity to troll for new partners. In his experience, the fresher the recruit, the more eager they were to please. He looked for men with determination in their gaze—ambitious men who wanted to go far. Men like Declan Munro.

At the thought of his nemesis, he cursed viciously. The welcome party had fast become his favorite hunting ground. The attendees were buffed and shiny and eager to please and most were more than a little awed to be spending a few moments in the company of their new boss. Despite his pleasant liaison with Eric, he was always on the lookout for a new diversion. It still left a sour taste in his mouth when he thought of how the last party had ended in his humiliation.

The phone near his elbow rang, interrupting his reverie. He reached for it and answered with his customary brusqueness.

"Yes?"

"Sh-she knows."

Ronald frowned at Chip's words and the fear that punctuated them. "What do you mean, *she* knows?" he replied, his voice sharp.

"The IA investigator. She knows. She knows everything. Why the hell didn't you tell me she was your fucking *niece?*"

Even though a feeling of dread unfurled in his gut, Ronald kept his tone neutral. "When did you speak with her?"

"Y-yesterday."

"*Yesterday?* Why didn't you call me?"

"It was late. Y-you'd already left the office. You've told me over and over never to call you at home."

Ronald bit back a savage curse and tried to get his burgeoning panic under control. "What did you tell her?"

Chip's voice turned whiny. "I didn't tell her anything. She'd already figured it all out."

"She knows about *us?*"

"Yes."

He sucked in a breath. "About Munro?"

"Yes."

"Eric?"

"Eric? What's Eric got to do with this? You're as bad as she is, going on about Eric all the time. Please, please don't tell me you're fucking him too..."

Ronald closed his eyes, his mind in chaos. He should have

cut Chip loose, like he'd planned. His carefully crafted world was about to come crashing down around him. One whisper would be enough to ruin him. He'd be worse than dead. He couldn't bear the thought.

An image of his niece materialized before him. Beautiful, smart and so hell-bent on the search for truth and justice, she'd never rest until she saw the wrong righted.

It was the reason he'd made sure she copped the Munro case. Her tenacity, dedication, determination and loyalty were all the qualities he'd relied upon. It was the way she was.

Now she knew the truth, she'd never let it go until she'd seen it through. He knew it as surely as he knew he couldn't let her do it. It was as simple as that. He only prayed she hadn't yet shared her suspicions with her superiors.

Chip had said he'd met with her late. It was possible she hadn't yet met with her boss. Ronald's only chance was to move fast.

He drew in a deep breath and held it until his lungs burned. The sensation cleared his head. At peace with his decision, he spoke again.

"Okay, Chip. Listen and listen well. I'm only going to tell you this once. This is what you're going to do."

CHAPTER 24

Clayton shook Declan's hand and turned to hug Chloe good-bye. She could tell from the warmth in his embrace that he'd made the adjustment regarding her status with his brother and accepted that she was now on their side. After closing the door behind Clayton, she turned to Declan.

"We have to go."

"Yeah, you're right."

Chloe hurried to collect her briefcase and Declan found his bike keys. Within minutes, they'd left his apartment. As agreed, Chloe drove her Honda and Declan climbed astride the Ducati. Together, they headed toward Parliament House.

The sun had begun its ascent. It was a little after eight. She couldn't be sure her uncle was in his office, but he'd always been an early riser and she wanted to keep the element of surprise on her side. She didn't want him to have time to think about his answers. She hoped he'd make the decision to tell her the truth...this time.

She sighed. There was nothing for it but to take a punt and hope for the best. It was all she could do.

At least she knew the IA Taskforce hadn't arrested him, yet. Webber had phoned a few minutes earlier and told her they'd run into a stumbling block: The Attorney General had been contacted and advised of the situation. He, in turn, had spoken to the Prime Minister.

Forward progress had been put on hold until a full briefing occurred.

Webber went onto explain that the Prime Minister was attending a high-level trade meeting that wasn't expected to finish until five, and no one expected an arrest to be made until sometime that evening.

The thought of how the day would unravel sent shards of nervousness arcing through her. Her heart thumped double time and anxiety tightened her throat. She still hadn't worked out what she was going to say.

She glanced in her rearview mirror and spied Declan on his bike about three car lengths behind her. His presence reassured her. For all her protestations that she was safe in her uncle's company, she was relieved Declan would be close by.

Drawing in a deep, fortifying breath, she steeled her nerves against the forthcoming confrontation. The impressive grandeur of Parliament House loomed ahead of her. As it had the during her previous visit two days earlier, the bright, morning sun glinted off the towering steel structure that started at the roofline and reached for the sky.

In less than ten minutes, and much too soon for her liking, she found herself slowing for the security guards who were perched inside a booth at the entrance to Parliament House and the underground car park. Another quick glance through her rearview mirror confirmed Declan had turned off in the direction of the public car park a short distance away. Chloe was confident he would do as he'd promised and if she needed him, all she would have to do was call.

Coming to a stop beside the security booth, she pressed the button on her armrest and lowered the window. She had her security pass at the ready. Recognizing her as the Minister's niece, the guard glanced cursorily at her credentials and waved her through.

With the working day not yet in full swing, finding a parking space inside the lot wasn't difficult. Within minutes, she located an empty spot a short distance from the bank of elevators.

She walked toward them and wiped sweaty palms on her skirt. Her nerves hadn't diminished over the course of her commute. If anything, they'd escalated. She swallowed in an effort to alleviate the dryness in her throat and prayed the meeting wouldn't be too traumatic. For either of them.

It wouldn't be easy for someone like her uncle to realize his secret had been discovered: a secret he'd kept hidden for more decades than she cared to consider.

The elevator arrived and the doors slid open without a sound. Stepping inside the plush glass-and-aluminium space, she hit the number of her uncle's floor and counted down the seconds to his floor.

All too soon, the elevator chimed and the doors slid open. Her belly took a somersault. Taking a big breath and squaring her shoulders, she marched down the corridor toward the Minister's Office before her courage could give out.

To say that her uncle was surprised to see her was an understatement, but he greeted her with his usual wide smile and effusive hug.

"Princess, fancy finding you in my neck of the woods. That's twice in one week! How lucky am I?"

Chloe looked around the well-appointed room. "Hello, Uncle Ronnie. We... We need to talk."

He frowned, but his expression remained unconcerned. "Of course. I've told you my door's always open."

Now that the moment was upon her, Chloe searched desperately for the right words. Despite the warm day unfolding outside, heavy damask curtains were drawn against the light, throwing the room into deep shadows. An antique lamp on the corner of her uncle's massive wooden desk shone a circle of feeble light around the office.

"Don't you want to open the curtains, Uncle? It's kind of dark in here."

"I don't mind the dark. I can think better that way."

Chloe's gaze was drawn to a familiar photograph of her aunt and her cousin that sat in its usual spot near her uncle's computer. Beside the picture was a black leather riding crop.

Her stomach somersaulted. Recognition and revulsion rushed through her, leaving her faint. Her uncle hurried to her side, concern clouding his eyes.

"Chloe, are you all right? You've gone pale. Here, take a seat. I'll fetch you a glass of water."

Before she could protest, he left the room. Chloe collapsed into the richly upholstered leather armchair that stood opposite the desk and willed her trembling to cease.

The riding crop.

Her riding crop. The one Charlie had spoken about. The one her uncle had assured her was kept on her cousin's nightstand.

Nausea swirled in her belly. If she'd needed any further proof that he'd lied to her—not once, but over and over again—there it was.

Still, it was possible her cousin had dropped by yesterday after a session at the stables. It was possible he hadn't lied about *everything*, but finding the crop next to his computer was damning just the same.

The door to the office opened and her uncle re-entered carrying a tall glass of iced water. With her thoughts still in turmoil, Chloe couldn't even muster a thank you.

"Where's Maria?" she asked.

"She's in Bali. She left yesterday morning for a couple of weeks. I forgot to tell you. She's gone over with a few of her university friends. They're kicking up their heels before they have to knuckle down to yearly exams."

Chloe's heart sank. It wasn't Maria who'd left the riding crop behind.

Her uncle moved to take a seat in the chair opposite her and adjusted his bulk until he was comfortable. He seemed unconcerned about her question and even less concerned about her lack of response.

He steepled his fingers and rested his chin on his hands, his expression thoughtful.

"Tell me what this is all about, Princess. It's very unlike you to come charging in here without notice. Are your parents all right? Has something happened?"

Chloe stared at him, knowing she had no choice but to say it. Gripping the chair with white-knuckled fingers, she blurted it out.

"Uncle Ronnie, I know you're homosexual. Or bisexual. Or...or something."

Heat scorched her face, her neck, her ears. Every part of her burned. Her uncle stared at her in shock, his eyes wide—his expression incredulous.

And then he laughed. Huge belly laughs that jiggled his formidable girth.

Chloe sat paralyzed, unable to speak, to even utter a sound. Had she miscalculated so badly? Was her uncle innocent of everything she'd thought? Or was he just a very good liar?

Confused and embarrassed, she blinked back tears. The Minister's expression sobered. He leaned forward and grasped her hands, his voice gentle. "Chloe, Chloe, Chloe, where on earth did you hear that? How could you even think something so preposterous?"

She pulled her hands away from his and looked down at her lap. Gathering her courage, she stared at him, her eyes narrowed in accusation.

"Yesterday, I-I met with Charlie Stanford. He told me he and you—that you and he...were...were lovers. I also spoke to Eric Stoltenberg. He said it was you who requested he access Declan Munro's personnel file. Declan told me about your...your approach to him at the party and how you made sexual advances toward him at the bar."

Her voice hitched. She took a deep breath and tried to slow the pounding of her heart. "It was you, Uncle Ronnie. It was *you*. All this time, I've been turning myself inside out wondering how a man as decent and honorable as Declan Munro could be guilty of such a heinous crime. All of the evidence pointed toward his guilt. I even spoke with you about it, about the questions I had and you *lied* to me. You looked me in the eye and lied to me. I almost ruined a man's life because of you. As long as I live, I will *never* forgive you."

The Minister merely shook his head slowly from side to side, his expression filled with sadness and regret.

"Dear, dear, dear, what some people will say in times of trouble. Charlie Stanford's your primary witness against the Munro boy, isn't he? The one who "apparently" discovered Munro's penchant for kiddie porn?"

Chloe's stomach clenched, but she nodded.

"I shouldn't be telling you this, but Stanford's in the process of being dishonorably discharged from the AFP. He's been under investigation for some time for drug dealing. Syringes were found in his locker, along with suspicious bags of white powder. An arrest is expected to be made any day. Once it gets out, his testimony will be worth squat."

Chloe's brow knitted in surprise. "Why didn't you tell me this on Tuesday?"

Her uncle shrugged. "I only found out about it yesterday afternoon. It's been a hush-hush undercover operation. They didn't want to scare away the players. Only the immediate people involved in the investigation know about it."

Chloe's mind spun.

Could her uncle be telling the truth? Was it possible Charlie had made it all up? Could he be that good a liar?

She wasn't prepared to dismiss her suspicions so quickly. "What about Eric Stoltenberg? You told me you had no idea why he'd requested access to personnel files. He told the HR manager at the time, *and* me yesterday, that he was acting on your orders. Are you going to tell me he's a liar, too?"

The Minister remained unmoved. "Eric Stoltenberg is in love with me. He has delusions that I return his feelings. I've done nothing to encourage him, but there you have it. The last time we spoke about it, I told him in no uncertain terms that I wasn't and never would be in love with him. He stormed out of my office in a fit of pique. I can only imagine this…revelation of his is nothing more than sour grapes."

Chloe tried desperately to hold onto her anger. She'd come there determined to confront him, certain in her knowledge that he was responsible for all that had befallen Declan—and more.

Unable to sit still, she jumped out of her chair and rounded on him, her anger resurfacing.

"And how do you explain Agent Munro's revelations? Is he deluded, too? Don't even try to convince me he lied. You told me you'd never met him."

Her uncle grimaced with annoyance. "I told you I couldn't *remember* meeting him. There's a difference, Princess."

"I don't believe you. It was only six months ago and I'm damn sure you'd remember approaching him for sex," she retorted, her breath coming fast.

"I'm sure I would too," he replied, his expression remaining calm.

"So...so you're denying it? Is that what you're doing? You're sitting there and calling Agent Munro a liar."

The Minister sighed and pushed away from his chair and closed the distance between them. Leaning close, he brushed an errant strand of hair off her face, his gaze once again filled with regret.

"You always did have an amazing imagination, Princess. From the time you were a little girl, you could keep us entertained with the most fantastical stories. Half the time, I had to remind myself they weren't true, but just some made-up, imaginary tale from a bright little girl who was smart enough to own the stars."

She stared at him with a sinking feeling. He'd been lying all along. No one forgot they'd propositioned someone for sex. Not unless they had something to hide. Like she'd told him, she'd never believe Declan hadn't told her the truth. Along with the evidence she'd obtained from Charlie and even Eric, it was obvious her uncle was caught up in a web of deceit so intricate that maybe even he could no longer grasp the complexity of it.

The harsh reality of the situation hit her anew like a slab of concrete.

Her uncle was responsible for framing Declan. He'd requested, cajoled, coerced Eric and Charlie to assist him in his endeavour and ultimately, had been prepared to sit back and ruin an innocent man's life.

And why?

Because his sexual advances had been rejected. Was he really such a narcissist? She couldn't believe she was even thinking of him in those terms. It was madness. Absolute insanity. And yet, sadly, she knew deep inside her it was true.

"I've heard enough," she said, determined to leave and never look back. She'd leave it to the taskforce to elicit the finer details. She had all she needed.

She collected her briefcase from off the floor where she'd left it and turned toward the door.

"It was all his own fault, you know."

She paused and her heart skipped a beat. She turned back around to face him. "Excuse me?"

"I said it was all his own fault. Declan Munro. He arrived at that function in the company of another man, another very good looking man. Add to that, the fact he was over thirty, buffed and beautiful and what was I expected to think?

"Of course I thought he was gay. It was a natural assumption. How was I to know the man he'd arrived with was his brother?"

Chloe stared at her uncle in horror, frozen in place.

"I made a move on him at the bar and he rebuffed me in the most humiliating way. Me, the Minister for Home Affairs, the man who could make or break his career. It was an unforgivable mistake and one I couldn't overlook. I was determined to make him pay."

Chloe shook her head with increasing vehemence. "Stop, please. Uncle Ronnie, please stop."

The Minister smiled. "But you were so eager to hear all the details, Princess. You've been hounding me for the truth from the moment you arrived." He took hold of her arm and dragged her across the room, forcing her into the chair she'd recently vacated.

"There. That's better. The least you can do is hear me out." He smiled again and moved slightly away.

"At first, I slunk away and licked my wounds, determined

to be more careful in the future, but then I discovered Declan Munro wasn't any ordinary AFP recruit. He was a member of a very prominent family, one with a long and enviable relationship with law enforcement. I assume you know his father was the first aboriginal appointed to the bench of the New South Wales District Court?"

Chloe bit her lip and nodded, praying her uncle's tirade would soon be over.

"It was then I experienced a little concern. Someone as well connected as Declan Munro could cause me a serious amount of trouble if he chose to speak about our unfortunate encounter. Someone like Declan Munro might find a sympathetic ear... I couldn't afford to take the risk. It was then I started out to destroy him."

He turned to Chloe, his arms outstretched in supplication. "Don't you *see?* I had no choice! It was either him, or me."

Tears formed in Chloe's eyes. She shook her head in disbelief. How could this be the uncle she'd known and loved all her life?

"Of course, there's nothing illegal about being gay, but I'd been hiding behind the protection of a long-standing marriage. It's an insult the voting public would be unlikely to forgive. I had your aunt and cousin to consider. My career in politics would be over. I could always try and brush off Munro's accusations as a simple misunderstanding—we'd been at a party, after all and the alcohol had flowed freely. I'd taken care to note that Munro had been drinking.

"But there were a couple of problems with this course of action. The first one was of course, that Munro had no reason to lie. With his background and impeccable service record, he would be considered a reliable source of information."

He drew in a deep breath and strode across the room. "The other reason had everything to do with me. I've lost count of the number of recruits I've approached over my years in this office. There are many who could come forward and support Munro's allegations, if it came to that. While I was confident most would remain loyal, there are a handful with whom I parted on let's say…less than friendly terms.

"I stewed over the dilemma for weeks and then, it came to me. Rather than wait and hope that Munro stayed quiet, I decided to preempt the battle. I decided to strike Munro where it would hurt the most, discrediting him to the point that no one, not even the lowliest member of the AFP, would believe a word he said. It wouldn't matter if a jury believed his protestations of innocence. The damage to his reputation would have already been done. Munro's life and career as he'd known it would be over." He chuckled.

Chloe felt sick.

"The plan was beyond brilliant," he enthused. "I realized I needed an ally in Munro's unit. I canvassed various options and stumbled across Charlie—or Chip as I'm fond of calling him. It was an added bonus to discover Chip was gay. It meant that not only would he be instrumental in bringing Declan Munro down, he could also be a plaything."

Chloe moaned in anguish. Her stomach rebelled at his words. She wanted to put her hands up over her ears and scream to block them out, but her hands remained frozen in her lap.

The Minister smiled. "We spent a thoroughly delightful month together before I approached him about the problem of Declan Munro. By then, Chip was ready to do anything I asked of him. And so it began…"

His grin widened and Chloe could tell he was lost in his memories. She eased herself out of the chair, intent on escaping the man she no longer recognized.

She made it to the door without incident, barely daring to breathe. Her uncle looked up, but remained where he was. His voice reached out to her where she stood outside in the corridor.

"As I said, Princess. Declan Munro had nobody but himself to blame."

CHAPTER 25

Chloe's hand shook uncontrollably as she swiped at the tears that coursed down her cheeks and stumbled out of the elevator. She headed toward her car. Somehow, she managed to turn the key in the ignition and get herself out of the parking station. The same security guard offered her a wave, but she barely registered his presence through the anguish that tore her apart. Exiting the car park, she drove barely a hundred yards before she pulled over onto the side of the road and gave into the pain that crippled her.

Her uncle had lived a lie, probably for most of his life. He'd lied to his family, his staff, his constituents. She didn't know if her aunt was wise to the subterfuge, but even if she was, that didn't excuse it.

What Chloe couldn't understand was why he'd gone to such lengths to hide his sexuality. They were living in the twenty-first century. Being gay was hardly a death sentence.

Sure, he might have to resign his ministerial position, but it seemed a small price to pay for the freedom to live his life true.

Chloe swallowed a sob. It wasn't her uncle's life-long deception and the knowledge that he was gay that caused the deep coldness that had settled in her belly. What had her limbs trembling like she was in the throes of a fever was knowing that her uncle had been prepared to ruin Declan's life over something as trivial as a knockback.

The realization horrified her. People received knockbacks all the time. Some mattered, some didn't. Some of them were forgotten quickly, some of them took a lot longer. The fact was, having someone turn you down was a part of life.

Declan had turned her uncle down. He'd passed on her uncle's offer to sleep with him. And her uncle had sought revenge.

He couldn't bear the thought of an underling knocking him back and telling him no. His actions were nothing more than that of a spoiled child who'd been refused a coveted toy. Was he really such a narcissist? The very thought of what he'd done made her ill.

Sucking in a lungful of air, Chloe fumbled for her phone. She punched in Declan's number.

He picked up after the first ring. "Chloe, thank Christ; how did it go?"

Fresh tears overwhelmed her and emotion tightened her throat. She swallowed and tried to speak. "He-he…"

"It's okay, sweetheart. It's okay. Where are you?" he asked.

"I've… I've just left his office. I'm on the side of the road, not far from the Hill."

"I'll be right there."

Chloe ended the call and dragged in a breath. Knowing Declan was nearby and ready to provide comfort calmed her frantic thoughts. Moments later, the sound of a motorbike snagged her attention. She smiled tremulously when he drew up behind her on his Ducati.

Charlie wiped the sweat off his forehead and upper lip and wished he hadn't finished the second bottle of rum. He could have done with a double shot right about now.

After telephoning the Master earlier, he'd spent the time since sitting in his pickup, not far from his Master's office, planning how to do his lover's bidding. He'd been there more almost an hour when he spied Declan on his midnight-black Panigale Ducati. He was heading toward Parliament House, less than two hundred yards from where Charlie was parked.

He was more than a little surprised that Declan would be in the vicinity of Parliament House. This early in the morning, the building was only open to parliamentary staff, or those with approved access to them.

He watched with interest as Declan came to a halt in the public car park right outside the building and parked the bike. After tugging off his helmet, he sat there, as if waiting for someone.

Intrigued, Charlie looked over his shoulder and then out his window to discover what might warrant Declan's attention, but he saw nothing out of the ordinary. Confused, he settled back against his seat and prepared to wait.

It was more than half an hour later, when Charlie heard the sound of the Ducati roar to life. He sat up and blinked to sharpen his gaze. Declan had halted beside a little red Honda that had appeared from the direction of the staff car park under Parliament House. It had pulled up on the shoulder of the road a little over a hundred yards away. Charlie watched as the door to the Honda opened. His jaw dropped open in shock.

The IA investigator climbed out of the car and fell into Declan's arms. He hugged her close, his lips moving against her hair, his hands caressing her back. Suddenly, everything dropped into place...

Declan was fucking the investigator. No wonder she'd gone after Charlie like a ferret down a hole. She was doing the defendant...

Another thought struck him.

Had the Master changed his mind? Had he summoned the investigator to his office to deal with himself? She was, after all, his niece. Had he doubted Charlie's ability to do the deed?

Fear and desperation surged through him. He had to prove himself worthy—of the Master and of his love. He focused yet again on the little red Honda and noticed Declan had climbed back onto the Ducati. He and the Honda were now moving out into the traffic.

Determined to show the Master his depth of love and loyalty, Charlie started the pickup and tailed them. His orders had been to take out the investigator, but right here and now, it seemed too good an opportunity to pass off to rid the world of both of them in one fell swoop. He only hoped he could manage it.

Flattening the accelerator, he sped along the lane that ran parallel to the one the Honda was in. Its indicator came on and the vehicle moved into the left-hand lane. Charlie smiled in delight. She was about two hundred feet in front of him and another two hundred from the nearest exit. The Ducati had dropped back, caught up in traffic, but it didn't matter. The investigator was his main target. He needed to stay focused.

His heart thumped hard. Once again sweat beaded his brow and across his upper lip and he swiped at them both with the back of his hand. Blood pounded in his ears. He stamped hard on the accelerator. His pickup leaped forward.

He closed the distance between him and the Honda, speeding past cars that were in the outside lane. Adrenaline surged through him. He was twenty feet away…ten…five… A wild, primeval yelp of triumph echoed in his ears.

The investigator turned and saw him, terror bursting across her face seconds before the side of his pickup slammed into the driver's side of her vehicle, pushing her off the road.

The squeal of metal on metal was ear splitting. Sparks flew between the vehicles and still he kept the accelerator pressed flat to the floor. He glanced ahead and saw the huge gum tree. A grin widened his mouth. The little Honda was headed straight for it.

CHAPTER 26

Declan maneuvered the bike through the gridlock of traffic, cursing under his breath as Chloe's Honda pulled ahead of him. He didn't know what had happened in her uncle's office, but he'd never seen such desolation on her face. She'd been almost beyond speech.

Reassuring himself that she wasn't hurt and that she was capable of driving home, he'd urged her to go directly to his apartment and assured her he'd be right behind her.

She'd nodded her agreement and he'd scrambled back onto his bike, eager to get her home and do whatever it took to remove the sadness in her eyes. He didn't want to admit it, but the blank expression on her face terrified him.

He glanced beside him and changed lanes, hoping to make up ground. A silver pickup ahead of him snagged his attention. He frowned as he recognized it. It was Charlie's, he was sure of it.

The pickup was traveling fast, faster than the posted speed limit. It was headed right for Chloe.

Misgivings stirred in his gut. They quickly morphed into panic. He shook his head from side to side and a scream climbed up his throat.

He opened up the throttle and urged the bike on faster, but he was too far away. He watched in horror as Charlie's pickup collided with the side of the little Honda and forced it into the gutter.

The sound of screeching metal reached him. No match

for the pickup, the Honda's wheels caught on the side of the curb and flipped up on its side. Seconds later, it slammed into a tree.

Shock and disbelief temporarily immobilized him. Chloe's terrified scream reached him over the cacophony of traffic and other noise. His blood ran cold.

"No, no, no, no, no!" he shouted, bringing the Ducati to a screeching halt. Leaping off, he tore toward the site of the accident. Smoke billowed from Chloe's car.

"Someone call a fucking ambulance!" he screamed, his gaze never straying from the mangled wreck that had once been a little red Honda.

He finally reached her and banged on the side of the car to get her attention. The driver's side window had shattered, but he could still see her through the crazed glass.

"Chloe? Can you hear me? For Christ's sake, answer me!"

He heaved on the door handle, but the battered and twisted metal didn't budge. He tried the rear passenger side door and had the same result. He banged the side of the car once again in an effort to get her attention.

"Chloe, answer me. Please, sweetheart. Please let me know you can hear me. I need to know you can hear me."

He spied the slightest movement of her head and his heart exploded with relief. The sound of sirens ricocheted through his brain. In some disconnected part of his mind, he registered the fact that emergency services were on their way.

Smoke continued to billow out from underneath the hood. He smelled the distinct odor of leaking fuel.

Christ, he had to get her out of there.

Racing around to the passenger side, he pulled up short when he realized the trunk of the tree had wedged itself firmly against the side of the car. There would be no way he could get past it.

Desperation and helplessness flooded through him. He fell to his knees and clawed at his hair. She was going to die and there was nothing he could do about it.

He jumped when a large hand landed on his shoulder.

"We've got it under control, mate. You need to move away."

Declan stared up at the fireman who held a thick hose in his hand.

"You don't understand," Declan implored the man. "She's still in there. You need to get her out. Please, God, you need to get her out."

"It's okay, we'll get her out. I promise you. Move away and let us do our job."

The fireman opened up the hose and blasted the front of the Honda. Within moments, the smoke died down and Declan collapsed in relief.

CHAPTER 27

Declan forced air into his laboring lungs. Everything moved in slow motion. He clenched his fists and tried hard to concentrate on the emergency services personnel that were working quickly to free Chloe from the wreckage of her car.

His mind shied away from the possibility her injuries could be fatal. He wasn't ready to contemplate that situation. She was alive. He's seen her head move. He was sure of it. Hurt, maybe, but alive. He refused to accept any other scenario.

He was surrounded by police vans and fire engines when he noticed an ambulance had arrived. Uniformed policemen wearing bright, high-visibility vests, directed traffic around the accident site. The smell of burnt rubber and engine oil permeated the air. It looked impossible that anyone could have survived inside the crumpled wreckage of Chloe's Honda where it lay twisted around the huge gum tree.

A gray-haired plain-clothes detective with an efficient manner approached him where he lay sprawled on the ground, right outside the cordoned-off area of the accident site.

"I understand you know the woman in the car," the man said.

Declan nodded. "Yeah." His voice was almost unrecognizable. He cleared his throat and tried again. "Yes, her name's Chloe Sabattini. She's a senior investigator with the AFP."

The detective paled. "Shit."

Declan understood how he felt.

"Who are you?" the detective asked.

"Federal Agent Declan Munro." Declan waited for some sign of recognition, but there was nothing. After taking down details in his notepad, the detective looked up at Declan again.

"Did you see anything? Do you know what caused the accident?"

Declan drew in a deep breath and tried to suppress the anger and guilt that threatened to overwhelm him. "Oh, yeah, I saw it all right. And there's one thing I'm certain of: This was no accident."

The strained growl of a hydraulic motor filled the air. A screech of protesting metal followed. Declan leaped up from his seat on the ground and watched in horror as pieces of Chloe's Honda were ripped apart by the metal teeth of the Jaws of Life.

A car door. A side panel. Part of the hood. The pieces of severed metal piled up on the side of the road.

Declan strained to catch a glimpse of Chloe. He spied a patch of clothing—the blouse she'd worn yesterday when she'd turned up at his apartment. The pale fabric was stained with blood.

His gut clenched in agony. There was so much blood.
Too much.

He gasped against the pain that tore through him. He couldn't bear it if she died. Not now. Not when they'd found each other. It wasn't fair. It fucking wasn't fair.

A shout went up and emergency personnel swarmed around the vehicle. Declan moved this way and that in an effort to see what was happening. A stretcher appeared and moments later, Chloe was lifted onto it.

Her eyes were closed. She lay motionless. His heart leaped in his throat. She was pale. So pale. Her hand hung limply over the side.

He wanted to go to her and cradle her in his arms and kiss her pain away. He took a step forward and then another. He didn't realize he'd approached the blue and white police tape until he felt a restraining hand on his shoulder. Spinning around, he came face to face with the detective he'd spoken to a few moments earlier.

"I'm sorry, but I can't let you move any closer. The officers need to do their job. Let them help her. They can do more for her than you can."

His words thrummed into Declan's head. They made sense in a disconnected, dispassionate way, even when he didn't want them to. He stepped back and the officer's arm fell away. Declan watched through pain-filled eyes as they loaded Chloe into the waiting ambulance.

"Where are they taking her?" he croaked through lips that were way past dry.

"Canberra Hospital."

The words had barely left the detective's mouth when Declan spun around and ran toward his bike, tugging on his helmet as he went. Throwing his leg over the seat, he pressed the ignition switch and gunned the throttle.

Deftly swerving around the gaggle of bystanders and parked traffic, he skirted the accident site and accelerated. Averting his gaze from what was left of Chloe's Honda, he headed toward the hospital and tried not to think about the impossibility of anyone surviving an accident marked by an almost-unrecognizable pile of wreckage. He clung to the fact the ambulance officers hadn't covered her body with a sheet.

Please, sweetheart... Please don't die on me. Please don't die on me.

The words repeated themselves in his head, a desperate mantra that moved in time with the rotation of his wheels. The noise of the traffic and the road around him receded and he heard nothing but the echo of his soul-wrenching plea.

In less time than he thought possible and with nothing but a hazy recollection of his journey there, he pulled into the parking lot of Canberra Hospital. Finding a vacant space, he parked and ran toward the emergency department. As much as he was anxious to find out about Chloe's condition, he was equally terrified some well-meaning stranger with a sympathetic face would be the one to tell him she hadn't made it. He bit his lip in an effort to stem his panic, once again turning away from the possibility she was dead.

The automatic doors to the emergency department slid open at his approach. It was still early and the emergency room was empty. With his helmet tucked under his arm, he located the buzzer that allowed him to communicate with the hospital staff beyond the closed doors. It was answered almost immediately.

"Emergency, can I help you?"

"I need to see Chloe Sabattini. She was brought in by ambulance a short while ago."

"Are you family?"

Declan paused, knowing if he told the truth, he'd be denied entrance.

"Yes, I'm her...husband," he replied and was immediately flooded with guilt. He'd get someone to contact Chloe's family at the earliest opportunity. If she had any. He was suddenly struck by how much he didn't know about her.

"Come in."

The door clicked and he pushed it open and found himself surrounded by the cold, sterile environment of the emergency ward. A middle-aged woman in a pale blue uniform bustled toward him.

"Mr Sabattini?"

Declan flushed. "Um...it's Munro. Sabattini is Chloe's maiden name."

The woman nodded understandingly. "Of course. I'm Vera, one of the registered nurses on duty. The doctor is still examining your wife. From what I can ascertain, she's a very lucky lady."

Relief surged through him, weakening his knees. He leaned against the wall for support.

"Oh, thank God! She's alive."

"Yes, she's alive but at the moment, she's unconscious. Her injuries, while not fatal, are very serious. She'll need surgery. The doctor will be around shortly to talk to you and obtain the necessary consents."

Nodding his head automatically, Declan turned away, his head spinning. There was no way he could sign a consent form. Whether he liked it or not, he wasn't her next of kin. He had no right to give consent. It was imperative he find out if she had any family living close by. Tugging out his cell phone, he dialed Clayton.

After giving his brother succinct instructions to locate Chloe's next of kin, he ended the call and tucked his phone back into his pocket. He drew in several deep breaths and scrubbed his fingers through his hair. The nurse said Chloe was alive. He'd concentrate on that and deal with her injuries later. She was alive. That's what mattered.

He found the nurse again and caught her attention. "When... When can I see her?"

Vera nodded and patted his hand. "Soon. The doctor will come and see you and let you know what's going on. I understand she has a couple of nasty fractures, among other things. Why don't you take a minute? Can I get you a glass of water?"

Declan shot her a grateful look. "Thanks, I'd appreciate that."

Vera padded away on silent, rubber-soled feet. Declan took the opportunity to bring his heart rate back under control. He didn't want to frighten Chloe with his panic, especially now that the reason for that panic had abated. She was alive. A few broken bones, not life threatening. She was going to be all right. He prayed it was true.

Returning a few moments later with a cup of water, Vera offered him the drink and waited for him to finish it.

"Right now... Feeling better?"

He nodded and squashed the paper cup in his hand. "Thank you."

"You're most welcome." She smiled. "You're not the first worried relative we've had in here."

He managed a small smile in reply.

"Now, if you'll just follow me, I'll take you to your wife.

She's down in Bay Three. The doctor's waiting to see you there."

Feeling much less anxious, Declan followed the nurse through the curtained ward. Various moans and groans and muffled whispers could be heard along the way and he was relieved when Vera finally came to a halt and eased back the curtain surrounding Chloe's bed.

He gasped when he saw her. He couldn't help it. Iridescent blue bruises and angry red abrasions criss-crossed her face. Her eyes were swollen shut. A deep cut on her cheek was already held together with a row of neat, black stitches and glistened with brownish antiseptic. Her arm was in a sling. The bedcovers had been tented over her legs. Declan dreaded to hear what damage they'd sustained.

But her chest rose and fell unaided and the relief that coursed through him left him weak.

"Oh, sweetheart. Thank Christ you're going to be all right." He rushed over to her side and pressed a soft kiss on her lips. She winced and turned away. Her eyelids fluttered, but remained closed.

"She's coming around," the doctor who stood nearby informed him. "It's a good sign. She sustained a head injury in the accident that knocked her unconscious, but fortunately, it doesn't appear too serious. The most severe of her injuries are to one of her legs."

Declan dragged his gaze away from Chloe's battered face and stared at the doctor. The man's expression was sober. A frisson of fear skittered along Declan's spine.

"H-how severe?"

"She's suffered multiple fractures to her right leg, including a compound fracture in her femur."

"And her arm?" he asked.

The doctor frowned. "Her arm?"

"Yes, it's in a sling."

"Oh, yes. Her arm. She dislocated her shoulder. We put it back in a little while ago. It's still in a sling so that she's mindful of it when she regains consciousness. The ligaments have been stretched. It will be sore for quite awhile."

"Are there any more injuries?"

"A couple of broken ribs, which we've strapped. Apart from that, there's not much more we can do with them. Again, she's going to feel it when she wakes up."

Declan turned away and stared at the woman he loved. She lay still and pale in the hospital bed. He watched the slight rising and falling of her chest and thanked God she'd been spared.

A murmur of voices outside the curtain snagged his attention. He glanced over his shoulder. The curtain was pulled aside and two plain-clothes detectives hovered at the end of the bed, notebooks at the ready. One of them was the officer Declan had spoken to at the scene. His badge identified him as Detective Sergeant Harris.

"I'm sorry to intrude, Agent Munro," Detective Harris said, "but it's important that we talk to you again. "We've spoken to a number of other witnesses. They all agree that this was no accident."

Declan's jaw tightened. He glanced down at Chloe and then returned his gaze to the officers. "Let's do this outside."

They moved away from Chloe's bed and walked a little way down the corridor where a trolley piled high with linen afforded a modicum of privacy.

Harris spoke again. "Do you have any idea who did this? We have a description of a silver-colored pickup that ran the Honda off the road. A couple of the witnesses said they saw a man behind the wheel."

Fury burned through him. His fists clenched. "Yeah, I know who did it all right and I know why. You need to put out a BOLO for Federal Agent Charles Stanford."

The other officer, younger and thinner than his partner, wore a badge that identified him as Detective Constable Allen. He scribbled in his notebook. A moment later, he looked up at Declan and frowned.

"A Federal Agent, you say? Are you sure?"

Declan narrowed his gaze. "There's no doubt in my mind."

"Did you see Agent Stanford behind the wheel of the pickup?"

Declan made an effort to hold onto his temper. "No, I didn't see him, but I recognized his truck. We... We worked together for a year. He drove that beast everywhere. I'd know it from miles away."

The officers shared a look and Declan knew exactly what they were thinking. Despite his best efforts, anger ignited inside him.

"Look, I know it was Stanford," he bit out. "Chloe—Agent Sabattini was in the middle of investigating him in relation to perjury charges and a heap of other things. She—"

Comprehension flooded Allen's face. His expression in his eyes grew decidedly colder. "Now I know who you are. I was wondering why you looked familiar. You're that copper who was charged with illegally accessing kiddie porn. I saw you on the TV. You've been committed to stand trial."

Harris tensed. He stared at Declan as if he was something so offensive, the man could hardly bring himself to look at him.

"Agent Munro... Yeah, now I know who you are," Harris' tone was thick with innuendo.

Anger tinged with desperation tightened their grip in Declan's gut.

"For Christ's sake, this isn't about me! Believe what you like, I'm not even going to try to convince you I didn't do it. Right now, the only thing you need to know is that the fucker who rammed his truck into the side of Agent Sabattini's Honda was Charlie Stanford."

They continued to look at him with suspicion. Declan dug his fingers into his hair in frustration.

"Call her superior, if you don't believe me. Detective Superintendent Tony Hammond at IA. He'll tell you all you need to know. Just be sure to tell him I said it was Agent Stanford behind the wheel. And for fuck's sake, do it *now*!"

Declan heard himself shouting, but was powerless to prevent it. Frustration, mixed with a healthy dose of fear that they'd ignore his information had annihilated his patience.

Stanford was still on the loose, escaping to God knows where, while Tweedle Dee and Tweedle Dum were eyeing him like he was worse than a fresh dog turd stuck to their shoe. From the time they'd recognized him, they hadn't even pretended they were interested in what he had to say.

Declan clenched his jaw to avoid saying anything further to antagonize them. He would achieve nothing by pissing them off. Taking a deep breath, he tried again.

"Listen, forget about me. The woman in that bed is lucky to be alive and the asshole who did this to her is still out there, roaming free. If you don't believe *me*, that's your choice, but at the very least, find Stanford and his truck. There's no way his pickup came out of that without sustaining damage. Find the truck and let it do the talking. Find it before it disappears, and along with it, your best chance to bring someone to justice. And while you're at it, take a closer look at Minister Sabattini."

Allen's eyes widened in surprise. "The Home Affairs Minister? You can't be serious?"

Declan stared hard at the men. "I'm not even going to pretend you'll believe a word I say, so take it to Hammond. He'll tell you everything you need to know and when you're through with him, you might arrange for a round-the-clock police presence outside Agent Sabattini's hospital room. I'll bet everything I have that Stanford, either acting on his own or pursuant to orders from someone else, just tried to kill her."

Declan's breath came fast. He glared at the officers, leaving them in no doubt about his anger that still simmered just below the surface. "There's nothing to say he won't be brave or stupid enough to try again."

With that, Declan pushed past them, no longer caring what they thought of him. They'd call Hammond, he was sure of it. Even if it was to satisfy their curiosity. Hammond would confirm what Declan had told them and they'd put out an alert to be on the lookout for Stanford. He only hoped it wouldn't be too late.

He wasn't entirely sure why he'd thrown in the line about the Minister. It was preposterous to even imagine Chloe's uncle could have ordered the hit. Declan had no evidence Stanford hadn't been acting alone, but the fact was, it was the Minister, out of a petty need for revenge, who had started Stanford on this course. It was the Minister who had loaded the gun: Stanford had merely fired the bullets.

Chloe had told Declan the taskforce expected to arrest her uncle later in the day. If Charlie had told the Minister of his last interview with Chloe—and it was almost certain he would have—the Minister had to know it was only a matter of time before his secrets were exposed. The game was up. His life as he knew it was over.

The man would be desperate, but would he be desperate enough to try to get rid of his own niece? It wasn't like the matter would go away just because Chloe was no longer around. Surely, the Minister knew that? Or maybe he didn't? Maybe he thought Chloe would come to him and seek answers, seek clarification from him, her beloved uncle, before she shared her discovery with her colleagues?

It wasn't too much of a stretch to imagine the Minister thinking like that. After all, it was exactly what Chloe had done: She'd gone to him for answers. The only thing he probably hadn't counted on was that she'd go to her boss and Declan first.

Looking up, Declan spied Chloe's doctor hurrying toward him, a clipboard in his hand.

"Mr Munro, I need a few minutes. We've prepped your wife for surgery. Whilst her circulation is not being impeded, the fractures are serious and need to be dealt with as soon as possible. I need you to sign the consent form."

A resurgence of guilt tightened his gut. He averted his gaze. "Um, I'm... I'm not—"

A loud wail of anguish sounded right behind him. He turned and saw a short, round Italian woman who looked about sixty barreling down the corridor.

"Where is she? Where is my daughter? Where's Chloe? My *baby!*"

The woman's howls rose in pitch. Declan stared at her and realized Chloe's next of kin had arrived. He stepped forward and held out his hand.

"Mrs Sabattini? I'm Agent Munro. I'm a friend of your daughter's. She right this way."

CHAPTER 28

Ronald tossed the contents of his drink down his throat and relished the slow burn of it all the way down to his stomach. The alcohol warmed him like nothing else did, especially after the turmoil of the last few days. Hell, what was he talking about? His life hadn't been the same since his encounter with Declan Munro.

Declan Munro. His nemesis. He should have told Stanford to take that prick out too, along with Chloe. It might not have been enough to prevent what was to come, but it would have made him feel better...

His fingers turned white around the fine crystal glass. His life had spiraled out of control. After years of an exhilarating existence beyond his wildest dreams, taking and giving without thought or consideration, over the last few days, he'd been dealt one blow after another.

He was dizzy from the speed at which his life had fallen apart and was barely gripping the edges of sanity with his fingernails. The worst of it was, he wasn't sure how to put an end to the madness, or even if he could.

He stared through the double French doors that led out into his wife's rose garden, his thoughts as black as the night that was not far away. The heavy scent of flowers wafted toward him on the gentle breeze, but he wasn't in the mood to appreciate it.

The phone on the desk pealed in the stillness, disrupting

his tumultuous thoughts. He strode over to it and snatched it up. "Yes?"

"It's done."

Anger seared his veins. Blood pounded in his ears. Knowing his wife had departed upstairs a few minutes earlier to take a shower, he made no effort to lower his voice.

"You fucking idiot! I saw the news reports on the television more than an hour ago. You didn't even have the brains to use someone else's pickup! What sort of a fucking imbecile are you?"

Charlie blubbered. "I'm sorry, Master. I-I didn't think. You told me to get rid of her. I-I only wanted to please you."

"Yeah, well, you fucked it up, Chip." His voice rose higher, along with his fury. "You fucked it up a right royal treat. You didn't even kill her."

"I-I hit her hard; I know I did. I drove straight into her. She hit the curb and flipped over. The car smashed into a tree. I couldn't have timed it better. There's no way she could have survived."

"Well, she fucking did, *Charles,*" he spat, intentionally using the name the man despised. "Her father's already called me to tell me the good news. She's lying in the Canberra Hospital, well and truly alive." His rage morphed into ice-cold fury. His voice dropped, became deadly. "Don't call me again, Charles. Don't *ever* fucking call me again. From now on, you're on your own."

———————

Nellie Sabattini's heart thudded so loudly she was sure her husband would hear it. Shock kept her momentarily frozen, then, fearful of discovery, she eased the door to the study shut. The tiny click as it closed was masked by a vicious curse and the sound of breaking glass on the other side of the door. Ignoring the urge to seek out its source, she turned away and stealthily made her way up the stairs.

CHAPTER 29

It was more than four hours and countless cups of coffee later, that Declan's phone vibrated in his pocket. Snatching it out, he answered it and almost collapsed in relief when a pleasant-sounding nurse informed him Chloe was out of recovery and was now resting peacefully in the orthopedic ward on the sixth floor. He hightailed it to the bank of elevators and then skidded to a halt when he spied Chloe's family huddled together in the waiting room. He took a deep breath and headed in their direction.

After fielding a barrage of questions from Chloe's mother, who'd introduced herself as Giovanna Sabattini, he'd repeated the process all over again when her father, two sisters and a brother arrived. It was obvious how much they loved her and by the time the interrogation was over, he'd convinced them he felt the same.

His admission had caught him by surprise. Until then, he hadn't voiced it, hadn't even really thought about it—at least, not in any concrete way. But as soon as the words were out of his mouth, he knew they were true. He'd never felt so connected to a woman before, as if they were one. It was soppy, sappy crap, but he couldn't help it: He'd fallen in love with Chloe.

The wonder of it had flooded through him, lighting him up from the inside. The only thing that managed to diminish his wide smile was the thought of her lying helpless and hurt on the operating table.

After bringing her family up to speed on the news she'd come through the surgery and giving relieved hugs all round, he headed back to the elevators and waited impatiently for the doors to open, her family close on his heels.

A nurse, sitting at a desk, gave them directions to Chloe's room and informed them she was awake. As they got closer to her door, he slowed his steps. His heart pounded with relief and a little apprehension. He told himself not to be stupid. He'd already seen the worst of it.

Chloe's family didn't feel any such reticence. They barreled in ahead of him amid muffled cries of anguish and relief. With an impatient shake of his head, he rounded the open doorway and stepped into her room, noting with annoyance the lack of a guard.

What the hell were they waiting for? A second attempt?

Wanting to vent his frustration at anyone who would listen, but needing to see Chloe more, he curbed his anger and stepped forward. A solitary hospital bed with its sides up kept her safe within its metal barriers. Fresh sheets and a blanket covered most of her body, with the exception of her arm that was still in a sling and rested by her side on top of the bedspread. Like it had in the emergency department, the bedclothes were held off her injured leg by a frame concealed beneath the covers.

Tears poured down her mother's cheeks. She quietly sobbed through a fist she'd jammed into her mouth. Declan moved closer. Chloe's eyes were still grossly swollen, but he saw her lashes flutter and realized she was awake. Pushing through the crowd of relatives, he moved to her side and reached for her uninjured hand.

"Oh, Christ, Chloe! I'm so glad to see you awake," he whispered. "You won't believe how scared I was. When I saw your car and you wouldn't answer me, I thought... Christ, I thought..."

Her bleary-eyed gaze found his and she tried to smile. "I'm o-okay."

"It's so good to see you awake," he choked.

"*Mm.*" She closed her eyes and took a breath. A few moments later, her eyes opened again. "W-where am I?"

"You're in Canberra Hospital. The ambulance brought you here after the accident."

Chloe grimaced.

Declan leaned closer. "Are you okay? Do you need something for the pain? Should I call someone?"

She shook her head a little. "No, really... I'm okay. The anaesthetic hasn't quite worn off yet. No doubt I'll be sore when it does."

Declan nodded. "You were very lucky."

Chloe offered another tiny smile. "That's what the doctor told me. I-I'm guessing my poor little Honda didn't come out of it quite so well."

"You're right about that." He paused and searched her face. "Are you up to talking about it?"

She sighed, but nodded slowly and struggled to sit up. "Ouch!"

"Lie still, sweetheart. Don't try to move. We don't have to do this now. Just take it easy."

"I want to know what happened."

Declan gazed at her. Do you remember anything?"

Chloe stared at him through the slit in her eyes. "I remember I was driving along the dual carriageway, not far from Parliament House. I remember you were behind me. A silver-colored pickup came toward me from the inside lane. I tried to swerve out of the way, but it kept coming at me." She drew in a shaky breath.

"The next thing I remember is the truck plowing into me. I-I hit the curb and went spinning through the air. I can still see the tree trunk. It was right in front of my face. After that, everything went black." Her voice hitched. A tear rolled down her cheek.

Listening to her slow, hesitant explanation, Declan's heart pounded in remembered fear. The sound of metal on metal; the sight of her Honda catapulting through the air; the screaming... *His* screaming.

He leaned closer and pressed a soft kiss on a tiny,

undamaged part of her face, reassuring himself she really was going to recover. "*Shh*, sweetheart. It's okay. Everything's okay."

Her uninjured hand moved and found his. She tilted her head toward him. "Did *you* see anything?"

Declan's breath caught. Dread weighed down his limbs. Slowly, he nodded.

Chloe closed her eyes. A few moments later, she opened them as wide as she could. She stared at him, through her bruised and puffy flesh. "Tell me."

CHAPTER 30

Charlie opened his bathroom cabinet and took out a syringe. With gloved hands, he carefully wiped it clean. After the Master's dig about his stupidity, he was determined that this time, he'd do it right.

Collecting a vial of fast-acting insulin from its usual place in his nightstand, he cleaned it in the same way and then dropped both items into a small leather pouch. Not many people knew he'd been a diabetic most of his life. Injecting himself with insulin was a daily event and one he'd become adept at. For him, it was a life-saving procedure; for someone without diabetes, it could be a death sentence.

He didn't know if Chloe Sabattini was a diabetic, but he was willing to bet she wasn't. The odds were in his favor. A large injection of insulin that went undiagnosed would be enough to get rid of her once and for all. The doctors would be at a loss to understand what was happening. They'd think it had something to do with her surgery. The best part of all was that no one would have a clue until it was too late.

He smiled. The beauty and simplicity of his plan took his breath away. He couldn't wait to see the Master afterwards, to accept his congratulations on making things right.

Dressed in casual clothes that wouldn't draw attention, he finished packing what he required and headed toward the door. Leaving his damaged pickup in the underground garage next door to his apartment building, he lifted his arm and flagged down a cab.

CHAPTER 31

Declan watched the regular rise and fall of Chloe's chest and was filled with relief. The doctor had stopped by an hour ago to check on her and had assured them she'd come through the surgery without any complications. He was confident over time, she'd make a full recovery.

A little while later, her breathing deepened and her hand fell away from his. He smiled tenderly and leaned over to brush a strand of hair off her forehead.

"Is she asleep?" Giovanna whispered.

Declan nodded and pitched his voice low. "I think so."

One of Chloe's sisters—the one who had introduced herself as Antonella and who looked so much like her mother it was a little disconcerting—moved closer.

"We might leave her to get some rest, Mama," she murmured.

Giovanna nodded. She leaned over and pressed a kiss against her daughter's cheek and then allowed herself to be drawn away. The rest of the family took their turn in saying goodbye. Within moments, he was alone with Chloe.

With a weary sigh, he sat down in the solitary armchair that stood a short distance from the bed. Leaning back, he drew in a deep breath and closed his eyes. It was nearly seven-thirty, but it felt like a lifetime had passed since he'd watched in horror as Chloe's car had been side-swiped and catapulted through the air. The memory of it played over and over in his mind. It would haunt him forever.

Knowing Charlie was responsible made him sick to his stomach, but he knew, as he hoped Chloe did, that neither of them were to blame. Charlie and her uncle were fully functioning adults capable of making their own choices. That their decisions were immoral, not to mention illegal and life threatening, didn't change anything.

The fact that they made the wrong choices was nobody's fault but their own.

Declan's phone vibrated in his pocket. In deference to Chloe and to the other patients, he'd switched it onto silent. He glanced down at the screen and saw it was Clayton and realized he hadn't thanked his brother for making contact with Chloe's family.

Declan stood and quietly made his way out of the room. Out of the corner of his eye, he saw that now a uniformed policeman stood outside Chloe's doorway. Relief surged through him. The detectives had spoken to Hammond.

He moved out of earshot before he answered the call. "Clay, how are you?"

"I'm fine. How are *you*? Better yet, how's Chloe?"

"She's good," he reassured his brother. "Well, not *good*, but you know what I mean. She's out of surgery and the doctor says she'll heal. It's only a matter of time now."

"Thank Christ for that. I'm so glad. I like her. I think I've even forgiven her for her part in this nightmare you've been caught up in."

Declan blinked at the sudden rush of emotion behind his eyes. "Yeah, me too," he quietly admitted. "I-I like her a lot."

Silence fell between them, but it was a comfortable silence as each brother digested and accepted the way things now were. A few moments later, Clayton spoke again.

"Did her family arrive? I got straight onto Hammond and told him what happened. He said he'd contact them."

Declan thought about Giovanna and smiled. She was all of five foot nothing, but more than made up for it with her spirit and determination. It wasn't until he'd repeatedly assured her he had only the most honorable intentions toward her daughter that she'd settled down enough to offer him a grudging smile.

"Yeah, they got here okay. They've been here almost as long as I have. They've only just left. By the way, thanks so much for getting onto Hammond. I didn't have a clue how to contact her next of kin or whether she even had any."

"No problem. It was nothing. I was happy to help."

"Yeah, well I appreciate it, anyway."

"What time are you leaving there? You must be tired as shit."

The stress and fatigue of the past hours suddenly weighed him down. He ran a tired hand over his face. "Yeah, I am."

"You ought to go home and get some rest. Chloe's going to need you firing on all cylinders when she gets out of hospital."

"You're right. She's asleep right now. The nurses told me she's still on some pretty heavy-duty sedatives. She'll probably sleep for most of the night."

"As I said, you ought to go home and get some rest. She's in good hands."

"You're right and now they have a guard outside her door, I'll rest a lot easier."

"Any word on Stanford? Have they brought him in yet?"

"No, at least, not that I've heard—but I'm guessing it's only a matter of time."

"Let's hope so. I can't wait for this whole nightmare to be over."

Declan closed his eyes against the surge of relief that filled his belly. "You and me both, little brother."

"I'm going to call Mom and Dad and let them know what's happening. They already know about you and Chloe. I filled them in earlier. It took some convincing, but I think Dad's even ready to call off the lawsuits."

Heat crept up Declan's neck, but he smiled, pleased. "Wow, he must be coming around. Thanks for going into bat for me, Clay. For both of us. And thanks for keeping them up to date. I-I really appreciate that." Declan's attention was snagged by the sight of Chloe's uncle on a television that was running in the visitor's room. Ronald Sabattini stood before a lectern and a row of microphones. The taskforce Chloe had mentioned earlier obviously hadn't yet arrested him.

The Minister's dark suit and tie matched his sober expression. His gaze skittered back and forth over the press gathered in front of him. The sound was down low, but there was no mistaking who it was.

"Well, I'll be damned…"

"What is it?"

"Chloe's uncle. He's on the television. I think he's going to give a press conference. I've got to go. I'll call you back later." Quickly ending the call, he strode up close to the screen in order to hear what was being said.

"Ladies and gentlemen, it's with a heavy heart that I stand here this evening to inform you that earlier today, there was what can only be described as an attempt on the life of my dear niece, Senior Investigator Chloe Sabattini." He paused and looked down at his notes before once again lifting his head to stare down the face of the camera.

"Around nine this morning, a silver-colored Ford F250 traveling north on the dual carriageway not far from Parliament House collided with my niece's vehicle. Police and emergency services responded immediately. Early investigations appear to indicate the collision was no accident. The suspect's vehicle has been identified as belonging to Federal Agent Charles Stanford."

There was a collective gasp from among the gathered media. Declan's gut clenched in shock.

"Agent Stanford has been giving evidence against Federal Agent Declan Munro in relation to the unauthorized access of computer files. My niece was the senior investigator on this case." His voice trembled with emotion. He paused and swiped at the moisture that had gathered in the corners of his eyes.

"It pains me to tell you that Chloe came to me earlier in the week with her concerns about Agent Stanford. While I listened to her, I didn't take her fears seriously and I will always regret it. If I had given them a little more consideration, perhaps she would not now be lying in a hospital bed fighting for her life."

Declan snorted and anger stirred in his veins. Trust the Minister to get maximum mileage out of the story.

"As for Agent Stanford," the Minister continued, "the police have issued an All Persons Bulletin for his arrest and we anticipate having him in custody very shortly. He will be dealt with according to the full force of the law."

"What were Investigator Sabattini's concerns regarding Agent Stanford?" a female journalist toward the front asked.

The Minister's lips compressed and he appeared to be weighing his answer.

"Agent Stanford's evidence was inconsistent. My niece was concerned Agent Stanford was lying and that he was framing Agent Munro." The Minister pursed his lips, as if deciding whether or not to continue. A few moments later, he raised his head and eyeballed the crowd of reporters assembled before him.

"What most of you don't know is that six months ago, my office was burgled."

Declan's heart skipped a beat and then pounded against his ribs. Blood rushed through his ears and he had to strain to hear the rest of Ronald Sabattini's story.

"Nothing appeared to have been stolen and so I made the decision not to get the police involved. I now believe it was Agent Stanford who trespassed into my office." He turned and stared straight at the camera. "I believe Agent Stanford stole the username and password belonging to Agent Munro and used this information to set him up."

Declan stilled, shock holding him paralyzed. He could barely draw breath.

"What about Agent Munro? Stanford was the prosecution's primary witness. Will the case against him be dropped?" another journalist asked.

Declan's breath caught. The Minister consulted his notes and then looked up.

"I expect so, but that will be a matter for the DPP. Now, if you'll excuse me, I must see to my family."

The press conference broke up and regular programing resumed. Declan turned away. Shock, disbelief and a quiet elation ran through his veins, but beneath it all, he couldn't help the uneasiness the Minister's words caused deep in his gut. The burglary in Sabattini's office sounded just a little too convenient.

Something wasn't right.

He turned away, disquieted, his head spinning. Only then, did he become aware of the man who stood behind him. It was the uniformed officer who'd been guarding the entry to Chloe's room.

Declan frowned. "What are you doing here? You're supposed to be guarding Agent Sabattini's room. Someone made an attempt on her life. You shouldn't—"

Out of the corner of his eye, Declan caught movement inside Chloe's room. He stared at her door and then his confusion morphed into panic.

The door was closed. He'd left it open; he was sure he had. He'd wanted to be able to hear her, in case she woke and needed him.

And now the door was closed...

He took off at a run.

CHAPTER 32

Charlie breathed in the pungent smell of disinfectant that was typical of every hospital he'd ever been in and grimaced. He'd always hated hospitals. The smell of them was the least of it.

Countless hours of his childhood had been spent in emergency wards. His mother was either too incompetent—or simply didn't care—to monitor his diabetes and ensure his insulin levels were adequate. He'd lost count of the number of times he'd gone hypo and ended up in a hospital.

It was past the end of visiting hours and he kept his gaze averted from the occasional doctor or nurse he passed in the corridor. Taking care to exert the authority he wore naturally after a decade as a police officer, he hoped any passersby would assume he was there on police business and leave him alone.

He'd learned long ago how important it was to keep up appearances. Most people saw what they wanted to see. No one in a hospital expected to see a murderer.

Pretending to be a concerned colleague, he'd called the hospital on his way and enquired about how the investigator was doing and what room she was in. He was counting on the fact that no one had yet wised up to the facts of the accident.

Whilst the switchboard operator was apologetic that she couldn't give out any details about Chloe's status, she happily advised him of the room number and told him he was welcome to visit her in the morning.

Charlie had chuckled quietly to himself from his seat in the back of the cab. There would be no visitors for Investigator Sabattini in the morning. At least, none that she would live to see...

Blinking away the memory, he focused on the job at hand. He glanced at the room numbers on each door. As he approached the one he sought, his steps slowed.

The place was quiet. He looked around, taking care to check behind him. He caught a glimpse of a man who was engrossed in the television. The man moved closer to the screen and Charlie froze.

Declan. Not far behind him, stood a uniformed officer.

Charlie's heart skipped a beat. He could barely hear over the sound of his blood as it pounded in his ears. He stood still, indecision gnawing at his gut. His gaze remained fixed on Declan, but the man he'd once thought of as a mate didn't move.

A surge of determination ran through him. He'd come here to kill her, just like the Master had asked. He wanted to give him a reason to take back his ugly words; he wanted to him proud.

Turning away, he strode toward the open doorway that led into Chloe's room. He closed the door quietly behind him and approached the bed.

She breathed deeply and evenly and he eased out his breath. He tugged the pouch containing the syringe and insulin out of his pocket and expertly drew up the contents of the vial until the syringe was full.

He moved closer to the bed and quietly located the rubber port that allowed substances to be added to the IV. With capable movements made efficient over years of practise, he slid the needle into the port and depressed the plunger.

With nobody the wiser, it wouldn't take long for it to be all over for Senior Investigator Sabattini. Charlie smiled with glee. He couldn't wait to tell the Master.

As quickly and quietly as he'd entered, he turned to leave and reached the door just as it flew open. It caught him in the chest. The syringe in his hand went flying and he gasped in surprise. Declan stared at him, fear and fury warring on his face.

"What the hell do you think you're doing? Get away from her, you fucking asshole."

Charlie raised his hands in a sign of surrender, relieved that Declan hadn't noticed the syringe.

"Calm down, Munro. I'm only paying my respects."

Declan's gaze narrowed on his hand and Charlie cursed under his breath. Too late, he remembered the vial.

Declan stared at the glass vial in Charlie's hand. It looked like it was empty. His blood ran cold. Without hesitation, he charged at the man he'd once called friend and pinned him against the wall.

"What the fuck have you given her, asshole?" he screamed, shaking Charlie by his shirtfront.

"Look, I found this!"

Declan looked behind him and saw the uniformed officer holding a syringe.

"It was on the floor over there."

Fear like he'd never known held Declan frozen in place. His attention was drawn back to Charlie when the man started laughing.

"You're too late," Stanford chuckled, shaking his head back and forth. "No one can save her now. You're too fucking late."

Declan whirled on his heel and charged out the doorway, yelling to the officer behind him. "Press the emergency button and don't let that murderer out of your sight."

Racing down the corridor, Declan shouted for help, his voice lifting with increasing desperation. Hospital staff came running from all directions. He offered them a garbled explanation.

A nurse grabbed a crash cart and raced toward Chloe's room. Declan followed, right on the heels of the medical staff and stared in horror at the sight of Chloe on the bed. She was as white as the bedsheet and lay deathly still. Her chest barely rose and fell with the shallowest of movements that seemed to take forever to repeat. For a moment, he was sure she'd actually stopped breathing.

"Everyone get out of the way," the doctor yelled. "We need to clear the room."

Declan stood rooted to the spot. Someone reached for his arm, but he shook them off roughly and moved out of reach.

The doctor looked at the monitor that displayed Chloe's blood pressure and pulse. He lifted her eyelids and shone a light into her eyes.

"Pupils are dilated and nonreactive. BP's eighty-over-fifty. She's unconscious. Does anyone know what she's been given?" he shouted.

Declan glanced at Charlie who was now straining against a set of handcuffs. The officer stood nearby. Finding his feet, Declan lunged forward.

"What the fuck have you given her?" he yelled for the second time. Charlie merely smiled. Spying the officer's gun, Declan snatched it out of the man's holster and held it against Charlie's temple.

"I want to know what you fucking gave her! *Answer* me!"

He waited a second...two. Charlie opened his mouth and then paused. Declan cocked the trigger.

"Okay, okay, put the gun down," Charlie said. "I only gave her insulin."

The medical staff immediately went into action. "I need blood glucose and insulin levels taken *stat*. Get me fifty milliliters of 50 percent dextrose bolus. We'll administer it intravenously and thereafter run a 5 percent dextrose infusion. Do we still have a cannula *in situ*?" the doctor asked.

"Yes," a nurse replied, while another one hurried out to do the doctor's bidding.

"Good, if we're going to have any hope of avoiding irreversible brain damage, we need to get that dextrose running ASAP."

In a blur of noise and movement, fear clutched at Declan's heart. He made a sound of distress low in his throat. The doctor's gaze swung over to where Declan stood near the doorway.

"Someone get those men out of here."

All of a sudden, hands were pushing him out of the room. He stumbled through the doorway, followed closely by Charlie and the officer.

The sound of the shouted orders that reached him from inside Chloe's room as the team worked over her echoed right down to Declan's soul. Fear and panic overwhelmed him and liquefied his limbs. He slowly collapsed to the floor.

Watching her husband bring his press conference to an end, Nellie Sabattini turned off the television and made her way upstairs. With movements that were calm and controlled, she removed her makeup, brushed her teeth and applied her night cream, just like she always did. Slipping into her favorite black satin and lace nightdress, she smoothed it over her still-lithe form and enjoyed the feel of its whisper-softness against her skin.

Despite her age, she'd worked hard to maintain her figure. Even after giving birth to Maria, she'd quickly regained her petite shape with a strict diet and a mountain of rigorous exercise.

Maria. Her baby. The one thing in her life that mattered.

For years, she'd been unaware that for most married couples, having sex once or twice a month was unusual. She'd been raised in a strict Italian family and was a good Catholic girl. Ronald Sabattini had taken her virginity on their wedding night. It never occurred to her to question the frequency of their couplings.

Once or twice a month soon extended to once or twice every six months. It seemed hardly any time at all had passed and they were lucky to have sex a couple of times a year.

After ten years of marriage, she finally found the courage to talk to her mother about her sex life, or lack thereof. Whilst her mother had expressed surprise, she'd been quick to assure Nellie that all men were different and had urged her to try harder to entice him to her bed.

Nellie had taken the advice to heart. For the next five years, she'd tried everything she could think of to attract her husband's interest. She read books on sexual positions she wouldn't even have imagined doing. She bought lingerie, perfume and videos. Nothing worked.

Finally, in desperation, she talked to him. She begged him to tell her what was wrong with her. Why, no matter what she did, he failed to find her desirable.

It was then that he'd told her.

Her marriage was a sham.

Unable to bear the shame of it, Nellie knew she had to hold her head high and soldier on. After all, what else was she to do? Explain to her friends and family that her husband was gay? That he'd been gay all his life?

She'd railed at him, screamed at him, begged him to tell her why he'd married her and he'd shouted back, tears streaming down his face, that he was a good Italian boy from a good Italian family. A family that went to Mass every Sunday of the year and twice on Christmas Day. "Coming out" simply wasn't an option.

Eventually, they'd called a truce. Nellie had agreed to go along with the subterfuge if he would give her a baby. At thirty-nine, it was never going to be easy and she struggled with the idea of Ronald being able to do what was necessary.

He struggled, too.

A month after she'd suggested it, he came to her with a proposition. There was a clinic in Sydney that specialized in IVF. Would she be interested in having them assist her to get pregnant?

Overjoyed at the prospect that her dream might soon be realized, they attended the clinic and followed the doctor's instructions. Her age was a disadvantage, but the fact that there was no physical reason she couldn't carry a baby to term was in their favor. It worked on the second attempt. Her only regret was that she'd left it so late to start.

The night Maria was born was the happiest of her life. The tiny fingers, the delicate hands, the mop of curly, black hair. Everything about her baby was perfect. She fell in love with her daughter and stayed that way. Maria had been the reason she stayed. For forty-two years, she'd stayed.

She'd stayed by his side. She'd stayed in his house. She'd stayed silent...

But no more... It was over.

He'd crossed a line. Maintaining his cover as a loving husband and father was one thing. The betrayal and murder of innocent people was something else.

She wanted no part of it.

———

It was late when Ronald switched the light off in his study and made his way upstairs. The light beneath his wife's bedroom door had been extinguished and a sigh of relief escaped his lips. He could do without further interrogation tonight. It was their wedding anniversary and he'd promised to take her out to dinner, but with all that had happened and with Chloe in the hospital, it hadn't worked out.

He continued down the hall to his room. Reaching his bedroom, he pushed open the door and felt his way along the wall for the light switch. Flicking it on, he turned toward the king-sized bed and started in surprise.

"What the hell are you doing in here?"

His wife remained silent and didn't move from her cross-legged position on his bed. He frowned and looked at her more closely. The lacy negligee barely covered her bountiful breasts. The indefinable expression in her eyes made him nervous.

"This is ridiculous," he blustered. "You haven't been in my bedroom for more than twenty years. What do you think you're doing?"

He strode toward his lavish walk-in closet and shrugged out of his jacket.

"I wouldn't do that if I were you."

He turned to face her, another angry retort on his lips. The words died in his mouth. Shock coursed through him.

The gun in Nellie's hand was steady and pointed directly at his heart.

"W-what are you doing? You can't be serious." He loathed the fear in his voice but was powerless to prevent it.

"Forty-two years, Ronald. I gave you forty-two years. And this is how you repay me? This is how you repay my sacrifice? With lies and treachery and deceit and betrayal and such monstrous acts of immorality I can barely even conceive of."

She climbed off the bed and walked toward him. The hand holding the gun didn't waver.

"You arranged to have your niece *murdered*. Your own flesh and blood! And for what? So that you could maintain this elaborate façade and continue to fulfil your own selfish needs?"

Panic nipped at the edges of his consciousness. He eased toward the door. She shook her head and Ronald found himself mimicking the action.

"No, Nellie. No. You have it all wrong."

"I don't think so, Ronald. For once in my life, I have it absolutely right."

She stood so close to him, he could see the flecks in her eyes. Her pupils were dilated and her breath came as fast as his. A pulse fluttered in the side of her neck. He did his best to stem the panic that threatened just below the surface.

"Give me the gun, Nellie. Give me the gun." He stretched out his hand toward her, hating to see how badly it trembled.

She looked at him with disgust and raised the gun. "Happy Anniversary."

The shot caught him squarely in the chest. Blood

bloomed instantly, staining the pristine whiteness of his shirt.

Nellie gaped in shock and turned to gaze in the direction of the doorway. She shrunk back against the bed in fear at the sight of an unfamiliar man.

"W-who? Who are y-you?" she stammered.

Eric Stoltenberg stared in fascination at the smoke that rose lazily from the end of the pistol. He still couldn't believe he'd done it. The pounding of footsteps in the hall drew his attention and he watched in bemusement as the room filled with heavily armed police officers, all shouting at once.

Someone knocked him to the ground and he fell hard. The gun was kicked out of his hand. Moments later, his arms were wrenched behind his back and handcuffs bit into his wrists. He watched it all in a daze, almost as if it was happening to someone else. The woman on the bed was hysterical. He wished someone would tell her to be quiet.

His gaze fixed on the Minister, where he lay motionless on the floor. In the noise and confusion, it appeared he'd been forgotten. Eric stared at the man he'd loved and noticed the slightest rise and fall of the Minister's chest.

Pain tore through him and he gasped at the agony it left in its wake.

He'd failed.

After everything he'd done, after the anguish he'd put himself through. The countless hours he'd debated the best course of action and had at last arrived at a decision...

The proof of his failure lay a few yards away. Despite the hole in the Minister's chest and the volumes of blood that had pooled beneath him, the man was still alive.

A cry of desolation forced its way up his throat. He opened his mouth to give it life and then he noticed it. A smile broke across his face. He blinked hard and opened his eyes, just to be sure. His smile widened.

The Minister's chest had stilled.

CHAPTER 33

Chloe struggled to a sitting position and reached for her crutches. More than six weeks had passed since the accident and most of her injuries had healed. The bruises had faded, her shoulder had repaired itself, her ribs had knit.

The only issue she had was with her leg, which was still encased in plaster from thigh to ankle. Whilst the doctors were happy with the way her bones were healing, the compound fracture had been severe and had required multiple screws and pins to hold the damaged bones together. She was still unable to bare weight on it and expected it to be that way for at least another fortnight.

Not that she was complaining. She was lucky to be alive. The police had impounded her little Honda as evidence. When she was finally allowed to inspect it, she'd barely recognized the pile of twisted metal that had once been her car. She was more than aware a few broken bones were a small price to pay.

Chloe made her way into the kitchen of Declan's apartment and reached for a bowl from the cupboard. Balancing on her crutches, she opened the refrigerator and pulled out the milk. Declan appeared from the direction of the bathroom, naked from the waist up, a towel draped low around his hips. When he spied her, he frowned and hurried toward her.

"What are you doing? I can help you. You shouldn't be

doing that." He took the bowl and bottle of milk out of her hand and placed them on the counter. Turning back to her, he shook his head.

"I know how frustrating this is for you, sweetheart, not being able to do things for yourself. But, it will only be for a little while longer, I promise. Until then, you need to call on me. I'm more than happy to help."

Chloe nodded. "I know, but you were in the shower and I was only trying to get breakfast." Frustration surged through her. "I feel so useless," she added, hoping he'd understand.

Moving closer, he put his arms around her and drew her against him. She took her weight on her good leg and leaned into him.

"I know. I can't imagine how exasperated you must feel. I think I would just about go crazy if I was on crutches for that long, but you need to be patient and allow your body to heal, like the doctor said." He pressed a kiss against her hair, as if to soften his words.

"Easy for you to say," Chloe grumbled against his naked chest. She breathed in deeply, loving the warm, spicy scent of him. She turned her face slightly and her lips grazed his nipple. She caught his sudden intake of breath.

Feeling naughty, she swiped her tongue over the sensitive nub. His arms tightened around her.

"Chloe." His voice held a warning.

She looked up at him and smiled, her eyes wide with innocence. "Yes?"

Declan shook his head at her. "Don't "yes" me. You know exactly what I'm talking about."

She battered her lashes. *"Do I?"* Her hand stole across his chest and then moved lower to caress the taut muscles of his belly. His skin contracted beneath her fingers. He stumbled a little and leaned back against the counter, his arms still secure around her.

"If you play with fire, you might get burned," he said.

"Mm, I see," she replied and sent him a smoldering look. "Who knows, it might be worth it?"

She tilted her head back and met his gaze, almost

gasping at the desire that burned in their depths. With her weight on her good leg, she reached up and traced the fullness of his lips. His mouth parted on a heavy sigh.

"Chloe..." Again, his voice held a warning.

"*Shh*," she whispered, sliding a hand from his cheek back down to his chest. "What are you afraid of?"

"You're still hurt. What if I—?"

She leaned into him and reached up with both hands. Tugging his head down to hers, she murmured against his lips, "You talk too much."

With that, she kissed him. Lightly at first and then, as he responded to her touch, she increased the pressure. She probed with her tongue and moaned aloud when he opened his mouth and granted her access.

Her hands once again were drawn to his chest and she explored the warmth of his skin. The lightest scattering of chest hair tickled her nose as she pressed her face against him and breathed deeply.

"You smell so good," she murmured. "All warm and spicy and male."

He smiled down at her. "I'm glad you like it."

"Oh, I like it all right. I like it a lot."

Declan stared down at her, his eyes dark with desire. With a groan, he bent down and lifted her into his arms, the crutches forgotten.

He strode down the hall and into his bedroom. Despite the fact they'd only recently climbed out of it, it was already neatly made. Chloe couldn't help but smile.

"It's only eight-thirty on a Sunday morning and you've already made the bed?"

Declan nuzzled the side of her neck. "What can I say? I like things tidy."

His mouth found the sensitive part right below her ear and she gasped. Fire burned through to her belly and lower.

Declan lowered her gently to the bed, mindful of her injured leg. When he joined her, she reached up and brought his mouth back to hers. Within seconds, the kiss ignited. His lips slanted across hers, tasting, seeking, taking.

She kissed him back and pressed herself closer against him, as close as her leg would allow.

His fingers nudged at the fabric of her bright yellow sundress. It had been purposefully chosen for the ease with which she was able to pull it on and off over her head and the bright color had simply made her smile. She couldn't wait to wear the hot pink blouse she'd kept stowed in the back of her closet for far too long.

Declan made short work of removing the dress and his hands went unerringly to her breasts. He rubbed her nipples through the thin fabric of her bra until they were puckered and hard.

She moaned.

With one hand, he reached behind her and unclasped her bra, freeing her breasts of their constraints. His lips quickly followed his fingertips, nipping and licking her nipples. His towel long discarded, she moved restlessly against the naked length of him. His hand stole across her belly and slid beneath her panties. When his fingers delved into the dewy softness between her legs, she gasped and turned her head from side to side from his sensual torment.

"Please, Declan."

"Please, what?" he murmured, his mouth intent on her breasts. He nuzzled first one and then the other. His tongue stole out and swiped across one of her nipples and she gasped again. Need spiraled down to her belly and ignited a path of desire. She moaned and moved against him, anxious to feel him inside her.

"I know, sweetheart... I know," he whispered, stroking her slick flesh. His finger parted her folds and found her clit—swollen, and oh so sensitive, When his fingers slid over its hard nub, she clutched at him, caught in a paradox of agony and ecstasy.

"Please, Declan. I need you inside me. *Please.*"

Moving slightly away from her, he reached over toward the nightstand and pulled out a condom. Ripping it open with his teeth, he quickly sheathed his cock and returned to her side.

Mindful of her plastered leg, he poised himself over her and nudged at her entrance. She squirmed and urged him forward.

He eased inside her, stretching her, filling her. A moment later, he began to move with long sure strokes. She clung to his shoulders and dug her fingernails into his skin, almost unable to bear the feelings that built deep within her core. With every movement of his hips, her need burned hotter.

"That's it, sweetheart. Let it go."

Declan's murmured words of encouragement were enough to tip her over the edge. She panted and moaned and gasped. Seconds later, she found her release.

Tightening his arms around her, Declan moved faster. His breath came harsher in her ear. She clung to him, urging him onward. With a shout of triumph, he climaxed.

It was long moments later before she was capable of speaking. "If that's what getting burned is all about, I'm all for it."

He turned on his side and grinned at her. "Minx."

She smiled back at him and sighed in contentment. At his insistence, she'd moved into his apartment after leaving the hospital. She wasn't foolish enough to think she could take care of herself without assistance and Declan was eager to help. Her mother had also offered, but something about having Declan close at hand was more than a little appealing.

She'd been told of Charlie's second attempt on her life by her boss. Hammond had attended upon her the day after it had happened, grave with concern. He also told her about the attempted arrest of her uncle and what they had found at his mansion.

It had been too much to take in and Chloe had sent him away feeling shocked and traumatized. Even now, she still found it hard to believe all that had happened. As if sensing her thoughts, Declan caressed her cheek with the back of his hand.

"What are you thinking?" he murmured, his expression filled with concern.

She sighed and told him the truth. "The thing with Charlie and Eric and my uncle. And even my aunt. I still can't conceive of how it all happened."

Declan drew her close against him. "Me either. I'm just grateful Stanford and Stoltenberg are locked up. At least you're safe from them."

Chloe shuddered. "I never would have dreamed Eric could be so violent. When I interviewed him, he seemed like a harmless boy."

"You just never know."

She thought of her uncle and aunt and the life of deception they'd lived for so many years. "You've certainly got that right," she said sadly.

"I hope you're not still blaming yourself?"

She unwittingly made a sound of distress in the back of her throat and then bit her tongue. Declan pulled gently away from her and sat up against the headboard.

"I thought we'd been over this, sweetheart?"

He said it gently, but tears still burned behind her eyes. He smoothed a lock of hair back from her forehead and her heart melted at the tenderness in his eyes.

She drew in a deep breath and let it out on another sigh. "My head knows you're right. It's my heart that will take a little more convincing."

He kissed her softly, gently as if trying to assuage the hurt that still lingered inside her. The hurt and confusion and pain on her father's face when he'd been told about his brother would stay with her forever.

But none of it was Declan's fault. Honorable, kind, smart and just downright gorgeous was the only way to describe him. He'd looked after her like she was the most precious thing in the world and she couldn't help but love him for it.

She loved him.

"When do you get your cast off?" Declan asked, interrupting her thoughts.

"Hopefully, in a fortnight. It will be good to get rid of the crutches and get back to normal. I hate to think how my garden's fared. Mom was going to see to my pot plants, but..." She shrugged and hoped he'd understand.

"You miss your apartment."

Chloe compressed her lips and nodded. "Yes, I do."

Declan's smile looked a little forced. "So what are you saying? You're sick of me, are you?"

Heat crept across her cheeks. She shook her head. "No, of course not. You've been wonderful, amazing. I couldn't have managed without you. I-I'm so grateful for everything that you did."

He frowned. "Grateful? I don't want your gratitude. Don't you know? I've fallen in love with you, Senior Investigator Sabattini."

Chloe stared at him, her eyes wide with disbelief. Her heart began to pound.

"Y-you *love* me? Are...are you sure?"

His frown darkened. "Of course I'm sure. I'm thirty-four years old. I think I've been around long enough to know how I feel. Having you around these past weeks, being able to take care of you—I want to be able to do that every day of our lives."

He drew in a deep breath, his gaze fixed on hers. "It wasn't until you were hurt that I realized how deeply I'd fallen for you, but since you've been here, in my home and in my heart, there's nothing about the idea of sharing my life with you, that doesn't feel right."

Hope and joy flooded through her. She grinned up at him. "You barely know me. You haven't even been to my apartment." She looked around the tidy room. "You're obviously a neat freak. I could be the biggest slob around."

The twinkle in his eye belied his heavy sigh. "You're right. I am a neat freak. It's a consequence of being nagged every day of my youth to pick up after myself and put my clothes away and keep my room tidy. I guess with seven kids in the house, Mom had to be a cleaning Nazi or else there would have been absolute chaos."

"Seven kids? You really have seven brothers and sisters?"

"Six, actually. I'm the seventh. And yeah, I have four brothers and two sisters."

Chloe shook her head, amazed. "The night we went for that bike ride, I peeked at a photograph in the spare room. I recognized your brothers and parents from the hearing and I could see the family resemblance between you and the girls, but I didn't think about the head count."

"Yep, there are five of us boys, starting with Tom. Then there are the babies—Josie and Chanel."

Chloe shook her head again. "Wow, what a family. I couldn't help but notice at the hearing how close you all appeared. It was nice to see them there, offering you their support."

"Yeah," Declan smiled. "It was. We've always gotten along. Clayton lives here in Canberra and Riley's up near Mom and Dad in northern New South Wales. Tom and Brandon are both in Sydney."

"Where are your sisters?"

"The girls share an apartment in Brisbane. They both went to Uni up there."

"What did they study?" Chloe asked, fascinated to know more about his family.

"Josie's a child psychologist and Chanel's a doctor."

Chloe heard the love and pride in his voice as he spoke of them and it warmed her through and through. Despite recent events, she still believed in family and always would.

"They're lucky to have you looking out for them. As am I," she added, holding his gaze.

Declan stared back at her, his eyes dark with emotion. "Does this mean you're considering moving in with me permanently?"

She nodded. "I'd love to."

His breath whooshed out. He chuckled and then laughed. "Really?"

"Yes, really. I've gotten used to being waited on hand and foot. Why would I move out now?"

"But what about your apartment, your garden?"

"I can always relocate my pot plants. You have a

decidedly nice balcony that could do with some greenery."

Her smile was reflected in his eyes. He bent his head and kissed her.

"I love you, Chloe Sabattini."

"I love you, too."

He pulled back and stared at her? "Really? Do you really? You don't have to say it just because—"

She pressed a finger to his lips. "Haven't I already told you, you talk too much? Of course I love you! How could I not? You're honest and caring and decent and proud. You're honorable and selfless and you genuinely care about other people. You love your family; you said you love kids. What's not to love about all that?"

His face filled with joy. He shook his head slowly back and forth. "I can't believe that through this entire nightmare, I've found you. I would never have believed it! If I had to go through it all again in order to have you, I would."

Chloe gasped. "That's... That's the most incredible thing I've ever heard. I-I don't know what to say."

"Don't say anything." Just kiss me and show me how much you love me."

Elation flooded through her. She couldn't stop the grin that stretched her lips wide. Moving closer, he drew her into his arms. Her lips found his and she set about showing him just how much she meant it.

EPILOGUE

Four months later

The opening bars of the entrance hymn pealed through the loudspeakers of St Patrick's Catholic Church and filtered through to Chloe where she waited with her father in the little room just off the narthex. Nerves jangled in her stomach. She smoothed down the panels of her white antique-satin-and-lace wedding dress and looked at herself in the full-length mirror. Her heart tightened with emotion at the woman who stared back at her.

Her hair was gathered into a loose knot at the base of her neck. Tiny, hot pink satin handmade roses were tucked amongst the strands. Artfully arranged tendrils escaped to frame her face and gave her a look of ethereal beauty.

Standing at her side, her father patted her hand and did his best to hold back his tears.

"Your mother's beside herself with joy to know she's lived to see your wedding day. She'd just about given up."

"How about you, Daddy? Are you happy?"

"I couldn't have chosen better for you myself." His voice was gruff with emotion. She tightened her grip on his arm and offered him a wobbly smile.

"Thank you, Daddy. You don't know how much that means to me."

He swiped at the tears that slid down his cheeks. "You

look beautiful, bambina. The prettiest bride I've ever seen."

Her smile widened and she brushed at the moisture in her eyes. "I bet you say that to all the girls."

"Just to my girls," he replied. His eyes twinkled, though they were still tinged with the sadness that had shadowed them ever since his brother's death. "Let's go and get you married."

As the music swelled, she entered the church on her father's arm. The congregation stood and turned as one to greet them. Declan's nieces, Cassie and Olivia, had gone in ahead of them and had strewn pink and white rose petals along the aisle. Chloe breathed in their heady fragrance.

Her sisters, Cathy and Antonella and her best friend, Savannah, all dressed in hot-pink satin, took their places at the front of the church. There wasn't a hint of Savannah's devastation over her recent breakup with Jonathan evident on her face. Her friend couldn't have looked happier.

Chloe's father led her slowly down the aisle. He nodded greetings to friends and family, his face glowing with pride.

Declan stood before the altar, waiting for her. His eyes shone with love and his soft smile was full of adoration. It seemed to take a lifetime, but at long last, she stood by his side. He tucked her hand in his and bent low to whisper in her ear.

"You're even more beautiful than I imagined. You're the woman of my dreams, the woman of my heart. And by the way, I *love* the pink."

The ceremony passed in a blur of heartfelt vows, gospel readings, hymns, happy tears and laughter. When it was over, Declan pulled her into his arms and kissed her to the sound of tumultuous applause. His entire family was crammed into the first five pews and from the smiles and catcalls emanating from his side of the church, they couldn't be more pleased.

Chloe looked across at her side of the church and smiled at her family gathered there. A shadow touched her heart at the thought of her uncle, but she made an effort to brush it away.

"Hey, beautiful, are you all right?"

Declan's gentle prodding brought her back to the present. She smiled and kissed him. The memories of those awful events, her family's anguish and shock over the tragedy, her own grief and devastation, would stay with her for a long time to come.

But today... Today was not a day for dark memories. Today was a day for overwhelming joy and celebration. The man she loved with all of her heart, had just been declared her husband. She clung to the thought.

"I'm great," she whispered. "Right now, I'm the happiest woman alive."

NOTE TO READERS

I do hope you have enjoyed reading Declan and Chloe's story. Having had a close family member suffer through a similar situation as Declan, it was a story near to my heart. As a lawyer, I firmly believe in one of the tenets of our criminal justice system that states a person is innocent until proven guilty. Where the system falls down is when a person's life can be ruined from nothing more substantial than mere allegations. Sadly, it happens all too often.

Please feel free to leave a review for The Betrayal. Every review is appreciated and really helps a new author like me.

The Deception is Book Five of the Munro Family Series and is Will and Savannah's story. You met Savannah in The Betrayal as Chloe's ambitious reporter friend. Savannah has had a difficult past and one you will discover in her story. I'm sure once you've read it, you'll agree with me that she more than deserves her happy ending.

Here's a sneak peek:

Ambitious newspaper journalist **Savannah O'Neill** *will do anything for a story, even if it means pretending to be a prostitute in Sydney's most exclusive brothel. She's there on a tip-off that underage girls are being held illegally and kept compliant with illicit drugs. What's more, unidentified bodies of young women have turned up in Sydney Harbour and at least one of them is linked to the brothel.*

Detective Will Rutledge has vowed to destroy the man he holds responsible for his brother's suicide. Vince Maranoa is the kingpin of Sydney's illegal drug industry: He's also the owner of the city's most exclusive brothel. Working undercover with the New South Wales Drug Enforcement Agency, Will is determined to put Maranoa behind bars.

When Savannah and Will cross paths at the brothel, there's an instant attraction, despite the fact she presumes he's a cohort of the crime boss and Will assumes she's a prostitute under Maranoa's employ.

With both of them determined to pursue their personal agendas to infiltrate the covert life of Maranoa, they will both be left gasping when the brothel's secrets are finally revealed...

The Deception will be available in July, 2014. If you would like to subscribe to my newsletter to receive news on upcoming Munro Family stories, release dates, book launches and other snippets, please go to my website at www.christaylorauthor.com.au and follow the link. I love to hear from my readers. Please feel free to contact me at christaylor@antmail.com.au Let me know who your favorite Munro family member is.

ABOUT THE AUTHOR

Chris Taylor grew up on a farm in north-west New South Wales, Australia. She always had a thirst for stories and recalls writing her first book at the ripe old age of eight. Always a lover of romance and happily-ever-afters, a career in criminal law sparked her interest in intrigue and suspense. For Chris to be able to combine romance with suspense in her books is a dream come true.

Chris is married to Linden and is the mother of five children. If not behind her computer, you can find her doing the school run, taxiing children to swimming lessons, football, ballet and cricket. In her spare time, Chris loves to read her favorite authors who include Richard North Patterson, Sandra Brown, Kathleen E Woodiwiss and Jude Devereaux.

You can find out more about Chris and sign up for her newsletter at her website:

http://www.christaylorauthor.com.au